THICKER THAN WATER

THICKER THAN WATER

JUDITH COLQUHOUN

Black Pepper
Melbourne, Australia

© Judith Colquhoun 2014

First published by *Black Pepper*
403 St Georges Road, North Fitzroy, Victoria 3068
blackpepperpublishing.com

National Library of Australia
Cataloguing-in-Publication data:

Colquhoun, Judith
Thicker than water / Judith Colquhoun

ISBN 978-1-876044-87-9 (paperback)

A823.4

Cover photograph: Lucia Rossi – *Water Profile*
Cover design: Gail Hannah

J udith Colquhoun was born in Queensland and raised in Sydney. She studied production at NIDA. Love and a job with ABC Television took her to Melbourne. She spent some time as a radio copywriter before joining the writing team for the television serial *Bellbird*. Thus began a forty year career of scriptwriting on shows such as *The Sullivans*, *Twenty Good Years*, *Skyways*, *GP*, *Something in the Air*, *Flying Doctors*, *MDA*, *The Man From Snowy River*, *Blue Heelers*, *A Country Practice*, *Home and Away* and *Neighbours*, and the children's series *Cornflakes for Tea*, *Zoo Family* and *Ocean Girl*. Judith is still (to her slight chagrin) best-known for killing Molly Jones in *A Country Practice*. Judith's television career resulted in five AWGIE awards and in 2007 she was a made a Life Member of the Australian Writers' Guild. She is married with two children and two grandchildren.

In 2009 she gave up scriptwriting to work on *Thicker Than Water*. Importantly for the novel, she had been a script consultant in Naples for the television serial *Un Posto al Sole*. Her experiences there contributed to the plot of *Thicker Than Water*.

Acknowledgements

The Australian Broadcasting Corporation commissioned me in 1997 to write a treatment for a telemovie which they hoped to make as an Australian-Italian co-production. We all loved the story but time passed and we realised that it was never going to happen. In 2009 the ABC very kindly gave me back the rights, allowing me to turn the treatment into a novel which became *Thicker Than Water*. I am immensely grateful for their generosity.

Many people have helped and supported me in various ways with the writing of this book. Chief among them are Anne and Alberto Sabato, Julian and Carolann Castagna and Salvatore (Sammy) Rao, who corrected my execrable Italian and shared insights and memories of the bel paese. Encouragement and advice when it was most needed came from Kevin Childs and Maureen Cooper and from my old scriptwriting mates, Luke Devenish and Scott Taylor. The generosity of Dr Damien Smith, AM, enabled me to see my computer screen. My family made coffee, poured wine, dealt with computer problems and were brave enough to offer constructive criticism. .

I am indebted to them all.

For John,
Remembering all our rich Italian days

Prologue

Lucy hoped the plane would not choose this particular moment to plummet from the sky. While the entrance to the underworld was, she knew, some forty kilometres west at Lago d'Averno (or so the Romans believed), this yawning crater beneath her was no doubt the back door. The whole of Alitalia Flight 312 could disappear in there without trace.

Lucy was not a good flyer.

She had tried everything available to combat her affliction: excessive alcohol, no alcohol, medication, meditation, appeals to the ex-Saint Christopher. She'd even spent a small fortune on one of those desensitisation courses the airlines offer. Nothing helped. She still boarded a plane as seldom as possible, with nightmares before and clenched knuckles throughout any flight.

So, clearly, this journey which seemed about to end in the gaping maw of an infamous volcano had not been undertaken on a whim. Lucy was not coming to the Mezzogiorno on holiday. She was not planning to savour the myriad delights of the Costiera Amalfitana, nor to study the remains of Graeco-Roman civilization which littered the area. Writers and artists had come here for centuries but she was neither. She was not even seeking a new lover or running away from an old one. No, her mission was altogether different. And the fact that she came in a Boeing instead of a chariot drawn by griffins should not have encouraged anyone to doubt the seriousness of her purpose. Lucy was Nemesis. She had come to settle a very old score.

The plane did not crash. It banked and turned and flew north-west, giving passengers on the left-hand side a stunning view of the Bay of Naples, before coming in to land safely at Capodichino.

Lucy was twelve thousand kilometres from Far-East Gippsland in the State of Victoria which is where her story had really begun.

One

Twenty-five years earlier, a bus left Bannon Creek, heading for Melbourne. Sitting, like Lucy, in a window seat, was a girl called Kate O'Connell.

There are parts of Far East Gippsland—Bannon Creek is not one of them—that are almost as beautiful as the Amalfi Coast. There are charming fishing villages where tourists flock in summer and if the smell of money is not as strong in Mallacoota, say, as it is in Positano (diluted as it will be with eucalypt and marijuana), it lingers all the same; while you'll find more Fords than Ferraris in the main street, any of the men in jeans and thongs could have a plane at the airstrip and an abalone licence worth several million dollars. It's a beer-and-barbie culture there, in what the tourist brochures like to call 'an unspoilt coastal wilderness.' And indeed you can swim at deserted beaches if you know where to look and there are wonderful picnic and walking spots in the vast reaches of Croajingalong National Park.

Inland a bit, where Kate grew up, was—and is—different.

Bannon Creek is proudly a timber town. It does not feature on picture postcards and tourists only stop for petrol. There is less interest in herbal cigarettes. The people are tough and hard-working, their inherent conservatism bolstered by a lack of educational opportunity and a suspicion of anyone born west of Bairnsdale. Salt of the earth or rednecks, depending on your point of view.

Kate's family fitted the mould perfectly, though Kate herself did not. Her dad, Stan, was foreman at the sawmill. Her mum, Joy, looked after Stan and five kids. Saturday, everyone went to the footy or the cricket and half of them got pissed. Sunday, after church or a good lie-in, they went to the pub or the bowling club and the same half got pissed again. The kids were left to their own devices which meant the boys ran wild and the girls hung out at the milkbar and gossiped. Except for Kate who stayed at home and buried her head in a book. It was not an exciting or enriching life, apart from the books, it's just what happened to be available.

Bannon Creek never wrapped its arms around Kate, never gave her any sense of belonging. By the time she was seven or eight she felt like an outsider. By the time she turned twelve she was working on an escape route. By then she knew she didn't like her family very much. She also knew—from the endless jibes about Miss Smartypants, who was too good for the rest of them—that they didn't like her.

She had thought that perhaps she was a changeling until she overheard her grandmother say she was 'just like Lucy.' Aunt Lucy, it turned out. Then she realised there must be an aberrant gene somewhere, fighting on the side of civilisation, which she had somehow inherited. She was sorry indeed to discover that Aunt Lucy was dead.

Kate did have allies in the town, at the local high school. Not amongst the students, who hated her guts, but amongst the staff. Leader of the pack was the formidable Liz Holden, head of English, who hovered over Kate like a stage mother, pushy and protective in turns. She offered extra assignments, books to read, enrichment programmes, even trips to Canberra for the odd exhibition—not that Kate was ever allowed to go. It was Liz who bullied Kate's parents into letting her stay on for Year Twelve, Liz who was utterly determined that Kate would go to university.

And Kate, seeing the prison gates swing wide, worked day and night and got the marks to do just that. Got the highest marks ever achieved by a student from her school. Liz bought champagne for the staffroom and *Brewer's Phrase and Fable* for Kate. Kate herself was quietly thrilled and more than a bit overwhelmed. Getting the marks was one thing; going off to live in the city, six hundred kilometres away, was something else. Lacking self-confidence, she did not set her sights too high but enrolled at Teacher's College. She too would become a mentor, a beacon of hope in some other godforsaken town.

Stan and Joy were dead against it. Kate had been offered a nice job in the office at the sawmill, good money, they thought she ought to take it. They thought she owed them.

'For what?' she wondered, quite sure she had never asked to be born and failing to remember a single moment of support or encouragement.

So she packed her suitcase with a clear conscience, promised to stay in touch with Liz and boarded the bus in the middle of the night. She was glad of that, the darkness hid her tears. Not that she was sorry to be leaving Bannon Creek but the freedom she had longed for seemed almost too much to handle. It wasn't until after Bairnsdale, the halfway mark, that she got a grip on herself.

She was fine by the time the sun came up. For a moment she even thought about her plans for the future, when she'd finished her degree, when she'd saved enough to take a break from teaching. Then she would really spread her wings, she would travel and write. That was the dream. To send Liz a postcard from London. A copy of her first book.

She smiled and saw that Melbourne was there ahead of her, beckoning through the morning haze. She could not know that in little more than a year the dream would be shattered.

Two

The nuns were not unkind; nor were they generous enough not to pass judgement. Since babies should ideally be born to two good Catholic parents, a single mother could hardly hope to make the grade. And if she was, like Kate, a Catholic, it only meant that she'd added a mortal sin to her shortcomings.

So the best thing all round was for Kate to have this baby adopted.

'Such a nice couple we've found,' said Sister Agatha. 'Very devout.'

'With a lovely house in Glen Waverley,' said Sister Jerome.

Kate wondered if you got a nice house for devotion.

'He's got a very good job in the public service,' said Sister Frances. 'Your baby would be blessed with every opportunity.'

'So the thing to do,' said Sister Agatha, summing up, 'is to beg God's forgiveness, put this youthful indiscretion behind you and get on with your life. Knowing your baby is in the best of hands.'

They all smiled encouragingly.

'Well?' said Sister Agatha.

Kate took a deep breath.

'The best hands for my baby,' said Kate firmly, 'are mine.'

The nuns said she was selfish. She had no idea how hard it would be to raise a child alone. Sister Agatha even went to Kate late one night and played the highest card of all.

'If you give the baby up you could resume your course,' she said. 'You could still be a teacher.'

Sister Agatha didn't know Kate at all, didn't know she'd spent a lifetime being the odd one out. She was therefore surprised when Kate resisted the pressure to fall into line.

Two days after her nineteenth birthday Kate went into labour.

Apart from the midwife and a doctor who came and went, she was quite alone.

She had not been at university long enough to make real friends and no one from Bannon Creek had the faintest idea where she was. She had thought of writing to Liz Holden but what would she say? 'I'm sorry, Liz, I've let you down, your golden girl is a miserable failure.' She couldn't do it. The time when she should have rung Liz was nine months ago. Liz might have been able to help her then.

No, she was flying solo. But soon there would be two of them. And this child she was carrying was going to have all the advantages that Kate herself had been denied. More advantages even than would have been found in the nice house in Glen Waverley. This child would be loved unconditionally. As for the father—he was gone and would not be missed. Kate was busy working on a story, a half-truth, to explain his absence. Really, she decided, the less said the better.

She didn't mean to cry out when the contractions first hit her. She had made up her mind that she was going to give birth in a calm and dignified way. But no one had told her how much it was going to hurt.

It was the little Italian nun, Sister Rita, not much older than Kate herself, who came rushing in. Ironic that it was her, the only Italian in the place. But she was—what was the word? Kate tried to remember—simpatica, that was it, so obviously all Italians were not the same. Any more than all nuns were the same. Rita, Kate remembered, had never joined in the chorus of disapproval.

She stayed with Kate and talked her through the labour.

'Should I call anyone?'

Kate shook her head.

'The father?'

'There's no father.'

Sister Rita brushed the hair from Kate's face.

'You're very bitter.'

'I have good reason.'

'Would it help to talk?'

'I don't think so.'

'Then I'll pray for you instead.'

'Thank you,' said Kate, thinking it couldn't hurt. 'Tell me. Why did you become a nun?'

Sister Rita smiled. 'Because I knew I would never find a man I could love as much as I loved God.'

Kate nodded. 'You make it sound almost sensible.'

At the end of six long hours, Kate was handed a small bundle with black hair and olive skin.

'A little girl,' said Sister Rita. 'Bellissima. What will you name her?'

'Lucy,' said Kate. 'Lucy Elizabeth O'Connell.'

Sister Rita approved. 'Lucia,' she said, 'Lucia Elisabetta. So easy if she ever goes to Italy.'

Kate smiled and didn't say that she fervently hoped her daughter would never go to Italy.

Three

Lucy, grown-up Lucy, was sitting in a room at a big city hospital. With her was a man called Geoff Harrington, who loved her mother. Behind the desk in front of them sat Kate's oncologist.

'Six weeks,' he said. 'Maybe eight. I'm sorry.'

'Can we take her home?'

'We could try some more chemo.'

'What would that achieve?'

'It might give her another month or two.'

'Might?' said Geoff. 'Or would?'

'We can never be sure.'

Lucy said, 'If she were your mother...?'

'I'd take her home.'

They thanked him and left and went to see Kate.

Lucy smiled brightly when they entered the ward. 'We're taking you home.'

'Thank God,' said Kate and smiled brightly too, even though she knew that a death sentence had just been passed.

'I've talked Lucy into staying for a bit,' said Geoff. 'Just till you're back on your feet again.'

'A couple of weeks,' said Kate, playing the game. 'I'm feeling better already.'

Geoff had been a widower for a long time when Kate first walked into his antiquarian bookshop. Lucy had just got her VCE results, good enough to get her into Arts at Melbourne University and Kate wanted something to mark the occasion. They spent a long time settling on a lovely old copy of Yeats' Collected Poems. Poetry, as Kate had explained, was important to both of them.

Geoff was drawn to Kate from the start. Now in her late-thirties, she was still a very attractive woman but it was more her mind that intrigued him, the fact that she loved books as he did, that he could not just talk to her but discuss things, argue, even disagree; and he enjoyed her dry wit. Above all he admired her independence, that she wasn't needy. It was because she demanded so little of him that he longed to give her everything but there was between them a most forbidding line of defences. This Kate had raised long ago in case her emotions should ever again go galloping off unchecked.

Fortunately Geoff was both patient and determined, a man who liked a challenge. He came to realise that his Herculean task was to convince Kate that men, all men, were not her enemy and some, himself among them, could indeed be trusted. His gentle perseverance was rewarded. Kate, who had never in her life enjoyed a real relationship, fell in love at last and moved into his large and pleasant California bungalow, not far from the beach at Elwood.

Lucy liked Geoff a lot and visited often. Childless himself, he treated her like the daughter he never had and was pleased when she came and brought her friends. There seemed nothing to mar Kate's happiness.

But she was not, as we have seen, beloved of the gods and this dream too was never destined to last.

They all knew it and for a while they tried not to mention it, hoping that if they ignored death it might still go away. But it wasn't easy; there was unfinished business to attend to.

Lucy found her mother sitting by an open window one afternoon, trying to catch the breeze from the bay. It was only October but unseasonably hot. Lucy noticed in the sunlight an auburn fuzz on Kate's head, soft like a baby's. Her hair was growing back after the chemo. Lucy wondered how long it would get. She fought back the tears.

'Get you anything?'

Kate shook her head.

'You looked like you were miles away.'

'I was thinking about Liz Holden.'

'Your English teacher?' Lucy was surprised. 'Do you want to get in touch with her or something?'

'I tried, Luce. Last year. She was killed in a car accident. I never got to explain.' She turned to Lucy. 'Don't put things off, darling. Don't think they can wait till tomorrow.' She sighed. 'She must have been so disappointed in me.'

'Because you got pregnant and dropped out of uni?'

'It was such a Bannon Creek sort of thing to do. I suppose she half expected it. I'm tired, I think I'll sleep for a bit.'

But Lucy had no intention of leaving it there. She chose a day when the morphine seemed to be doing its stuff.

'How come it took you so long?'

'To do what?'

'Find Geoff. Or someone like him. I can't believe you didn't have offers.'

'I just wasn't interested.'

'Or maybe you were too hurt?'

'Can we leave it?'

'Not unless you promise not to die on me. Like Liz did. You know?'

'I can't answer your questions, Lucy.'

'About my father?'

'There's nothing to say.'

'I know he walked out on you, mum. But you did have a relationship—or I wouldn't be here. You must have felt something for him.'

Kate just shook her head.

'I understand that you can't forgive him. But one day I might want to find him.'

'Please, Lucy. Listen to me. You don't understand. And you don't want to find him. Let it be.'

Lucy left, hurt and angry. It was the closest they'd come to a row for a long time. She arranged to meet Simone, her best friend since schooldays.

'I don't know, Sim, I'm starting think he must be a serial killer.'

'Maybe he's a priest,' said Sim and almost got a smile. 'You've tried Geoffrey?'

'He just evades the question.'

'So he knows more than he's saying.'

'Maybe.'

Sim stirred her coffee for a moment or two. 'Luce? Your mum's got a lot on her plate right now. All those painful memories... perhaps it's not the time?'

'She's dying, Sim. How much time do I have?'

'Do you want to spend it fighting with her?'

Lucy didn't. Instead she clung to the absurd hope that Kate would go into remission and then, at some later date, reveal what she so desperately wanted to know.

Even Geoff, as gently as he could, suggested that Lucy had a right to know where she came from, however unpleasant the facts.

'I can't do it,' said Kate.

'You should do it,' said Geoff. 'You know you should.'

It didn't happen. Kate grew weaker, the pain more intense. The nurse came more often, suggested Kate go into palliative care. 'St John of God,' she said. 'We could get her in there tomorrow.'

'No!' from Lucy.

'They're absolutely wonderful.' The nurse looked at her patient. 'What do you think, Kate?'

Geoff didn't wait for Kate's answer. 'We'd rather keep her home.'

When the nurse had gone Kate managed to whisper 'I'm glad you didn't hand me over to the nuns again.'

Geoff squeezed her hand. 'Wouldn't do that to you.'

Lucy watched this little interplay, puzzled.

'Someone going to fill me in?'

'Just an old joke,' said Kate quickly.

Lucy got up and walked out.

Geoff took a deep breath. 'God forbid, Kate, but you could die tonight. So I'm going to be brutal. She's grown-up. She wants the truth. And yes, the telling will be painful for both of you. But you need to do it while you still have time. So I'm going to send her back in here. Alright?'

And finally, Kate nodded.

Four

It was painful. And what Lucy learnt was not quite what she had expected. When Kate hit the big smoke that autumn morning, fresh out of Bannon Creek, she was as green as the first new growth that followed a bushfire. She was clever but naïve, pretty but unsophisticated, completely lacking in street smarts. Even at the hostel where she boarded, where most of the other students were also from the bush, she found it hard to fit in. Not to put too fine a point on it, Kate was well aware that she'd made it to uni against all the odds; second-rate country high school, second-rate family of hicks and philistines. She felt she was there on sufferance and sometimes wondered if Liz ever realised how hard it was going to be.

The course wasn't a problem, she worked hard and did well, found much of it really easy, in fact. But there was no time for socialising, for making friends. Her student allowance was not enough to live on and there was no help from home so she got a part-time job in a coffee shop in Carlton.

Kate didn't mind the work and she enjoyed chatting to the customers. The owners of the place, Italians, were nice to her and she got free meals. And then their nephew, Paolo, arrived from Campania. He was to stay with his aunt and uncle for a while, work there until he got a proper job and the rest of his family arrived.

Paolo was a gorgeous southern boy with a very cute accent and exquisite manners. To compare him to the Bannon Creek boys was like comparing a dragonfly to a slug. He made flirting an art-form. He flirted with Kate over the cappuccino machine. It wasn't long before he persuaded her to go to the movies with him, to see an Italian film. It was just about the most exotic thing Kate had ever done.

He raped her on the way home.

Kate paused there in the telling and looked at her daughter. Lucy, tears pricking her eyes, concentrated on her mother's arm, lying on the sheet. She saw how thin it was now and dotted with petechia, the flecks of blood under the skin from broken capillaries which the nurse had reluctantly admitted was not a good sign. She took her mother's hand in hers.

'Go on,' she managed to say.

Kate told Lucy how she somehow got back to the hostel from the park where Paolo had taken her; how she had stood under the shower for nearly two hours, scrubbing herself; how she'd finally crawled into bed and tried to work out what to do.

So naïve. Of course she should have gone to the police—or a rape crisis centre, if she'd known such places existed.

Instead she went to her local priest. She told him she wanted Paolo charged. And he talked her out of it. He said that since she knew the boy it would look bad for her, mud would be thrown, some of it would stick. He would go to see the family. Best if Kate went home for the holidays and forgot about it.

Kate went home but Liz was away and there was no one she could talk to. She almost confided in her mother but felt she wouldn't be believed and gave up on the idea. By the time she returned to Melbourne she knew she was pregnant.

The aunt and uncle were no help. Before they had been so friendly, treated Kate almost like one of the family. Now she was an outsider, more than that, a threat. They told her the boy had gone back to Italy, the family had changed their minds and were no longer emigrating. They refused to give Kate an address or to pass on any message. Kate should forget that Paolo had ever existed.

'Forget?' said Lucy. 'Forget?'

'It was a bit hard,' said Kate, 'in the circumstances.'

'At least I know where I get my olive skin and black hair.'

Kate just nodded.

'Is this where the nuns come in?' asked Lucy.

'St Joseph's Maternity Home.'

'Why there?'

'Well I couldn't go home. It would have given them all such

13

pleasure. How are the mighty fallen. And I was still too much of a Catholic to consider abortion.'

'I would have had one. But I'm glad you didn't.'

Kate almost smiled. 'So I went to see Father Ignatius again. And he referred me to St Joey's.'

'Thus absolving himself of all responsibility.'

'He had a point, Lucy. The courts could be hell for rape victims back then. Especially if you didn't have a good lawyer to back you up. I don't blame him so much.'

'Well no. He wasn't the one who did that to you. Raped you. Ended all your dreams, stole your career, forced you to become a single mother, years and years of living on nothing so I could have what you never did—'

She broke off, filled with rage at the injustice of it all. There was a long silence then.

'You see why I didn't want to tell you? I've got anger enough for both of us, darling. Let me take it with me. It's over now. My beautiful girl, I wouldn't have swapped any career in the world for you.'

Kate died three days later.

Geoff put the notice in *The Age*. Lucy decided it ought to go in *The Herald Sun* as well, she couldn't imagine the Bannon Creek mob reading *The Age*. But either they didn't see it or they didn't care because none of them came to the funeral. Which was a relief for two reasons: Kate wouldn't have wanted them there and it gave Lucy an excuse to visit—something she hadn't done since she was ten years old.

Geoff felt he should go with her but Lucy reassured him.

'I've talked Simone into coming. And you need some time to yourself.' She left him a bottle of malt whisky and hit the road.

Five

'So what's this trip in aid of?' They were at Lakes Entrance and Sim was stuffing her face with fish and chips.

'I think it's time they knew the truth.'

'You think they'll revise their opinion of Kate?'

'I don't know. Shouldn't they?'

'Oh they should,' said Sim. 'Just don't count on it.'

Lucy was mulling that over as she opened the gate to her grandmother's house, the same gate that Kate had swung on as a toddler, before her eyes had been opened to the possibility that realms of gold existed outside this town.

Given the no-show at the funeral, Lucy wasn't sure what to expect when she knocked on the door; resentment perhaps, even hostility. What she got was pretty much indifference. She prompted the sort of response that might have been generated by an ad on the telly for some long-forgotten product.

Her grandmother opened the door.

'Hello, Gran,' she said. 'It's Lucy. How are you?'

'Well I never,' said her grandmother, 'Lucy. After all this time.' She yelled into the house. 'Stan! It's Lucy!' Then she turned back to the near-stranger on her doorstep. 'I suppose you'd better come in.'

Lucy went in. No kisses, no hugs. She was ushered into the living-room where Stan was absorbed in the racing guide.

'Hi, Granddad.'

'Gawd,' he said. 'Lucy. What the hell are you doing in Bannon Creek?'

'Kate died,' said Lucy. 'Your daughter Kate, remember? It was in the paper. And I left a message on the answering machine.'

'Oh, is that what it was. Couldn't really understand it,' said Joy.

'Don't read the papers any more,' said Stan. 'Except for the sport.'

'All bad news these days. People dying.'

'Yes. Like Kate.'

'Cancer, was it?' Her grandfather.

'Yes.'

'Got to die of something,' said Joy.

'She was forty-four,' said Lucy.

'It's all that pollution in the city,' said Stan, lighting a fag. 'She shoulda stayed at home.'

'She went to get an education,' said Lucy, trying to keep her voice even.

'Got you instead,' said Joy.

'She was raped,' said Lucy. 'That's how she got me.'

Joy and Stan exchanged a glance. This was news and they had no idea how they should respond to it.

'Never heard that one before,' said Stan, like it was a joke in poor taste.

'Takes two to tango, I always say,' said Joy.

'Perhaps you didn't hear me. She was raped. An Italian boy called Paolo. He forced himself on her in a park. Held her down. Raped her.'

'Then why didn't she tell someone?'

Lucy had had enough. She felt murdering her grandparents would not help to avenge her mother.

'Who would she have told?' She got up. 'I shouldn't have come. I wanted you to understand. But it's too late. Do you know, there were a lot of people at her funeral. Nearly a hundred of them. Including her partner. They all loved her dearly. I wonder why you could never love her at all?'

'Of course we loved her!' said Joy indignantly, following Lucy to the door. 'It's just she made it that hard! Always so up herself!'

'She wasn't up herself, Gran. She was a little girl and she was just different. She couldn't help it any more than a gum can help being different from a wattle. And you should have been proud of her instead of driving her away.'

And with that Lucy herself drove away from Far-East Gippsland, or rather her friend Simone drove through the night while Lucy cried, not for herself, but for her mother's misfortune in being born into the wrong family. And when she finally stopped crying, somewhere west of Bairnsdale, she wiped Bannon Creek from her mind.

Six

It didn't take Lucy very long to formulate a plan. She discussed it with Geoff and found him sympathetic—because she was her mother's daughter and he loved her—and disapproving, because he was older and sensible and practical and could not see that any good would come of it.

Simone agreed with Geoff.

What Lucy had in mind, of course, was to find her bastard of a father.

Geoff wondered what she hoped to achieve. 'You'd never get a case against him, even if he were still in Australia.'

'I know. It's not about that.'

What Lucy had in mind, if she ever found her father, was to do everything in her power to destroy him. Whatever life he had built for himself back in Italy, she would do her best to demolish; whatever relationships he had established over the years, she would tear apart. That's what she intended. But it's not what she said to Geoff.

'I just need to confront him.'

'After all this time?'

'He ruined her life, Geoff. She'd fought so hard for her dream, to get away to a place where she fitted in, where it wasn't a sin to be clever, where people talked about ideas. And he snatched that away from her. He never said sorry. He was never held accountable at all. I want to make him face up to that at last.'

Geoff was not deceived. He sighed. 'Look. Alright. I take your point. But Lucy—fifty million Italians? Do you even know his surname?'

Lucy shook her head. 'Do you?'

'She never mentioned it.'

18

'I'll find out. And I'll find him. Please, Geoff. Don't fight me. Help me. Do it for Kate.'

'Kate would turn in her grave.'

'No. She'd wish me buona fortuna.'

'What?'

'I've started Italian lessons. I haven't got very far. Wish I'd done it at school instead of French.'

Geoff stopped fighting her. Nor did he tell her that Kate would never, ever have given her blessing to this venture and that he did so himself only so he could keep Lucy close and, in that way, perhaps a little safer.

Lucy changed her name by deed poll to Harrington and applied for a new passport.

'I hope you don't mind that I used your name.'

Geoff, who was quietly pleased, hugged her. 'But why change it at all?'

'I just think it's a good idea. You know, if I do find him.'

Lucy started with St Joseph's Maternity Home—except that it was now full of old people with dementia. Lucy had made an appointment and found herself at the convent next door, explaining her mission to the Mother Superior, how she was trying to locate her father. The Mother Superior was helpful, one or two nuns remained from those days, if she could wait a few minutes?

Lucy waited nearly an hour. A little dark-haired nun finally arrived, full of apologies.

'I am so sorry, we had an escape.'

Lucy looked startled.

'I know, it sounds as if we keep prisoners. But some of our— clients, we must call them now, some of our clients go wandering, you see, and there's a very busy road, you might have noticed?'

Lucy had. She smiled.

'That which was lost is found?'

The little nun grinned. 'Indeed. I'm Sister Rita, how can I help you?'

'Lucy O'Connell. I was born here twenty-four years ago. My mother was Kate O'Connell.'

'Yes, I know.'

'You remember her?'

'I do. And I remember you. My first birth after I came here. I'm a nurse, you see. How is your mother?'

'She died six months ago.'

Sister Rita crossed herself. 'I am sorry. I liked her so much. She was very strong.'

'Can you tell me, Sister—did she have any visitors while she was here?'

'None at all.'

'Did she ever mention who my father was?'

'No. I did ask. I thought she might want us to get in touch. She wouldn't have it. I remember thinking she was very bitter and she said she had good reason.'

'She did.'

'You want to find your father.'

'Yes.'

'I wish I could help,' said Sister Rita. 'It's not good to let old wounds fester, is it?'

'No. It's not.'

'Maybe Father Ignatius could tell you more. He was the one who sent your mother to us.'

'Is he still alive, then?'

'Oh, yes, very much alive. You'll find him at St Benedict's.'

She showed Lucy to the door, chatting, 'When you were born, how familiar you looked! The hair, the skin—just like my little sisters. I wouldn't be surprised, you know, if your father turned out to be Italian!'

Lucy forced a smile.

'I'll pray for you, Lucia Elisabetta,' said Sister Rita. 'For a happy outcome.'

Like her mother all those years before, Lucy thanked her and thought it would take a lot more than prayer.

Father Ignatius was away on retreat. She had to wait another week before she could see him. He was not like Sister Rita. He must have been nearly seventy and he seemed unwilling to help her at all.

'Kate O'Connell,' he said. 'Goodness me.'

'You remember her, then.'

'Well. Just a little.'

Lucy didn't think priests were supposed to lie.

'I'm sure you remember quite clearly. She came to you for help when she was raped. You talked her out of going to the police and referred her to St Joseph's.'

'The courts could be brutal back then.'

'The rape was brutal. You told Kate you would speak to the boy's family. Did you do that?'

'I believe I did.'

'Paolo, he was called. And since he was my father I want his surname, please. And his address if you have it.'

'I'm a priest, I can't divulge information like that.'

'You didn't get it in the confessional, Father Ignatius. So you can tell me. Surely I have a right to know.'

Perhaps the retreat had wearied him. Or perhaps it had been about Seeking the Truth. Father Ignatius suddenly stopped playing games.

'His name was Paolo Esposito. He was sent back to Italy in disgrace after what he did to your mother. I honestly have no idea where he is now. His aunt and uncle moved to Doncaster I think, when they retired. They may be able to help you, their name is Resteghini. But don't expect too much from them. To some extent, he ruined their lives too.'

'I can only ask.'

'Miss O'Connell, I can see that you are angry. I understand that. I would not give Kate the same advice today. Paolo should have faced up to what he did.'

'It's never too late, Father, is it? Thank you for your help.'

Lucy left. She suspected that she now had a priest as well as a nun praying for her in her endeavours. She wondered if it needed faith on her part to make it work.

She found the address in Doncaster without too much trouble and decided to risk turning up unannounced. Bad decision.

A small group of elderly Italians were busy in the open garage as

Lucy walked up the drive. One of the women came to meet her, waving dripping red arms and leaving globs of whatever it was in her wake.

'Not interested! All good Catholics! Wasting your time!'

It took Lucy a moment, then she smiled.

'I'm not a Jehovah's Witness,' she said. 'Nothing like that. I haven't come to talk about the Lord Jesus.'

'Oh,' said the woman. 'What then?'

'Mrs Resteghini?'

'Grazia Resteghini. Yes.'

'I'm Lucy O'Connell. My mother Kate once worked for you. In the café in Carlton?'

Grazia looked suddenly wary. 'Lots of people worked for us.'

'I'm sure you remember, Kate,' said Lucy gently. 'She went out with your nephew Paolo. Please can I talk to you just for a minute?'

'We're busy,' said Grazia, 'making the sauce.'

She waved a hand towards the garage—the copper, the boxes of fruit and bottles, the strange little crushing machine—and Lucy realised that the red stuff was tomato pulp and that there would, by day's end, be enough sauce to stock a small supermarket.

'Maybe I can help.'

'You ever made sauce before?'

'No. But I'd love to learn.'

Grazia was dismissive. 'It's hard work.' She turned to the others, muttered something in Italian which Lucy had no hope of understanding and beckoned her to follow.

'Five minutes,' said Grazia when they entered the kitchen. 'Once you start on the tomatoes, you can't stop.'

'I just want to ask you a few questions.'

Grazia grunted and started to prepare coffee for the saucemakers. Lucy wasn't sure if she was to be offered one or not.

'My mother died some months ago. Now I want to find my father. Paolo Esposito. Your nephew.'

'How do I know that Paolo is your father? You could be anyone! Where is the proof?'

Since Grazia had so recently proclaimed her faith, Lucy decided to

22

play up her Catholic credentials.

'It was Father Ignatius who told me where to find you,' she said. 'He believes me. The nuns at St Joseph's believe me.'

She picked up a photo from the dresser—Grazia and two other girls, taken long ago.

'You and your sisters?'

Grazia busied herself with the coffee.

'I bet the one in the middle is Paolo's mother, am I right? Funny, she looks just like me, don't you think?'

Grazia turned to her then. 'Why do you want to cause trouble, eh? After all this time? Do you think we didn't suffer enough because of that boy? My sisters are in Italy still because of him! Mauro and I— we have lived our lives cut off from our family for forty years!'

'My mother knows all about that, Grazia. She had no one at all. Paolo raped her and left her pregnant and ran off back home. She had to leave university and bring up his child with no help from anyone.'

Grazia clutched at straws. 'He was just a boy. He made a mistake.'

'He committed a crime. An act of violence. But he is still my father. I hope he has changed. And I have a right to find out. Especially now, when I have no one else.'

If that was a lie, it wasn't much of a one, thought Lucy, since she had no intention of ever contacting Kate's family again.

She looked at Grazia, pleaded with her. 'I am going to Italy. I just want his address. Old wounds should be healed.'

There was a long pause.

'I'm sorry,' said Grazia. 'I can't help you.'

'Won't help me.'

'You don't want a father. Or healing either. You want revenge. Isn't that so? And to get it you will hurt a lot of innocent people.'

'I hope not. But if I do, so be it. That will be his fault, not mine. And I will find him, because it's important for both of us. We both need to understand our past. I'm sorry you can't see that.'

Once again, Lucy left without what she had come for. What was it with her relatives, she thought, that made them all so pig-headed and contrary? She was getting into her car when Grazia arrived, panting.

'It's too much, you understand? What you ask. But here. At least take this.' And she thrust a bottle of tomato sauce into Lucy's hand and was gone.

Lucy felt the anger rising within her. Were they mad, these Italians? Did they think they could buy her off with—tomato sauce? She was tempted to smash it in the gutter. 'Gente di merda,' she thought as she drove away, glad that she could at least swear in Italian. Why oh why had she gone? Why hadn't she asked Simone to go for her? Now they even knew what she looked like.

'That's what I achieved,' she said to Geoff, holding out the sauce when she got home. She was shaking so much he had to grab it before she dropped it. 'All I did was show my hand. I bet Grazia's already writing to her nephew.'

In this Lucy was correct. No sooner was the last seal clamped on to the last bottle of sauce than Grazia, claiming a headache, excused herself from the usual celebration and went to write a letter. It was 1996 and she did not have email; she used a little blue aerogramme to send the news to Paolo that he not only had a daughter but she was likely to turn up on his doorstep in the not too distant future.

'Stai attento, Paolo,' she wrote. 'Be on your guard. This girl looks like your mother.' That wretched photo, it was true, there was no denying the likeness. She finished the letter. 'Make no mistake, she is out to cause trouble, I'm sure of it.' And who knew where it would end, she thought, as she sealed the envelope. She looked up to see her husband standing in the doorway.

'What?'

'That girl. She's family.'

'Non svegliare il can che dorme, Mauro.' Let sleeping dogs lie.

Mauro shook his head. He did not agree with his wife. Paolo, for his part, when he got the letter, burnt it. And tried—with less than total success—to put it out of his mind. Which had always been his way of dealing with the unpleasant things in life.

Seven

Lucy went on with her preparations. The fact that it was going to be hard to find her father did not daunt her; she wouldn't accept that it might be impossible. She would visit every Esposito on the Italian peninsula if necessary.

Geoff tried the National Archives on her behalf. A helpful young man explained that the records they needed—patchy at the best of times—were currently being computerised and were unavailable. He'd see what he could do but didn't hold out much hope. It was possible—just possible—that some immigration records might still be held in Rome.

Lucy went to the Italian Consulate—she had to go anyway for her visa—and met Simone afterwards. They lunched in Carlton as they had in their uni days, as Kate had in hers.

'How did you go?'

Lucy groaned. 'Do you know how many Italians are called Esposito?'

'Lots?'

'It's like Smith or Jones. Or Nguyen if you're Vietnamese. Common as mud. Before unification, abandoned children were all given the name Esposito.'

'Shows a singular lack of imagination.'

'Elsa—the woman who helped with my visa—said it was especially common in Naples, in fact it's a pretty sure bet that anyone called Esposito has Neapolitan ancestry.'

'What, Neapolitans made a habit of dumping their kids?'

Lucy shrugged. 'I guess they were poor. And desperate. Anyway, I've changed my plans a bit, and I'm going to start there.'

Simone stared. 'In Naples!'

'Why not?'

'Well. You know... like you just said. Isn't it terribly poor and full of slums and run by the Mafia?'

'I think it's called the Camorra in Naples. And anyway, I was talking about a hundred years ago!'

'Has it changed?'

'I'm sure it has. I got some brochures and it looks quite beautiful.'

'Yeah, well anywhere looks beautiful in travel brochures. Probably even Bannon Creek.'

Lucy fiddled with her lunch. 'Sim? Stop being so negative?'

'I'm not negative about Italy, I'd kill to be going to Italy, heavens, you know me, "Is Italian, is good," that's my motto. I'm green with envy. But nobody goes to Naples!'

'Well Mum did mention Campania. I've got a feeling it's right. And anyway, you talk like I'm going on a holiday. I'm not.'

'Well no. Of course not. But won't you just be going through phone books or something? Couldn't you start in—I don't know. Tuscany?'

Lucy chose to ignore that. 'The Bay of Naples is famous, that's where Capri is.'

Simone sighed. 'Okay. Just so long as you don't get mugged or shot or sold into slavery.'

She ordered coffee for them both then looked at Lucy's face, all the excitement gone out of it.

'I'm sorry. I'm worried about you, okay? So is Geoff, he told me. Just promise that if you need a hand you'll ring me. I could always come over.'

'You've got a thesis to write.'

'It can wait. Luce, don't be cross. I didn't mean to be negative. It'll be fine. I'm sure it will. Like you said—Capri. And hey, Pompeii. Fantastic! Whether you find him or not. Your bastard of a father.'

Sim had been Lucy's best friend since prep at Clifton Hill Primary. And although she was smiling brightly now Lucy suddenly realised that Sim didn't want her to find Paolo, that Sim was afraid for her as Kate had been and as Geoff probably was and she felt a little fear shoot up inside herself about this mission. But she put it aside and would not give into it and refused to even consider it again. In that

26

she was both her mother's and her father's daughter.

Instead, taking command of the situation, she called at the library on the way home. And was surprised to find how many people had written books on Italy, how many people seemed to absolutely adore the place. She felt rather put out, knowing there was little chance that she herself would join the chorus of adulation.

She was staying with Geoff until she left in order to save money, and he looked surprised when she arrived home, staggering under the weight of the books she'd borrowed.

'You're going to read all those before you leave?'

'Research. On Naples.'

'Ah.'

'Don't say 'ah' like that. I thought you might help me.'

'Gladly. Um, why Naples?'

'Esposito. It's a Neapolitan name. So I'm going there first. Well, first after the embassy in Rome.'

'I see.'

'Sim says nobody goes to Naples.'

'Well you're going to prove her wrong, aren't you?'

Lucy could see why her mother had loved him so much. They sat down after dinner and pored over the books.

'I just want to get a feel for the place,' Lucy said. 'The guy at the Consulate made it sound quite daunting. And Sim didn't help.'

Nor did the guide books. They were ambivalent, defensive even.

'Not an easy city to like,' read Geoff. 'Large, dirty and crime-infested. Spend as little time here as possible. Oh dear.'

'I don't expect to like it,' said Lucy. 'It's going to be full of Italians, like Paolo. I want to know what to expect, that's all.'

'I know some lovely Italians,' said Geoff.

'Some of your best friends?'

Geoff just smiled.

Lucy read on. 'Anyway, this is a bit more optimistic: 'Few places on earth inspire such fierce loyalties.'

'Better,' Geoff agreed. 'And after all, most of this stuff was written for Americans.'

'Does that make a difference?'

'Oh heavens yes, you know Americans. It's all about the plumbing.'

'I see,' said Lucy, who didn't, quite.

'It's worth remembering,' said Geoff, 'that almost everyone wanted Naples at one time or another. The Greeks and Romans, the Byzantines, the Goths, the Normans, the Swabians, the Angevins, the Bourbons.'

'You left out the Aragonese.'

'So I did. And wasn't it part of The Grand Tour? For the English upper classes?'

'Oh, yes, absolutely.'

'So it must have had something going for it.'

They read on for a while, opening a second bottle of wine. Geoff finally broke the silence. 'Goethe liked the place, listen to this: 'Naples is a paradise... everyone lives in a sort of intoxicated self-forgetfulness.'

'Maybe that's what Paolo's doing.'

'What will you do if you don't find him?'

'Come home. Well I've only got a semester's leave anyway, after that it's back to the classroom or lose my job.'

Geoff looked surprised. 'You'd get another job.'

'What I'm doing—it's not an obsession, Geoff.'

'I'm glad to hear it. I thought it might have turned into one.'

'Honestly, no. It's not like I'm searching for my roots or anything. I'm doing this for my mother.'

Geoff nodded. 'Something I've been wanting to say.'

Lucy knew what was coming. 'And I'm okay for funds.'

'You're going to Europe, Lucy. Italy's not some third-world country, it's expensive.'

'I'll manage, really I will.'

'I've got a couple of thousand dollars for you. I want you to take it.'

'I couldn't possibly!'

'Why couldn't you possibly? You want me to lie awake at night worrying? You want Kate to come back and haunt me for letting you go at all?'

'She wouldn't dare.'

'Be gracious for once. Thank the nice man and take his money.'

Lucy kissed his cheek and agreed to take the money. She was rewarded with a line by Barbara Grizzutti Harrison in *Italian Days*: 'We have loved the Mezzogiorno and live at psychic high noon.'

'Promising,' she said. 'Not—as I've said—that it matters.'

She meant it. While liking Italy might make things easier, she couldn't help feeling that an admiration for anything Italian—Puccini excepted, perhaps—would be an insult to Kate's memory. But she went to bed feeling a little more relaxed. Because if she were completely honest with herself, the fear she had felt at lunchtime was not a new thing but had snuck into her being some time ago and was now starting to grow apace, and shake her confidence in this entire enterprise.

She went to sleep with the words of an old song going around in her head, one that Simone's grandmother used to sing, a silly song about the isle of Capri, and finding a girl there beneath the shade of an old walnut tree. But in her dreams the tree was on the edge of a cliff and what she found in its shade was Paolo and he fought her off with great determination. She woke as she was about to plunge into the sea beside three huge rocks.

She told Geoff about the dream next morning, in part to dispel the fearfulness it had aroused. He just smiled.

'Tiberius. He got a mention last night, remember?'

Lucy did remember, and felt a bit foolish.

'In fact, there's no proof that he ever tossed anyone over a cliff. He wasn't as bad as he's painted.'

Lucy flared. 'Are you trying to tell me something?'

Geoff shook his head. 'Lucy, I'm with you, okay? Just because I think Tiberius has had a bad press, I'm not calling for a general amnesty.'

'Sorry. I think I'm getting a bit nervous.'

'And no wonder. You're going overseas for the first time. By yourself. Not to have fun but on a difficult quest.'

'You make me feel like Don Quixote.'

'Brave, I hope. Not foolish.'

Lucy sighed. 'Tell me honestly. Do you think I've got a hope in hell of finding him?'

'Maybe you should go to St Pat's and light a candle.'

'For divine guidance? I would if I thought it would do any good.'

'Or you could wait till Rome and go to St Peter's.'

'You've been there of course.'

'A long time ago. I was planning to go back. With Kate.'

'Were you hoping she'd find her faith again?'

'Of course. I believe in miracles.'

Geoff was still a practising Catholic. He and Kate had argued about it long and hard, without rancour, enjoying the intellectual point-scoring.

'So what's it like?'

'St Peter's? Very big. Very grand. You'll like the Pantheon better, it'll appeal to your atheistic leanings.' He smiled. 'I wouldn't be surprised if God preferred it as well.'

Lucy was packing a few days later, with Simone's help.

'You've got to carry it, Luce, remember that.'

'It's not like I'm just going to loll about on a beach! And anyway, it'll still be cold.'

'One sweater, one jacket. You want more, you buy it.'

'I'm made of money now?'

'You know what they charge for excess baggage? Besides, you'll look at all those Italian chicks and want to chuck your clothes in the nearest charity bin.' She gave a critical look at a shirt Lucy was folding. 'Or is that where they came from?'

'I've been saving, Sim. What do you think teachers get paid anyway?'

'You've just spurred me on to finish my thesis.'

And then they heard Geoff calling, sounding quite excited. It was only a small miracle, he said, but Lucy's instincts had been right. Geoff's helpful young man from the National Archives had sent him a fax that afternoon. A Paolo Esposito, aged 21 at the time, had arrived in Australia from Italy in July 1972.

'And this,' said Geoff, waving the fax, is a copy of his entry certificate.'

'I don't suppose,' said Lucy, 'that it happens by any chance to say where he came from? It wouldn't do that, would it, Geoff?'

Geoff smiled. 'Mention is made of Pozzuoli.'

'Where?'

'It's just around the bay from Naples. Like I said, your instincts were right.'

Lucy hugged him and hugged Simone.

'Of course there's no saying he went back to Pozzuoli.'

'But it's somewhere to start, isn't it?'

'I'd be saying a little prayer to San Gennaro if I were you.'

Lucy and Sim exchanged a look.

'St Januarius. He was martyred at Pozzuoli, he's the patron saint of Naples. His head's in the cathedral there.'

The girls looked appalled. 'His head?'

'And some of his blood. On certain feast days it liquefies. Then the locals know that Vesuvius won't erupt for a while.'

'Superstitious rubbish,' said Sim.

'Probably,' said Geoff equably. 'All the same—doesn't hurt to hedge your bets.'

Lucy resisted the urge to rush out to the nearest church and finished her packing. The last thing to go in her pack was the photo of her mother which usually stood on her bedside table. She'd bought a folding leather frame for it—now it could be displayed or not, as she felt appropriate. Two days later, Geoff and Sim took her to the airport. Geoff gave her Norman Lewis's *Naples '44* to read on the flight. Sim gave her a book called *Getting It Right In Italy*. Her G.P. gave her a mild sedative. And thus armed, Lucy kissed them both and disappeared through the doors to the departure lounge.

The flight was long, the food bad, she'd seen both the movies and the child in the row behind was brat enough to put her off parenthood for life. Add to this her innate fear and the trip was only a couple of steps short of hell. She was saved by the doctor's little pills and those two well-chosen books.

Norman Lewis, she discovered, was a wonderful writer whose love for Italy and the Italians—forged in the misery and deprivations of wartime Naples—she found inspiring. Sim's book proved that her destination was indeed a foreign country and they did things very differently there. Together they kept her mind occupied and her fingernails more or less intact until she landed some twenty-six hours later on Italian soil.

The journey Kate had hoped her daughter would never make had begun.

Eight

Lucy gave herself three days in Rome. She went to the Embassy, letting them know who she was and vaguely what she was doing, in case she did get mugged or sold into slavery.

They couldn't help much; their records had all been sent home to Australia. 'Let me guess,' said Lucy. 'It's all being computerised.'

'Exactly right,' said Samantha, the young Australian-Italian who was doing her best to be helpful. 'If you're trying to put some foliage on the family tree, honestly I'd leave it a year or two. It's a mess right now.'

'Un grande casino, huh?'

'Not bad, how long have you been learning?'

Lucy smiled. 'Three months.'

Samantha took pity on her. 'Look. You want some advice? Best thing to do, when you get to Pozzuoli go straight to the Ufficio dell'Anagrafe and ask there. Everyone in Italy has to have an official place of residence. Doesn't mean they actually live there of course, but it's a start.'

Lucy thanked her, it was something. And then she walked the streets with a feeling of déjà vu. St Peter's, the Forum, the Spanish Steps, the Colosseum, the Trevi Fountain—what Australian hadn't seen them in books and brochures or stuck their likeness on the fridge in the form of postcards from peripatetic friends? Even the ghastly Vittorio Emmanuele Monument was as familiar as Uluru, if somewhat easier to climb. Geoff was right, though—the enormous vaulted space of the Pantheon was sublime.

And she went to the Protestant Cemetery, il Cimitero Acattolico, early one day when it was still damp with dew under the cypresses. Geoff had told her about it too, had made her promise not to miss it and here she was, paying her respects to Keats and Shelley.

Poor Keats first. She stood by his grave and marvelled at the quiet; there was a surprising amount of birdsong but little could be heard of the noisy city that lay just outside the wall. She wondered how one of the world's greatest poets could die so embittered that he wouldn't even allow his name on his tombstone. Had he no inkling how history would treat him? Perhaps not. He had always seemed so full of melancholy to Lucy, rich and sensuous, yes, but in a sort of end-of-things way. Or so she had thought.

Shelley, on the other hand... and she went to find his grave, consulting the map in her guide book. Oh, yes, altogether different. Percy Bysshe Shelley. Cor Cordium, heart of all hearts, yes, that was it. And some of Ariel's song from *The Tempest*:

Nothing of him doth fade,
But doth suffer a sea-change
Into something rich and strange.

And suddenly Lucy was thinking of her mother, who like Keats and Shelley and so many here, had died before her time; the mother who had given her a love of poetry and encouraged her to learn her favourites off by heart because, Kate had said, if you ever find yourself in a dark and lonely place, it's good to have a poem to keep you company.

Lucy thought now how Kate would have loved this place, which was neither dark nor lonely, would have loved to see it, even if it was in Italy. But Kate never got further than New Zealand, where Geoff took her for a holiday when her illness was suspected but not yet diagnosed. It was the first and only time she left Australia.

Nine

When Kate left St Joseph's Maternity Home with two-week-old Lucy, she was sure of just one thing. Nothing and no-one would ever come between them. She realised she had to earn a living; she was not the sort of girl who could ever be happy living on handouts. So she would need a job, and someone to look after Lucy while she was doing that job. But she would be a good mother, the very best mother, no questions would ever be asked about her ability to raise her child.

There was a bookstore in Carlton, new and second-hand books, it was a place Kate had haunted during her first and only student year and she liked the old Jewish couple who ran it. She saw them putting a sign in the window one day, 'Assistant Wanted', and went straight in. If there was one thing Kate knew about, it was books. Fortunately, she could also type, since all the girls at Bannon High learnt to type and all the boys did woodwork, it not being expected that many of them would Go On To Greater Things. So in spite of—or perhaps because of—having Lucy in a sling against her breast, she got the job.

When her new employers enquired about her babysitting arrangements, and it became clear that Kate hadn't got that far, Esther Freeman took it upon herself to make a phone call. Within the hour, Kate and Lucy were on a tram heading for Brunswick and a visit to Isobel Reed. Isobel—known as Saint Bel to many in Brunswick—ran a small child-minding centre. She'd begun it as a means of keeping her large Edwardian house when she found herself suddenly widowed with two toddlers of her own. That was over twenty years ago. She liked Kate. Kate liked her. And when Lucy was left in Isobel's capable arms the following Monday morning, Kate was the only one who cried.

And so began the first five years of Lucy's life, and Kate's as a single mother. Lucy lacked a father but not much else. If the succession of dingy flats they lived in were less than ideal, Kate and Isobel Reed were always there to provide stability. As for Kate, the job was alright, the Freemans were kind and there was plenty to read. And she had her beautiful daughter. She would probably have been wiser to get out of Carlton, to go to St Kilda or Frankston or Dandenong, away from the milling students and the sandstone colleges, the green lawns and the leafy walks and the noisy pubs, and all the other reminders of what might have been. But she stayed there, surrounded by the university, like a sailor thrown overboard from some mighty vessel, left to struggle in tumultuous seas.

It was Esther Freeman who gave her a long-term goal when, in 1973, Gough Whitlam introduced the single mother's benefit.

'You will apply, Kate?' she asked.

'I don't know. I don't think so. I'd rather work.'

'Just what I said to Roy. She is not the type to live on handouts. All the same... you should think about the future.'

Kate smiled. She thought about little else.

'I mean—three years, Lucy goes to school, yes?'

'It still seems a long way away.'

'It's nothing. A job in a school—that would be ideal, no? Then you are free in the holidays.'

'Are you trying to get rid of me?'

'Never. But for you, it would be best. Think about it. There are jobs beside teaching.'

Kate not only thought about it, she did some research and she prepared herself, studying at night by correspondence, gaining a diploma in office management. And when Lucy started school, she bid farewell to the Freemans and went to work at the local high school. It wasn't a very well-paid job and in fact Kate didn't enjoy it as much as the bookshop, but the library was a good one and the hours were perfect and she counted herself lucky.

Or so she had told Lucy, never once mentioning how hard and at times how lonely, her life had been. For most of the time it was just the two of them and Lucy didn't mind that. Nor did she really notice that for all the years of her childhood, no man ever set foot inside their flat.

Lucy was a bright child and a pretty one. She did well at school like her mother before her and she had, in Simone Richards, a best friend who provided her with another family, one that treated Lucy almost as their own, even took her on the occasional holiday with them. Perhaps it was this that saved Lucy, gave her some sense of normality. It also implanted in her a longing for a proper family of her own which she rarely articulated and then only to herself. It seemed an impossible dream, like winning the lottery.

In time—in a long time—the Richards even became friendly with Kate, though not to the point of ever inviting her to dinner, nothing like that. Perhaps they did ask her and got tired of the refusals; Kate was always working, always studying, always, perhaps, afraid of—what? Rejection?

It was only when Lucy was going through Kate's things after her death, and read her diary, that she finally understood. It was not a proper diary, Kate never had time for that, sometimes whole weeks were missing, sometimes there was just a line, 'too tired,' something like that. But she had wanted to be a writer, and what she did put down was enough. More than enough to make Lucy determined to see this through to the end.

Ten

Thinking about her mother, there by Shelley's grave, in the blessed quiet of the Protestant Cemetery in Rome, Lucy found herself in tears.

'It does get to you, doesn't it?' said a very English voice and Lucy looked up to find a woman perhaps in her fifties smiling at her but also clutching a handkerchief.

'I didn't expect to cry.' She didn't add that she was thinking about her mother.

'I always cry. They were so young. And so monstrously talented. Keats or Shelley?'

'I'm a Shelley girl.'

'And I. Such a romantic. Though he treated his women and children abominably.'

'My mother liked to remind me of that.'

'A realist as well as a romantic?'

Lucy could only nod, afraid the tears would flow again. The woman waited a few moments.

'Your first visit, then?'

'My first visit to Italy.'

'I do hope you find what you are looking for.'

Lucy wondered if everyone could just see straight through her, read her like an open book. How, if that were so, would she ever get to find Paolo? Get close to him, as she planned, without his knowing her identity? He'd see her coming from miles away. The woman must have sensed her disquiet.

'You're not the usual backpacker,' she said, 'I can tell that much. Enjoy this bel paese, my dear. Embrace it. You'll find it has much to offer.'

And she was gone, quickly lost to sight amidst the spring flowers and the scattered tombs of all those adopted Romans. Lucy wondered if she would ever find it in her heart to embrace the beautiful country. And if its offerings would include a missing father, if it would in due course deliver him up to her.

Rome was tantalising but it was just a stopover, she still had a long way to go. The phrase stuck in her mind from her last Italian lesson: c'è ancora molta strada. She was glad something had stuck; she could understand only a little in the bars and restaurants she'd been to and asking directions was a minor embarrassment. But people were kind and tried to be helpful and she managed to get by.

So it was that Lucy Harrington, formerly O'Connell, came to be on Alitalia Flight 312, which finally disgorged its passengers through gate lounge four at Capodichino, the airport which services Naples.

Mad, bad, glorious Napoli.

Eleven

Lucy caught the bus into centro, staring out the window, trying to take it all in and finding that it was, somehow, just exactly what she'd expected: the motorini and their suicidal riders, the cars, the bars, the cigarette sellers on every corner, the old buildings crowded together, walls covered in washing and fat bunches of wisteria; the impossibly narrow streets, winding down towards the bay, the glimpses of that blue, blue water. And hovering over it all, the black hump of Vesuvius over which she had flown less than an hour before, staring down into its crater, fearful that it might choose just that moment to end its fifty years of quiescence. It was all so Italian—and yes, she'd just been in Rome but this seemed revved up several notches. What was that about psychic high noon?

She did not want to like it. This was enemy territory. She tried very hard not to be seduced.

The youth hostel at Mergellina, which Lucy found easily enough, was like youth hostels everywhere, providing the bare necessities with a minimum of style. But it was clean and—as she knew from assiduous study of city maps—on the right side of Naples for Pozzuoli.

She claimed a bottom bunk then returned to the reception desk and asked about the best way to get there. It was not difficult—just another bus. Or of course she could hire a motorino or even a car.

Lucy laughed out loud. She was a good driver but she had watched the traffic in Rome in stunned disbelief and from the little, the very little she had seen since arriving in Naples it was even worse here, it was total chaos. The rules, if they existed, were unfathomable. Seat belts were scorned, kids sat in the front on mum's knee and every driver held a cigarette in one hand while pressing on the horn with the other, so how they actually manoeuvred the car was a mystery—perhaps with their knees. When did the bus leave, again?

The guy on reception was helpful. There were many buses, it seemed, Pozzuoli was just down the road. Was she going to see the Solfatara? Lucy, having no idea what he was talking about, shook her head.

'I'm going to the Ufficio dell'Anagrafe.'

'Ah. Next to the Municipio. The town hall.'

'Municipio.' Lucy repeated it.

'Correct.'

'Grazie. I will go tomorrow. Domani.'

The truth was she couldn't face Pozzuoli today. She was tired and she knew how much effort it would require if no-one spoke much English—and why should they at a government office? More than that, she feared the disappointment that would come if Paolo Esposito—her Paolo Esposito—were unknown there.

She went back to her room to grab a jacket and ventured out, deciding a walk to get a feel for the city might do her good. She could also, she realised, use a more detailed guide book. Solfatara? She had no idea and cursed herself for not asking.

She walked for an hour or so, avoiding the dog shit which seemed to be everywhere, amazed by the number of people—a gardener here, a window-cleaner there, who actually sang as they worked, did they all aspire to be opera singers?—and stopping to buy two more guide books. She stopped for coffee too, sitting in a bar with a view of that impossibly blue bay and tried again not to be impressed.

She found herself watching a pair of teenagers. Velcroed together at hip and lip on a stationary motorino, both of them so beautiful Lucy kept looking around for the cameras, they finally completed their display of eternal devotion and roared off through the traffic, no helmets of course. Lucy, feeling a bit like a voyeur—except that the pair had been so blatant—was suddenly lonely. She bought a postcard and wrote a funny note to Simone and then headed back to the hostel.

She sat on her bunk and considered the options for dinner. To go out to some trattoria alone, sit and eat alone—the prospect wasn't inviting. The hostel restaurant was open and even this early in the season there was bound to be someone else there. She'd just settled on this less scary option when the door opened and three blondes burst into the room, shedding enormous backpacks as they came.

Scandinavian. Had to be, with that hair and those tans.

'Hello,' said the first, in near accentless English. 'I am Mette, pleased to meet you.'

'Trine.'

'Dorte. We are Danish.'

'Hello. I'm Lucy.'

'Ah! Fantastic! Australian.'

They all smiled hugely and began stowing their gear.

Lucy smiled too. They had that effect. 'How did you know?'

'You Australians; the accent! Everywhere! Good travellers.'

'After university, we go Downunder.'

Dorte—or was it Trine?—said something in Danish.

'She's starving,' said Mette for Lucy's benefit.

'We are in Naples, we must have pizza, yes? You will join us?'

'I was going to eat in the restaurant here.'

'You can't! The choice will be pasta and pasta.'

'And just possibly pasta.'

'With tomato sauce.'

'Or without.'

'We go to Piazza Sannazzaro,' said Mette, who seemed to be the leader. 'We eat pizza amongst the petrol pumps. Recommended by your Lonely Planet Guide Book.'

They stood there smiling at her, clearly wanting her to join them.

'I think,' said Trine, 'you have much on your mind, yes? Come and relax for a bit.'

'They say the pizzerie in Sannazzaro are just as good as Brandi.'

'And much cheaper. No servizio, no coperto.'

'Brandi?'

'It's famous. They're supposed to have invented the pizza Margherita. Come, Lucy, come and tell us about Australia.'

Lucy lost the argument going on in her head, which told her she was not here to enjoy herself, and the four of them walked down to the Piazza Sannazzaro.

The tables were set up outdoors amongst the petrol pumps, now fortunately closed for the day, but with the cars still roaring past of course. Lucy couldn't help wondering what a Melbourne health inspector would make of it all. But Trine spoke fluent Italian and the waiters fell over themselves to assist with their order.

The pizza, when it came, was better than any Lucy had eaten back home. She was startled though, to suddenly find beside her plate a key ring with a small red horn attached.

'Please pay what you think is worth' it said on one side and on the reverse, 'The blessings of all the saints.'

Lucy looked around and saw a woman of indeterminate age, dressed in skirt and shawl, standing there, nodding and smiling. She looked at the girls.

'What on earth...?'

The waiter sprang to her aid. 'She's begging, signorina. You buy or not, is no matter. Except...'

'Except—what? It will feed her starving children?'

Mette grinned and said in English, 'More likely pay off the new Fiat, begging's an art-form here, Lucy.'

But the waiter understood her and shook his head. He pointed to the horn. 'Is for good luck, signorina.'

'Really?'

'Sì, signorina.'

'I see,' said Lucy, who didn't. 'In that case...' And she forked out three thousand lire and the woman almost curtsied and disappeared.

'I hope it does bring me luck.' Lucy shoved the thing in her pocket.

The girls looked at her curiously. 'You are going to need luck?'

Lucy told them, briefly, that she was here to look up some family connections, and expected that it might be difficult. They accepted the story and then raved about Pompeii, where they had spent the day. After that it was all Australia—where should they go, what should they see, how much could you cover in six months. The four of them drank a litre of passable wine and walked back to the hostel licking lemon gelati.

Lucy was sorry to find they were off on the ferry to Sicily next morning.

She did not sleep much. Rome had been noisy but Naples was something else, a full cacophony: the ceaseless traffic and insistent sirens; the human voices, laughing, shouting, singing, and any number of unidentified bangings and clangings. It went on till dawn. The Danes slept through it—perhaps they'd had time to acclimatise.

Lucy was up early, her nerves on edge. Craving coffee, she went out to find a bar and bumped into Mette, on the same mission. They walked down to the water together and sat gazing out into dense fog. The head of Vesuvius could just be seen poking through and down off the NATO base loomed the huge bulk of an American aircraft carrier.

'Capri is out there somewhere,' said Mette.

'Hiding in a cocktail of deadly pollutants?'

The Danish girl smiled. 'Just fog. Pliny The Younger wrote about it, back in the first century.'

'So it's one hundred percent natural?'

'As they say in the ads? Let us hope so.'

'I must read Pliny,' said Lucy.

'Oh yes! Before you go to Pompeii. His description is brilliant.'

Lucy just nodded.

'I forget. You are not here to sightsee.'

'Maybe Pompeii. If there's time.'

'Try. It's...' She threw up her hands.

'Amazing?'

'There is nothing like it. Nothing. Find the time. Promise me.'

'I'll try.'

Mette looked at her sympathetically.

'These family connections. They must be very important, I think.'

Lucy nodded.

'I hope it works out. I hope you have good news when we see you in Australia.'

Lucy forced a smile. 'Me too.'

They finished their coffee just as Dorte and Trine arrived. More coffee and cornetti too. The sun was warm, the water was blue and the fishermen had nearly finished unloading their boats. Picture postcard stuff. Lucy went right on trying to hate it while the Danes extolled the beauties of the Aeolian Islands. Was she sure she wouldn't come with them? Back at the hostel, they all exchanged addresses, there were hugs and kisses and her new friends were gone.

Lucy felt the loneliness engulf her again. In fact, she had longed to go with them, to head off to sunny Sicily. Suddenly, too late, she was desperate for someone to confide in, someone to share the task ahead. She fought back the urge to ring Simone. It was the middle of the night back home, which didn't matter but calls from Italy cost a small fortune, which did.

Instead, she summoned up all her courage and found her way to the bus stop. She had wasted most of the morning already, it was time to act.

Twelve

The guide books had given her a glimpse into Pozzuoli's fabled past. It might now seem little more than an outer suburb of Naples but once—ah, once!—it had been a great trading city, a mighty port for the whole Mediterranean. Not much sign of its former glory now, as the bus rumbled past abandoned apartment buildings. They puzzled Lucy, there were so many of them. The old man sitting next to her saw her staring.

'Terremoto,' he said.

'Earthquake?'

'Sì. Ottanta-tre.'

An earthquake thirteen years ago and they still hadn't been repaired? Was this modern Europe or not?

The bus stopped and she remembered 'municipio' and asked the driver for directions. She passed more ruins as she walked there but these, being Roman, escaped criticism. She found the town hall and nearby, as promised, was the Ufficio dell'Anagrafe.

Lucy took a deep breath. She wished, too late, that she had asked Trine to write her a note, explaining her mission. Wished it even more when the man behind the counter failed repeatedly to understand her request.

'Aspetta!' he finally commanded and disappeared through a door into the nether regions of the office. Lucy waited. And waited. She waited a good hour while people came and went. She presumed the grumpy old man had forgotten her. Gone for caffè, perhaps. Gone to find someone who spoke English. Lucy did not expect him to speak English, there was no reason on earth why he should, the onus was entirely on Lucy herself to understand the locals, she admitted that. But a modicum of regret that he was unable to help—that would have been nice.

What happened next was not nice at all. Someone—a girl younger than Lucy herself—lowered the grille that protected the staff of the Ufficio dell'Anagrafe from thieves, bomb-throwing camorristi and crazed Australians. Lowered it with a deafening thud and disappeared.

'Hey!' Lucy called. 'Hey! What about me?'

The girl stuck her head back just long enough to point to a sign and then was gone again, shutting the door firmly behind her. Lucy checked out the sign and learned that the office was closed between 13.00 and 16.00.

They had gone off to do whatever Italians do with their three-hour lunchbreak. Lucy cursed a culture which still indulged in the siesta. She cursed her wasted morning, forgetting how much she had enjoyed the company of her Danish friends. She cursed the rude and thoughtless staff of the Ufficio dell'Anagrafe and she cursed her own ignorance. And when she had finished cursing she burst into tears of frustration.

She caught the bus back to Naples, she was damned if she was going to hang around Pozzuoli. She should of course have gone to see some of its sights, the Temple of Serapis perhaps, or the Solfatara, which she now knew to be an extinct volcano, complete with fumaroles and boiling mud so exactly how extinct was it? Knowing her luck, she'd only have to visit for the whole thing to burst into life with the strength of a thousand Hiroshimas. The fact that it hadn't done so for a couple of thousand years only increased the possibility in Lucy's mind.

The bus was crowded, standing room only. An old lady put her head on Lucy's shoulder and dozed off. Lucy was so busy wondering how to deal with this unaccustomed invasion of her personal space that she missed her stop. She decided it was fate and stayed on the bus until the old lady, apparently not asleep at all, got off somewhere in via Toledo. Lucy followed.

After coffee and a panino she felt a bit better and decided a walk would do her good. The shops were all selling clothes she could never afford but it didn't hurt to look and the names sang their siren song—Armani, Valentino, Bruno Magli, Versace, Ferragamo. Such elegant little shops. Simone would have been drooling. Unlike the Ufficio dell'Anagrafe most of them were open. Did they ever have sales? This was hardly the poverty-stricken Naples she'd been warned about.

After an hour or two she got tired of feeling covetous and turned down a side-street and just wandered. Unknowingly she crossed Spaccanapoli, perhaps the most famous street in Naples, with its cafes and craft shops and churches, and entered the poorer regions beyond. This was more like the Naples of her imaginings, lives crowded and impoverished, spilling from dwellings of just one or two rooms out on to the street. She was trying to imagine what it would be like, living with so little privacy, when she felt a hand on her arm.

In an instant, all the dire warnings about Naples came back to her; all the stories of druggings and muggings and murders; at the very least she was, she knew, about to lose her wallet, her passport... she just hoped he didn't have a knife... it was all her own stupidity, what was she doing, wandering around these back streets by herself?

She spun around wildly to confront her assailant. He was a young man. He was pointing, saying something in English.

'Your earrings, signorina—'

Lucy jerked her arm free and took off. She was damned if he was having her earrings! The young man ran after her, she could hear his feet on the paving stones. He was tall, he had long legs, he was faster, much faster than she. Did he have a gun?

He grabbed her shoulder. Alright! He could have them, he could have anything.

'Please, signorina...'

Panic-stricken, Lucy started to take off her earrings. 'Take them. They were my mother's. But take them, you bastard.'

'Signorina—'

'Take what you like...' She was shaking all over.

'Signorina! I do not want your earrings, okay? Please listen?' He held up both hands, backed off a little. 'I try to help you.'

Lucy stared. 'Help me?'

'Gold jewellery in this part of Napoli—bad idea. Very bad. The scippatori rip those from your ears. Please—for now. Place them in your bag?'

Lucy, still in shock, still wondering if he didn't have another agenda, did as she was told. And finally managed to speak.

'You care what happens to me? Why?'

Now it was the young man's turn to look confused.

'This is my city, signorina. You are a visitor. I do not wish that you have a bad experience here.'

'And that's all?'

'That is all. Buona sera.'

He gave a little bow and turned to leave. And Lucy, released from the sudden fear of a mugging, suddenly realised how utterly ungracious she had been.

'No, please, a moment. I'm sorry. That was very kind of you. It's just... it's just...'

It was just that she was falling apart, she thought angrily. She couldn't explain, even to herself, why she had been so frightened. The thing was, she hadn't realised, back home in Melbourne, quite how hard this whole business was going to be, and how difficult she was going to find it on her own. If Simone had been with her, this young man would never have frightened her, not for a second; by now they would have been flirting with him. She hated feeling so vulnerable, she despised herself for it. No longer comfortable in her own skin, she felt that she had become, in this foreign country, a mere shadow of the confident, feisty girl she had been.

The young man was holding out his hand.

'I am Stefano Falanga,' he said. 'I gave you a fright, I apologise. Perhaps I buy you a coffee, yes? You should sit down a moment.' He waved to a bar in the small piazza nearby.

Lucy wanted nothing more than to sit down. She'd been walking for hours and her feet hurt and she thought a shot of caffeine might just prevent a humiliating rush of tears. She shook his hand.

'Lucy Harrington. Thank you, but I am fine.'

'We could sit, if you like, at separate tables.'

Now he was laughing at her. She felt like an idiot. 'Thank you. A coffee would be great.'

They sat, he ordered coffee. He smiled. He no longer resembled a sinister camorrista, he was just a nice Italian boy, perhaps a little older than Lucy herself, with dark wavy hair and brown eyes and olive skin, very Neapolitan. Lucy tried to make conversation, to show she was not quite so gauche as she must appear. She forced a smile.

'How did you know I'm a visitor?'

He looked amazed. 'Because... it is...'

'Obvious.'

He nodded. 'You are not English. Australian?'

'My accent?'

'Partly. I have met a few Australian girls.'

I bet you have, Lucy thought to herself. And Yanks and Canadians and New Zealanders, pick up a tourist here and there, have a fling, you Italian men, you are all the same...

'And you do not have a good day. Can I help?'

Why was he being so damned nice? 'I'm fine, really. Just a bit tired.'

He gave her a look, a raised eyebrow, he didn't believe her. 'You have just arrived then in Napoli?'

'I got here yesterday.'

'There is much to see.'

'My guidebook says there are thirty-eight churches I mustn't miss.'

'Not to say two volcanoes.' Stefano grinned.

'Two?'

'The live one—' with a nod towards Vesuvio '—and the dead one at Pozzuoli. La Solfatara.'

'Oh. Pozzuoli. I was there this morning. But not at the Solfatara.'

'You must go back. It's amazing.'

Lucy shivered. 'I haven't much time for sight-seeing.' Especially not in Pozzuoli.

'Oh. I assumed...'

'I'm doing some research.'

'Into?'

She felt like saying it was none of his business. But that would be churlish, he was just being friendly. He probably thought it was for a thesis.

'It's—well, it's a family matter.'

'I see.' The coffee came.

'So you will not go to Pompeii, to Capri, to Cumae, to Sorrento...?'

'I—I don't know.'

'The Costiera Amalfitana—it is so beautiful it takes your breath away. Even mine and I live here all my life. To go home without seeing it—che peccato.'

Lucy felt she was being absurdly secretive again. She knew she needed help and here, possibly, was someone who could provide it. It was ridiculous to go on mistrusting the entire Italian race, after all, what could Stefano do to her? Try to race her off? Here in this little piazza, in broad daylight? He wouldn't get far. What harm could there be in talking to him? Still she hesitated. But perhaps Stefano felt that the walls were beginning to crumble. Or perhaps he didn't give up easily.

'I work for my father,' he said. 'I complete my degree in architecture but do you know how many architects there are in Napoli? Six just in our palazzo! No work if you are not Palladio. So for now—my father's Agenzia Immobiliare. How you say it? Real estate. Good thing is, I can take time off if Australian signorina need assistance. Some help with this—research. So she has time left to see this bel paese.'

He did not smile. He looked concerned that she might indeed miss the chance to see his beautiful country. That phrase again.

'Really... I'm okay. I can manage.'

Manage? Oh, sure. She was doing just brilliantly.

'Truly? You can do this research with—how many words of Italian?'

Lucy looked at him. 'About twenty.'

Stefano called the waiter and ordered more coffee. 'Allora. That means—'

'I know what 'allora' means. You all say it all the time.'

'We do?'

Lucy nodded. 'Just like us. Only we say 'Well, then'.'

'Well then, Lucy. Tell me, how can I help you? This research—it is study? University?'

'No.' Lucy paused for a moment. And then she told him. Not everything, of course. But enough; about her search for an unknown father and how everything was conspiring against her. Everything and everyone, including that stronza in Pozzuoli who had banged the grille down and gone to lunch.

'That is one of your twenty words? "Stronza?" Very useful.'

Lucy of course was already regretting that she'd told him anything at all. Was this what had happened to Kate? Alone and lonely in Melbourne, had she started off by confiding in the charming Paolo?

Lucy could have kicked herself. She was grown up, she was educated, she was supposed to have a few street smarts. What the hell was she doing, telling her life story—even the edited version—to some complete stranger? To a bloody Italian!

'Now you mock me.'

'No, truly, Italian bureaucracy—' he threw his hands up '—it is full of persons one could call "stronzo." Or some other words I can teach you.'

'I have a dictionary.'

'A teacher is better. Finish your coffee. I have a Vespa. We go to Pozzuoli, yes? To the Ufficio dell'Anagrafe. I talk to them about your Paolo Esposito.'

'Oh, I couldn't possibly. I'm sure you have work to do.'

'Much work, most important. I do it tomorrow.'

He stood up. 'We leave now, we are there when they open, yes?'

And Lucy, who had no intention of going anywhere at all with Stefano Falanga, soon found herself on the back of his Vespa, heading far too fast along via Coroglio towards Pozzuoli, with the gulf on her left and the Campi Flegrei, the burning fields which had inspired Homer and Virgil and so many others to wax lyrical, stretching inland on her right. Fitting that the entrance to hell was supposedly in there somewhere. If she did manage to find Paolo, she'd know where to take him.

Thirteen

They pulled up outside the Ufficio dell'Anagrafe as the doors opened; perfect timing. And what a difference it made, dealing with his own tribe, to the stronzo-turned-nice-guy on the other side of the counter. Such service he offered! He was even charming to Lucy. For Stefano he managed to find no less than thirteen Paolo Espositos of roughly the right age whose registered addresses were all in Pozzuoli.

They copied the addresses and departed with what Lucy considered unnecessarily extravagant expressions of gratitude. She made a mental note to be extra nice to the migrant kids in her classes when she finally got back to teaching. She was starting to understand how it felt to be a stranger in a strange land, a second-class invisible nobody.

Stefano was speaking. 'I think we must start tomorrow. Visit them one by one.'

'Why not today?'

'Wrong time. Your Paolo will be at work.'

'Perhaps not. Perhaps he's rich and retired and lolling about his swimming pool.'

Stefano gave her a look. 'You wish, huh?'

'I don't care. I just think he might be the type.'

'Why?'

Lucy shrugged.

'Is not Australia. Not so many people have swimming pools, Lucy.'

'No. I suppose not. It's just the image I have of him.'

'I thought you don't know this father?'

'I don't. I've never met him, I told you.'

'But already you do not seem to like him. Why?'

Lucy wished, fervently, that she could learn to be more circumspect; to keep her thoughts to herself, to be an altogether more private person.

'Please. Can't we start today? It would be such a help if you were there, at least for the first two or three.'

Stefano shook his head. 'Lucy, I will come until we find this Paolo. But we cannot just go knocking on doors, to ask "Are you the father that Lucy does not like very much?"'

'Well, no. Of course not. We need some excuse.'

'Esatto!'

'Like...?'

'I do not know.'

'Maybe... Jehovah's Witnesses?'

'I am Catholic,' said Stefano. 'I am not so good at talking about Gesù Cristo.'

'But Catholics believe in Jesus.'

'We believe, of course. But we do not have the need to tell everyone about—you know—our special relationship?'

'You'd still do it better than me,' said Lucy, 'I'm an atheist.'

Stefano was surprised, even a little shocked. 'Really?'

'Really.'

He let it pass. They had arrived at yet another bar, he was ordering yet more coffee.

'How much of this stuff do you drink in a day?'

'Five, six cups. Is good for you.'

'Good for you?'

Stefano grinned. 'Better than—what you call it? 'Veg-e-mitty?''

'Mite. Vegemite.'

'I tried it once.' He shuddered.

'We're given it when we're babies. We become addicted.'

'It's so salty!'

'And anchovies aren't?'

'Toccato!' Lucy looked blank. 'Touché.'

'Oh. Right. Touché. So. Back to our cover story. Perhaps we are doing market research?'

'It's possible... but I have a better idea I think. We have television

54

programme here, *Carràmba Che Sorpresa*. Everyone knows it, very popular. They organise reunions, you know? The parents see again their son who has lived for thirty years in Argentina?'

'And we are doing what exactly?'

'Finding all his cousins, his schoolfriends, to be part of it. On the list is this Paolo, yes? They went together to Australia?'

Even Lucy could see that it was perfect. And Stefano was all enthusiasm.

'Okay, maybe we try one or two. Make a beginning. Like you say, perhaps he is rich, he does not work giovedì. Your twenty words—'

'Include the days of the week.'

'Very good.' He seemed to enjoy teasing her. Lucy didn't really care. She was just glad to be doing something positive. Stefano consulted the list of addresses.

'These two,' he said, 'we start here, easy to find.'

They got back on the motorino, Lucy hanging on for dear life again, glad that at least Stefano was not one of those idiot Italians who refused to wear a helmet; that he even had a spare one for her. Well he would have; she was not the first girl, even the first Australian girl, to occupy the pillion seat. It didn't matter, this was strictly business.

They rode through winding streets, skirting a busy market and ended up outside a rundown block of apartments in a part of town that had clearly seen better days. If her father lived here, Lucy thought, he wasn't doing all that well for himself. There was no lift and they walked up to the fourth floor and paused outside the open door of Number 6. They could see a bed with an old man who appeared to be sleeping; beside the bed was a wheelchair and a commode. Stefano looked at Lucy who shook her head. They were about to go away when a woman arrived with a basket of laundry.

Stefano got in first with such a torrent of Italian that Lucy barely understood. There were some angry words from the woman, apologies from Stefano, a few conciliatory phrases on both sides and then they departed.

'Well?' Lucy asked as they trudged downstairs.

'He's her husband.'

'Husband? But he must be seventy, at least.'

'Fifty-four. He's got MS.'

'All the same... has he ever been to Australia?'

'They never leave Italy. They have the tickets for America when Paolo got sick. One good thing—she believes the story about *Carràmba Che Sorpresa.*'

'Good. I mean... oh, shit. It seems awful, intruding on someone like that.'

'Because he was sick?'

'It's such an awful thing, MS.'

'His wife thinks so. She is full of—how do you say it, risentimento.'

'Resentment?'

'Resentment, yes. Our two languages—so similar!'

'Sometimes. Do you blame her?'

'The wife? He's her husband. It's her duty to look after him. It's worse for him, yes?'

'I suppose so.'

Lucy thought, privately, that it all depended. Some invalids were saints, some tyrants. It was no life for either of those Espositos—Espositi?—confined as they must be most of the time to that dingy flat. She wished it had been Paolo; she could have gone away knowing he'd been punished enough.

The second apartment was nicer, in a an old and elegant block, painted pink and white with shuttered windows and a large arched door on the ground floor through which, Lucy surmised, carriages must once have entered. The signora who greeted them was also nicer and she too bought the story about *Carràmba Che Sorpresa.*

But her Paolo was not Lucy's; he was away in Munich, visiting his mother, who was German, a widow now, living with Paolo's older sister... regrettably, they had never been to Australia.

Lucy expected Stefano to call a halt then but he seemed to have got into the spirit of it and they went to more addresses on their list, another three, by which time the lights were coming on all around the bay and the sun was doing quite spectacular things over Capo Miseno. But their efforts were not rewarded. Twice their knocks went unanswered; once, the Paolo Esposito who opened the door was so clearly, so joyously, so outrageously gay that they left him to enjoy his aperitivo in peace before Stefano had even mentioned *Carràmba Che Sorpresa.*

Lucy herself called a halt then. She felt she had taken up more than enough of Stefano's time; he must have much to do, plans for the evening, his mamma was no doubt expecting him for dinner... she even wondered if she should offer to pay him, and settled for suggesting a contribution towards the fuel for the Vespa...

Wrong. Horribly wrong. She could tell from the look on his face.

'I'm sorry... you are offended.'

'I see you need help. I offer. I do not want to be paid.'

'It was just for the petrol. It's expensive. In my country we—'

'Lucy, this is my country. We have a saying, 'paese che vai, usanza che trovi.' You know how that translates?'

Lucy shook her head.

'"When in Rome, do as Romans do." Okay?'

'Okay. Can I say thank you?'

'"Thank you" is alright. Accepted. Now please get on, I take you back to Mergellina. Unless you like to have dinner with me.'

As usual, Lucy's gut reaction was to say no—and that's what she did. Refuse first, regret later. Stefano seemed to have been expecting the knockback, he just smiled and gave one of his infuriating little shrugs. It was a terrifying ride back of course—was he deliberately going faster than ever just to pay her back?—but the sunset over that fabled shore made the prospect of imminent death bearable. In no time she was deposited safely at the door of the hostel.

'I collect you in the morning,' he said. 'Ten o'clock. We search again.'

Lucy tried to hide her relief that he would be there to help her. 'I thought you had to work tomorrow?'

'No, it can wait, I talk to my father. By the way—here the food they say is terrible. I hope you do not get the mal di stomaco. Ci vediamo, Lucy!' The Vespa roared away.

Fourteen

H e was right about the food. And the stomach ache. Lucy had a terrible night, her confused dreams—about some Italian game show hosted by her father—punctuated by frequent trips to the bathroom. She dragged herself from her bunk in the morning, looking and feeling terrible, and wished she could contact Stefano and tell him not to come. But she hadn't thought to ask for his number. Even the weather matched her mood; the promise of the sunset had not been fulfilled and the day was cool with gusts of rain coming in off the bay.

Lucy saw Stefano pull up, plastered a bright smile on her face and went out to meet him. He took one look at her and shook his head. It was getting to be a habit.

'So tell me. What did you eat last night?'

'Cassuola di pesce.'

'But that has tomatoes!' From his tone he might have been saying, 'But that has arsenic!'

'So? What have tomatoes got to do with it?'

'You do not eat seafood with red sauce at night. It's very bad for your health, it will make you sick! I should have warned you.'

Lucy nearly laughed out loud. 'Stefano, you did warn me. You said the food was terrible and you were right. But it wasn't the tomatoes, for heavens sake, I probably got a bad mussel.'

'Australians, you not understand, l'apparato digerente... um, la digestione?'

'Digestion.'

'Esatto. And now you look like you die.'

Close to death or not, Lucy was getting cross. 'That is absolute rubbish. We are familiar with tomatoes, we have them in Australia. We eat them morning, noon and night. With seafood if we want.

And they have never, ever made me sick! But seafood that is off...'
'Off?'

Lucy sighed. It was all getting too hard.

'Bad seafood makes you ill. Shellfish especially. The cassuola was full of shellfish.'

Stefano shrugged. 'Allora. I think you are too sick to argue.'

That at least was true. He wondered if she would rather go back to bed, he could return later, but Lucy, afraid that he might never come back and she'd be left to deal with all those Espositi alone, gritted her teeth and insisted she'd be fine.

She wasn't fine and the ride to Pozzuoli was a nightmare. Lucy closed her eyes and hung on and prayed for deliverance. It came at the bar to which Stefano guided her. It came, thick and black, at the bottom of a small cup. Caffè corretto. She did not want to drink it but she was too sick to argue and, amazingly, the combination of strong coffee and stronger grappa soon worked its magic. She felt that she would, just possibly, live.

The palazzo—any large building, Lucy had learnt by now, was confusingly called a palazzo—was not far from the seafront in via Roma. It was undistinguished but well-kept. Stefano was pressing the bell of the entry phone when the portiere accosted them.

'Non c'è nessuno in casa.' Even Lucy understood that no one was home. And expected the conversation to be short. But Stefano went ahead with his Carràmba spiel and next, she gathered, they were talking football—prompted, perhaps, by the portiere's Napoli t-shirt. She recognised a few words, calcio and squadra, and there was a lot of earnest manly chat while Lucy herself just smiled politely. And then it was ci vediamo all round and he was waving them off.

'Very interesting,' said Stefano. 'Caffè, yes?'

It was at least forty minutes since the last coffee so Lucy thought no doubt Stefano needed one. She settled for mineral water.

'You seemed to get on with the portiere.'

'Everyone likes to talk football. People here are very passionate.'

'Not just here.'

'In Australia?'

'Oh yes.'

'That man is pazzo. Mad. He thinks Napoli can beat Juve tomorrow. I wish was true.'

'And the owner of the apartment? Is there a Paolo Esposito?'

'Once were two Paolos, father and son. But papà died, now the young one comes to visit, you know? I think perhaps this is what you look for.'

'Really? Why?'

Stefano shrugged. 'A feeling.'

Lucy thought it wasn't much to go on. He seemed to sense her disappointment.

'We will come back. The lady return for lunch, he said. Perhaps then you meet your grandmother, Lucy.'

Lucy shivered.

'You do not wish this?'

Lucy no longer knew what she wished. To declare her hand to an elderly and unknown Italian was out of the question. She did not want more tomato sauce, she just wanted Paolo's address. But she couldn't say that to Stefano.

'Of course.'

'Good. To pass the time, I show you the Solfatara, yes?'

The rain had eased to a fine mist. The Solfatara may have become extinct thousands of years ago but it did not seem that way to Lucy when she saw the fumaroles dotting its vast crater and the jets of bubbling mud and felt the heat underneath her feet. Stefano threw a rock in the air and when it landed the whole earth reverberated with the sound.

'Is it hollow underneath, some sort of cavern?'

He shook his head and was explaining how the gases corroded the rocks, forming millions of little cavities which in turn were responsible for the echoing sound, when Lucy looked up and gasped. Coming through the mist, like something from a Fellini film, was a line of young men in long black cassocks and wide-brimmed hats. One after another they appeared through the gloom and then she saw that they were little more than boys. Gradually they began to break ranks, to run around and skylark.

'Seminarians?'

Stefano grinned. 'Out of prison for a little.'

'They seem so young!'

'Many go straight after school.' He paused. 'I almost go myself.'

Lucy was stunned, it was the last thing she would have expected. He was defensive.

'It's not a bad life.'

'But surely you must have a calling. A vocation.'

'Has nothing to do with God. You see yourself helping people. Saying the mass. Holding hand of the dying. A romantic notion.'

'Oh.'

'I realised in time how stupid it was.'

Lucy suspected there was more to it but didn't like to press him. They walked to a vantage point above the crater, until the young trainee priests were just so many black dots. A watery sun was struggling through the mist, enough to give them a view out to Capo Miseno and beyond to Procida and Ischia.

'Is beautiful, yes?'

'Yes.'

The whole damn country was beautiful, yes, alright. She knew that before she came. And this young man was perhaps that rare thing, a genuinely decent human being who had no motive other than a desire to help her. And then Lucy realised she was being unfair again; genuinely decent people had not been rare in her life at all. The problem of course was admitting an Italian into their ranks.

'There is something wrong?'

Lucy denied it. The Vespa was now some distance away. By the time they reached it, she was vaguely hungry, a good sign that the bad mussel or the red sauce, or possibly both, had given up the fight with her digestive system. They ate a panino and watched the fishermen cleaning their boats and then it was time to head back to the via Roma.

Fifteen

The portiere was nowhere to be seen but the bell was answered and a pleasant voice told them to come up.

Stefano's 'feeling' had been right. Lucy knew it as soon as she saw the woman who opened the door. She could have been no-one but Grazia Resteghini's sister. The middle one in the photo on that table in Doncaster. The same high cheekbones, the heavy eyebrows, the slightly aquiline nose. Lucy tried to pull herself together while Stefano introduced her, his 'colleague from the BBC,' to her grandmother. She could feel the woman's eyes on her or thought she could. She avoided her gaze and tried to look interested and business-like while Stefano launched into the Carràmba rubbish yet again: they were tracing all the friends and relations of a guy who'd gone to Australia, they were bringing him home to see his mamma, Paolo Esposito was on the list, had known him in Australia, they weren't sure if it was the right Paolo...

And suddenly Lucy couldn't take it another minute. She tapped Stefano's arm, pleaded an urgent need for fresh air, excused herself and fled.

Stefano, when he found her by the Vespa forty minutes later, was not happy.

'Diavolo, Lucy! I do not understand you! Why do you run away?'

If she'd been expecting sympathy, it obviously wasn't coming. Nor, she had to admit, did she deserve it. She had run away, overcome by a blind and suffocating panic. She did not know what had happened. She did not know where the strong, determined Lucy who had boarded that plane at Tullamarine had gone to. The fact was that seeing the elegant, grey-haired woman who was, almost certainly, her grandmother had thrown her completely.

'Eh? Lucy?' He was waiting for an answer. Lucy said nothing. 'I told the signora how sick you are. She is preoccupata. Worried. Wants to make you some camomilla. She is a nice lady.'

Lucy nodded. 'And the son?'

'I have the address. I'm not sure I will give it to you.'

'What?'

'Because you lied. You were not so sick, not at all. If she is your nonna, Lucy, why don't you want to talk to her?'

'It's complicated, Stefano.'

How to explain? All those years with just her and Kate and a little share of Sim's family. No brothers or sisters of her own, no aunts and uncles and cousins. No grandparents either, in any real sense. Oh, she got a card on her birthday, every year with the same four words, 'Love, Gran and Granddad.' And there had been the abortive trip to Bannon Creek when Lucy was ten.

It was her grandfather's sixtieth birthday, she'd been delirious with excitement. She and Kate went on the bus, it took seven hours but she didn't care, she was going to meet her relations. At last she would have Family. Like George in the Famous Five books she read so avidly, she'd have cousins to play with and amazing, exciting things might happen.

Which isn't quite how it turned out. The cousins, prompted, stirred themselves enough to say hello and invite Lucy down the creek to get some yabbies. On the way she got pushed into a steaming pile of cow manure. Lucy knew it would be really smart to laugh this off but she was only ten and she was wearing a new pair of white jeans that Kate had bought for this special weekend. It was the other kids who laughed.

Lucy wore a borrowed dress to her granddad's birthday barbecue, not that anyone would have noticed because an hour in, most of the guests were off their faces. The afternoon dragged on, the music got louder, the salads wilted, the flies danced on the meat and the pile of stubbies grew higher. When it became obvious that the cake would never be cut, Kate took Lucy back to the motel in the main street where they were staying and Lucy did not protest. Cheap and tawdry as it was, it seemed like heaven.

'Luce?'

'Mm?'

'I'm sorry.'

'It's not your fault, mum.'

'We shouldn't have come.'

'Why don't they like us?'

'They don't dislike us. It's just we're all different, you know? Interested in different things.'

'Shouldn't matter. Not in a family.'

'Sometimes people just don't get on, darling. It can't be helped.' Kate did not mention, but Lucy knew, that no-one, not even Kate's mother, had asked a single question about their life in Melbourne. They got an early bus home.

This is what Lucy was thinking about, sitting by the Vespa in Pozzuoli fourteen years later, the feelings that had torn her apart on that long, long ride back to Melbourne, the yearning for a family that she knew even then, at the age of ten, was lost to her. The sight of this new grandmother, so utterly different—perhaps—to Joy O'Connell, had revived that childish hope that maybe, after all, she still belonged somewhere, to someone. And even though it couldn't be, because Paolo Esposito had made it impossible, the thought was overwhelming. But she couldn't tell Stefano any of that without telling him the whole story. And she wasn't ready to confide in him yet.

She looked at his angry face, this young man who'd gone out of his way to help her. Whatever his motives, he deserved better treatment than he'd got from her.

'I'm sorry. I'm really sorry. I didn't mean to cause you embarrassment.'

'So. It's alright then. You are sorry.'

Lucy didn't know what to say, how to bridge the rapidly widening gulf.

'I do not understand, Lucy. You say you want to find your papà. But I think this is only part of story. You do not trust me.'

'I will tell you this much then, Stefano. I do want to find my father. But I don't want him to know who I am. Not at first, anyway.'

Stefano looked bewildered. 'Why not?'

'I need to find out who and what he has become.'

Stefano realised then that this was indeed serious. He wished she would trust him, he found Lucy quite a challenge and now the possibilities surrounding this long lost father intrigued him.

He realised she was close to tears and was gentle.

'He did something bad, yes?'

'Yes.'

'Okay. We say no more. This evening you come to my house, my mother wish to cook you a proper Italian cena, yes? And we make plans to visit Stella del Mare.'

'Stella del Mare? This is where Paolo lives?'

Stefano nodded. He explained that it was way down the coast, in the Cilento, over a hundred and fifty kilometres. Lucy almost smiled and Stefano wondered why. She explained that even two hundred kilometres was hardly way down the coast, at least not where she came from. But she said she would love to accept his mother's invitation and then she would think about what to do next.

Stefano, who was learning fast, wisely refrained from telling her he had it all planned. He left her at the hostel, with a promise to collect her again at seven.

Lucy knew enough about Italians to realise that it was quite an honour to be invited to Stefano's home. She knew enough about bella figura from reading *How To Get It Right In Italy* to realise that what she wore and how she behaved would matter, if the whole of Australia were not to be confined to some cultural wasteland. She consulted the book again now, blessing Sim for her thoughtfulness, and learned that a cake would be an appropriate gift for her hostess. Gianni, on duty at reception, pointed her towards the nearest pasticceria. She chose an elaborate chocolate and hazelnut confection and watched in amazement while it was gift-wrapped in multiple layers of colourful foil and tied with several metres of ribbon. Only in Italy.

Back at the hostel again, she washed her hair, dressed with care—a skirt, a shirt, her only pair of heels—and waited for Stefano. And waited and waited. Eight-o'clock. Eight-fifteen. She was sitting in the foyer where she could see the outside world. And hear it, every time the door opened. Was there any city in the world as noisy as Naples? Tonight it seemed worse than ever. If they'd just take their hands off their car horns for a second, that might help. It was, Lucy had to admit, a busy time of day. Even the hostel was busy, getting into gear for the coming high season. The mini-bus that met the train from Rome came and went twice. The second time the driver looked stressed, Lucy noticed. He wasn't the only one. It was a quarter to nine. Where the hell was Stefano? Had she misunderstood him? Got the whole invitation wrong? Or maybe Signora Falanga was not so happy to entertain this stranger after all. Ridiculous anyway, that Stefano was still living at home, what was he, twenty-six or seven? No doubt la mamma still washed his underdaks, cooked his favourite pasta sauce, probably put the paste on his toothbrush... god help the poor woman who married him, she'd be nothing more than a slave.

It was almost nine, she was about to give up, she thought she'd just check with Gianni and make quite sure there wasn't a message for her, when Stefano arrived. He was smiling.

'Lucy, come, quickly, we are late.'

She couldn't believe it. 'I've been waiting an hour and a half, Stefano. I know we're late. You don't think an apology might be in order?'

'But it's not my fault. You must have heard.'

'Heard what?'

'The traffic! Senti!'

He held the door open and again she heard it alright, the ceaseless din, the car horns, the police sirens. 'Che casino! A big ingorgo stradale—how do you say in English? Traffic...?'

'Jam?'

'Yes! Jam. Enormous! You could not tell?'

'It just seemed a bit worse than usual.'

'The beep-beep. This is what people do.'

'And you couldn't get through on the Vespa?'

'My mother made me bring her car. She said you would—you know.' He waved a hand at the skirt and heels. 'Not easy on a motorino. So—andiamo?'

Feeling she couldn't put a foot right, Lucy followed him out to

Signora Falanga's Alfa Giulietta. But if the evening had not got off to a good start, it rapidly improved.

The Falangas gave her a warm welcome. Stefano's parents, younger brother and grandmother were there. The apartment was immaculate and Signora Falanga apologised several times for its terrible state, as every Italian housewife feels compelled to do. The meal was very Neapolitan—mozzarella, pasta, swordfish, all cooked to perfection. They finished with Lucy's cake, which had clearly been a good choice. Everyone expressed a polite interest in her quest but they were careful not to pry; she wondered if Stefano had primed them. And then photos were produced of Laura, his sister, married to an Englishman and living in London. Stefano had spent a year with them, this was where he had polished his schoolboy English. They had two small children and Lucy saw the glow on the senior Falangas' faces when the infants were mentioned. Family. It was everywhere and everything in this home and the evening, pleasant as it was, only served to remind Lucy, for the second time that day, of all that she had missed.

It was just what she needed. These nice people had managed to rekindle her anger, her sense of injustice and outrage. Tomorrow she would hire a car. She would manage the driving, it couldn't be that hard, millions of other tourists did it. She would head south and find Paolo.

Sixteen

S he was profuse in her thanks when Stefano dropped her back at the hostel. 'Your family, they're lovely. And you, Stefano—I don't know how to thank you for all you've done. Not just for helping me to find where Paolo lives. It's more than that. You've given me the courage to go on. And I'll always be grateful.'

He looked bewildered. 'I don't understand. You talk like it's goodbye.'

'Well yes. For now. I have taken so much of your time. And you have work to do. But I'm sure we'll meet again sometime.' She was talking too quickly, hoping he would accept her decision to go on alone, that they could part friends. She was half-expecting—and dreading—a scene, here on the pavement outside the hostel. What she got was worse, far worse.

'Are all Australians like you? Do they deceive people, use them, how do you say, throw them away when they get what they want? It's not what I expected, that you would take advantage, Lucy. I say addio, then, e buona fortuna.'

He was back in the car, the door slammed before Lucy could frame a response. She had supposed he would be annoyed. She had not anticipated that icy anger, that hurt. Only then did she realise that he actually cared, if not for her personally then at least that this quest, of which she had told him so little, should have a successful outcome.

Stefano got home and found, to his chagrin, that his mother, Mariateresa, was still in the kitchen and eager to talk about his nice Australian friend. Lucy had made a good impression, the whole family liked her. They were, however, puzzled about this search for her father; did it not all seem a little strange? Stefano agreed that it did. Mariateresa wondered if perhaps it was about an inheritance.

Stefano thought a murder was more like it. She looked alarmed. He tried to laugh it off; he really hadn't a clue, Lucy hadn't said much, he thought she was hurt and angry, that was all he knew. His mother looked at him shrewdly.

'And you, Stefano. You are hurt and angry too?'

'Australians. They are impossible. Not like us.'

'She is half Italian, no?'

'She doesn't seem it. Goodnight, mamma.'

And he escaped to bed, but not to sleep. He *was* hurt. And angry. He'd gone out of his way to help and felt he'd received precious little thanks for his efforts. But he also knew that he'd wanted something in return from Lucy Harrington and even though it wasn't such a big thing, the very fact of it sullied his noble gesture somewhat and made him feel he'd been less than honest with her.

Back at the hostel in Mergellina, Lucy did not sleep either. She lay in her bunk, glad the room was empty that night, and asked herself why had she behaved so badly towards Stefano? He didn't deserve it, she had to admit that much and it would have done no real harm to tell him the truth. Would it? She just knew that she could not. Why, however—that was the difficult question. It wasn't because she was ashamed, she knew that much with certainty. It wasn't shame that had brought her to Italy but righteous anger and a burning desire for vengeance. That would be hard to explain, of course, and perhaps Stefano would not understand; might even think it had all been partly Kate's fault, that she had in some way 'asked for it'. It was, heaven knew, a common enough attitude back home even now and Lucy suspected the same would hold true in this macho country. Almost as bad would be telling Stefano and having him try to talk her out of following her plan. He might well adopt the line taken by Father Ignatius and Grazia Resteghini, that no good would come of it and a lot of innocent people might be hurt.

And so it went on during the long night, many questions and few answers, until somewhere around three in the morning things suddenly became a little clearer and then Lucy slept, her dreams accompanied by the never-ending opera that is Naples.

In the morning she wrote two letters, packed and checked out of the hostel. She found Stefano parking the Vespa. She would have avoided him but it was impossible.

'Ciao,' was all he said.

'Ciao. You are still angry.'

'Of course I am angry.'

'I've written you a letter. I have tried to explain.' Lucy held it out to him. 'There is also one for your mother. It was a lovely night, I wanted to thank her. I'll post it.'

'No need, I take it. Italian post—probably never get there.' Lucy gave him the second letter. A long pause followed. 'This letter—it says why you do not trust me? Why you must go alone to the Cilento, a stupid thing to do with your twenty words of Italian, down there is not like Amalfi Coast, you know.'

Lucy wondered if he was psychic, if he knew how much she wanted to give in, to say alright, yes, come with me. She remembered the long night, the arguments she'd had with herself, the sudden realisation that she had to do this alone.

'Stefano,' she said, 'this has nothing to do with trust. It would be so much easier if you came. So much nicer too. But I am not doing this for myself. And it is not my story to tell.'

He thought about that. 'Is a pilgrimage you make? Or vendetta?'

'Something like that.'

'Which?'

'Both.'

He shrugged. He was not happy. But he seemed to accept it. 'You go on the bus?'

'I'm hiring a car.'

The look on his face said it all. He insisted on taking her to a car-hire place where she would not be robbed blind. He would not hear of the Cinquecento she wanted to hire, it was too small, it did not have enough power for the roads she'd be using, he wanted her to get a Lancia but agreed finally to a Fiat Punto. And then he took her for a drive, or rather made Lucy take him for a drive. They hadn't gone five hundred metres before she managed to take the wing mirror off a shiny new Audi parked in the one-way street. She was mortified and started to stop.

'No, no, no, keep driving!' yelled Stefano, 'was his fault, stupido!'

'His fault? How do you work that out?'

'He should bend the mirror in. A lesson, yes, you remember?' Lucy, shaking, thought she might, indeed, remember. Her next mistake was to stop at a stop sign.

'No, no! Drive! The car behind go straight into you!'

'You're telling me to ignore the traffic signs?'

'Not ignore, Lucy. They are—' he searched for the word— 'advisory. An indication, yes?' Ah, so that was it. Advisory traffic signs, perhaps you might like to consider stopping here, perhaps not, suit yourself. What a splendid idea, Lucy wondered what the constabulary back in Melbourne would think of it. Stefano finally ordered her to stop, not far from the entrance to the A3, the gateway to the south.

'I leave you here.' She nodded and managed to stop her hands shaking. In vain she protested that this was miles from the car hire place where they'd left the Vespa. Stefano said he'd find his own way back far more easily than she would ever again find the autostrada. It was true but she was loath to admit it and so they had another argument. Lucy had intended to go by the coast road but Stefano threw up his hands. Did she not know that the area around Portici and Torre del Greco was the most heavily populated in Europe? And the road very narrow? An ingorgo and she'd be there for a week. Nothing to see anyway. Much better to take the autostrada, turn off when she saw the signs for Castellammare, then take the N145 to Sorrento and the Amalfi Coast. She demurred once more; she had thought of stopping at Pompeii... Stefano sighed. Did she know anything about Pompeii? It was Lucy's turn to get angry.

She had a feeling this driving lesson, all these instructions, the dire warnings, were designed to make her aware of her shortcomings, to doubt her ability to see this expedition through, to ensure that she felt like a very inadequate foreigner. 'I know a great deal about Pompeii,' she said stiffly.

'Then you have booked somewhere to stay,' he said. 'Because you will need three days to see it.'

Lucy, who had intended to give it three hours, said in that case

Pompeii, having waited two thousand years for her visit, could wait a little longer. They stood there like two quarrelling lovers, Lucy thought, except they weren't lovers, they were friends, they should have been good friends by now, and that made it worse. Lucy held out her hand.

'Thank you again. For everything.'

Stefano ignored the hand. 'You are in Italy now.' He kissed her on both cheeks, an air-kiss which she hated, a cold formality. Then he produced a hand-written card from his pocket. 'In case you decide, after all, that I can be useful.' He turned away, stopped, looked back.

'Remember to drive on the right.' Then he was gone and she was alone. She got back into the Fiat, resisted the impulse to burst into tears, to drive it back to the hire place, to ring Qantas and go home. Instead she did up her seat belt, started the engine and crept out into the traffic, heading for the A3 which, if the gods were kind, would take her in the direction of Paolo Esposito.

While Stefano stopped at the first bar he came to, ordered a coffee and read her letter. It was just a note, really, another apology, and an explanation of sorts but it told him only what she had already said outside the hostel: that she wished he could come with her, that she wanted to be honest with him but the story wasn't hers to tell. He tried hard to read between the lines and began to see that Paolo Esposito must have caused more than the usual anguish when he abandoned Lucy and her mother but the details, of course, eluded him. He gave up finally, caught a bus back to the car hire place, retrieved the Vespa and went to work with the father he loved in the job he hated. Some days he wondered if he'd made the right decision leaving the seminary. He felt he could have faked the necessary belief quite as easily as he faked an enthusiasm for selling real estate.

Seventeen

The Piazza Tasso in Sorrento, with its fine display of brilliant red callistemons, was a place to make any Australian just a little bit homesick, the more so one in Lucy's present frame of mind. Only an hour had passed since she'd said goodbye to Stefano but it seemed like a lifetime and had she been religious, she might have been in the nearby church, giving thanks that she was still alive. Instead, she was picking at a plate of the ubiquitous spaghetti alle cozze, wondering why she had ordered it, wondering if she would, in fact, ever eat again.

The trip had been horrendous. Of the scenery she'd seen nothing, so intent had she been on keeping the Fiat away from the assorted maniacs with whom she shared the road. Lucy was no slouch behind the wheel but this wasn't driving, this was a blood sport. She had passed only one car and that because her curiosity got the better of her: why was it, alone, doing less than a hundred and fifty? She glanced across at the driver and discovered the reason—he had the newspaper spread across the steering wheel, over his hands, and was reading as he drove. And it had only got worse after she left the motorway; then she'd had to deal with the 'advisory' traffic signs. She began to understand Stefano's surprise when she mentioned hiring a car. Motoring on these roads required a period of adjustment.

The waiter was asking a question, the meal, was there something wrong? Lucy felt like screaming that yes, every damn thing was wrong, she was a nervous wreck, she was lonely and homesick and the bottlebrushes weren't helping. But he looked so concerned she did no such thing but assured him the pasta was buonissima, grazie and forced herself to eat. And in fact it can't have been too bad because after a while she did feel a little better and decided that, having missed Pompeii, she might as well at least have a look around

Sorrento before she faced the N145 once more.

A short walk led her to a terrace and peering over the balustrade, she looked down on to Marina Grande far below, alive with bathers and small boats. She held her breath, watching a diver plunge into the clear water, sure it was far too shallow and he would break his neck—and watched in amazement as he continued on down for two or three metres. She marvelled at the clarity that, even from this height, made each small rock on the seabed distinguishable from its neighbour. It would be bliss to swim in such a transparent sea. She looked out across the gulf to Ischia and back to Naples and the looming bulk of Vesuvius and thought, not for the first time, how much easier it might have been if her father had come from some damp industrial town in the English midlands. Easier to maintain the rage when you weren't continually seduced by landscapes made for gods and lovers.

It was impossible to hate Sorrento and Lucy gave up after a while, even promising herself a return visit as she reluctantly headed back to the Fiat. She consulted her map again and found that Stella del Mare was less than 100 kilometres away. The road was winding, certainly, and she might conceivably want to stop once or twice for a look at the famous Amalfi Coast, but she'd make it this afternoon for sure. She set off with renewed confidence which lasted until the small town of Sant'Àgata sui Due Golfi. There she had a puncture. Where, she thought, as she got out to survey the damage, was the Royal Automobile Club of Victoria when you needed it? She could see a service station a hundred metres down the road. She locked the car carefully, took her shoulder bag and was about to set off—by which time a small group of helpful young males was gathering, each one pointing to the flat tyre and earnestly proclaiming his ability to change it in no time. Lucy was uncomfortable. They were too insistent by far. She shook her head, thanked them, politely refused their offers and a couple drifted away. The others, however, three of them, would not take no for an answer. They were young, still in their teens and full of bravado. And then one reached out and snatched Lucy's car keys from her hand.

It was a simple thing; no doubt he intended to open the boot, to take out the spare tyre. He was showing off, nothing more, he would be the one to help the pretty foreigner. But Lucy felt trapped, they were forcing themselves upon her, they wouldn't listen to her, wouldn't go away—and in her mind she was not on the Sorrentine Peninsula, she was imagining a summer's night in Melbourne twenty-five years before. Was this how it had been? She tried to grab the keys back but the boys just laughed. So friendly at first, they were taunting her now, like hunters who sensed that their prey was at least wounded. Lucy couldn't believe how the atmosphere had changed. All this because of a flat tyre? It was absurd. It was totally ridiculous. And with that something snapped and the old Lucy, schoolteacher Lucy, so used to handling a roomful of teenaged boys with testosterone levels off the Richter scale, reasserted herself. At the same moment a black BMW glided to a halt beside her.

'You obnoxious little creep!' she bellowed. 'Give me those keys! Dammi le chiavi!'

Her request was reinforced with a torrent of Italian, delivered in a loud and very authoritarian voice by the driver of the BMW. Out of the car, he showed himself to be a man in his mid-forties, pleasant-looking and immaculately dressed. The boy with the keys thrust them into Lucy's hand.

'Scusi, signorina.' They all melted away.

'Thank you,' Lucy said to the stranger, trying to appear in control.

He smiled. 'A pleasure, signorina. Though I'm not sure you needed assistance.' His English was excellent. He grinned. '"Obnoxious little creep." This I like.'

'I think they actually wanted to help. They were just a bit—pushy.'

'Showing off. Let us get your tyre changed.' A procedure he managed to accomplish without getting so much as a speck of dust on his perfectly-tailored suit, thanks only in part to a mat and a pair of gloves which were no doubt kept in the boot for just such an emergency. Lucy made a note to describe to Geoff how it was done. She was effusive with her thanks, and sensible enough not to offend him with offers of payment. She was vague about her plans and he suggested that the Greek ruins at Paestum were not to be missed and Agropoli might be good for a stopover. The eager tourist, she looked

75

at the map where he indicated and agreed it all sounded splendid. He finally shook her hand firmly and roared off in the Beemer at an enviable speed. A nice man, much the same age, she surmised, as her father. Which led her to wonder yet again what he would be like, this Paolo who owned a restaurant in the seaside town of Stella del Mare.

Lucy had driven the Great Ocean Road in Victoria many times. Sim's family had a shack at Eastern View where they used to go for holidays. It was also where you took visitors from overseas—down the coast and back through the Grampians for the best scenery the state had to offer. The Great Ocean Road was—and is—a highway you treat with respect. It hugs the coast with cliffs on both sides, it twists and turns, there's a lot of traffic, including trailers with boats and caravans, and quite often you'll find cars parked in unexpected places, especially when there are whales to be seen. Some people, timid drivers, avoid it. Lucy enjoyed the challenge and expected to enjoy the drive around the Amalfi Coast as well. But the N163 which hugs the Costiera Amalfitana is not the Great Ocean Road.

The bends are more frequent and very much sharper and the traffic is heavier and—naturally—goes at twice the speed. If you do find a vantage point where it's safe to pull off and admire the view, you might be in for a big surprise. Lucy stopped, shaking after a near miss with the bus from Ravello, and stepped on to a platform built out at right-angles from a sheer escarpment. She looked out towards Capri, a hazy shape on that shining blueness, and felt she was hanging suspended between sea and sky. She almost laughed out loud with the sheer joy of it. Then she looked across to the cliff face next to her and thought she had stumbled upon the Positano tip. The assortment of rubbish defacing that achingly beautiful place included—she counted them—six mattresses.

Lucy had not yet had much experience of Italian mattresses but the ones at the hostel fitted the usual pattern, being incredibly lumpy things constructed of horsehair and offcuts from building sites. As she had seen, at regular intervals these objects of torture were hauled out on to balconies, where dedicated housewives wielding cane beaters disposed of every last dust mite with commendable vigour. Obviously, given this treatment, the mattresses didn't last long (probably the women didn't either) and when their short lives were over, this was apparently where they ended up—dumped unceremoniously over the nearest cliff. And if that happened to mar a lookout on the Amalfi Coast, like the one at which she stood, so be it. Lucy would have wept except that it was not her country and she thought instead that it was just like the Italians to ruin everything—and then hated herself for being so childish and mean-spirited. Trying to recover her good mood, she got back into the car and set off again.

Way ahead of her, the black BMW was only thirty kilometres from its destination at Stella del Mare.

Eighteen

Lucy did not want to stop at Paestum. Even when she saw those magnificent ruins suddenly appear before her, rising magically from the plain, she felt she ought to continue her journey. After all, they had been there even longer than Pompeii and like Pompeii, would no doubt overlook the insult if she passed them by for now.

However, she wanted to arrive in Stella del Mare somewhere around mealtime, giving herself the perfect excuse for visiting the restaurant. And if she went on now, it would be far too early for dinner. Italian dinner, that is, since no one in the south seemed to eat before nine o'clock. She could of course go to Stella del Mare, find somewhere to stay and then have dinner... Lucy finally gave up this ridiculous debate, admitted she was scared silly and that lunchtime would be a far better time to arrive, offering better chances for a quick getaway should one be needed. She therefore parked the car with all the other tourist cars and buses, and got out to admire the glory that had been Greece.

Licking a gelato, Lucy wandered around viewing the architecture on display from around 500 B.C., and comparing it to that of her home town. She wondered which of Melbourne's buildings might survive for two and half millennia and struggled to come up with anything. Maybe the Shrine. Maybe the Exhibition Building. She doubted it. She longed for Kate to appear beside her so they could debate the subject. Then, as advised by her benefactor in the BMW, she drove on to Agropoli and found a camping ground near the beach with so called 'chalets' for hire. And here she booked in for the night.

Lucy managed to negotiate a local supermarket and buy pasta, prosciutto, cheese and wine. She hesitated over the reddest tomatoes she'd ever seen. They looked wonderful but a red sauce at night, what was she thinking of? She could almost hear Stefano carrying on about mal di stomaco. But Stefano was back in Naples and she didn't want to eat another meal in a restaurant, she wanted some time alone to think and to plan. She bought the tomatoes and made her sauce and very good it was. Unlike the wine, which was local and obviously an acquired taste; regretfully, Lucy tipped it down her tiny sink.

She could have done with a drink. She had to admit she was getting nervous about what awaited her at Stella del Mare. The 'what-ifs' going through her mind were endless. What if her father recognised her immediately, refused to even speak to her, ordered her out of his restaurant, called the carabinieri? What if her grandmother, forewarned by Grazia Resteghini, had already been on the phone? What if—and Geoff had prepared her for this—Paolo told another story completely, made Kate a willing partner, or the one who had ended the relationship? Unlikely, of course, but it could happen. How would she defend her mother? What if there happened to be a large family who rallied to his side, would she have the strength to stand up to all of them?

In the beginning it had been part of Lucy's plan to denounce Paolo to his family if he had one but this was something she didn't like to dwell on. She could see the injustice if she were to hurt either his unsuspecting wife or worse, their children. But since there had been no justice for Kate, or for Lucy herself for that matter, perhaps she would just have to harden her heart.

While Lucy was pondering all of this, Roberto Lucattini, the owner of the BMW, was in Stella del Mare, in the bar of a restaurant called Il Veliero, which means sailing-ship in Italian. He was having a drink with his old friend, Paolo Esposito, and sailing was not the only thing the two had done together. They had first met as kids at elementary school in Pozzuoli and had stuck together until the day Paolo departed for Australia. By then Roberto was already at university, studying law. Now he owned a practice in the nearest large town and lived in Stella del Mare. He was recounting the story of the damsel in distress he had rescued that afternoon.

'Australiana?'

'I think so. The accent. And she was—you know how they are.

Gutsy.'

Paolo's curiosity was aroused but he tried to sound only minimally interested. 'Did she give a name? Was she pretty?'

'No name. Could have been a local to look at. Dark hair, olive skin. Yes, pretty. Maybe she'll come on to Stella del Mare, you can see for yourself.'

Paolo smiled and refilled their glasses and fervently hoped she would not come. Not that this girl could be Lucia, the daughter he'd been half-expecting for several months now, the daughter that Grazia had warned him about. It wasn't possible. But he touched the table all the same with his index and little fingers and Roberto saw him— saw him fare le corna as the Italians call it, ward off the evil eye—and called him on it. Paolo laughed it off, said that someone had walked on his grave and changed the subject to the season ahead. Bookings were promising, perhaps it would be a good one.

Lucy finally went to bed, hoping for no more than a good night's sleep. She had barely dozed off when the disco started. Just in time, before she did something that might have strained Italian-Australian relations for years, she remembered the earplugs so thoughtfully provided by Qantas. And after that, in spite of a mattress made of horsehair and off-cuts from a building site, she passed out.

In the morning she found the post office. She thought of ringing Stefano but knew he'd take it as a sign of capitulation and be on the damn Vespa before you could say Oddio no! Instead, and with some difficulty, she put a call through to Australia. It was a terrible extravagance but she just had to hear Geoff's calm, measured tones. On this of all days, she needed to know that her cheer squad back home was geared for action.

'Lucy! Is something wrong?' Not so calm at all.

'Did you get my aerogramme?'

'Yes, I did. So quick, I was amazed. I read it to Sim over the phone.'

'Un miracolo. Geoff, I want you to light me a candle.'

'You!? Have they converted you?'

'Today's the day. I know where he lives, I'm going there. To his restaurant.'

'Oh, Lucy. I wish I were there.'

'Yeah. Me too.'

'Are you all alone? This Stefano—'

'I left him in Naples, I thought it was better. Geoff, just tell Sim, will you? And send me good vibes, the pair of you?'

'My dear girl, we'll do that, naturally, but is there anything else?'

'Nope. Just wanted to hear your voice. You know, a bit of home.'

'Be brave. Be sensible. You'll be fine. And let us know how it goes. Soon. Reverse the charges, ring any time, middle of the night, it doesn't matter, promise me.'

'I promise. And thanks, Geoff. Ciao for now.'

'Ciao, Luce. Stammi bene!'

'What?'

'I'm learning too.' The phone clicked.

Well of course he was. She hung up, smiling, feeling a whole lot better. She delayed her departure as long as possible with a swim and hair-washing and two unwanted coffees and finally hit the road, where she annoyed the other motorists as she dawdled south. She contemplated buying a copy of *Il Mattino* to spread over the steering wheel, so they would better understand her slow progression, but decided she would rather arrive in one piece than worry about what the locals thought of her driving skills. Did that come under bella figura? Probably and if so, too bad.

She was still too early.

The drive had been easier than she expected, the traffic was lighter down here, the Cilento being neither so fashionable with tourists nor so accessible as the Amalfi coast. That small tower on the headland looming in front of her—Stefano had mentioned something like that, the Saracens was it?—marked the entrance to Stella del Mare. She was nearly there. She drove through a tunnel in the headland—how Italians loved their gallerie, she thought, never go around when you could barge straight through—and there it was, smaller than she had expected but undeniably pretty, with a harbour on her right for the fishing boats, followed by a long white beach, while on her left the town spread up the rise and the steeper hill behind, disappearing who knew where in the mountains beyond.

Stella del Mare, the town where Paolo Esposito had chosen to hide his crime from the world. Though it seemed unlikely that Paolo himself felt there was any crime to hide.

Lucy drove slowly along the main street. The first building she passed was a large and ugly hotel, a glass and concrete block with balconies on the seaward side. It was quite out of keeping with the rest of the town where the buildings were mostly local stone with shuttered windows and nearly all, at this time of year, swathed in purple and magenta bougainvillea. After the hotel came the usual shops and cafes and bars, a Banca del Lavoro and a post office on the small piazza and further on, right on the beach, a restaurant called Il Veliero. Lucy caught her breath at the sight of it and stopped for a moment.

It looked nice; more than nice. It looked inviting. The sort of place you'd choose for a long lunch with a lover, bodies still warm and salty after a morning at the beach, a place to linger over cold white wine and fish that still held the tang of the sea. Not at all the home of a monster. Lucy, needing time to think, drove on until civilisation ended with a bar and disco, Il Delfino Nero, at the farthest end of the beach. Then she did a u-turn, came back and found a park near the piazza. There was a tourist office and she went in and consulted the accommodation lists. There were three or four places in her price range; if she wasn't too fussy she was sure to find something. She wrote down some addresses and picked up a local map. And then she looked at her watch and saw that it was half-past twelve. Not late enough, not really, but she worried that if she put off her lunch much longer she would lose courage altogether. So she drove back to Il Veliero.

It was hard now to find a parking spot which she took as a good sign that the place might be crowded. A local kid ushered her into a place and, having learnt the ropes from Stefano, she gave him a smile and a thousand lire; worth it to know the car would be there, undamaged, when she returned. She looked at the restaurant and there were indeed people going in the door, quite a few people, but she did not join them, deciding instead to go for a walk first, like a soldier seeks to familiarise himself with the territory on which he may later do battle.

The restaurant was bigger than it had first appeared, or at least the building was. When she got to view it side on, Lucy could see that the large front balcony was repeated and the land had been excavated enough to make a huge basement area, so it was effectively three stories at the back with an orchard and a big vegetable garden behind, all beautifully kept. She thought perhaps the family, if there were one, lived on the premises, or perhaps they had rooms to let. Paolo was doing okay for himself if he owned this lot. Alright, it wasn't Positano—and she hadn't even driven down into Positano, she had just smelt the money from the clifftop—but all the same, not too bad.

It was really getting quite hot; no wonder there were so many people on the beach. And no wonder many of those were now heading for the shady terrace of Il Veliero. Not the sort of crowd they would get in the height of summer but a good number even so and quite enough to make her inconspicuous, or so Lucy hoped.

But then she hadn't counted on Roberto Lucattini who, since it was such a splendid day, had shut his office early and headed home to take his wife out to lunch for their anniversary.

Nineteen

Lucy entered the restaurant, noticing as she did a sign on the window that said staff were needed for the summer. She tried to stay in control of her feelings as she waited to be seated. She told herself firmly that it was ridiculous to be nervous; Paolo would have no idea she was coming and could not possibly recognise her in any case. So she bore a passing resemblance to his mother; so probably did thousands of other Italian girls. Dark hair, olive skin—it was common as mud down here in the south and back home too. Even her green eyes were not unusual. Relax, Lucy, you're just another young Australian, off exploring the world like millions before you, no other agenda.

'Sono sola,' she was saying to the waitress, a young woman barely out of her teens.

The girl smiled. 'No problem,' she said in heavily accented English and was leading Lucy to a small table by the window when a voice hailed them from the bar. 'Signorina! We meet again!'

The waitress looked at Lucy in surprise. 'You know Roberto?' Lucy shook her head but Roberto beckoned, she was being ushered over to the bar, was shaking his hand while a torrent of words poured over her, English, Italian, it may as well have been Urdu.

'Signorina, what a co-incidence.' He turned to Paolo. 'The girl I was telling you about.'

The man glanced at her, smiled politely. Late forties, thick hair greying, a somewhat lined face with brown eyes and a slightly aquiline nose, a muscular man who was used to hard work and exercise. And still good-looking. It had to be him. Was it? It couldn't be. Not someone so normal. Roberto was addressing her. 'Did you go to Paestum, did you stay in Agropoli?'

'Thank you—yes. Excellent advice.' And thank god she had taken it, for it made her footloose-tourist cover story more believable.

'And now you are here, in Stella del Mare. But forgive me. I am Roberto Lucattini... this is my wife, Ornella—we celebrate our anniversary—'

'Auguri, signora. Lucy Harrington.'

'—and this is my friend, Paolo Esposito, who owns this excellent establishment.'

Paolo was holding out his hand. Lucy could not take it. She felt a wave of revulsion so strong she was afraid she might be physically sick. She gripped the edge of the bar instead and fought it. Thought of her mother and why she was here and fought it harder than she'd ever fought anything in her life and managed to regain control.

'I'm sorry. I feel a bit faint. I didn't sleep much, a disco, you know? At the camping ground. So much noise... and then the drive...'

Roberto translated. Ornella Lucattini was all kindness, the girl needed food, to sit down. Lucy, who was sure that any food would choke her, agreed that lunch was just the thing. She thanked Roberto again for his help, assured them all she was finding the Cilento very beautiful and let the waitress—who introduced herself as Paolo's daughter, Chiara—lead her to the table.

She ordered something from the menu, the first thing she recognised, which happened to be gamberi, prawns—there was a restaurant in Carlton called Il Gambero, it had been there forever. And while she waited she watched her half-sister go about her duties and watched her father, now joined by a woman who was presumably his wife, celebrate with their friends and she thought it was like a real-life episode of *Carràmba Che Sorpresa* that she had found herself in except that would probably be vaguely amusing and this wasn't, not remotely, this was a nightmare and not the scenario she had planned at all. She had imagined herself so calm and in control and totally anonymous. Instead she was a trembling mess and all that was going through her head, ridiculously, was Casablanca and the wonder that of all the bars in all the world, this was the one that Roberto Lucattini had to come to. She knew that Paolo was occasionally looking in her direction; was he putting two and two together and coming up with four?

Paolo, in fact, was trying to convince himself that the number was anything but four, because that was what he wanted to believe. Grazia had said the girl was called Lucy O'Connell but Lucy was hardly unusual and this one called herself Harrington. And anyway, surely she wouldn't just turn up for lunch, this long lost daughter. She'd phone, demand a meeting, make a scene, gran passione would be unleashed... but Paolo was imagining how an Italian might do it and Lucy was only half Italian and that half had been buried since birth in a totally Australian culture.

Neither Paolo nor Lucy were aware that Ornella Lucattini also occasionally glanced in Lucy's direction. If they had, they might have put it down to the concern she'd displayed earlier. In fact she was trying to work out where on earth she had seen this girl before.

The prawns came and Lucy knew she must eat them or questions would be asked. She sipped her water and forced herself to swallow. She took a map from her bag and pretended to consult it while she ate but the place names danced in front of her eyes. She looked instead out through the glass at the diners on the terrace, laughing and relaxed, and beyond to the beach and the sea and thought of Kate and Geoff and how they would have enjoyed it and of all that her mother had never experienced, all the little things like eating fish by the seaside with someone you love when you are young and life stretches before you with its infinite possibilities.

Lucy was into her teens before she really began to comprehend all that was absent from Kate's life. She still didn't know why it was missing, and wouldn't until after her mother's death, when she read her diary. It was the diary, as much as the trip to Bannon Creek, which had brought Lucy to this place: this restaurant by a sunny beach in southern Italy in the early summer of 1996. Lucy had cried angry tears when her mother had told her how she came to be born. She wept far more bitterly when she read Kate's diary because only then did she realise how utterly alone and friendless Kate had been, with nowhere to go in the world but the hated house in Far East Gippsland.

Lucy shuddered now as she tried to avoid looking at the man who had brought about all this misery and the words she had read came back to her.

17th I've been home—no, not home, just here again where I came from—for three weeks. Father Ignatius said I should try to put it all behind me. I don't think Father Ignatius has ever been raped...

19th ...I stay in my room, reading. All my life I've escaped into books, what would I have done without libraries? I tell them I have to study. The thing is I can't bear to go out. To see people. I know it's probably irrational but I'm afraid I might find myself alone with men, with a man. Even here in Bannon Creek, in the street or the post office, anywhere. I feel that what I am—'rape victim'—is written all over me and that I'll therefore somehow appear available. And there are always, will forever be, people who are going to say I asked for it.

23rd I didn't sleep at all last night. I keep thinking, was it my fault? Not altogether, but partly. Because I didn't say 'no' loudly or clearly enough. Well I couldn't. I tried but no sound came out. It was like that girl at school, Jeannie, who was epileptic, who tried to talk when she was having a seizure but she couldn't, it was like that. It was like drowning. But I did push him, hard, and I scratched his face—he must have known from that I didn't want him to do it. He must have...

There was much more, page after page, and through it all the self-doubt grew and her self-esteem crumbled away. When a pregnant Kate went back to Melbourne, it was not just her Catholic upbringing which made her agree to St Joseph's. The nuns offered a society of women and a degree of anonymity which was not available anywhere else. For this, she was prepared to suffer their religiosity and their condemnation or, which was worse, their clumsy attempts at her salvation. There were one or two, like Sister Rita, with enough compassion to offer nothing more than the hand of friendship but Kate was already too damaged to reach out and accept it, was already building the walls which would stay in place for the best part of twenty years, keeping her safe and depriving her of much that would have alleviated the tedium of her life.

That was what had happened. That was how the tiny spark that had illuminated Kate's life and put her on the bus from Bannon Creek and borne her away, promising so much, had been stamped out. And Lucy looked up and saw the man who had done the stamping approach her table and wished that, like Nemesis of old, she had a sword in her hand and the power to exact justice there and then. But she had only a knife and fork and no wish to look ridiculous. So she smiled.

'You feel better, signorina?'

The accent was heavy, there was clearly not much chance to practice his English down here. 'Thank you, much better.'

'And the prawns—is good?'

'Excellent. Buonissimi.'

He seemed pleased that she was pleased. 'Very fresh. You like something else, dolce?'

'Thank you, no. Just an espresso.'

Lucy didn't want the coffee, she wanted out of there. But after the bad start she didn't want to appear in a hurry, she wanted to play it right, to leave without arousing any suspicions if she could. She noticed that Roberto had moved away from the table and was at the bar taking a phone call while the two women were still in animated conversation. A pity, it left Paolo free to perform his duties as padrone. He returned with her coffee.

'You stay in Stella del Mare, signorina?'

'Perhaps, I'm not sure. I haven't got long, I'm meeting a friend in Brindisi in a few days, we're going to Greece.'

'Greece? You do not stay in Italy?' There was no hiding the surprise in his voice. Surprise—or relief?

Lucy burbled. 'I wish I could—such a beautiful country. But I've only got three months. I have to be back in Australia for my dad's fiftieth birthday, I promised, you see.'

'A big occasion, most important. I understand.' And he smiled with what seemed like genuine warmth, wished her a pleasant time for the rest of her stay in a mixture of English and Italian, and left her to her coffee.

Having paid her bill, Lucy headed to the door. A young boy, nine or ten, opened it with a flourish. Lucy thanked him and found she was looking into eyes as green as her own, a replica of her own. But the cheeky smile must have been all his father's.

'See you later, signorina.'

Lucy made her escape. Back in the car she tried to push the disturbing image of the boy out of her mind. A wife, a daughter, and such a young son, she had somehow never expected that. She wondered what the hell she was going to do now. The lies had been a handy cover and she was rather amazed at how easily they had tumbled from her lips. She'd always been a lousy liar, it had got her into trouble at school and it got her into trouble still—even the little white lies that smooth everyday social intercourse did not come easily to her and her friends knew better than to ask Lucy if their bums looked big in anything unless they wanted the ungarnished truth. Yet here she was lying through her teeth without a qualm and while it had been a temporary fix she soon realised it was likely to make things very much more difficult in the long run when the lies, like a crooked seam, would have to be unpicked. But that at least could be put off until another day.

Far more pressing was where she was going to stay that night. Instinct told her to get out of Stella del Mare. She needed time and space to rethink her course of action since that damn flat tyre had made her battle plans redundant. She looked at the map but nothing leapt out at her. She looked at the sea, shining and still and still impossibly blue and realised how different it was, this Mediterranean, from the seas she had grown up with, which crashed and banged and hurled themselves, green and white and glittering, at the shore. She drove out of Stella del Mare and turning left, headed for the hills.

Twenty

S he drove for two hours without actually getting all that far. For one thing she took a wrong turn and found herself heading not south-east, as she had planned, but north-east.

This happened after she had stopped in a largish town to call Geoff. He answered after two rings, he must have been waiting by the phone. She gave him a faithful rendition of the day's events thus far, omitting only the details of the imaginary father and his birthday. He agreed that she'd done the right thing giving herself some space and offered support in any form that it might be needed. Lucy hung up feeling that he was all the father she would ever need and it was then, going over the call in her head instead of paying attention to the road signs, that she headed in the wrong direction. By the time she realised her mistake she decided it didn't really matter and kept going.

The road rapidly became steeper and narrower, down to just a couple of metres in parts, as it wound its way ever higher—the N167 was starting to look like a freeway. Every few kilometres there was another small town or village and Lucy could only wonder how they managed to build up there even today, let alone hundreds of years ago. It was as though some giant had picked up a handful of buildings and slapped them on to the side of the mountain wherever the fancy took him. Most had stuck but not all, for the ruins of past landslides were everywhere, and one village came in 'old' and 'new' versions, moved before natural forces pushed it into the valley below.

She stopped there in the old part, in Roscigno Vecchio, and wandered for a little while around its abandoned buildings, now falling into decay but each with that amazing view away to the mountains in the east. How the people who had called this home must have hated leaving. The ancient well under a huge old maple tree still held cold, clear water and Lucy refilled her empty San Pellegrino bottle, feeling all the time that she was being watched. She heard a noise and turned quickly but saw no one. She felt a little spooked and suddenly realised how alone she was and headed back to her car. It was then that she saw her—an old woman dressed in what had perhaps been the local costume, leading a donkey with panniers full of firewood. Anywhere else and Lucy would have been looking for the film crew but not here.

'Buona sera, signora,' she said and smiled but the woman ignored her and Lucy didn't dare to get out her camera, afraid it would be taken as an insult.

With nowhere to stay in Roscigno, either Vecchio or Nuovo, Lucy continued her journey. But the road was getting steeper and the towns and villages were now fewer and further apart. She should have expected this; it was a vast national park, after all. She was starting to worry that she might have to sleep in the car when she arrived in a small village called Monte Santa Caterina. Although there were at least three Saint Catherines, and Lucy didn't know which, if any, had particular responsibility for her mother, and was herself in any case a non-believer, she nevertheless decided to accept the name as an auspicious sign. This decision may have been prompted by the fact that it was now after six and it had been a momentous day and Lucy was very tired and rather fancied un aperitivo. Which sounded so much nicer than admitting to herself that she'd kill for a drink.

She therefore found a park not far from the inevitable piazza and got out. Santa Caterina wasn't big enough to boast a tourist office and there was no sign of a hotel or any other accommodation that Lucy could see. So she went into a bar and ordered a Peroni, her accent causing the entire company to turn and stare, and when the beer came, she asked in the best Italian she could manage if there was anywhere in town that she could stay. The barman didn't understand a word. Lucy tried again.

'Per stanotte—una camera.' She was miming as she spoke, head on her hands in the universal sign of sleep. 'Un albergo, una pensione... in qualche posto, anywhere!'

The man looked perplexed. And suddenly there was a woman at

his side, laughing, and everyone else was talking and laughing too. They had all got it, everyone except the one guy Lucy had asked.

'Mi dispiace, signorina,' the girl said in Italian, but slowly and with many gestures so Lucy could follow. 'I'm sorry. He doesn't hear so well. You need a bed, yes? Somewhere to stay?'

A grateful Lucy said indeed she did. It seemed there was not much on offer, just one pensione. But it was clean, comfortable... they could phone Signora Bianchi, see if she had a room? Lucy sipped her beer while the call was made. She was in luck—a room was available. It was just two streets back from the piazza. The woman drew a small map, wrote the address on it and gave it to Lucy.

'Australiana?'

'Sì.'

While Lucy finished her beer the woman explained she had a cousin in Sydney, she hadn't seen him for thirty years. One day, God willing, she might get out there... at least that's what Lucy thought she said. She recommended the trattoria opposite if Lucy needed a meal later on. Then Lucy wished the assembled company 'buona sera' and went to find her lodgings.

Signora Bianchi was perhaps seventy but looked older, bent as she was with arthritis, her skin as brown as the ancient beech trees in her garden. But she was friendly enough and explained to Lucy, in Italian with a few words of English, that she was a widow and childless and let out her two spare rooms to the few visitors who made their way to Monte Santa Caterina. She led the way up the narrow staircase, indicated a bathroom on the landing, and finally opened the door into a small but spotless room. The view from the window, of the sun going down over those same valleys and hills through which Lucy had driven all afternoon, was breathtaking. Lucy did not care what the mattress was like, this would do beautifully. She paid the signora and finally found herself alone.

She would have to eat but not yet. She pulled a sweater from her backpack and put it on. The breeze coming through the open window was cool enough to remind her she was now over six hundred metres above sea level and a long way from Il Veliero. She couldn't believe how quiet it was. A couple of children shouting to one another, the sound of cattle drifting up from the valley below where, perhaps, it was milking time... that was about it. How un-Italian!

There was one thing Lucy knew she ought to do this evening. Stefano deserved a phone call almost as much as Geoff had. After all, without his help she would probably still be searching for Paolo's address, might not even know if he were still alive. And also—go on, be honest, she told herself—it would be nice to hear his voice again, even if he shouted at her or, worse than that, adopted the icy tone he had used when she last saw him.

Signora Bianchi insisted on giving her a key, even though Lucy tried to explain that she would not be late, and she walked back to the village square. There was a public telephone on the bottom corner, before the piazza ended in a sort of parapet. This formed its fourth side and prevented the locals from falling to their deaths down a steep escarpment, while also affording views—more valleys and mountains—to the east of the ridge on which the village was built. It was all very beautiful but this was Italy and Lucy expected nothing less. She looked over the edge and yes, far down below was a pile of rubbish. Not in the best frame of mind for the task, she went into the phone booth and called Stefano.

'Pronto, sono Stefano.'

'It's me. Lucy.'

'Ah. Lucia. Come va la vita?'

Not what Lucy was expecting. Not 'how wonderful to hear your voice, I've been worried about you.' Not even 'You stupid girl, why haven't you rung, I thought you'd been kidnapped.' Just, 'How's things?' Stefano the cool. Well two could play at that game.

'Oh, fine, yes. Thanks.' She was buggered if she was going to speak Italian. 'I'm up in the Cilento, it's beautiful. Little village called Santa Caterina.'

That gave him a jolt. 'What? You are supposed to be in Stella del Mare, your father, what happened?'

'I saw him today. Long story. He doesn't know I was there. At least—I don't think he does.'

'You did not speak with him?'

'Only to order lunch. I'll go back. I just wanted to say thank you again. The directions—everything. I wouldn't have found him without you.'

'It's my pleasure to help. I told you—'

He broke off.

'What?'

'Nothing.'

'How is your work? Do you sell a lot of houses?'

'I sell nothing. I hate immobili.'

'Real estate.'

'That. Yes. I think perhaps I will go back to the seminary.'

'Oh, Stefano. Don't be ridiculous.'

'Why is it ridiculous?'

'Because you have no vocation. You're not suited to it.'

'What I am suited for is not possible. Lucy?'

'Yes?'

'You would not like me to come down there?'

Oh yes, she would. She would love it. Someone in her corner, to help her plan a new attack. Someone to laugh with, to share a meal with... to sit with and watch the sun go down over those amazing mountains...

'No really, Stefano. I'll stay here for a day or two, then I'll go back to Stella del Mare.' She laughed and said, without meaning it, 'They need staff, I might even apply for a job.'

'With no Italian?'

'It's getting better. Buona notte, ci vediamo uno di questi giorni.'

She hung up. And wished she hadn't. One of these days? What was wrong with tomorrow? She nearly rang back. So did Stefano but he was too angry. Instead he rang his sister Laura in London and talked to her for a very long time about women in general and ones with Anglo sensibilities in particular. Laura, an avvocato by training, worked in IT and knew quite a few ex-pat Australians. What Stefano learnt was that they were very independent; that he should be patient; that he must not under any circumstances sulk and that Lucy probably thought it weird beyond belief that he still lived at home so he should invent a good reason for this if he wanted the relationship to prosper.

Lucy, with no one to give her such cross-cultural advice, went to the trattoria and ordered a pasta e patate which, when it came, was not really all that good. Though perhaps it wasn't the fault of the chef as several other customers seemed to enjoy it without complaint.

Twenty One

At around midnight, when the rising moon found a pathway straight through her window and on to her pillow, Lucy debated getting up to close the shutters. Instead she lay there and watched its progress across the sky, and remembered two lines from a poem that Kate had loved:

> *That orbèd maiden, with white fire laden,*
> *Whom mortals call the moon...*

Shelley again. Lucy thought about the Protestant Cemetery and the woman she had spoken to. She could do with someone to speak to now, someone who understood English, she hadn't realised how exhausting it would be, trying to make yourself understood all day, everyday, in a language not your own, a language you barely spoke. She realised, just in time, that she was in danger of feeling sorry for herself. No one, she told herself briskly, had forced her to come here. She had choices, so many choices. And Kate had had so few.

For most of her adult life, Kate had never gone to bars or restaurants; had not even accepted dinner invitations. For years she had hardly gone out at all. It was not just her lack of money and her meagre wardrobe; it was her complete lack of self-esteem. She could never get over the feeling that she'd be found out, exposed, held up to ridicule—though for what she could not have said. What she needed was help—she needed it like the Vietnam veterans, so many of whom were then coming home to denial or outright rejection— but like them she didn't even know she needed it, let alone where to get it. All this, too, Lucy discovered from her diaries.

And then came the one little entry—and Lucy allowed herself to be a little fanciful since the crystal clear sky had won her over and she was now out of bed and sitting by the window as she thought back over it all—one entry which had shone forth like a small bright star and had marked the change:

Liz Evans, the librarian—funny it should be another Liz—saw me reading Stefan Zweig's *Beware of Pity*. I suppose it's not often read these days but she loves it too as it turns out and we got talking. And she's persuaded me to join her book club. It's a women only thing and they don't go on too late so Lucy should be alright...

Lucy was about fourteen by then. She remembered how her mother had broached the subject. Would Lucy mind if she went to this book club, it was just once a month, she'd have to do her homework next door that evening. And Lucy, so delighted to see her mum doing something vaguely normal, like going out, having a hobby, would have done her homework underwater if that was what it had taken. It was the beginning of the thaw. Spring did not arrive for another four years when Geoff came on the scene but at least, by then, Kate had made some friends. No wonder she loved books so much.

As Lucy was trying to get to sleep at last, music started up from the house next door—she was getting used to the fact that Italians ate late and partied even later. Now she was sorry she hadn't closed the window because the song which drifted through it banished all thought of Shelley's orbèd maiden, though it too was about the moon, a bad moon this time, on the rise.

Lucy shivered. Normally she didn't mind a bit of old Creedence Clearwater, heavens they'd been around forever, they had to be doing something right. But that song? 'Bad Moon Rising'? With its warnings of storm and earthquake to herald the end of things? With its apocalyptic predictions of doom?

The moon, the real moon, sailed out of sight. Lucy shut her eyes and told herself very firmly that she didn't believe in omens any more than she believed in saints, that the one made no more sense than the other and that tomorrow would doubtless be fraught with as yet unforeseen problems so she needed to sleep. And when Creedence moved on to 'Who'll Stop the Rain?' she did sleep, though not before wondering whatever had happened to 'O Sole Mio', which would have been less surprising in these parts than decades-old American rock.

When Lucy woke she wondered for a minute where on earth she was. Then it all came back and the day ahead loomed, filled with the necessity to make decisions which, at the moment, seemed totally beyond her. She had coffee and a cornetto at the bar and then opted for a walk to the sanctuary of Saint Catherine, a distance—according to the marker—of five kilometres. She thought it would give her both exercise and time to think and hoped she wasn't supposed to make the pilgrimage on her knees or something. She thought it unlikely. Saint Catherine, any of the Saints Catherine—and she still didn't know which was honoured by this town but they were all most assuredly women—would not make such absurd demands of the faithful. In any case, it would have been impossible. Before long the path, which had started out as wide as a bicycle track under the beech trees, became a series of steps and Lucy was not so much walking as climbing, the steps ever steeper and closer together, the track clinging to a rock face on one side while the drop on the other fell away through a wooded slope to the village below.

For a while the going got easier through an alpine meadow and Lucy sat for a few minutes and caught her breath and admired the view which was, yes, spectacular. She was getting the exercise she wanted but the problem of how to return to Stella del Mare and, once there, exactly what to do about Paolo was no nearer resolution. Had he lived alone it would have been easy. Lucy knew she could not kill him and didn't want to but she could destroy him by other means, she could find out what mattered to him and take that away, whether it was money, power, reputation or just some little thing he loved. But Paolo had a family and that, she suspected, was the thing that he loved, the one thing that mattered.

So she was back to the question which continued to trouble her: could Lucy hurt him without directly hurting that family who were in no way to blame for what had happened to Kate and in all probability knew nothing whatsoever about it? Could she in fact carry out her strike without any collateral damage?

She knew it couldn't be done. What hurt Paolo would hurt them. Would hurt the girl, Chiara, who had been so pleasant. Would hurt the small boy with the green eyes.

Lucy herself had been hurt by Paolo's act against her mother. Hadn't she? Well, she had been born. She had grown up without a father. But then, if that's all you've known... could you really call it suffering? Look at all those saints—the Catherines had actually got off fairly lightly but what about her own one, what about Lucy? Tortured and having her eyes put out? That was suffering if you like. Not that it ever really happened, of course, but as an example...

Confused, conflicted, Lucy got up and continued on her way. The brief respite afforded by the small meadow was soon over; the steps began again and continued until a small clearing in the forest, back from the cliff face, revealed a tiny domed structure which was the sanctuary. Inside, on the far wall, was a crucifix, and on the right a large and rather garishly painted statue of Saint Catherine, holding a large bunch of white lilies. From the inscription, and the story of her life thoughtfully written on the wall, Lucy discovered that this was Catherine of Siena, a mystic but also apparently something of a fourteenth century diplomat and never one to take a back seat. She lit a candle out of respect rather than belief, and turned to leave. She did not think St Catherine could help her but she did marvel at how the workmen who built this little shrine had accomplished their task. That was a miracle indeed, because even if they had dug the stone from the ground nearby, everything else to finish and furnish it, and the tools to do so, must have been carried up here on someone's back. She could have done with a bit of their faith.

She took her time going back to the village. She thought she would probably stay another night. She knew that returning to Stella del Mare with some vague story about liking the place just wasn't good enough. She was going to get one chance at this and she didn't want to blow it. On the other hand, her time was limited, she couldn't afford to waste it swanning around southern Italy chatting up the saints.

She had a panino for lunch, bought some postcards and wrote on them then went back to the pensione, where she found Signora Bianchi in the kitchen, ironing linen. Lucy had never in her life seen anyone ironing sheets, let alone an elderly woman with such severe arthritis she could neither stand upright nor straighten her hands. She could not bear to watch it now. But she knew, from reading and anecdote, that someone like Signora Bianchi would be fastidious about her house and her linen too, would be mortified if it weren't as immaculate as the Virgin.

She stood in the doorway watching for a few moments, not sure if her return had even been noted. Then she spoke gently, searching desperately for the Italian she needed. 'Signora? Si prego... posso essere d'aiuto?'

Signora Bianchi looked horrified—not, Lucy gathered, because of her Italian, but at the mere thought of a paying guest taking charge of her iron. Lucy tried to persuade her; Signora Bianchi fought back. It took nearly ten minutes—given the shortage of vocabulary—for Lucy to convince her hostess that she actually enjoyed ironing; that she had some things to think about and needed a bit of quiet time to do it; that she was homesick and ironing would comfort her (a desperate ploy, that one) and that Signora Bianchi reminded her of her grandmother and she would like to do it on that account (a total lie.) Signora Bianchi gave in with a thousand thanks and went out to potter in her vegetable garden.

Lucy ironed to the accompaniment, not of a rock band but of someone aiming for higher things, perhaps to stand in for Pavarotti who had already been announced for performances of *Tosca* in Naples at the end of the year. Whoever this person was, Lucy thought, c'è ancora molta strada da fare, as he continued to torture 'E Lucevan le Stelle'.

Oh, well, she thought, he probably knew what lay ahead. Opera singers, psychiatrists, Jesuit priests—they all had extraordinarily long apprenticeships to serve. Perhaps he would make it. She had thought herself about striving for higher things, doing a master's degree as Sim was now, then a doctorate but couldn't, as yet, see the point; she enjoyed teaching, she didn't want to be an academic. Maybe she would do it when she was old and tired of instilling a love of Shakespeare and a well-constructed phrase into a roomful of hormone-charged teenagers. For the moment there were more pressing things to concern her.

Like the intricate pattern on the pillow case she was ironing, which must surely have been made for someone's trousseau long ago, when people still had such a thing as a trousseau, because it was all roses and love-knots. Lucy imagined all the heads that had lain upon it, including Signora Bianchi's, there beside her late husband, whose plain, somewhat serious face adorned several photos scattered around the house. He was in uniform in most of them and in one Signora Bianchi gazed at him adoringly. So it had most likely been a happy marriage, which brought Lucy to Paolo. She realised she didn't even know his wife's name but they too had looked happy, content with their lot, that was it, yesterday at lunch with their friends. Of course appearances can be deceptive but not, Lucy felt, in this case. She had worked in a lot of restaurants in her student days and there was an easy conviviality in Il Veliero which she knew very well only ever filtered down from the top. It made for the sort of place that was not only good to eat at but fun to work at—or as near to fun as waiting at tables could ever get.

And that was it. What yesterday on the phone to Stefano had merely been bravado seemed now, as Lucy ran the iron across a football field of white linen, like an excellent plan. She would indeed take up waitressing again and wheedle her way into a job. She would have to concoct a tissue of lies to undo the ones she'd told already but that shouldn't be hard, she was getting good at lying. Straight into the lions' den, that was the way to go. They needed staff, they had the sign up. And she was a damn good waitress, she could prove that easily enough and she could point out what an asset it would be to have an English-speaker around.

Once inside the tent, Lucy felt sure she'd find a way to get to Paolo. She'd dig around and discover his Achilles heel and then she'd exact her revenge and if others got hurt as a consequence so be it. It was not for her that the bad moon was rising.

Lucy forced a last wrinkle from the final sheet. Signora Bianchi came in from the courtyard and almost wept with gratitude to see the ironing finished. She made tea in Lucy's honour and produced some almond biscuits and they tried, the two of them, to make conversation. It was not as hard as it might have been. Lucy, who had studied not only French but also some Latin at school, was quite a good linguist and was, as she'd boasted to Stefano, picking up more Italian every day. And Signora Bianchi had finished high school and thus spoke proper Italian and not just the local dialect Lucy had heard in the bar and found totally incomprehensible. So although progress was slow Lucy learnt that the late Signor Bianchi had been a maresciallo in the carabinieri, which explained the uniform. He was born in Santa Caterina but he and Alessandra Primerano, as she was then, had met when he was stationed in Castellabate. He used to come down to Stella del Mare where Alessandra's family lived. He was a good man and she missed him still, even after five years.

Lucy said he looked like a very loving husband. She asked if the signora still had family in Stella del Mare and for some time there was no reply. Finally Signora Bianchi said there was a niece but she no longer kept in touch. And then, to Lucy's consternation, a tear slid down her cheek. They both chose to ignore it.

Such a pity, Lucy said. Signora Bianchi sighed. 'Una bella ragazza. Noi—' She crossed her index fingers tightly. 'Like so?'

'You were close?'

'Close. Yes. Silvana like my daughter when her mother dies.'

'And then something happened?'

'È sposata.'

'She got married?'

'Yes. And her husband...' An eloquent shake of Signora Bianchi's head said it all. 'But... she is innamorata.'

She gave Lucy a long look. 'Everyone like Paolo, signorina. Is just me not trust him. And this Silvana can't forgive. Capisce?'

Capisce? Oh, she most certainly did understand! That is—if it was him. But it had to be, it was, Lucy knew it was. This woman's niece was married to her father and yes it was a co-incidence but wasn't life full of them, wasn't it all about six degrees of separation?

Signora Bianchi was still talking, trying to explain, saying that she was perhaps just a stupid woman, but she'd heard things about Paolo, rumours of uno scandalo, and she'd asked him to his face and he'd been evasive and she expected a man to be honest like her Giuseppe. So the rift had grown between them, between the aunt and the beloved niece and now it was irreparable. She, Alessandra, stayed up here in the mountains in her husband's country, crippled in body and very much alone while down on the coast Silvana was apparently happy to immerse herself in her family and forget the woman who had helped to raise her. Lucy thought how sad it was; the more so when you thought about the ridiculously short distance between them. It's not like they were separated by the vast spaces of Australia. She sighed. Who was it who'd remarked that God gives us our relatives, thank God we can choose our friends?

Signora Bianchi was asking where Lucy intended to go next. Lucy, practising her new cover story, said she wasn't sure. Down to the coast, perhaps down to Reggio... it depended whether her friend, who appeared to have fallen in love too, was going to meet up with her or not. But she had enjoyed her little visit to these beautiful mountains and she had enjoyed doing Signora Bianchi's ironing, she'd had a very peaceful afternoon. And indeed she had.

She ate at the little trattoria again that evening and found the food excellent. And neither rising moons nor rousing bands nor tremulous tenors kept her awake; not even the thought of her possible new role as a waiter at Il Veliero disturbed her dreamless sleep. A ten kilometre hike and an afternoon's ironing are better than any narcotic. She didn't even wake when a massive storm broke over the Cilento and sent torrents of rain and rock down the scarred hillsides.

Twenty Two

As Lucy prepared to leave Monte Santa Caterina next morning, back in Naples a nervous Stefano Falanga was taking a phone call from someone at the studios of La RAI, Radiotelevisione Italiana.

Stefano might have trained as an architect but he had long ago fallen in love with il mondo dello spettacolo, with show business. What he dearly wanted was to be a designer—theatre, film, television—and this call, arranging an interview, was a chance to get his foot in the door. The programme now in the planning stage was a co-production with, oddly enough, an Australian company. Stefano didn't give himself a hope in hell of getting the position, he had no raccomandazione, no one to pull strings on his behalf, but he intended to try nonetheless. His application was the little secret he had kept from Lucy and, in fact, from his father, who lived in hope that Stefano would yet learn to love the real estate business and one day take over Falanga Immobiliare S.r.l. (It was not, however, a secret to his mother; mothers have a curious habit of finding out such things.)

Stefano did not know if there would be Australians at the interview, nor how he should go about impressing them if there were. It was still a week away. He could ring his sister Laura. He could also go on what would doubtless be a wild goose chase and try to find Lucy. He wasn't sure if he dared though he did feel that one good turn deserved another and he had certainly helped her—was it too much to ask for a little advice in return? Or would she think that was the only reason he had offered his assistance in the first place? Laura would have told him not to be ridiculous but Laura didn't know how deep were Lucy's suspicions about Italian men.

While Stefano wrestled with this dilemma and pretended to show an interest in selling an over-priced apartment in Vomero to an obnoxious Milanese, Lucy bid farewell to Signora Bianchi, trying to suggest that she not give up on Silvana because women should be above petty vendettas (and save themselves for important ones, though she didn't even attempt to spell that out).

Signora Bianchi kissed her on both cheeks and gave her a hug and said she was una ragazza molto simpatica, like Silvana used to be, and she hoped perhaps Lucy might come back one day. Lucy hoped so too and held the signora's knotted hands and suggested, gently, that a rheumatologist in Salerno might be able to help her. Signora Bianchi said it was troppo lontano, too far, and Lucy laughed at that as she'd laughed at Stefano and told her to think about it because she could not come every week to do the ironing.

Lucy's feelings of bonhomie had completely vanished by the time she had travelled thirty kilometres down towards the coast. For one thing, she wasn't really heading towards the coast at all but rather driving parallel to it; the storm had caused landslides and everywhere the signs were out, 'FRANA' and 'CADUTA MASSI', falling rocks. It was hard driving, with detour after detour and she very nearly invoked the ex-St Christopher again.

The conditions were not helped by the fact that she was again being eaten by nerves. She would have given a great deal to have Sim there with her. Someone who saw the world as she did, who'd give her honest advice and make her laugh, someone who spoke English! She wondered how she had ever thought she was brave enough to do this alone. And yet... and yet there was no other way. And so she kept on driving and somehow avoided falling rocks and came around a bend and there was that blue, blue sea again and the sun came out and she thought of Kate and like a nun, renewed her vows.

But she still dawdled, making several stops which were, she knew, no more than delaying tactics—she needed nothing at all, for instance, from the market in Stio but it was pleasant to walk and pretend, just for a while, that she was nothing but a tourist. Finally, finally, having driven in a vast arc through the mountains, she saw the Saracen tower ahead of her. She drove through the tunnel and she was back in Stella del Mare, with its boat harbour, its beautiful beach, its ugly hotel and the restaurant owned by her next of kin.

Lucy decided she would stay at the one camping ground. She thought it would look more casual, less planned than a pensione. It was closer than she would have liked to the slightly seedy Il Delfino Nero but she had her ear-plugs so she booked a chalet and went for a swim. In the evening she went to Il Veliero for dinner.

She knew as soon as she arrived that the gods had at last decided to smile on her. The place was in chaos. After a long wait a flustered Chiara greeted her.

'You back? No go in la Grecia?'

'I don't think so, no. Change of plan. A busy night?'

'Un disastro. I am sorry. For now, no place. You wait?'

'Of course. Has something happened?'

Chiara waved to a couple of long tables. 'The bus—is not normal for us, to take, you know? But there was una frana?'

'A landslide? I've been up in the mountains, landslides everywhere. So you have to feed a busload of tourists, yes?'

'Esatto.' It was Silvana who answered, who was also working and who explained that, not only had the landslide given them unforeseen customers, it had prevented two of their staff from turning up for work. She was apologetic, they would try to get the signorina a table very soon, perhaps a drink at the bar in the meantime?

'Ha capito?' Chiara was worried that Lucy might not have understood but Lucy had got the gist of it well enough and was trying to look suitably upset on their behalf. But all she could hear was opportunity knocking.

'Look. Let me help? When I was at university I worked as a waitress, I have experience. Ho fatto esperienza.' She indicated the long tables. 'And those people—French, yes?' Now she did smile. 'Parlo francese.' Which was true enough, she did speak French, even if it was a little rusty.

Chiara looked at her mother, said something very quickly in Italian and Silvana nodded vigorously. 'You do this? We pay you, naturalmente.'

'You can give me a meal later. Have you got a spare—?' She mimed an apron.

106

The evening passed very quickly. Waiting was apparently like riding a bicycle—one of the skills that, once learnt, was not forgotten. Lucy took over the tables of stranded bus passengers. They were having a set menu with limited choices which made it easier and her French also came back to her—she was able to understand their requests and sympathise with their position. In fact, she achieved exactly what she had hoped, she charmed the pants off everyone, including Paolo, who stopped her just once to offer lavish thanks for her assistance. It was an effort but she hoped she appeared natural as she told him she was having fun.

Lucy was good, there was no doubt about it. And if Paolo hadn't noticed for himself, Silvana commented on the fact more than once. So much better with the customers than the absent Concetta. So much more competent than the absent Marco. All of which was true and Paolo could see where it might lead. He felt a frisson of fear, like the tremor which presaged an earthquake. He had lived through earthquakes. In 1980, when the Irpinia earthquake struck, he was best man at a wedding in Teora. The town was destroyed. Sixteen years later he still sometimes woke with the taste of dust in his mouth, fighting to free himself from the bedclothes.

He looked around at his family. He could see Andrea in the kitchen, cadging dessert from Enrico, the chef; Silvana and Chiara, busy working the floor; Rosaria upstairs he hoped, studying for her final exams (though you never knew with Rosaria). This was his world. He had made it without much help, had worked absurdly hard, seven days a week for many, many years to build it, had damaged his health and nearly gone broke more than once in the process. It was as though he were trying, through his own labour, to expunge some demon within. People had thought he was mad, to build such a beautiful restaurant in a sleepy little town like Stella del Mare; now they were envious as more and more tourists came to the Cilento. And then Mario Moretti arrived and built his big hotel at the end of the beach and Stella del Mare was well and truly on the map. Well, to be honest some people said it was ruined, but that depended on what you liked, of course, the simple things or the high life. And who you wanted for your neighbours. Mario and Paolo had for a time maintained a thin veneer of civility in their daily intercourse. Neither Paolo nor Silvana trusted Mario an inch, they knew his kind and who his friends were. Everyone in Campania knew it. There were people like Mario Moretti and his friends all over the Mezzogiorno, all over Italy. Paolo knew, and Silvana suspected, that the veneer of civility, like the ozone layer, was dangerously thin.

This then was Paolo's little universe and he was, in the main, well pleased with it. He knew there were clouds gathering on the horizon and a storm would come but this was something he understood. There was nothing he could do to stop it, only God could do that. Lucy he didn't understand at all. Was she just another Australian tourist, friendly and helpful, or a threat on a new front? Had she in fact come to bring his universe crashing down? Paolo wished the Sibyl at Cumae were still dispensing advice, he'd have gone to her in a heartbeat. But she'd shut up shop a couple of thousand years earlier.

Subtlety had never been part of Paolo's make-up. When they were all having something to eat after the kitchen had finally closed, he turned to Lucy and asked about her friend, the one she was to meet in Brindisi—were they still going to Greece?

Lucy said she doubted it. She explained that Susie had an English boyfriend. They'd broken up but now he was back on the scene and she'd decided to remain with him in London. Lucy didn't want to go to Greece on her own, she thought she'd rather stay here and see a bit more of Italy; maybe even stay in one place for a while and actually get to know the Italians a little. Of course Susie and the boyfriend could break up again...!

Chiara and Silvana both laughed at this. So did Rosaria who had taken a break from her studies and come down to join them. A stunningly pretty girl, she was supposed to be the linguist of the family but her English was actually worse than Chiara's. Lucy, the schoolteacher, suspected a lack of application. She agreed that it was a hard language to learn but told them she'd had migrant students from Asia and the middle-east who'd conquered it in just three months. But then they'd had no choice.

Rosaria just rolled her eyes. It was, she declared, una lingua impossibile. Silvana shook her head, what was impossible was Rosaria's laziness. And that's when Chiara, who'd taken a real liking to Lucy, had her brilliant idea—the one Lucy had been hoping someone else would come up with.

Chiara, of course, was suggesting that Lucy stayed in Stella del Mare and—since she wanted to get to know the Italians—took the vacant position at Il Veliero. Silvana thought it would be marvellous but was sure Lucy wouldn't be interested; Rosaria seemed keen because Lucy could help with her English and Andrea said she could do his compiti, his homework, any time she liked, he thought she was really cool. Lucy, already in love with Andrea, was laughing and protesting when Paolo, trying to hide his panic, asked loudly if they were all quite mad, it was out of the question!

Silence. Silvana suggested mildly that it was at least an idea worth discussing. Paolo backpedalled. He merely meant that Lucy, he was sure, had no permesso di lavoro, no work permit, so how could they employ her? This pronouncement was greeted with the derision it deserved. This was Italy, since when did a small thing like government regulations stop anyone from doing anything? Silvana said that naturally they would pay Lucy in cash. She had proved what a good waitress she was. They needed someone badly. And they could put on the window a sign to say that French and English were both spoken here, a decided asset. Paolo was left with nowhere to go. He turned to Lucy. What did she think?

Lucy, all too aware of Paolo's eyes on her, said she would have to think about it, perhaps she could give them an answer tomorrow? 'Rispondo domani?' It was coming, the Italian. All those lessons she had crammed in were paying off. Or was it as everyone said, there was nothing like total immersion?

Back at the camping ground, Lucy rang Geoff, since it was still afternoon in Australia. Being with a family had, as usual, made her lonely and she had the excuse of needing to bring him up to date. Geoff was supportive but cautionary. She knew nothing about these people. If they suspected for one moment that she was there to do them harm... Lucy tried to reassure him. She did not intend to stab Paolo while he slept. She'd come to upset his peaceful existence, that was all.

Geoff chose his words carefully. 'But you've no idea how?'

'To be honest, no, not yet. But I'm sure it'll come to me when the time's right. I'll just have to be patient.'

The only problem she could see was the daily proximity to Paolo but she would just have to cope with that. Geoff, not reassured at all, wanted to get on the next flight but Lucy talked him out of it with the promise of regular phone calls and finally hung up, leaving Geoff to reach for his bottle of single malt.

He was becoming increasingly concerned about this expedition of Lucy's. He had never expected her to get in this deep. He'd been worried about a confrontation, worried that Paolo might threaten her, even harm her. Now he was equally worried about what she might do to Paolo, that she'd get carried away by some mad and dangerous scheme. Geoff was not only a devout Catholic but a devout Christian and could never in his heart of hearts believe in vengeance, which was God's prerogative. Geoff was a New Testament man through and through, big on forgiveness. He did not want Lucy to burn in hell and he did not want to visit her in some dingy Italian gaol—and though these were the sort of thoughts that came to him only at three o'clock in the morning and vanished in the bright light of day, they were coming a lot more often. He wished she had never gone to bloody Italy. He wanted her here, a link with his beloved Kate.

In bed at the camping ground in bloody Italy, Lucy marvelled at how things had fallen into place and thanked her lucky stars, or rather the unstable hills, for the landslide which had made it happen. She could not know it then but it would not be the last time that a shifting mass of earth and rock would change the course of her life.

She talked to her mother that night. She didn't feel foolish as she did it, though she had no illusions that Kate could actually hear her. Having no god to give her a benison, Lucy wanted her mother's blessing and felt sure that she had it.

She thought back to the time that she privately called Kate's Coming Out: the year when Kate had blossomed as her friendship with Liz Evans grew. The other women in that little group, impressed by Kate's knowledge of books and writers, had gradually drawn her into their circle and this is turn gave her what she had never known—some self-esteem. Lucy was only a teenager then, but a sensitive one, and she watched and was happy for the mother she loved. But the preceding years, those fifteen lost years, had to be paid for.

Lucy felt now that she was on the brink of achieving her goal. It would still take time, perhaps quite a lot of time, and certainly the details remained unclear. But she was confident that justice would be done, that retribution would be delivered. Nemesis had stopped her chariot at the gate of Paolo Esposito and tomorrow she would enter his house.

Twenty Three

It was a clear, bright morning. The shining sea shone, the sand was already dazzling and it was too late in the season for the icy tramontana to come down from the north. Nor was there any sign that the sand-filled scirocco might come howling over from Africa. It would, therefore, in all likelihood, be another perfect day in the Cilento. And busy enough at Il Veliero to keep Lucy on her toes should she report for duty. She decided they could wait for a while, it wouldn't be wise to appear too keen, and went in search of breakfast.

There was a little bar in the piazza—Lucy assumed there was a little bar in every piazza in Italy—and she sat outside to enjoy her coffee and cornetto. She watched a man setting umbrellas up on the beach, red and yellow ones in two long lines. Later in the day people would hire these umbrellas and gain the right to place a deckchair underneath and occupy a spot of sand. She imagined the riots there would be back home if anyone tried to take ownership of a beach and charge people to sit on it. She sighed. 'Paese che vai...'

She must have spoken out loud without realising because she got an answer. 'So what do you find different and not like this morning?'

'Stefano? Stefano!' She was shocked, amazed, delighted. Trying hard not to show the delight. 'What on earth... I mean, che diavolo! Where did you come from? Cioè...' But she could not think of the Italian at all.

Stefano was pleased by her reaction. He felt it was a good start. All the way down from Naples, which he had left while Lucy was still sound asleep, he had worried about how she'd react to his arrival. At one point he had almost turned around and gone back. But then there would have been the problem of how his father would react.

Stefano wasn't close to his father, Guido, they were too different in temperament for that, but he loved him. Perhaps it was love born of duty but it was none the less real for that and he tried to make a success of his role in the business. Guido, however, wasn't deceived and was now ready to bow to the inevitable. At dinner the previous evening, primed by his wife, he had mentioned the job interview; hiding his disappointment, he suggested that Stefano talk to his Australian friend about how best to approach it. A pity, he said, if Stefano did not give it his best shot. It had, it seemed, been a night for parental blessings.

So Stefano had ridden down to Stella del Mare, hoping to find Lucy back from her inexplicable visit to the mountains, and here she was.

'I have come to check you are okay. Not buried under a landslide.'

'No, perfectly safe. It's nice to see you.'

'You come back today?'

'Last night. I had dinner again at Il Veliero.'

'You met your father?'

'Well—yes and no.'

Stefano threw up his hands. 'I do not understand. Yes and no—what is this? I expected by now a big reunion, yes? Everybody very happy. You want me to organise it?'

'No! Stefano, please. I'll do this my way. You must not say anything. Niente! Stai zitto. It is—come si dice?—it is imperativo!'

He laughed at that. Lucy glared. 'This is funny?'

'I am sorry. But you do not say "imperativo" except to talk of things grammatica, yes? You say "essenziale."'

'Alright! Allora! È essenziale!'

'Your Italian is much better. I think many more than twenty words, yes?'

'Oh yes. Possibly as many as fifty.'

'Do not be cross. We correct each other, we learn. Insieme.'

'Together.'

He nodded. 'Un altro?' He pointed to her coffee, she nodded and he disappeared into the bar. Lucy watched him go. She was quite surprised at the strength of her feelings on seeing him again. She told herself it was just the pleasure of being with someone who would, for a little while, alleviate her loneliness. Even if they bickered and fought all the time, they were mostly on the same wave length. She did actually like Stefano and wondered why she was so determined to keep him at arm's length. Had she tried, she would not have had to search too deeply to find the answer.

Lucy had never had a real relationship with a man. That is to say, she'd been out with men and once or twice had even talked herself into sleeping with them but it had always ended disastrously—usually with Lucy being called a frigid bitch. She had often conceded, alone and in tears, that it was very likely true. There was something, a lack of trust, that made her hold back. She was always too afraid to let herself go, too afraid of losing control. When she stayed at Sim's flat in Fitzroy, which she frequently did, they'd be kept awake by the couple next door whose love-making was accompanied by the loud moans and cries of an ecstasy Lucy had only ever imagined and which, to be honest, left her faintly uncomfortable. Not so Sim, who would bang on the wall and tell them to shut up and please get it over with. Next morning, she'd discuss it with Lucy (who wished she wouldn't) and speculate as to whether the girl had really managed the three or five or whatever orgasms or whether she was so keen on the guy she was faking it.

A psychologist might have concluded that Lucy's unease was something she had inherited, or rather learned, from her mother. Something absorbed, as if by osmosis and despite Kate's every effort to prevent it, from the day she was born, like a child might unwittingly inherit its mother's fear of spiders. One thing was certain, whatever had caused this particular trait in Lucy's make-up, learning the details of her birth had done nothing to alleviate it. It was just as well that Stefano, in grave danger of falling in love with her, didn't know what lay ahead of him. He didn't yet realise it would be his task to convince Lucy that men, especially Italian men, were not her enemy and some, himself among them, could indeed be trusted. Geoff had perhaps had the easier job.

Stefano, not being clairvoyant, didn't get back on his Vespa. Instead he listened, with some impatience, while they drank their coffee and Lucy told him about the mountains of the Cilento and how beautiful they were. She was surprised to discover he had never actually driven up there himself. But before she became too critical she remembered that there were many places in Victoria where she had never been—Philip Island with its famous colony of penguins was one—and they had to agree that tourists often saw more of a country, albeit superficially, than the locals ever did. She told him about Signora Bianchi too—though not about the connection with Silvana—and he was vastly amused at the thought of her doing the ironing. He said that was very Australian.

'Australian?'

'Yes.'

'Why?'

But he couldn't explain why. So she let it go and told him about the chaos at the restaurant the night before and how again she had helped out—she supposed that too was Australian—but it had achieved its purpose. She'd been offered a job and she planned to accept it.

Stefano was utterly bewildered, a state which Lucy's presence seemed to frequently induce. He had thought she was joking about a job. Why, he demanded to know, didn't she just say who she was?

'Please. You know I can't tell you that.'

Stefano wasn't angry any more, he was troubled. He decided he no longer wanted to know her plans, he was getting to be afraid of what she might say, afraid that it might make whatever was growing between them impossible. He was worried that he was in any case about to destroy it himself but he too had his dreams, and he had to take the risk.

'Alright. I don't ask any more. There is something else instead.'

'Go on.'

'Is my turn to ask for help.'

'From me?'

'Yes.'

'Dimmi.' She waited.

And then he talked about why he had been attracted to the priesthood, how it was not a vocation, as he had at first imagined, but a love of things theatrical, for what was the mass if not a grand theatrical performance with the priest the star of the show? It was the

115

robes, the incense, the shimmering candlelight, the processions and above all the music—these were the things that had drawn him in. And when he realised that, which he did the first time he went to the opera, then of course he gave up on the idea and went off to study architecture instead.

It was Lucy's turn to be bewildered. 'Even though you knew there were already too many architects?'

Stefano shrugged. He loved design. He was good at it. Maybe design would get him into the theatre. Or even film. Or even, to start with, television... which, as it turned out, was what he needed her help with.

Lucy stared. Television? She was a schoolteacher. She knew nothing about television—except that most of it was rubbish. Stefano agreed, most of it was indeed merda. But one had to start somewhere. And he told her about the Australians who had come to La RAI and had kindly granted him an interview and how he was sure he would blow this amazing opportunity if she refused to help him because he had no raccomandazione, none. Niente di niente.

Lucy had no idea what he was talking about.

Stefano thought she was angry. 'You think I only helped you so I can ask you to help me.'

Now she was angry, she was furious. 'What sort of person do you think I am, Stefano? That I only help someone I'm indebted to?'

'That is raccomandazione.'

'I think you had better explain.'

So Stefano told her how things worked in Italy, how it was never what but who you knew, that got you a job such as this.

'So you need someone to pull a few strings, right?'

'Exactly, yes, you have this too?'

'Well. A bit.'

'Here it is essential. Someone who knows somebody. Or better, someone who owes somebody.' Especially, Stefano explained, it was essential in Naples, where the studios of la RAI in via Marconi had seen very little production for a very long time. The competition would be fierce. And he had so little experience, only some amateur productions—how could he hope to impress them without raccomandazione?'

'Well not by whingeing, that's for sure.'

'"Whingeing?" This means?'

Hard to explain such a very Australian concept. 'You think there will be Australians at this interview?'

'I do not know. If it's Italians only I have no hope.'

'Because of the—raccomandazione?'

He nodded. Lucy could see this job meant a great deal to him. She knew nothing about the show or the production company and didn't see how she could help in the least. But she did feel she owed it to him to try.

'Listen. Senti. Gli australiani preferiscono...' Stefano was smiling encouragement and she managed to continue in Italian for a while before lapsing back into English. 'Australians like people who are confident, you know? Who have great enthusiasm and will work very hard. You must tell them how much you want the job. They will like that.'

'Yes?' Stefano seemed doubtful.

'Absolutely.'

'Okay. Thank you. I want the job. I have much enthusiasm, yes?'

'Yes.'

'And I work very, very hard.'

'Exactly. And take any examples of your work to show them.'

'Is enough?'

'I don't know, Stefano. Smile, shake their hands, be friendly. The show—you know what it is?'

'I think telenovela?'

'Huh?'

'A, what you call soap opera?'

'Honestly? Oh my God, I don't believe it! Not *Neighbours* in Italian! Oh, they couldn't!' Lucy collapsed into laughter.

Lucy and Sim had grown up with *Neighbours*, the classic but soapiest of Australian soap operas, watched by millions. They had followed it in primary school and all through their teens. It was still going strong though Lucy hadn't seen it for years now. The whole idea of her compatriots exporting it, or something like it, to the

Italians, was just hilarious. It was so unsexy, so unsophisticated, so suburban. But then again, she supposed, why not? The English adored it.

Stefano was crestfallen. 'What is so amusing?'

'Nothing. In Australia we make very good soaps. I hope you get the job, Stefano, I really do.'

But she could see that he was hurt. She had somehow belittled this dream job of his and now she felt awful.

'Listen. Like you said. You have to start somewhere. You get the job at la RAI, it's a beginning, yes? What about me? I'll be waiting on tables. Una cameriera.'

He nodded but he did not smile. He wished he had never come. He had expected her to be angry, she got angry so easily, but he had not expected her to laugh at him. It was unbearable. And she saw all this in his face.

'Stefano. I'm sorry. You take me too seriously. We Australians... we joke a lot. We make fun of each other. It's just our way.'

'I try to understand you, Lucy. I cannot. This I regret. I like you, I want for us to be friends but—' He threw up his hands. 'I wish that day in Spaccanapoli had never happened.'

'Then I would still be in the Ufficio dell'Anagrafe in Pozzuoli. Trying to make myself understood.'

Rosaria could not possibly have chosen a worse moment to saunter past. It would have to be Rosaria—who should in fact have been at school—or perhaps it was a good thing because it did at least stop them saying things they would no doubt later regret. She came straight up and greeted Lucy, waited to be introduced to her 'friend' and wanted to know if Lucy had made a decision about working in the restaurant. Lucy said she had and would come to see Paolo in a little while.

Rosaria squealed with delight. 'You do it, Lucia, I have certain! Soon I speak very good the English, mamma happy. Also joyful me. Good you got nice Italian boy, Lucia, ciao!'

And she was gone. 'Now I know how I sound in Italian,' Lucy said and pulled a face. 'And trust her to go off with the wrong impression.'

'Oh?'

'She thinks you're my boyfriend.'

'She is—how old? Eighteen? She thinks a man and a woman must have a relationship. Tonight I will tell her we are, as you say, just friends.'

'You're staying tonight?' The tension, which Rosaria had managed to break, was rising again.

'Please do not worry, I don't mean with you. I have a small tent, I will sleep at the camping park.'

Lucy couldn't help smiling, in spite of herself. 'That's where I am.' Stefano didn't smile, he didn't approve at all.

'By yourself? It's not good, Lucy, not suitable at all. We find somewhere else for you. Tell your father you start work tomorrow, you need time to find accommodations, yes?'

'No "s." It's singular. "Accommodation."'

'Thank you. Lucy...?'

'Yes?'

'I do not know what you do here. But I worry about you. My family also. We like you. I want for you a good outcome. That is all.'

Lucy wanted to lean over and kiss him on the cheek but even such casual intimacy was too difficult, she was afraid that it would be misconstrued. So she didn't.

'I'm glad you came, Stefano. I need a friend. I need one now and I think very soon I'm going to need one even more. I will ring Australia and find out what I can about the production. I've thought of someone who might be able to help.'

'Forget it, it's not important.'

'It's important to you. And you are my friend so it's important to me. We'll do that now and then I'll go and see Paolo. I can't promise anything but Geoff used to make documentaries. It was a long time ago but I think he's still got friends in the industry.'

So she rang Geoff for the second time in twenty-four hours, getting him out of bed, which he didn't mind because he was relieved to learn that Stefano had come down from Naples to check on her, since he couldn't do it himself. He promised to see what he could find out. Lucy finally got off the phone smiling.

'I think he approves of you,' she said. 'He'll do what he can. We've got to ring back tomorrow.'

'This is very kind.'

'No, he's just glad you're keeping an eye on me. He worries too.'

And now it was her turn to see Paolo, she couldn't put it off any longer. Stefano sensed her reluctance. Was she quite sure she wanted to take this job instead of just telling her father who she was?

Lucy said she was sure but not with the assurance she had intended. Stefano gave her a look. She laughed and said she was worried that she'd drop a plate of prawns into someone's lap. It had happened to her once, at a very posh restaurant in Melbourne, the waiter had been so mortified that she'd ended up comforting him. Stefano, going along with it, asked what 'posh' meant and Lucy launched into the usual explanation about the English travelling to and from India, Port Out, Starboard Home, in the days of the old P & O steamships.

'English,' said Stefano. 'Completamente strano.' But he had at least distracted her.

He dropped her off on the Vespa. 'In bocca al lupo,' he said, because he would not risk giving her bad luck by wishing her good. 'I will meet you at the camping park, I have things I must do.' She was left there outside Il Veliero, wondering what his business could be in Stella del Mare.

Twenty Four

P aolo saw Lucy coming. He had hoped all night that she wouldn't but Rosaria had already told him to expect her. He put a good face on it. So did Lucy.

'Buongiorno, Lucia.'

'Buongiorno.'

They were both glad when Chiara and Silvana came into the empty restaurant. Rosaria, presumably, had at last gone to school and Andrea had no doubt been there for hours since classes began, Lucy knew, at eight. She was rather sorry that he wasn't part of the welcoming committee.

Chiara spoke first. 'Rosaria says you take the job, yes?'

'Yes. If you still want me.'

They were all smiling, even, she was careful to notice, Paolo. Of course they wanted her, they needed her badly, when could she start? Lucy asked if tomorrow would be alright, today a friend of her cousin's had arrived from Naples, she would like to spend some time with him. There, she thought, get in first, forestall any questions.

Paolo said tomorrow they were closed, it was Tuesday, their one day off for the week, but the day after would be good. He would need to get her details, just in case the Guardia di Finanza or some such came and asked questions, unlikely but one never knew, he could see her passport?

Lucy produced it and Paolo wrote down the relevant details. He expressed a little surprise that she had come straight to the south, most tourists went first to Venice and Florence after Rome, but Lucy reminded him of her original plan to continue on to Greece. Besides, she said, she thought it wiser to see the south first before it got too hot, and then travel north as the temperature rose. Which everyone agreed was indeed sensible. This was all achieved with a mixture of bad Italian and worse English and much waving of hands. It seemed to work, they even agreed on an hourly rate acceptable to both parties and Lucy promised to equip herself with a black skirt and a couple of white shirts.

They parted with what Lucy sensed was genuine warmth on the part of the women. She had no way of knowing what Paolo was feeling. She still hoped desperately that he believed her cover story. She forced herself to be casually friendly with him and thought she pulled it off.

Paolo, for his part, had looked at Lucy's passport and had been only mildly comforted. Yes, it was in the name of Harrington. But he still felt that her trip from Melbourne to Rome to Naples was hardly the usual path for a young Australian traveller with no particular ties to Italy. On the other hand, what did he know? Perhaps Italy was flavour of the month over there now, not very likely but anything was possible.

Given a choice, Paolo would not have employed Lucy. Refusing, however, would have been difficult, with Silvana convinced the australiana had been sent to them in their hour of need by a thoughtful Deity. Paolo was not an imaginative man and he could think of no excuse that would make sense to his wife. The truth was out of the question.

After the Irpinia earthquake, he had almost told her what had happened in Australia but he loved her too much to risk it. He still did. There had been the occasional affair in twenty-four years of marriage, that went without saying, but none that had meant a thing, he had always gone home to Silvana and always would. He was clever enough to know that she was his safe harbour.

Lucy returned to the camping ground quite pleased with her morning's work. Things were going according to plan and if they were also getting just a little scary, well that was to be expected. She was inside the tent. Now she could begin to search for whatever it was that would make Paolo vulnerable and bring about his downfall.

She did not have to wait long for Stefano. His tent was already pitched on a site not far from her chalet, he'd got a spot as close as possible in case, he said, there was any trouble. She told him she was now employed and he was annoyed that she hadn't bargained for more money—they would have expected it, he said, she was being ripped off. After a week she must insist on more.

'And your business in Stella del Mare?'

'Successful. I have found you somewhere to stay.'

'What?'

Stefano was pleased. Permanent accommodation was hard to come by at this time of the year but he couldn't go back to Naples and leave her in a camping ground. In another week the place would be crowded and dirty; worse, it would be full of polentoni who were not to be trusted, anything could happen.

'Hey!' said Lucy, 'Hold it, who are these 'polentoni'?'

'Northerners. They do not know how to treat women. They are maleducati. Very rude.'

Lucy took a deep breath. 'I think there are good and bad everywhere, Stefano. I can look after myself.'

'Please. It is just a very small appartamento. What in London is called a bed-sit, yes? We say un monolocale. And I can negotiate for you an excellent price, come and see?' He was pleading with her and Lucy knew he did not find that easy. On the other hand, she didn't want to be beholden to him—not more than she was already. And then she realised she was automatically responding in the negative again, why did she always do that? Stefano wanted to help her, he was just being kind, after all, he was the real estate expert. And it wasn't as if she had to sleep with him if she said yes. Did she?

'Okay, why not? I'd love to see it. Thanks.' There, it was done. Not so hard after all.

The apartment was on the top floor of an old three-storey block up the hill behind the town, a good way from Paolo's restaurant. The building was square and ugly, with pink paint peeling from its walls. Nothing of historic significance here, no memory of Greek or Roman or Moor, just another lump of jerry-built concrete. No lift either and Lucy felt as she climbed the stairs that she could probably do without a gym membership. She was quite unimpressed until the landlord opened the door and flung it wide and then she knew she'd take it.

It was just a long, large, rather shabby room with a door leading to a small bathroom at one end, a bed, a table, a couple of chairs and basic cooking facilities. And, of course, the obligatory, to die-for view, put there to seduce any passing foreigner; a view up the coast, down the coast and out to sea, which could even be enjoyed from a tiny balcony. Lucy loved it all. It would, she knew instinctively, be a bolt-hole, a haven. She tried, as Stefano had coached her, not to look too impressed while Stefano himself loudly pointed out all the bad features. The landlord, aware of the game being played, promised to replace one or two small items and a deal was eventually struck. He would have the lease prepared and Lucy could move in tomorrow.

Alone with Stefano, Lucy was full of gratitude. He said she could thank him by letting him take her out to dinner and she agreed but first they went in Lucy's car to Castellabate and shopped for a black skirt and two white shirts. Lucy would have grabbed the first thing she saw but this was Italy and limited though the options were in such a small place, Stefano managed to find three shops he could drag her into and made her try everything on and model it for him before he was satisfied.

'What do you want?' he asked when she dared to protest. 'That people think Australians do not care about bella figura? That skirt—it's 'orrible, Lucy. The cut—can you not see?'

Lucy didn't think the cut would matter under a long black waiter's apron but when even the shop assistant agreed with Stefano she went along with it and paid twice the price for something better. Over the inevitable coffee, Stefano broached another subject. He wanted to get her a small present, a cellulare, a mobile phone. He got quite annoyed when she started to say no before he had even finished. He had agreed not to ask her business with her father and he wouldn't. That did not mean he would stop worrying. If she had a phone he could at least ring her. More importantly, she could ring him, discreetly, if she needed him. It would not cost much—it's not as though she'd be making calls all over Italy.

That turned into a two-coffee-and-one-beer argument which Stefano won, although Lucy insisted on paying for the phone herself until she found she couldn't really afford it, not if she was going to extend the hire of the car, at which point Stefano used his superior language skills to conclude the deal and leave her with no option but to let him hand over his credit card.

It took them another half hour at the post office to make their call to Australia. Lucy handed the phone to Stefano and made him talk to Geoff himself.

'Signor 'arrington? Stefano Falanga, ciao.'

Geoff insisted on first names and regretted that he did not have a great deal to tell Stefano. The production was indeed a soap opera. An old friend who was still a television director had passed on a couple of tips.

'First up don't ever tell them you want to work in film. They will think you are—how can I put this?'

Stefano hazarded a guess. 'A 'wanker' is perhaps the word?'

'That's the one,' said Geoff.

'I see,' said Stefano, who desperately wanted to work in film one day. 'No talk about film.'

'Be enthusiastic. Tell them how much you love television. You want to be a designer, yes?'

'Indeed.'

'Let them know you understand what a designer does. That your role is first and foremost to leave room for the cameras to move.'

'This is not obvious?'

'Apparently not. I'm sorry, it's probably not much help.'

'No, it's fantastic. Thank you so much.'

'If I hear anything else I'll let you know. Good luck with it. And Stefano. Thank you so much for helping Lucy. It means a great deal to me.'

'It is my pleasure. My very great pleasure. Thank you again. Arrivederci.'

Geoff hung up the phone back in Melbourne and thought it was as he had expected. The boy was in love with Lucy. And he knew what Kate would think about that. But he sounded nice enough. He did not sound like a rapist.

Stefano told Lucy that Geoff had been very helpful. Inwardly he felt more nervous than ever and wondered if he would bother even going to the interview.

Paolo was also trying to keep his nerves at bay and had found an excuse to drop in on his friend Roberto Lucattini. He told Roberto about hiring Lucy and pretended to be concerned that she did not have the necessary permesso di lavoro. Like Paolo's family, Roberto was amused by this unexpected display of civic responsibility. So rare a thing was it—not just from Paolo but from anyone at all on the entire Italian peninsula—that he was privately forced to consider what had brought it on. And couldn't for a minute imagine anything sufficiently serious.

His wife Ornella however, who had joined them for an aperitivo, could. Because she was starting to think she knew where she had seen Lucy Harrington. If indeed that was her name. But for now she said nothing. Paolo was her cousin, after all.

Twenty Five

Stefano took Lucy to a tiny hamlet back up the coast and off the main road where, because it was such a balmy evening, they elected to eat outside at tables that were simply stuck into the sand and where, as the evening drew on and the tide came in, the water grew ever closer to their feet. Lucy slipped her sandals off and dug her toes into the sand and thought how delightful it was. She thought also how this place—like the pizzerie in Piazza Sannazzaro—would never be allowed back home in Australia because some over-zealous health inspector would take great pleasure in closing the place down, citing Regulation 136B, paragraph 2(iii). Stefano was surprised when she told him, he thought that sounded very German, not like he imagined Australia at all.

'So how do you imagine it?'

'Very carefree, you know? 'Appy-go-lucky. Like everyone is always in vacanza and a bit—irresponsible?'

'You'd be so disappointed. We're quite staid these days.'

'Staid?'

'Respectable. Law-abiding. It's you lot, you Italians, who have no respect for the rules. What is it you say, "fai come ti pare?" Do what you like.?'

'You think those idiot politicians deserve our respect?'

'You voted for them! You think it is good to dump your rubbish over a cliff and refuse to pay any taxes?'

'I pay taxes! Sometimes.'

'You will if you get a job with the Australians. They might surprise you in other ways, too.'

'Like?'

'We are not so happy-go-lucky any more. We work very hard.'

'I think Australians want only an easy time.' He was stirring but she still took the bait.

'You're talking shit, Stefano. Am I having an easy time?'

'You are an exception. In every way.'

Lucy let it pass and got stuck into the plate of alici, the little marinated anchovies lined up in a glistening row in front of her. Stefano wisely changed the subject.

'So. This new family. How are they?'

'How are they?'

'What sort of people?'

'I hardly know them.'

'But you have a little impression, yes?'

'I'd rather not talk about Paolo.'

'Leave him then. The others, I am interested, is all.'

'Silvana is his wife. Not sure about her. She wants me there, I don't know why.'

'Perhaps because they are busy. You work hard.' He paused just a moment. 'Perhaps Signora Bianchi telephone, tell her how good you iron.'

Lucy was startled for a moment, but saw that he was smiling, it was just a little joke, he couldn't possibly be aware of the connection between those women. She grinned back.

'Very funny. Anyway, Silvana's okay, we'll see. Chiara, the older girl, I like a lot. She's smart, Chiara, works hard, gets on with it. She's close to Silvana. Andrea, the boy, is just a kid, but adorable. They all spoil him rotten, no doubt he'll be insufferable in a few years.'

'Un mammone. A mamma's boy.'

'Not just mamma's, everyone's. Even the staff spoil him. And then there's Rosaria. She's a total airhead, bone lazy but so beautiful what does it matter?'

'No more beautiful than you, Lucia.'

Lucy laughed again. 'Oh please.'

'It's true.'

'Me? Stefano, you saw her, she is gorgeous. I'm just...' She shook her head. She thought he was mad but deep inside she was just a tiny bit flattered. Actually, quite a lot flattered. But she was unused to compliments, because she never allowed men close enough to pay them, so she felt flustered by the remark and was glad that the second course arrived.

The seafood (no tomatoes) was excellent. While they ate it, Stefano talked about Naples, about the endemic corruption which it seemed would always be part of life there, about 'see-Naples-and-die' and how what the phrase really meant was that once you had seen Naples it was okay to die, because then the arc of life was complete. He loved Naples and said while it was sometimes impossibly hard to live there, it was also impossibly hard to leave, as all the thousands of émigrés had discovered. Lucy said without thinking that the Italians and the Irish had a lot in common and Stefano agreed that they did and asked if she had Irish ancestors then? And Lucy had to admit that yes, like an awful lot of Australians, she did.

Then Stefano waded out into what he sensed were deep and dangerous waters, though he did not know why they should be, and he asked about Lucy's life in Australia, about her family, about what it had been like, growing up without a father. Lucy tried to make light of it.

'Nothing like Naples, that's for sure!'

'No?'

'It was just us, Stefano. My mother and me in a small flat. No relations, not many friends to start with. There was no money to go out, to entertain. It was very, very quiet. We read heaps of books, the English classics and plays and novels and poetry. Sometimes, not often, we went to see a film.'

He couldn't understand at all. 'But your grandparents?'

'Six hundred kilometres away. They didn't like my mother—not even when she was a little girl. And she didn't like them.'

'So no cousins either? No uncles, aunts?'

Lucy shook her head. 'I had my friend Sim and her family. One or two others.'

'This... this is sad. Che catastrofe.'

'A catastrophe? No, it wasn't that bad. Not for me, my mother did everything she could for me. I adored her.'

'And her? There was no one for her?'

'Not until Geoff.'

'The man who helps me and worries about you. He is, I think, like a father?'

'Sort of. A father, and a friend.'

'But you have taken his name.'

'Yes.'

'I understand.' A matter of expediency. So her Italian family wouldn't know who she was.

'I'm very close to Geoff. I would trust him with my life.'

'You find this hard, to trust people.' It was a statement.

'Do I? How do you know?'

'You are always—I don't know how to say it. Poco espansiva... you hold back, that is it. Like you are afraid to let the world know how you feel. Afraid sometime someone might touch you.'

Lucy stared at her plate. It was like he was reading her soul. She hated him. She wanted to hate him.

'Lucy?'

'I think this is possibly the best—what did you say the fish was called, sarago? I think it's the best sarago I've ever tasted.' And the only sarago she'd ever tasted.

'Lucy, you do it again.'

She whispered, 'Don't.'

Stefano could have kicked himself. Mentally he did kick himself. They finished the meal and talked about Lucy's new job and Stefano's prospective one and the things they had to do tomorrow. They had coffee and limoncello and then they drove back to Stella del Mare and the camping ground where Stefano bid Lucy sogni d'oro, sweet dreams. He had one last question before he left her.

'What was your name before you changed it?'

'O'Connell.'

'O'Connell. Yes, I see. A good Irish name.'

Then they both went to their separate beds and slept badly. Stefano spent the night in his stifling little tent wondering how he would ever get through to this girl. He sensed that the task would be long and difficult but the last two days had convinced him that she was worth the effort. He did not mind a challenge or he would already have settled down to earn an adequate if dull living with

Falanga Immobiliare S.r.l.

Lucy lay in her slightly more comfortable chalet wondering, yet again, why she didn't just give up the struggle and present herself, like some wandering nomad, at the door of his tent. And knew that the reasons were twofold. Firstly, she was frightened; it was bound to end in disaster because that was what had always happened in the past. And secondly—and far, far more importantly—she had not come to Italy to fall in love. She did not like Italy and she did not like Italians. There was certainly—and this she knew to be true—no way on earth she could ever live here. And Stefano—he had said as much that night—could never live anywhere but chaotic Naples, home of the baroque gone mad or bad, depending on your point of view. It was therefore quite senseless to begin something that on every count could only end in tears. She was not here for herself, she was here for Kate. The Sirens might be singing out there on their rocks, for this was their old playground, but Lucy was refusing to listen. They would not lure her from her course, she would keep her hand firmly on the tiller. It was hard.

The next day she moved into her apartment, what Stefano called her Piccolo Nido, her little nest. He wanted her to unpack, wanted to see her settled but she wouldn't have it. Even the small degree of intimacy that would be involved, his sensing her clothes, her make-up, her underwear—it was too much, it was too soon. Stefano, seeing this and trying to practice a patience that did not come easily, suggested they go and do some shopping instead, he could at least make sure she wasn't robbed before he left.

They shopped, they swam, they had lunch. Tomatoes were allowed. They talked of everything that was unimportant. They returned to Il Nido and Stefano carried the shopping upstairs: coffee, pasta, fruit, milk, all the necessities. Plus a packet of cornflakes. He had teased her unmercifully when she bought it. So Australian! He thought it was hilarious, and shook his head again now when it came out of the bag.

'Stefano? Don't.'

'But Lucy, it is food for—what are they called, le galline?' He imitated a chicken.

'We call them chooks.'

'Chooks? No, hens, that is it.'

'They're chooks in Australia. They don't eat cornflakes, we do.'

'Va bene. If cornflakes make you so beautiful, is okay.'

Lucy decided to treat that as a joke too, though he did not look as though he were joking. 'The thing is, you can eat them in your pyjamas. To go to a bar for breakfast, you have to get dressed. Australians are lazy.'

'Yesterday you tell me how hard they work.'

'At work they work. The rest of the time they are lazy.'

'Why do you always make a joke?'

'I don't always.'

'So. Only with me?'

'Only when I don't know what else to say.'

'Or you like to change the subject?'

Lucy met his gaze then and gave a little shrug that might have been acquiescence.

'Oh Lucy. Lucia...' It sounded so different in Italian. He pronounced it with the soft Neapolitan 'c'. It sounded like a ripple curling around a sandy rock. It was just a word. He turned it into a caress. He held her for just a moment, tilted her face up to his but did not kiss her.

'Whatever this thing is you plan—be careful, you promise?'

She nodded.

'I call tomorrow.'

He left then. Twice on the stairs he almost turned and ran back but forced himself to continue. Stefano, like Geoff, was getting just a little paranoid, was seeing headlines in *Il Mattino*. They featured Lucy being dragged off to the Questura but for what, he could not imagine.

Lucy felt quite bereft once he had gone but decided that, tempting though it was, she must not wallow in self-pity. Tomorrow she had to report for duty. She should get her house in order, practise some Italian verbs and have an early night. She took her mother's photo from her backpack and placed it by her bed. She had no idea really what the next day would bring. It might herald the outbreak of hostilities but she suspected a period of phoney war was on the cards and in this she'd be proved correct.

Twenty Six

L ucy presented herself at the restaurant the next morning, in time for her first shift. Silvana greeted her warmly, speaking slowly in Italian and ushered her into the kitchen. It was cooler and cloudy today, they were not expecting to be so busy, there should be time for Lucy to familiarise herself with the menu. Enrico took her through it and explained the southern dishes which were unfamiliar. He was surprised by her knowledge until she informed him that Melbourne was full of Italian restaurants, most of them even run by Italians.

There was a great basket of seafood on the bench and this Paolo had bought early that morning from the local fishermen. Enrico held the selection up for her one by one so she could learn the names, sgombro, polipo, calamaro, cozze.

She joined in. '...Gamberi, vongole, orata, sarago. È buono, il sarago.' Especially if eaten on an incoming tide, with your bare toes stuck in the damp sand.

'Brava!' Enrico and Silvana both clapped her little performance. Lucy, suddenly embarrassed, wished she had shut up.

By the time they were done Concetta and Marco had arrived and the full complement of staff was ready for action. Concetta, a local woman who was probably not as old as she looked, said hello and little else. Marco, barely out of his teens, started to flirt in the first five seconds and met schoolteacher-Lucy for his troubles.

Lunch passed without incident. Lucy only got one order wrong and redeemed herself with a Canadian couple who were relieved to find someone who spoke English. Lucy did not uncover any skeletons in the Esposito cupboard. She knew Paolo was watching her every move. She hoped she was less obvious as she watched him.

Lucy was about to leave for the afternoon break when Silvana stopped her. 'You have somewhere to stay now?'

'Yes. A bedsit at the other end of town. It's fine. I've got a mobile phone too, I should give you the number.' She wrote it out quickly, better the phone number than the address, for some reason she wanted that place to herself. Ridiculous, she knew, in a town this size everyone would know in three days where she lived. They probably knew already.

When she put the key in her door soon after, it occurred to her, as it hadn't the day before when Stefano was still there, that this was the first time she had lived alone since her mother came home to die. She had always been happy in her own company but there was an added element to it now; once inside these walls, she could cease acting and be herself again. Here she did not have to be on her guard, it was not just a matter of relaxing, it was about feeling safe. It was a new and not altogether pleasant sensation, needing to feel safe instead of taking it for granted.

She opened the window to let the sea breeze in and lay on the bed and allowed herself to think about Stefano in spite of having no intention, none whatsoever, of allowing their relationship to develop into anything beyond friendship. But the fact that she was here, in the Cilento, in this little flat, with a job in her father's restaurant—it was all due to him and she owed him and she hoped one day she could repay him. She hoped he got the job at La RAI if that's what he wanted. He deserved it. He was nice. He was more than nice. He was—oh for God's sake, he was sexy, funny, charming, generous, good to his parents—and no one said her name like he did, Lucia... why did he have to be one of them? Her buzzer rang. She leapt up from the bed, had he come back?

'Yes? Pronto?'

'Lucia? It's Andrea, ciao, I come up yes?'

Her heart sank. So much for privacy. 'Sure Andrea. Avanti.' Not even two days.

He was grinning from ear to ear when she let him in. 'How did you find me?' she asked. 'I was trying to keep this place a secret.'

'No one else knows. My friend Dario saw you move in, he told me. Hey, this is cool, great view.'

'I like it. And please—slowly, yes?' She was having trouble keeping up with the torrent of Italian.

Andrea was inspecting everything, even her clothes. Italians, Lucy had noticed before, were not too much concerned about invading personal space. 'You don't have much stuff.'

'I'm travelling.'

He turned to her then, suddenly serious and spoke in his schoolboy English. 'But you no travel now, you stay yes? Please, Lucia?'

'You want me to stay?'

He nodded, solemn now.

'Why?'

'You help Rosaria.'

'She hasn't asked me to help her.' And never will, Lucy thought to herself, lazy little sod.

'We see.' He grinned then and reverted to Italian. 'Dario says your boyfriend is very good-looking.'

'He's not my boyfriend.'

'Yes he is, you are engaged!' Except the word he used was 'fidanzati', which it seemed to Lucy covered just about the entire gamut of Italian boy-girl relationships. She let it go. He was just playing the role of annoying little brother. Never having had one before, she found it both novel and amusing.

Andrea sat down at her table then and asked if she was busy. Lucy, taken aback, said she'd intended to have a rest.

'Are you very, very tired?'

'Well. Not that tired, I suppose.'

He pulled an exercise book from the backpack he'd been carrying. 'I've got this English homework. It'll only take a minute. Please, Lucia.'

So that was it! How long had this kid known her? The sheer nerve of it amazed her. And yet... he was smiling at her as though he somehow knew he had a right to ask, and those green eyes were gazing into hers, appealing to ties he could not have known existed, and Lucy caved.

'I'll help you, Andrea. But I will not—not—do it for you. Get it?'

'Okay.'

They worked for nearly two hours. Lucy explained the vagaries of several English verbs. She helped the boy to understand that since 'ough' could be pronounced at least five different ways in English and that was just off the top of her head, getting it wrong was not the end of the world. She was about to start on the use of the apostrophe but Andrea said his head was spinning and maybe that would do for one day. He said she was a very good teacher, better than the one he had at school but Lucy was quick to point out that she only had one student. She knew what it was like to have twenty-five of them in a room.

And then Andrea started asking questions about her life at home in Melbourne. What were Australian schools like and where had she gone to school and did she have brothers and sisters and on and on. And the more he asked the harder Lucy found it to convince herself that this was just childish curiosity. He was only ten and to him she was something a bit exotic, she knew that, a stranger from the other side of the world. It would have been odd if he hadn't been curious. But a nagging voice kept asking what ten-year-old cared so much about his homework that he wanted to spend a whole afternoon on it? And why had he come to her when he barely knew her and had he indeed come of his own volition or had he been sent to spy?

Well two could play at that game, she thought and although she felt quite ridiculous—a feeling she was getting used to since coming to Italy—she asked Andrea, ever so casually, about his life, had they always lived in Stella del Mare and did he like it or would he prefer to live in the city, in Salerno say, or Napoli?

Andrea laughed at that, cities weren't for him, not yet anyway. It was nice to go for a day or two, to the movies and stuff like that, but for now he was happy here. Too many crooks in Naples, they'd rip your arm off just to steal your watch.

'No crooks in Stella del Mare?'

'Not that sort. Maybe a couple of kids who pinch things from tourists. Only the big guys here.'

'What do you mean, the big guys?'

'Nothing. Dad says things sometimes. Dad's an assessore.'

'Sorry?'

'In the giunta comunale. They are chosen by il sindaco.'

'Ah. The mayor. That's interesting. So your dad is on the council. That's what we call it in English.'

'Yeah, consiglio.'

Stefano rang then and Lucy sent Andrea away with a promise to help him again some other time.

'Ciao, Stefano!' he yelled at the phone, before letting himself out with a wave.

'You have a visitor already? I am jealous.'

She couldn't believe how good it was to hear his voice. 'Andrea came for help with his homework. Well. He asked for help and that's what he got. I hope... you know...'

'There was not another agenda?'

'He's only ten. He's curious, that's all.'

'He asked a lot of questions?'

'About home. Yes. And I told a lot of—not lies, exactly. Half-truths. I hope I can remember what I said. Paolo's on the council. He's a member of the giunta, or whatever it's called.'

'It's like the executive.'

'Big fish in a little pond, then?'

'What? Oh! I see. Yes.'

'Andrea also says there are big crooks in Stella del Mare.' She laughed. Stefano didn't.

'This is Campania, Lucy. Big crooks everywhere. But they will not affect you. It is not because of them I don't sleep.' And then he spent a long time telling her how worried he was instead of saying what he really wanted to but she sensed what was coming and changed the subject to his interview, just four days away. Stefano was not so much nervous now as resigned to missing out and nothing Lucy said seemed to give him any hope.

'You could always come to Australia for a while. We don't have so many architects.'

'I don't know anyone in Australia.'

'You know me.'

'But—I couldn't.'

'Why not?'

He didn't know why not. Lucy hoped it wasn't because he couldn't bear to leave home and was foolish enough to suggest as much.

'Perhaps you would not know how to look after yourself, since your mamma does such a good job.'

Even though Laura had warned him, Stefano was wounded. 'I stay at home because is cheaper, Lucy. I can save money. Apartments not so easy to get.'

He was so sensitive. Lucy wished she had shut up. 'I know, I know. It's what Italians do, it's alright!'

'Is not like I am a prisoner, I come, I go as I please.'

'Of course. I understand. But Stefano?'

'Yes?' He sounded wary.

'Napoli—it is not the entire world. One day you'll have to get out into the rest of it.'

'You tease me again.'

'Never. Now I have to go back to work.'

When she returned for the evening shift, she found Silvana waiting for her, full of apologies for Andrea's rudeness in going to her home uninvited. Lucy laughed it off, her fears that he'd been sent on some mission of discovery allayed, and in the days that followed his visits became a regular event, and he taunted Rosaria with his newfound English phrases.

Lucy would have enjoyed the work at Il Veliero if there had not been the need to play a role. She was not secretive by nature and while the deception was necessary, she found it both trying and tiring. And while she got on well with Chiara, forging a relationship with Rosaria was a different matter. Perhaps it was simply the fact that Lucy had Rosaria's number and the girl knew it and resented it. Suddenly, here was an adult she could neither impress with her looks nor beguile with her charms, who actually saw her for what she was. Hardly surprising then that Rosaria became the first Esposito to rue the arrival of Lucy Harrington.

The second was Paolo's cousin, Ornella Lucattini.

Twenty Seven

Ornella had thought long and hard about the visit she was making to her aunt Michela. She had discussed it at length on the telephone with her mother, Lisa, in Torino and was even now going over the pros and cons as she drove her Fiat Brava to Naples.

Ornella, Paolo's cousin and childhood confidante, was also the keeper of his darkest secret, although he was not aware of the fact. Of all the family resident in Italy, only she knew the true version—or as close to the truth as anyone but the participants could get—of what had happened on that night in Melbourne when Paolo Esposito took Kate O'Connell to the cinema.

Many, many years ago Ornella had visited her aunt and uncle in Australia. They were still in Carlton then and the coffee shop had expanded to become a full-blown restaurant. One night after closing, when Mauro had gone to bed, Grazia spoke of her joy at seeing Ornella, her regret that they had so little contact with the family. If only things had turned out as they had all expected. It was during this conversation that the story of Paolo's 'youthful indiscretion' came out.

Ornella, by then considering marriage to Paolo's best friend (whom she loved deeply), was shocked. It did not sound like a youthful indiscretion to her, it sounded like rape and she said so. It was Grazia's turn to be shocked. How could she say such a thing about her own flesh and blood? The girl had thrown herself at Paolo, she was a silly little kid from the bush—burina was the word she used, a country bumpkin—and no doubt she was asking for it. Not that Paolo was blameless, Grazia wasn't saying that, but he'd paid for it, they all had, over and over. One unfortunate incident and so many lives change...

Ornella had let it go. This, she sensed, was an argument she would never win. She would just be told she wasn't there, she didn't understand. In fact, when she got home, she felt she understood only too clearly: the whole family was involved in a conspiracy, not only of silence but of self-delusion. Paolo had not committed rape, he had made a mistake. On his return, he had pretended that he had not liked Australia. Michela had proclaimed—vociferously—that she had never wanted to go there in the first place and Paolo senior had suddenly discovered an unexpected business opportunity he could not possibly forego. (Surprisingly, it was his son who managed to turn it into a success, showing an entrepreneurial skill that none had thought he possessed. It provided the capital for his first little bar.) And thus had the unpleasantness been put behind them.

Ornella's father, not long after, had accepted a promotion with Fiat and this had brought about the move to the company's headquarters in Torino. Ornella went ahead and married Roberto. She never told him what Paolo had done. She thought often of the girl called Kate and wondered what had happened to her and her baby. She prayed for them and thus became part of the conspiracy herself, despising herself for it. But Ornella had grown up, like Paolo and Roberto, in the back streets of Pozzuoli and would do nothing to send anyone back there. Of all their classmates, she could think of less than a dozen who had really made it. They, the three of them, had been blessed indeed. Or perhaps they had made their own luck. These days, Ornella looked at the world and found her faith sorely tested. And anyway, Paolo she felt was paying—had perhaps already paid—for his sins.

So far as Ornella knew, Paolo's wife Silvana was in total ignorance of the skeleton in the family cupboard. (Or was deliberately choosing to be obtuse.) Silvana had fallen out with her aunt at the time of her engagement, Ornella knew that. Zia Alessandra did not approve of Paolo but no one had ever seemed sure of the reason. No one except Ornella that is, and she kept her feelings to herself. But it was obvious to her. Alessandra was married to a mareschiallo after all, an honest and incorruptible maresciallo, which was quite a rare thing and she no doubt shared his high standards. Having heard the whole story, or enough of it, she would have expected Paolo to be both open and contrite and he'd failed on both counts. Ornella thought Alessandra had been given a pretty raw deal.

Ornella felt a black cloud descending—or maybe a bad moon rising—the moment Lucy walked into Il Veliero. It took her a while to remember Grazia's treasured photo which she had seen so long ago in Australia: the three young women, Grazia herself, Michela and Lisa. The resemblance between that young Michela and Lucy was uncanny. When she did recall it, then everything fell into place.

Passing the trip off to her husband as necessary for the acquisition of new summer sandals, Ornella was now on her way to Naples, to the apartment in Pozzuoli recently visited out of nowhere by the team from *Carràmba Che Sorpresa*.

Ornella, who knew it was too late by far to awaken sleeping dogs, was going to warn Michela that a long-lost granddaughter had at last arrived on the scene.

Michela's reaction, when she heard the news, was not at all what Ornella had expected. She was not upset, she did not call on the Virgin for assistance, she did not demand that the family rally for war. She simply chose not to believe it.

'But she could be anyone, Ornella! You know what Australians are like! The globe is littered with them!'

'When Australian girls come to Italy, zia, they go to Venezia, Firenze, Roma. She came straight here and then to Stella del Mare. Like a homing pigeon.'

'You told me. She explained that! Her friend. And then she takes the job. Simple.'

'And the fact she looks exactly—exactly—like you?'

'Ornella! It's nothing. A photograph. A million girls look like that. You are mistaken.'

'Paolo is worried.'

'Paolo has reason to be worried. But not about this so-called daughter. How is he?'

'I think not so good. But he doesn't let on. Silvana though, she watches him like a hawk.'

'I'm glad someone does. And Rosaria?'

'We all know Rosaria.'

Rosaria's grandmother sighed. 'It's a pity she was born with looks.' Ornella thought that since Rosaria had clearly not been given brains the looks were actually a good thing but she just smiled.

'Rosa will do okay. With luck she'll marry a fortune and you can retire to a nice villa on Capri.' They finished their lunch and went shopping. On the drive home, Ornella marvelled at her family's ability to stick its collective head in the sand and play ostrich and started inventing excuses for another little trip she would need to make soon.

Of all this Lucy knew next to nothing. She did know that Paolo and Ornella were cousins because Andrea had told her. And she was aware that her father was not in perfect health because some days under the olive skin and the tan there was the greyness that only came with pain and with which she was all too familiar. But since no one ever made the slightest reference to it, she got the impression the subject of his illness, whatever it might be, was taboo. She would not allow herself to feel sorry for him but it was difficult.

Lucy's ideas of justice had never extended to the inflicting of physical pain and she did not yet realise how much she would have to change to succeed in the role in which she had cast herself. Nor did she understand how very different at its core was the society in which she had been raised to this one in the Mezzogiorno. She would soon learn.

There was a lot of talk in the restaurant about the giunta comunale. The family discussed it. So, around the bar, did Paolo's friends and associates. Lucy's Italian wasn't good enough to follow the fine detail but she did learn enough to know that the sindaco, the mayor, was ill and might be forced to stand down. Should that happen, there would be pressure on Paolo to take his place, since they belonged to the same party. Lucy got the impression that Paolo was keen to have the job. She couldn't understand why. He was far from well himself. Did he want the prestige? Did he fancy wearing that ridiculous ribbon around his waist on high days and holidays? It was Stefano who explained.

'Mayors have power, Lucy, they issue contracts for construction, you know? For the roads. They can close down a place which does not obey its licence... many things. You see? It's not just presenting medals to schoolchildren, to the football team.'

'I understand.'

'You say he wants this?'

'I think so. I'm not sure.'

'It's maybe not such an easy decision.'

'Why?'

'It's complicated. Like everything in Campania. Interesting to see what he does, your father. If it happens. Now I must go. You wish me in bocca al lupo, yes?'

It was his interview. 'Of course. I'll be thinking of you all afternoon. But you'll be fine. Call me when it's over.'

He didn't call. Lucy had no idea how they would organise these things. Surely all the applicants would be interviewed and then a decision would be made. Or would it be done on the spot? Had Stefano missed out and been told already? Should she ring him and commiserate? How would he take it? Perhaps he just wanted time to himself. Lucy kept looking at the phone, willing it to ring and it finally did, just before she had to leave for her evening shift, but it was Geoff's voice at the other end. He advised patience. He pointed out that Stefano, right now, might just possibly hate all Australians.

They talked about other things, about Andrea's English lessons and Paolo's possible bid to become mayor.

'What makes you think he wants the job?' Geoff asked.

'Just an impression.'

'Perhaps he feels he should do it.'

'Why would he?'

'I don't know? Sense of duty?'

Lucy didn't think it likely. Paolo? Duty? She shook her head. She never considered either that her prejudices might be getting in the way of her judgement or that she had not been in Campania long enough to understand how this foreign country worked.

She did think, however, that Geoff might be right about Stefano. Perhaps he was just hurt and bitterly disappointed. She would leave it until the next day to ring him. Aware of added tensions in the air at Il Veliero, she was glad when her shift finally finished. Pleading a headache, she refused a nightcap with Chiara and went home. Just as well, because she had a guest waiting at Il Nido.

Twenty Eight

S tefano had found the interview as daunting as he had expected, though not in the way he had expected. There were four people present: two Italians, one of whom was the head of design, and two very easy-going Australians. They were introduced by first names and he missed their titles but thought one of them—he wasn't sure which—was the executive producer. It was their very enthusiasm which threw him (in spite of Lucy's warnings), their air of genuine excitement about the project, like this was absolutely the greatest thing since—well, since the introduction of television.

They looked at his meagre portfolio, asked about his, virtually non-existent, experience. He expressed his eagerness to join them, to be a part of the project. They asked what he thought about the role of a designer and he gave them some stuff about attempting to heighten the drama while creating a world the viewer would accept as real. He also mentioned leaving room for the cameras to move. The Australians smiled and said it was a great answer.

The producer or whatever he was said they had to be honest—actually there was no longer an opening in design. But they desperately needed a production assistant. If he wanted to get into television, it was really fantastic experience and the job was his. Stefano didn't know whether to laugh or cry.

'Look,' said the head Australian guy, the capo. 'Not what you were after, I know that. But we really need a local for this, especially an English-speaking local. You'd be ideal. So think about it, okay? Let us know tomorrow?'

Stefano agreed to call them tomorrow. He thanked them and left, got on his Vespa and here he was, waiting on Lucy's doorstep, when she got home.

'I hope you do not mind. I need to talk.'

Lucy didn't mind at all. 'I'll have to get you a key. It's about the job, then?'

He nodded.

'What happened? We can talk in Italian if you like. If you speak very slowly.'

'I must practice my English.'

'That means you got it, yes? Fantastic! Well done!'

She was so pleased for him she actually gave him a hug. 'We should have a drink.'

'I have some wine.'

He opened the wine but he did not seem as thrilled as she expected.

'What is it? I thought you'd be over the moon. Do you say that?'

'We say in the seventh heaven. Al settimo cielo.'

'But you're not.'

He sighed and told her the whole story. 'I do not know what I should do. The money is shit. But this Australian guy say it's good experience, great opportunity, blah, blah, blah.'

To be honest, Lucy couldn't see the problem. But she wasn't about to say so. 'Well it isn't a design job, which is what you wanted. But something like television—a field where so many people want to work—it's probably good just to be in there, you know? Then when something comes up, you're on the spot. At least I'm pretty sure that's how it works back home.'

Stefano seemed unconvinced. 'I got it because I speak English, Lucy. Nothing else.'

'You don't know that.'

'They say so. Said so.'

'You're getting the chance to show what you can do!'

'I wanted the chance to show I can design.'

'And maybe you will.' Why wasn't he proud of his language skills, for heaven's sake? 'Look at it this way. Would it be better than selling real estate?'

'Anything is better than selling real estate.'

'Then why not give it a go?'

'What if I am no good? Make of myself a complete fool?'

147

'Stefano! How could you? They understand you have no experience! Just take a risk for once! In fact—there is no risk. If it doesn't work out, you can always go back to working for your father.'

'I can't.'

'Why not?'

'He says, if I do this, I am on my own. He will hire someone else.'

Smart Guido, Lucy thought. Aloud, she said gently, 'Perhaps this is his way of telling you to take it.'

'Or perhaps he tries to make me feel guilty and stay.'

Lucy shook her head. 'You Italians. Everything has to be such a drama! Why is it so hard, it's just a job, not a life sentence. Do what you want, follow your heart!'

'I am not brave enough for that.' He looked at her and ran his fingers through his hair, releasing the curls which had been flattened by his helmet on the long ride down. Lucy knew that she was not brave enough either though should he stay the night...

'I think you ought to take the job,' she said.

'I think I should get a job in Stella del Mare. Where I can look after you.'

'I need looking after?'

Stefano didn't know the answer to that. He'd heard rumours in Stella del Mare about the growing feud between Paolo Esposito and Mario Moretti. The talk, if it were true, did not bode well for peaceful co-existence, for Mario was a man who liked to get his own way. On the other hand, he couldn't imagine that anyone, least of all Lucy, was in any physical danger. No one knew she was Paolo's daughter. And this wasn't Naples.

'Stefano? You haven't answered the question.'

'Of course you need someone to look after you. You are a helpless straniera. Alone in the wicked Mezzogiorno.'

Lucy nearly tipped her wine over him but he restrained her. They only had one bottle.

'Please—be careful, that is all. Stai attenta. Keep open your eyes?'

'I will. I am doing that anyway.'

He looked at her again, hoping that now, at last, she might confide in him.

It didn't happen. She sensed his disappointment yet again.

'I'm sorry.'

'No. It's alright. Whenever.'

She thought it was a good time to change the subject back to the soap opera. 'The job, then. You'll decide tomorrow?'

'I will take the job.'

'Fantastic.' She was really pleased.

'As you say—not a life sentence.'

'Exactly.'

'And I do not wish you to think I am a—I do not know the word in English.'

'A wimp. A pappamolle.'

He was surprised. 'Where do you learn this?'

'Andrea.'

Stefano grinned. 'I speak to that boy.' He got up.

'You're not riding back to Naples?'

'Lucia! It is two o'clock. In the morning. I have a place at the camping ground.'

She felt really bad. Inhospitable. 'You can stay if you like. The bed's big enough. I mean—to sleep. You know.'

'I know what you mean. And I am an ordinary man. I change my mind about seminary, remember? I see you for disgusting cornflakes.' The door closed behind him.

They had breakfast together—warm cornetti fat with lemon cream—and then he headed back to Naples. Lucy knew this game could not go on forever. Their relationship had to be clarified, one way or the other. Or ended. But she could not bear the thought of ending it. Was that just fear of loneliness, of being left to fight single-handed? Or did it mean that they were already way past friendship, that there was no turning back to something so easy and comfortable? And the minute she said it to herself she knew it was absurd because there had never been anything comfortable between them, not since the moment he'd stopped her in that little street beyond Spaccanapoli. What they had was rather something so unpredictable that neither of them quite dared to grasp it, it was like an electric fence that might or might not have current running through it; like a beautiful mushroom that was perhaps a delicious amanita caesarea or could equally well be a death cap.

Lucy had no gold standard against which to judge her feelings. But whatever emotion was creeping up on her now, love or something like it, she knew only that the timing couldn't be worse.

She still had no idea how she was going to make Paolo pay for his crime. While her anger and her sense of injustice continued to burn brightly, the problem of collateral damage was still there. It was even more troublesome now that she knew—as she had not known when she first considered it up in Monte Santa Caterina—that Andrea idolised his father. But then, as she kept telling herself, Paolo had no right to hero-worship. It was tricky. She would just have to toughen up.

For a few days nothing much happened. Stefano started at la RAI and bemoaned the fact that he was unlikely to see much of Lucy because the Australians seemed happy to work all day and all night. But he thought, once he got the hang of things, that he would like it, though he had so much to learn.

Lucy was pleased for him. She herself was getting the hang of things at Il Veliero. Sometimes she felt as if she were a student again, with a summer job down on the Surf Coast back home. The family seemed to think she was happy. Paolo actually asked one day about her father's birthday—was she still planning to be home for it? And Lucy, who had once been the world's worst liar, glibly told him that her dad had been invited to join the crew of a yacht sailing to Vanuatu and so maybe there wouldn't be a party after all, at least not in the near future.

'He likes then to sail, your papà?'

'Oh, yes,' said Lucy, 'he loves it more than anything. That's why I stopped at your restaurant—when I saw the name, Il Veliero, I thought of him.' She was pleased with that. She thought it sounded pretty convincing. And Paolo, who needed some good news at that moment, was inclined to believe her.

Next day however, when Lucy arrived at the restaurant for work, the tension was undeniable. Enrico, usually so genial, was in a filthy mood, muttering to himself about how in twenty years he'd never been spoken to so rudely. He made his displeasure apparent in the food, which generated several complaints. Paolo and Silvana both disappeared when the place was at its busiest, leaving Chiara to cope as maître d' and only Lucy and Concetta to handle the floor. It was not good.

Lucy had no idea what was going on and nobody enlightened her. She wondered if the mayor had finally been carted off to hospital or had even died and if the pressure was again on Paolo. It was the only thing she could think of. Once again she was glad when her shift ended and she could escape back to Il Nido. She desperately hoped that Andrea would not turn up, demanding help with his English homework, she wasn't in the mood, she didn't think even he could make her laugh today. But it wasn't Andrea who eventually came, it was Chiara.

'I want to apologise, Lucy, today was terrible. Everyone so sconvolto—how do you say it? Upset?'

'It's okay. You've got problems, that's alright. It's none of my business, it happens in every family.'

'Not like this.'

'It does you know.' She smiled but Chiara wasn't comforted.

Lucy wasn't sure why she had really come. She offered coffee, camomile, orange juice. Chiara asked for water. When Lucy took the glass to her she noticed that Chiara, normally so self-controlled, was fighting back tears. She felt awful then, that she hadn't seen it, hadn't guessed that Chiara just wanted someone to talk to, a shoulder to cry on. She sat down beside her, this half-sister she liked so much who was, after all, barely twenty even though she often seemed so much older. Or was that just in comparison to the feckless Rosaria?

'Chiara? Cry if you want to. Sometimes it helps. Who's going to see you here?'

But Chiara was made of sterner stuff than that. She took the tissue Lucy proffered and blew her nose and sipped the water and declared herself okay.

'Oh Lucy. I try, you know, get on with her. We are sisters, I love her. But she make me so mad!'

So that was it. Nothing to do with politics, just Rosaria up to her usual tricks, she was behind all the family angst and Enrico's tantrums and the less than satisfied customers. Lucy hoped she wasn't pregnant or worse still, that she hadn't run away to Hollywood.

'What's Rosaria done?'

Chiara rolled her eyes. 'Soon she must take the maturità—her final exams, you know?' Lucy nodded. 'Two months ago they tell her she will never pass. Not unless she works very hard.'

'Which she doesn't do.'

'Esatto! And today our parents are called to the school and the teachers inform them of this. Mamma mia!'

'Bad, huh?'

'Un gran casino. Because they want that Rosaria goes to university. Now she must repeat the whole year.'

'And she's refusing.'

Chiara nodded miserably.

'I don't see how they can make her, Chiara. I mean—what's the point? She's not really cut out for uni anyway, as far as I can see. Why not let her do what she wants?'

'Because Rosa always does what she wants. And papà says adesso basta. In English I think, enough is enough.'

'I see.' And for once, Lucy was on Paolo's side. Make the girl graduate from high school at least, make her work for something, or she would go through life assuming that her looks would get her everything her heart desired. And when her looks had gone—what then?

'Lucy?'

Lucy knew what was coming. 'I can't do it, Chiara. Not in—how long is it? A month or so?'

'Three weeks. But you are professoressa. And her English is the problem. Other subjects she can just—what do you say—scratch through?'

'Scrape through. Chiara, I'd like to help. Honestly. But you're asking for a miracle.'

'Lucy, I tell you something. Since you come, for me is like having a big sister. I know one day you go home. But for now is really nice.

Just this one thing—please? I know you not cattolica—you teach and I will look after miracle. Will you try?'

So Lucy said that if Paolo and Silvana agreed—and if Rosaria promised to work like she had never worked before—then yes, she would try. Privately, she cursed herself for being an idiot. She had come here to make Paolo's life easier now? And why hadn't she just said no? It was her usual response when in doubt. She had no answer for that.

Beginning the next day, Lucy no longer did the midday shift in the restaurant. Instead, she spent the afternoons with Rosaria upstairs in the family's private living area. They worked in a seldom-used dining-room lit by a mauve chandelier, with a marble-topped table and huge matching sideboard. Lucy thought it was delightfully Italian and wondered, not for the first time, how a country that produced some of the world's best design could also come up with—well, this.

Paolo and Silvana were pleased with the arrangement and effusive in their gratitude. Since Lucy was now working in her professional capacity as a teacher, they even insisted on paying her more. Lucy soon felt she was earning every lira because Rosaria was anything but an easy student.

For the first day or two, everything was punctuated with 'Non capisco,' her favourite phrase, or 'È troppo difficile!' Lucy soon put a stop to that.

'If you must complain, Rosa, please do it in English. But in fact you understand more than you think and none of it is all that difficult. You just don't want to try.'

Rosaria sulked. She even managed to squeeze out a few tears. 'Why you so cruel, Lucia? I no care if fail. Università—this not for me.'

'Then what do you want to do?'

'I go in America.'

'To do what?'

'To work in fashion.'

'Why not Milan? Paris? London? Why America?'

'Is a long way from here!'

'I see. Then you'll need to speak English, won't you?'

'I have already English good enough.'

'Rosa. Your English is shit. The Americans won't understand you. They will think you're an illiterate peasant. Understand? Una contadina analfabeta? Can we get back to the passive voice?'

It wasn't a lot of fun for either of them but Lucy was a good teacher and soon realised that part of Rosa's problem was, strangely enough, a total lack of self-confidence. She had convinced herself that she could not learn English and, ergo, it was proving impossible. Lucy tried a gentler approach, got fashion magazines and had Rosa translate them into English, kept the conversation to topics she thought might interest the girl, clothes, music, travel. Lucy talked about her own days at university and what a great time she'd had, exaggerating the social life by a factor of about ten. It was hard to know if they were making any progress but at least the atmosphere in the room upstairs was less tense.

The following Tuesday, when the restaurant was closed, a visitor arrived from Naples. Had Lucy known about this she would have begged for the day off, would have feigned illness, would have simply not shown up. But she did not know because no one had thought to tell her and by the time she found out it was much too late to flee.

Twenty Nine

It was a pity that Michela Esposito had only one son. It meant that Paolo, forced to be the repository of all her hopes and dreams, was spoilt as a child and had to suffer the burden of unrealistic expectations thereafter. In Michela's eyes, he could do no wrong, or if he did do wrong, she would find a way to excuse and forgive. Australia, and all that had happened there, was long ago and long forgotten—or had been until Ornella stirred it all up again. Damn Ornella, jumping at shadows, why couldn't she just let things be?

Michela did not for a minute think that the girl from Australia would resemble her in any way. She was sure Ornella was mistaken; people were always seeing likenesses where none existed, they'd show you a baby photo, exclaiming 'just like his father!' when in truth the child looked more like the pope or indeed the local greengrocer. But all the same, Michela's curiosity was piqued and when she heard that Lucy was not only working in the restaurant but was now also coaching Rosaria for her exams, it gave her the perfect excuse for a family visit. She rang Silvana and suggested she pop down to give Rosaria some encouragement.

Normally, Lucy would eat lunch upstairs with Rosaria, to maximise their time together. Lucy would make it an opportunity to encourage conversation when she hoped Rosa might be a little more relaxed. On this particular Tuesday, however, Silvana took her aside. She explained that Rosaria's grandmother was coming from Naples for lunch. They would all eat together, Lucy must join them, then she and Rosa could go upstairs and get on with their lesson.

Lucy did her best to hide her consternation.

'No, no, it's very kind, but I couldn't intrude, it's a family occasion. Truly, I'll come back later.'

Silvana wouldn't hear of it. 'Lucia, you are almost family anyway.

And she wishes to meet you. She is nice, Paolo's mother, she has not much English but you will like her. Please?' And Lucy had no choice but to graciously accept.

Inwardly, she thought that if today was the day for the big revelation, then so be it. Perhaps fate was taking a hand at last and making decisions for her. She had no doubt that Michela would recognise her. It was only a few weeks, nothing had changed but her Italian and although she was proud of the fluency she'd gained it was still not enough to fool anyone except maybe some other tourist. So she tried to be brave and get on with Rosaria's lesson while they waited for nonna to arrive but inside she was full of trepidation.

The lesson, if you could call it that, was in any case a waste of time. Rosaria wasn't paying attention and Lucy assumed she was excited about seeing her grandmother. Perhaps, unlike her own, she was of the variety that arrived, present-laden and smiling, to dote on her adored grandchildren.

Not so. Rosaria, it seemed, was as anxious as Lucy to avoid the coming lunch and suggested they disappear. She even suggested it in English, thereby no doubt hoping to win Lucy's agreement. Which she might well have done but for her very bad timing—alas, Michela was already pulling into the car-park and Chiara was on the stairs, calling them to come down. Rosaria pulled a face. She was going to get a lecture, she was sure of it. Her nonna would get that disappointed look she did so well. She would sigh and talk about the value of a university education. It would all be too, too unbearable! Lucy refrained from adding 'and so, so justifiable' because for once she felt united in a common cause with Rosa. Instead, she sent her down and said she'd follow in just a moment. She went to the bathroom and tried to compose herself with some deep breathing. She decided to play it straight and leave the running to Michela. After all, the team from *Carràmba Che Sorpresa* would have interviewed hundreds of people, they could not be expected to remember those who were not even used on the show.

She felt she had made the right decision when she finally made her way downstairs and Paolo introduced her to his mother. Michela was charming, full of praise for Lucy's efforts in helping Rosaria and expressing the hope that she was finding time to see some of the country. There was no sign of recognition that Lucy could see, though she felt that her grandmother's eyes were on her constantly, in a way that was more than just politeness to a stranger. Her grandmother; for the second time she wrestled with the concept that this woman was her flesh and blood and wanted it and didn't want it.

Michela, for her part, was tantalised by a feeling of déjà vu; she had met the girl before, she was sure of it and it had nothing to do with old photographs and nor did she see in Lucy a younger version of herself. It was something else and it bothered her. She did not immediately connect her with the visit from a certain television show.

The chat continued over an aperitivo and then everyone sat down to lunch, during which Rosaria did indeed have to endure a gentle lecture from her nonna about the wisdom of applying due diligence and temporary self-denial in the pursuit of a university education. Her sister Chiara had done it, her little brother was showing every sign of doing it—did Rosaria want to be the only Esposito who would never graduate?

Chiara and Andrea both showed great diligence in clearing the table. They seemed embarrassed for their sister and it was brought home to Lucy that in spite of their differences they were still close. However much they might criticise their sibling, that did not give anyone else a licence to do the same.

Rosaria herself looked like she couldn't care less and perhaps only Lucy knew it was an act. Lucy thought if this was Michela's idea of encouragement she had missed the mark by a country mile. But then Michela changed tack and promised a shopping expedition to Rome if Rosa could manage a pass. Rosa said her nonna's money was unfortunately safe. Michela looked puzzled. Was she giving up already then? Saying she had no hope at all? In spite of her parents paying for a tutor?

Silence from Rosaria. Michela turned to Lucy. Did she also think that the cause was lost, that Rosaria was bound to fail?

Lucy was annoyed. She hadn't wanted to be here and she hardly felt it was the right time for a parent-teacher interview. She said quickly that Rosa was working hard and doing her best, they would just have to wait and see. She started to say something else but was interrupted by the arrival of Ornella and Roberto, who'd been invited for coffee. Roberto, once the greetings were over, took Paolo aside and it soon became clear that the mayor was in hospital and not expected to last the day. The news took the heat off Rosaria; the discussion was now all about politics and whether Paolo should or should not accept the position when, inevitably, it became his for the taking.

Lucy was fascinated, she rather hoped Paolo would become mayor because it might give her a chance to denounce him. She began to get the feeling though, that she had been mistaken, that he did not want the job at all and was being pushed into accepting it by others. It was his body language which told her this, her Italian wasn't good enough to keep up with the chatter. She also knew that it wouldn't look good to appear too interested, especially with Michela's eyes still on her. She suggested that she and Rosaria go back to work, said goodbye and headed for the stairs. Michela followed her.

'A moment!' Lucy was forced to stop. 'I didn't mean to put you on the spot before, Lucia. We all appreciate your efforts to help Rosaria.'

'I hope I can help her, signora.'

'You were going to say something—when my niece arrived?'

'Oh. It wasn't important.'

'Please.'

Damn you, thought Lucy. 'It's just that I don't think Rosa is the sort of girl to respond well to pressure.'

'I see. You have known my granddaughter for—how long? A few weeks?'

'That's true, signora. And I have taught—and helped—hundreds just like her. Good afternoon, it was nice to meet you.'

And Lucy made her escape upstairs, knowing that her grandmother didn't like her very much and almost certainly either knew who she was or at least suspected the truth. Oh well. She certainly hadn't come here to be loved. Michela watched her go and again had that flash of déjà vu, a feeling that the scene or one like it

158

had been played out before. Was it perhaps in her own home back in Pozzuoli? But Silvana was calling her.

Rosaria was feeling, if not loving then at least grateful, when Lucy joined her.

'You defend me, Lucy. To nonna. I have very much gratitude.'

'Better to say, 'I am grateful'.'

'I am grateful.'

They got on with the lesson and the rest of the afternoon was productive but the day, overall, left Lucy unsettled. Back at her little apartment she tried to sort out her tangled feelings.

It wasn't actually all that difficult; it was more a case of her not wanting to accept the conclusion to which she came. So she rang Geoff, hoping he might give her a different answer.

'I don't know where I'm going, Geoff. I don't have the faintest idea how to achieve what I came to do.'

'You thought it was going to be easy?'

'I don't know what I thought.'

'It's not enough to just confront Paolo?'

'He'd wring his hands and say he's tried to make up for it. He probably believes it. Only the kids would get hurt. Andrea worships the ground he walks on.'

'What does Stefano think?'

'He doesn't even know why I'm here.'

'Maybe it's time you told him.'

'He wouldn't understand. He'd think I was totally mad.'

'You know what your problem is. You've found yourself a family.'

'You're all the family I need.'

'Not true, Luce.'

'Tell me what to do.'

'You could always come home.'

'Give up?'

'Let go. Not the same thing.'

'I'm not ready for that.'

'No, of course you aren't.' He sighed, he did worry about her. 'But every day you stay will make it harder. Because every day you are getting more involved in these people's lives. They're your flesh and blood, my dear, they were bound to get under your skin. Weren't they?'

'My grandmother doesn't even like me.'

'And you're just a bit hurt, right?'

'How do you do that? Read me like a book?'

'Because you're so like your mother.'

And then she told him that Paolo would almost certainly become mayor and that might give her an opportunity to dish some dirt. Geoff tried to sound a note of caution, saying she could not prove anything and Paolo was on his home turf, but Lucy was sure the hint of scandal would be enough.

If Lucy was comforted by the conversation, Geoff was not. He felt she was forgetting that Italy wasn't Australia; sex scandals there, he was sure, were not judged with the same self-righteous, finger-pointing morality that prevailed in predominantly Anglo countries. He smiled to himself, he could just hear Lucy: 'It's because they can all toddle off to confession, say a few novenas and be done with it.' Geoff thought confession had a lot going for it.

The two weeks that followed weren't easy ones, not for Lucy nor for anyone connected to her. Lucy did not see Stefano because in the studios in via Marconi one crisis followed another with monotonous regularity and even on his days off he was expected to be available so he had to stay in Naples. He rang Lucy daily, not to complain but to—what was the phrase she had taught him? To let off steam, that was it. The show—it was a disaster. Or perhaps not. Stefano himself thought it was going okay but the Australians weren't happy, the bosses at la RAI in Rome weren't happy, there were not enough writers, not enough directors and those idiot designers, had they left enough room for the cameras to move? Of course not. Lucy laughed and tried to console him.

'And what about you, Stef? You miss the real estate?'

'I do not.'

'Ah. So, overall, it's going okay?'

'Lucy, it's totally crazy. But I enjoy very much. It's hard work but also never boring.'

'Good.'

'Except I am not seeing you. And I miss you.'

'I miss you too.'

'Veramente?'

'Sì.'

There was a pause. 'Lucy?'

'Yes?'

'Could you not come to Napoli?'

'Perhaps when Rosa's exams are over.'

'It will kill me to wait this long.' Lucy said she doubted it but failed to tell him that she couldn't, to her deep chagrin, get him out of her mind for more than ten minutes; failed to mention that everytime a Vespa pulled up outside the restaurant she wondered if it were him. She felt it was utterly childish, she was behaving like a teenager but Rosa, being Rosa, wondered too and would find some reason to go to window and peer out and then shake her head so soulfully that Lucy had to laugh in spite of herself.

'He's working, Rosa. And we should be too.'

At least the atmosphere in the grandiose dining-room was degrees warmer since the visit from Michela. Spring might have passed but Rosaria, like some late-blooming shrub, produced abundant new growth in the form of English vocabulary and syntax. She did not find it easy; she was in fact working very hard—which meant that Lucy had not exactly lied to Michela after all but had merely been a bit premature. Lucy suspected it was all too little too late but hid her doubts and was outwardly optimistic.

There were other tensions. Paolo bowed to pressure and became mayor. His children were proud. His wife, if she had concerns, hid them well and his friends, Roberto and Ornella included, were delighted. The feeling, so Lucy gathered, was that at last they had someone strong running the show, someone decent, a man of integrity. Things would be different from now on. Lucy was sceptical. In her experience, when politicians—even at this local level—talked about 'things being different', they usually meant for themselves. Nonetheless, she felt it would look odd if she didn't offer her congratulations.

This simple act brought its own problems. Lucy still could not bring herself to touch Paolo, to kiss him on both cheeks in the Italian way was impossible. And because it was impossible to do it to him, she tried not to do it to anyone, at least not in Stella del Mare, though she did make an exception of the children. Instead, she was quick to put out her hand. Hardly 'paese che vai,' and she was sure they must think she was very cold and stand-offish but she couldn't help it. She knew she would have to get over it, Stefano had called her on it though she was not that way with him. She just said she felt awkward, all this kissing and touching was not her, Australians didn't do that.

'All Australians?'

'Most Australians.'

So she made sure she had her hands full of dishes when she congratulated Paolo. She was surprised when he asked her what she thought about his new position. She tried to be non-committal.

'I'm sure it's not an easy job,' she said. 'A bit of a juggling act, I suppose. Trying to keep a lot of people happy.'

'You are very—' He searched for the word. 'Astute, yes? Is true. It takes much time. I hope you not go back in Australia just yet.'

'I haven't made any plans.'

'Good. We need you. I do have plans, Lucia, we are soon very busy.'

Lucy thought what an odd situation it was, to be needed, trusted, by someone she was plotting against. There were times when she found it hard to believe that Paolo didn't know who she was; more likely he had taught himself to believe whatever was most convenient.

Whatever Paolo's plans were, Lucy didn't think Silvana approved of them. She was still friendly enough but so much quieter these days and seemed preoccupied with some problem far more pressing than the daily running of Il Veliero. It was Chiara who finally gave Lucy an explanation.

'I don't see why you can't know. Papà, he will buy Il Delfino Nero. And mamma, she worries. His health, Lucy, is not so good, and now he is sindaco, is all too much.' Lucy could see why Paolo wanted her to stay on, at least in the short term. She was good at her job and more reliable, she knew, than the rest of the hired help. Perhaps the best way to hurt him would be to up and leave!

But Paolo did not buy Il Delfino Nero. Although Roberto had drawn up the contract and already held Paolo's deposit, Mario Moretti made a last minute offer and bought it from under Paolo's nose. Lucy was the only person who didn't understand why Paolo, furious as he was, didn't fight it. She assumed that Italian law was different. Or maybe, just maybe, Silvana had been very persuasive? But no; Silvana was as angry as Paolo. Italy, Italians—she would never understand them.

She put the whole business out of her mind and concentrated on Rosa's exam, now just three days away. She spent a couple of hours going through old exam papers and decided a miracle was needed. She would ring Geoff, her favourite Catholic, and ask him to pray for one, Rosaria deserved that much. And then, because the night was hot, she poured herself a glass of prosecco and went to sit on her tiny balcony and gaze at the sea and ponder on what she was doing and becoming: an atheist seeking miracles, a woman afraid of loving, a Nemesis failing to deliver judgement. She was not happy.

Thirty

Stefano, when she talked to him, was not happy either—not when he heard about Paolo's new problems.

'This will not be good for Paolo, to have his enemy at both ends of the beach.'

'I know they don't like each other, Stefano, but enemy? You think Moretti is—'

Stefano cut her off. 'Lucy! Of course they are enemies, all the world knows this, even I, a stranger, know it. If you understood Italian better, you would know it too.'

'But can it make that much difference? That Moretti owns the nightclub?'

'You think he will leave that rundown heap of shit the way it is? He will spend big money, add a proper ristorante—you will see.'

'The restaurant at his hotel is very bad. You said so yourself.'

'But looks glamorous, yes? And the food—what do the tourists know? They think is local, authentic.' He swore. 'Maybe the freezer bag is local, there is factory in Salerno.'

'Making bags for frozen food?' Lucy almost laughed. But it wasn't really funny.

'I feel sorry for Paolo.' There was no reply. 'Lucy?'

'He has a lot of problems, I can see that.' But she did not say that she was sorry for him too.

'Rosaria—when is her exam finished?'

'She has English on Friday. It's the last.'

'And then I can see you?'

'Perhaps I can get some time off.'

'You have earned this. You want I should speak to Paolo?'

'No! I'll see what I can do.'

Rosaria called at Lucy's on her way home after the exam. Lucy

164

didn't need to ask how it had gone.

'Maybe you did better than you think.'

Rosaria shook her head. The exam had been terrible, all the kids agreed, even the really bright ones. She had failed for certain. It wasn't fair. She had tried, Lucy knew she had tried. Well she wasn't going back to school, they would have to drag her there kicking and screaming. She was inconsolable.

She said none of this to her parents, however. She told them the exam was hard, everyone said so, but that meant they would have to adjust the marks. She actually appeared optimistic. Lucy, who heard it all from Chiara, assumed she just couldn't face confessing the awful truth. Or perhaps she didn't want to add to her parents' already considerable worries.

Stefano had been right about Mario Moretti: it appeared he had big plans for the rundown bar and disco and was wasting no time in putting them into action. In a very short time it had been given a quick paint job and renamed Il Delfino Blu. It was, to say the least, eye-catching. More importantly, extensive re-building seemed to be underway. No plans for this had been submitted to the council, Mario apparently feeling such niceties were unnecessary and this left Paolo, as mayor, with another headache: to ignore the matter or pursue it and risk the consequences. Of course half the buildings in Italy, let alone the Mezzogiorno, had gone up without proper planning permission but Paolo had stood for and been elected on a platform of opposition to such practices. It was therefore hard for him not to pursue the matter. On the other hand, if he did pursue it, not only was his self-interest evident, there were risks involved. And if he stood aside and left it to others, then they would be exposed to those risks. And only Paolo himself knew how great the risks were. He was still seeking advice from his few trusted associates, a pointless exercise really since they didn't have the whole story.

All this Chiara had tried to explain to Lucy who was finding, as the days went by, that the longer she spent in this place the more foreign it became. It was as if the Italy and the Italians she had heard so much about, the culture which had been transplanted and adopted so enthusiastically in Australia, belonged somewhere else altogether and had little to do with the people amongst whom she now found herself. Lucy was also reluctant, given the present tensions at the restaurant, to ask for a day off. In the end though she had no choice, her tooth demanded it. She broke a crown she'd had since a silly accident on a school camp three years earlier. Then it was the paddle of an over-exuberant year nine learning to kayak; this time, more simply, one of Enrico's excellent almond biscotti. He was mortified but Lucy should of course have dunked the biscuit in her coffee or her Strega, which was what it was intended for, and then all would have been well. The trouble was, she found it faintly disgusting, this constant dunking of food the Italians went in for, to her there was something childish about it, something redolent of English nurseries and nannies, boiled eggs and toast soldiers, tomato soup with floating squares of bread and butter. She couldn't understand why they did it and so there she was, in urgent need of dental assistance.

Silvana offered to ring her dentist in Agropoli but Lucy, grasping at a memory from her dinner with Stefano's family, said that he had an uncle who was a dentist in Naples and if they didn't mind she would perhaps go up and see him.

Stefano did not sound as sorry as he might have about her tooth. 'This is not so bad, Lucy. My uncle is a very good dentist. He will fix the tooth and I will see you.'

'Do you think he'll be able to fit me in?'

'Lucy. It's family. If someone else must be cancelled...' Lucy could almost hear him shrug over the phone.

'Tell him I have insurance, Stef. The money is not a problem.' And she silently thanked Geoff who'd insisted on top level travel insurance before she set foot outside Australia.

'No problem anyway. Please, tell me you will get the train?'

She did get the train. Chiara took her to Agropoli and she caught it there. It wasn't the drive up the coast that bothered her but the thought of weaving her way right through Naples at the other end. So much easier to find Stefano, who had scrounged a day off work, waiting at Stazione Centrale with the Vespa.

They went straight to via Chiaia where zio Tiberio, Stefano's uncle on his mother's side, patched the crown expertly and chatted to Lucy in a continuous stream of Italian to which she, having a mouth full of wadding, was unable to reply. Which was just as well because the man's knowledge of Australian history and politics was formidable and she was afraid she might have let her country down badly. Stefano enjoyed her discomfiture enormously and kept assuring his uncle that they would have dinner sometime when he and Lucy could enjoy a real debate.

'Where did he learn all that?' she asked after the ordeal was over. 'Not at university?'

'No, is just an interest. Since he was a kid, he learn about the Antipodes, you know? He thinks Australia has great system of government, very democratic. This is true, yes?'

'Ah—compared to what?'

'Rest of the world?'

'I'd say we're maybe in the top fifty?'

'This is all? I think zio not agree. But he's very pleased when I tell him I have Australian girlfriend. Now I show you some of Naples you have not seen.'

Lucy let the 'girlfriend' pass without comment. 'I should book in at the hostel.' She should have known better.

'Lucy, you stay with us or you deeply offend my mother. She has already made the bed in my sister's room. We go now and visit some churches.'

'Churches?'

'Why not? If you feel up to it. Be good for your soul.' So Lucy finally made a start on those thirty-eight must-see churches, beginning, appropriately for a city which had embraced the baroque so passionately, with Gesù Nuovo. After its magnificent excesses, the Gothic simplicity of Santa Chiara came as something of a relief. Stepping out into the famed majolica cloisters she couldn't believe her eyes.

'Tomatoes?'

'You forget, Lucy. During the war Neapolitans starved. They live on rats, on grass. Here is a nice garden, it's not to be wasted.' And indeed, the crop was doing well. Lucy gave the Catholics a brownie point for practicality and found it rather endearing. She bought a postcard in the church shop and couldn't help looking around to see if they sold passata. Perhaps, she thought, if it were blessed... Holy Passata from Santa Chiara, what a good little money-spinner that might be. She was smiling at the thought and Stefano wanted to share the joke but she wouldn't tell him, she didn't want him to think she was mocking his religion. But when he did drag it out of her he laughed heartily and said they should seek out whoever was in charge these days and make them a business proposition.

They were having a good day. When Lucy slipped on the ubiquitous lava paving stones and Stefano grabbed her hand to stop her falling, and went on holding it, she did not find an excuse to let go. They went to the Chapel of Sansevero and gazed in awe at its treasures, including the Cristo Velato. How had he done it, the sculptor Sammartino, how had he worked the marble to make it so nearly transparent? It seemed, yes, miraculous, and Lucy thought she could understand why the Neapolitans were all so damn religious, it—religion—was everywhere, you could not escape it. And then Stefano took her to via San Gregorio Armeno which was busy with shoppers even though it was summer and she wondered what on earth it was like in December. This was where the makers of presepi, the famous Neapolitan nativity scenes, made and sold their wares and Lucy could have spent the whole day there, among the thousands of tiny—and not so tiny—items. Here were Mary and Joseph, shepherds and shop-keepers, magi and musicians, priests and pizza-makers and asses and oxen by the score. There was produce enough to feed a miniature multitude—bunches of grapes and fat prosciutti and baskets of lemons and crates of fish. And it came, all of it, in both the best and the worst of all possible taste: in one shop an exquisitely-crafted terracotta angel, worth a year's wages; in the next a chubby-cheeked plastic baby Jesus with a halo of twinkling party-lights, a snip at ten thousand lire. Lucy found it all endlessly fascinating.

'You should be here at Christmas. You could make your own presepe.'

'I might take one home. Start a new fashion in Melbourne.'

'It's not a fashion, Lucy. It's an ancient tradition.'

Lucy took umbrage at that. 'We have Christmas cribs too. We just don't have the whole village. We don't have Pulcinella dropping in. And lemon-sellers and chooks and the rest of it.'

'Ah. Chooks. Like this, yes?' And he stopped to buy her a little wire cage full of tiny brown and white chickens and when they finally sat down for coffee he produced another package and it was one of the angels she had so admired, a beautiful thing. She was speechless. How had he managed to buy it without her knowledge? He laughed. Neapolitans could do that, speak with their hands and their eyes, a nod of the head and the deal was done. Easy. But of course, perhaps she didn't want it, seeing that it was a religious symbol...

Lucy declared that it had great cultural and artistic merit and then, more honestly, admitted to having a bit of a thing about angels.

'You are sure you are completely lapsed Catholic?'

'Oh yes, quite sure. It's not that I believe in angels, see. I just like the idea of them. Flitting about, you know? Being useful?'

'Useful.'

'Yes. It'd be really nice if they did exist. Comforting.' She sighed. 'But they don't. And no amount of clapping will change that. Or praying I suppose, that'd be more appropriate for angels.'

'I am lost.'

'Angels, fairies, they're much the same. I'll give you Peter Pan to read.'

'Oh! Peter Pan! Yes, I have read. My sister's children. Angels, Tinkerbell... I see how you are thinking.' I see it, he thought, and I will never understand this crazy girl in a million years.

'But this angel,' Lucy said, gently fingering the one she had been given, 'I will treasure always.'

She was truly touched and thanked him sincerely but as she looked at him she knew yet again that Stefano wanted more than her thanks, that he wanted at the very least her trust and probably a great deal more and suddenly realised she was holding out now for the simplest of reasons, she was afraid of losing him.

As usual, he was the perfect gentleman and changed the subject. (Now and then Lucy wondered if that were his true nature, or if he somehow knew about Paolo already and was determined to show her how different he was. But he could not possibly know, so she concluded he must be naturally polite and sensitive.) Stefano was saying that they would have an aperitif with the family but he planned to take her out to dinner, to an old part of Naples that he thought she would like and he hoped that was okay. Lucy, her thoughts in turmoil, said it would be great.

They went then to a bar in Santa Lucia, down on the seafront, and met up with some of Stefano's colleagues from La RAI. Lucy, who hadn't expected this, enjoyed herself. The group included one of the Australians, a man named Chris from Adelaide, and Lucy relished the chance to talk for even a short time to someone from home. Chris clearly enjoyed it too since he'd picked up virtually no Italian and was jealous of Lucy's skills. Lucy could feel Stefano's eyes on her and found herself wondering—hoping?—that he was also jealous. Most of the others had some English so the conversation flowed and it soon became evident that they were all proud of the production, in spite of its many problems; when she made a joke about Australia exporting soaps to the world, it wasn't her compatriot who sprang to its defence but Giovanna, one of the storyliners.

'The world should thank you, Lucy. For keeping half the population off Prozac.' Lucy joined in the laughter and had to admit it was very likely true. Chris, teasing her, asked if she was by any chance a television snob and she admitted that was possibly true as well and promised to wait until she'd seen the show before she cast judgement. She was almost sorry when Stefano said it was time they were leaving, it had been nice to talk about something so totally disconnected from Stella del Mare.

As they said their goodbyes and headed back to the Vespa, however, there was a connection to Stella del Mare which neither of them noticed. Sitting with a friend at an outdoor table not twenty metres away, Michela was watching Lucy. And seeing her with Stefano she finally remembered where she had first seen the girl. It was in her own living-room. *Che sorpresa* indeed!

Thirty One

Stefano took Lucy that evening to one of the little seafood restaurants at Marechiaro. He knew the staff, who teased him about his new ragazza from Australia and gave them the best table with an uninterrupted view of the sea. Vincenzo, the waiter, brought the large basket containing the catch of the day and although he recommended some fine orata Lucy would not be swayed from having sarago. She smiled at Stefano and he thought that if a little sea bream could be taken as a sign then perhaps things were finally looking up.

Marechiaro, once and still a fishing village, though now subsumed into greater Naples, is a romantic place, as romantic as its name, and especially so at sunset. Lucy and Stefano sat there and drank their wine and ate the excellent meal that Vincenzo brought them while the sun slowly disappeared in a showy display of gold and pink and purple and the lights came on across the bay.

'What are you thinking?' Stefano asked.

'How beautiful it is. How many people must have sat here over the centuries and said to each other 'just look at it.' How do you say 'across the water' Stefano? It's not attraverso, is it?'

'Not unless you go in boat, no. If you mean like the lights it's al di là del mare.' But he wasn't looking at the sea, he was looking at Lucy and thinking that l'aldilà also meant the afterlife and that's where this damn girl would end up sending him. Fortunately Vincenzo arrived with the good news that his nonna had made rum babà this morning and would they perhaps like some? Stefano said they most assuredly would and told Lucy she was in for a treat, it was the best babà in Naples.

Lucy thought he was probably right. It was quite delicious, a wedge of cake impossibly light and airy oozing rum-soaked syrup.

While they were eating it a singer appeared, moving between the tables. He was actually quite good and accompanied himself not on the mandolin, as Lucy would have expected, but on a guitar. He was singing 'Funiculì, Funiculà'. She smiled. 'What else?'

'You know it's about a railway?'

Lucy was surprised. 'What, a real funicular?'

'Of course, up the side of Vesuvio. It closed after the eruption of 1944.'

'I had no idea.' The song came to an end and Stefano waved the man over and spoke to him quickly in Neapolitan. He seemed reluctant but Stefano slipped him twenty-thousand lire which he pocketed. He nodded to Lucy, moved back a little and began to sing. Lucy didn't know 'Santa Lucia Luntana' and couldn't follow the words, since they too were in dialect, but the singer put his heart into it and there was no mistaking the yearning in his voice and Lucy thought she understood. When the applause, which was lengthy—for this was not a place where tourists came—had died down, Lucy said, 'It's beautiful. Very sad. It's an emigrants' song, isn't it? They are homesick. Full of what you call la nostalgia.'

Stefano nodded. 'Santa Lucia is their last glimpse of Napoli as they sail away. How did you know?'

'I told you we have a lot in common. The Irish sailed away too. And wrote songs about going home.'

'I think it's not possible, you know, to be truly happy away from your own land.'

'All those Italians who made it in America? They were not happy?'

'Rich and happy is not the same.'

'In my country, we are all immigrants, except for the aboriginals. But we are happy, most of us. It's not about place, it's a state of mind.'

'You are happy, Lucia?'

She thought she would be when she had done what she came for but she couldn't say that. 'We're getting very serious.'

Stefano wanted to get serious, wanted to tell her how he felt about her and beg her to confide in him but he knew it wasn't the time and was starting to doubt if there ever would be a time. So instead he smiled and stood up and held out his hand to her. 'Come then, I will show you something not serious.'

They had his mother's Alfa and in it Stefano drove Lucy slowly up to Capo Posillipo, where there were cars parked all along the side of the road, with here and there amongst them a stall selling gelato or cold drinks. There were few people to be seen and to Lucy's amazement, all the cars had their windows totally covered in newspaper. She looked at Stefano, puzzled.

'What?'

'You can't guess?'

Lucy shook her head. And then she noticed one car, a little Cinquecento, gently rocking. She stared. 'They're not...?'

Stefano laughed. 'They all live at home. They have nowhere else to go. It's private.'

'Private?'

'Well. More than the beach. Yes?'

Yes? He wasn't suggesting, surely, that they, the two of them... Lucy glanced at the back seat, she couldn't help it, in case a pile of newspapers lurked there. She didn't know what to say, what to think. And then she saw Stefano's horrified face.

'Lucy! O Dio, no! I did not mean that! Not for one minute! I thought you would think this is funny, they're just kids, you know? Teenagers. I want to make you laugh is all. Oh Lucy. You really think I make love to you in the back seat of a car? With *Il Mattino* on the window?'

They drove home in silence. Lucy was acutely aware that she'd wrecked a beautiful evening, a near perfect day (if a perfect day could ever include a trip to the dentist) while Stefano was thinking he had done much the same thing. He parked the car but neither of them got out. They knew if they left it at that the damage might be too hard to repair.

'I'm sorry,' Lucy said. 'I should have realised.'

'No, it was my fault. Not to explain first.' He paused. 'Will we ever get it right?'

'I don't know.'

'What do you want to do, Lucy?'

Go home, she thought. That's what her head was telling her. To go home to her own place, not to find happiness but the comfort that's bred of familiarity, that comes with knowing who you are and where you fit in. Kate, if she were here, would forgive her. But her heart told her something else altogether.

'I've made such a mess of things,' she said. 'And now I'm afraid I will lose you.'

He pulled her close to him then and held her tightly and told her she was wrong, so wrong, and he kissed her on the mouth, gently at first and then less so and for the first time in her life Lucy responded with genuine passion and found that she did not, could not despise all Italian men, least of all this one.

They went inside then. They were not, as Stefano had said, going to make love in his mother's Giulietta. With or without newspaper over the windows. They said goodnight and Lucy dutifully went off to Laura's room and lay between the perfectly ironed sheets and wondered what the hell she was doing. Why had she ever allowed Stefano to insinuate himself into her life? To the point where she was not only inclined to depend on him, which was bad enough, but where she also, undeniably, had feelings for him. It wasn't as if she hadn't seen this coming but she'd made no effort, none at all, to remove herself from the danger and now it was too late. Now, when she should have all her energies concentrated on the task before her, here was this huge distraction; this falling-in-love thing, unnecessary, unwanted, a disaster of her own making. She felt the prick of tears behind her eyelids; she felt young and foolish and vulnerable. It was a long time before she fell asleep and when she did she had horrible dreams in which she was plunging into the sea off Marechiaro while pages of *Il Mattino* rained down upon her, pink and gold and purple in the sunset and Stefano grew ever smaller far above her.

Stefano did not dream. He spent the night wondering what it was that Lucy had made a mess of and as happens when sleep eludes us and the hours before dawn become interminable, his imaginings grew out of all proportion until he was again afraid for her. He thought that if he could keep her in Naples another day she might, after their physical closeness, at last confide in him.

174

He was still trying to persuade her to stay while they waited for her train next morning. 'Please, Lucy. We need to talk. The whole night, I worry about you.'

'There's no need. I'll work things out.'

'I can help you, no?'

She shook her head.

'Alright. No talk. But stay one more day. I will ring them. Tell them you break another tooth.'

Lucy managed a smile. 'I wish I could.'

'Lucy? Stop saying no, no, no?'

And she looked at him, and he seemed so earnest and so caring that her resolve begun to crumble and she would very likely have given in if her seldom-used mobile phone hadn't rung. It was Chiara, speaking Italian so fast Lucy had trouble keeping up.

'Lucy? You are coming back this morning, please, you must!'

'I'm coming, I'm at the station, what's the matter?'

'It's Rosaria, the most terrible thing! She didn't come home last night, she's disappeared! We are sick with worry.'

Stefano took Lucy to the platform. He wanted to go with her but they both realised there was nothing he could do, probably nothing that anyone could do except offer moral support. Rosaria hadn't been missing for long. She'd gone shopping with a friend yesterday and hadn't returned. It was going to be a matter of waiting.

'We will hope that Rosa has a guarding angel,' Stefano said.

'Guardian.'

'Sorry, yes. Guardian.' The train was about to leave. Lucy got on, found a seat and waved to him through the window and then he was gone. In a sudden moment of panic, she thought she had left her angel, the one Stefano had bought her, on her bed at his house. She groped around in her bag and was so relieved to find it there she almost cried. It was then that she realised how much she was dreading this return to Stella del Mare.

The high drama that awaited, the soul-searching, the recriminations—these were to be expected. But if, heaven forbid, this were not just some waywardness on Rosaria's part, or some minor accident, but something serious—what then? The thought came unbidden and she tried to banish it but couldn't: was fate going to do her work for her? Because she knew that if anything happened to Rosaria then she, Lucy, would be on the first flight home.

Chiara met her at Agropoli. No, there was no more news. They'd rung all her friends, all the hospitals, no one knew anything. They couldn't understand it, people didn't just vanish into thin air.

But of course people did. Everyday, all over the world, that's exactly what happened.

'How is Silvana?'

Chiara wiped her eyes. 'She tries to be brave. For papà. He is very distressed.'

The restaurant was closed. Inside, the faithful Enrico manned the Gaggia behind the bar. Andrea sat looking lost and bewildered at the foot of the stairs, watching his parents as though they were alien beings whose behaviour he couldn't quite fathom. This was not surprising; the heat of their argument—and they seldom argued—excluded him entirely.

'It makes no sense,' Silvana was saying. 'Why would they do it, we are not even rich!'

'Kidnappers might think we are rich! Sometimes they take the wrong person! It is possible, Silvana!' He was distraught, that much was obvious, clutching at straws, any straw. And then he saw, they both saw that Chiara and Lucy had arrived. To Lucy's surprise Paolo went straight to her and ignoring the usual space she kept between them, kissed her. 'It is good you are here, we need someone sensible.'

And then Silvana also embraced her and Andrea came to whisper that he was so glad she was back and Enrico waved at the Gaggia and she nodded, yes, thank you, coffee would be great.

And she felt a complete fraud.

For one thing—sensible? Lucy O'Connell Harrington? How her friends back home would laugh at that. She could see Sim rolling around on the floor. At work, Lucy was notorious for sitting crossed-legged on her desk to teach; even in her twenties, she liked to go to Luna Park after dinner in St Kilda... no, not especially sensible. Or she wouldn't be here.

But mostly she felt a fraud because these people were treating her like family and she was family except that she hadn't bothered to let them know. And she was starting to see how terribly dishonest that was. But for the moment all she could do was try to help. Get through this and then return to her own agenda.

'It's not possible that Rosa has just decided she wants some time to herself?'

Silvana saw straight through that. 'You are saying she might have run away?'

'I don't know. I think we have to look at every possibility.'

'She would do this to her parents? Deliberately?' It was Paolo. He seemed to find the idea inconceivable. That annoyed Lucy; didn't he realise that Rosa was grown up now, she was not his baby girl any more?

Lucy asked about Rosa's exams. 'She hasn't got the results, has she?'

'Not yet,' said Silvana. 'But she seemed fairly happy about it. I don't think she'd run away over that.' Lucy's doubt must have shown. 'You don't agree, Lucy?'

Lucy looked at their anxious faces and felt the time for keeping confidences was probably over. 'She came to see me straight after her last exam. The English. She was really upset. It was very hard, they all said so, but she's quite sure that she's failed. She didn't want to worry you. Not at the moment.'

There was a long silence. Then Chiara spoke. 'This changes things, I think. Rosa might have gone to stay with a friend somewhere until... I don't know...'

'Until what?' said Paolo.

'She could make some plans,' Chiara said—bravely, Lucy thought.

'You make it sound like she's frightened of us. This is ridiculous, we are her parents! Another hour, that's all, then I call the police.'

Lucy went home briefly to change since the day was getting hotter and rang Stefano. He was inclined to agree that Rosaria might well have gone to stay with a friend though it did seem odd that she hadn't rung. As for a kidnapping, yes, they happened but no one had been in touch, no demand had been made for a ransom, somehow it didn't seem likely. That was Camorra stuff. Lucy wasn't sure if he really believed this; whether he did or not she drove back to Il Veliero feeling quite a bit better. Then she saw the police car parked by the front door. Sick with dread, she hurried inside. There were two cops, one Lucy recognised from the local station, but they had not come with bad news. Paolo had summoned them and now, as Lucy walked in, was explaining rather forcefully why they had to find his daughter.

'I should never have become mayor. I was told not to accept it, I was warned... don't you see?'

The younger cop, Vito, a nice boy but not the brightest, a bit of a joke in town as Lucy knew, looked faintly puzzled. But the Comandante got it alright, and so did Silvana, who had gone quite pale.

'You were threatened, Signor Esposito?' the Comandante asked.

'There were hints. Some phone calls. "To accept this position would be most unwise..." That sort of thing.'

'You want to name names?'

'We both know the town dogs could do that, Comandante. And I'll leave it to them. But you must see now why I am so concerned?'

'All the same... no phone call. No ransom note.' He shook his head. 'I'm a father too. And a lovely girl like this...' He indicated a photo which Lucy saw was now on the nearest table. 'She would have a boyfriend, yes? Perhaps she's with him?'

It was Chiara who spoke, quite angry. 'My sister has many friends. Boys and girls. No one special. No one she would...' She pulled a face. 'They have all just finished the maturità. There was no time for relationships!' She almost spat out the word.

'Then what do you think has happened, signorina?'

'We don't know. We are asking you to find out.'

Silvana found her voice. 'We are asking for your help.'

The Comandante was almost condescending. 'Well of course, signora. That is why we are here.'

Lucy vowed that in future she would be less ready to criticise the police back home. On the other hand, she had to admit there was probably not a lot that the cops here could do. There was no evidence of foul play or even of misadventure and it wasn't as if the

Cilento were dripping with CCTV. They departed with Rosa's photo and a promise to set the usual procedures in motion, whatever that might mean. Paolo slammed the door behind them.

'Probably Moretti has paid them off as well!'

Silvana had managed to hold herself together while they were there. Now she was weeping. 'Why didn't you tell me, Paolo?'

'So two of us would lie awake all night?'

'You should have said no when they asked you to be mayor. I had my fears, I should have spoken out! Instead, I encouraged you.'

'I was hoping to do something good, Silvana. To change things even a little, it has to start somewhere! You agreed with me...'

For all that her heart went out to Chiara and Andrea, Lucy found it hard then to be in the same room as their parents. She was truly sorry for Silvana, she'd be sorry for any parent going through such a nightmare, even she supposed, for Paolo. But to hear Paolo speak of doing good, of playing the public benefactor, that was—well, oxymoronic. And then there was the love between them, so strong it was almost palpable, the love that Kate had gone without for so much of her life. Funny, Lucy thought, how at the very time when her sympathies for the family should have been strongest, a little thing could send her anger flooding back to the surface. She'd been afraid, when she was with Stefano, that the anger was dying and she was glad to rediscover it now, alive and well. Perhaps it would not have reared its head had Lucy been less certain that Rosaria was alive and well.

Ornella and Roberto arrived then and Lucy went to the kitchen to help Enrico prepare some food. He was grateful—no one had eaten all day and it was time they did. Lucy was making up some antipasti when she overheard Ornella talking to Paolo in the office next door.

'I know you would not admit it to Silvana, you would say anything to save her worry. But are you being blackmailed?'

Paolo sounded genuinely shocked. 'Blackmailed? Over what?'

'Are you?'

'No! Absolutely no! Threats only—like I told you. Like I told that bastard cop.'

Ornella put her arms around him then and hugged him. 'I had to ask, Paolo. Roberto is worried, we both are.'

Lucy moved away, she didn't want to hear any more. Her hands were shaking as she dished out the alici, the olives. Blackmail. Was there an uglier word than that? Ricatto. Even in Italian it was harsh. She had learnt it from the newspapers she made herself read everyday.

She and Enrico put the food on the table. They needn't have bothered, it was barely touched. Neither Silvana nor Paolo took their eyes off the phone and every time it rang, which it did often, the room went quiet. But the calls were all for the restaurant or the voices at the other end were Rosaria's schoolfriends, anxious for news but containing too a frisson of excitement that something this strange and possibly terrible was happening to one of their own.

And then, with her usual exquisite timing, Michela arrived.

Thirty Two

Michela was upset, there was no question of that, but she was tough as old boots, Lucy had to hand it to her. She insisted on hearing the whole story, she asked questions, and then she declared that since they clearly had no idea, as yet, what had happened, they should all eat, because God only knew what lay ahead. Bullying and cajoling by turns, she got the family to the table. Enrico had been sent home by now and Michela asked Lucy to help her with the pasta. Out of sight in the kitchen, she turned on Lucy like a rattlesnake.

'Was this your doing?'

Lucy nearly dropped the bowl she was carrying. 'What?'

'Was it? Do you know where she is?'

Michela's voice was venomous. It took all Lucy's courage, all her willpower, not to once again turn and flee. She put the bowl down carefully, slowly. She was frightened. And she was furious. 'I was in Napoli, signora. With my friend who works in television. And I will put such wild accusations down to your understandable state of mind.' And then she went on preparing the pasta, hoping her hands weren't shaking too obviously, hoping the mention of Stefano's job, by now no lie, would explain *Carrambà Che Sorpresa*.

'I am watching you, Lucia.' And Michela turned on her heel and left Lucy to do the pasta on her own.

The evening wore on. Lucy didn't know whether to stay or go. She found it hard being there in the same room as Michela and had a desperate need to talk to Geoff. At around ten she found Chiara out on the terrace.

'I'm going down to the piazza, Chiara. I need to make a call home. To Australia.'

'You could do it here.'

'I don't want to tie up the phone.'

'Will you come back?'

'If you want me to. If there is anything I can do to help.'

'I think she is dead.'

'I'm sure she's not.'

'Truly? You think so?'

'Truly.' At that point Lucy did believe it, though she couldn't have said why.

'Please come back.'

'Of course.' Lucy decided to walk to the piazza. It wasn't far, the night was balmy and she needed some quiet time on her own. She thought about grandmothers, about the special relationship Sim had with hers and which Lucy had always envied, feeling it had an almost storybook quality. Sim's grandmother was the sort you confided in when you'd had a row with your parents; the sort who took you to the ballet and quietly introduced you to the glories of a good gin and tonic long before those same parents thought it appropriate. Lucy's own luck in the grandmother department, she realised, was not about to change. She wondered why it was that she aroused either indifference or animosity in them when all she had ever wanted was a hint of affection. Oh well, she had lived without it long enough and could continue to do so. She fished out her phone card and entered the empty booth, knowing Geoff would supply affection in abundance.

She caught him, as she had hoped, on a lunch break and told him the whole story. Geoff, good at hiding his feelings, did not let on how much it worried him and kept his voice calm and measured. He agreed that it was far too early for despair over Rosa and expressed his concern about Michela.

'She sounds a formidable woman.'

'She must know who I am. She hates me.'

'Maybe she's playing games with you, Lucy. Trying to get a reaction.'

'If you'd seen her, Geoff. Heard her... she'd have done well at the Inquisition.'

'But you stayed cool. You let her call the shots.'

'I was seething inside. I still am! She's my grandmother, how dare she cast me as the villain!'

Geoff felt a little better. Fighting Lucy was back. 'Luce? I wish I were there. I hate that you're on your own. Sim and I—we talk about it all the time. If you want—'

'No.' Lucy interrupted him. 'You are not to get on a plane. I just needed someone to talk to.'

'Stefano?'

'He's lovely, he bought me an angel, but I wanted to talk Australian.'

'So what are you going to do now?'

'I don't know. I said I'd go back. Chiara wants me to.'

'You're close to her, Lucy. To all three of them. Chiara, Andrea, Rosaria—you're never going to have any other siblings. Concentrate on them for now. Get through this crisis. Then worry about your own agenda.'

'That's your advice?'

'Yes.' He was afraid he'd upset her.

'It's good advice. I'll take it.'

'Keep me posted?'

'Of course. As soon as we know anything. Thanks Geoff.'

Geoff hung up, musing over the thought of Lucy with an angel. He hoped it kept her safe. As an extra precaution he walked to the church around the corner and prayed both for Lucy and for the missing Rosaria. And for the soul of his beloved Kate whom he missed not less but more with every passing day.

Lucy, walking back to Il Veliero in the dark, was also missing her mother and rather wishing she hadn't told Geoff not to come. There were so many things she needed to talk about and no one at all with whom to have the conversation. Letters wouldn't cut it, what was needed was a long night with a bottle of wine and no interruptions.

Blackmail, that was one of the things. Ever since Ornella had mentioned it to Paolo, it had lurked there at the back of Lucy's mind, gnawing away like some termite. What she had had in mind for Paolo—that was not blackmail. She wanted to expose him for what he was, yes, make him face up to what he had done—but there had never been any question of demanding money or threatening his family. What she'd had in mind—still had in mind—was very different. Wasn't it?

She looked at the moon, a tiny crescent and wondered where Rosaria was and if by any chance she was looking at it too. She had to be right about Rosaria because any other alternative...

'Signorina?' A hand landed on her shoulder and Lucy pulled away in a panic, spinning around once again to confront an unknown assailant. But this was not Spaccanapoli in broad daylight, this was a near deserted road on a dark night and it was not Stefano's concerned face she found herself looking at but Mario Moretti's. And Mario had company, one of his sidekicks, a beefy young man with a scarred neck whom Lucy had seen hanging around the hotel.

'I startled you.'

'Yes!'

His Italian, even Lucy could tell, was surprisingly educated. 'I apologise. Also that I do not speak English. We haven't met, I am Mario Moretti. And you are Lucy. From Australia.'

Lucy said nothing. Was she supposed to be impressed? The whole town knew who she was by now.

'I've heard—everyone has heard—about Rosaria. A terrible business. I do not like to intrude. But I'm a father too. Please— convey to the family my hopes for their daughter's safe return.'

Lucy just stared at him, dumbfounded. Could he possibly be serious? He wished her goodnight and continued on his way, Nico— yes, that was his name, Nico Barone—giving her a smirk and following his master like a faithful puppy.

Lucy stumbled into the restaurant without being quite sure how she had got there. Her reappearance startled everyone. Chiara went to her side but it was Paolo who spoke.

'You have heard something?'

Lucy shook her head and took a deep breath. 'I saw Mario Moretti. He sends you his hopes for Rosa's safe return.' She realised how preposterous it sounded. She was trembling all over now and Chiara had to grab a chair for her but still Michela swooped.

'You saw Moretti? And where did this meeting take place?'

Lucy hated her then, hated her with a bitter loathing. 'In the street, signora. I was walking back. He stopped me. He accosted me. He and one of his henchmen.'

'I don't understand. Why would he talk to you?'

'Perhaps you should ask him, signora! I was too frightened. He did say he didn't want to intrude.'

Silvana glared at her mother-in-law. 'Michela? What are you doing?'

'It's the stress,' said Ornella smoothly. 'Shall I make some camomile? We are not ourselves.'

Ah, camomile, thought Lucy to herself, Italian cure-all, while at the same time admitting that she too had succumbed to its soothing charms. She did not see the look that passed between Ornella and Michela as Ornella went over to the bar. Lucy still thought that any interest her grandmother might have in her, any inkling as to her true identity, was based on the visit by the putative team from *Carràmba Che Sorpresa*.

They all had camomile. Chiara, who had been at school with Moretti's daughter, ventured to suggest that perhaps his message had been sincere. The idea was not well received. Roberto and Paolo rang all the hospitals once again and checked in with the police. The night crept on.

Up in Chiara's room, the two girls talked for a while. 'She drives me insane, Lucy, but I can't imagine not having a sister.' Lucy, who was only just beginning to understand what having a sister might be like, put an arm around her.

'Do you honestly still think she's alive?' asked Chiara.

'Yes,' said Lucy, but with less conviction than before. If she was alive, why didn't the wretched girl get in touch with them? A phone call, a message of some sort, how hard was that?

Chiara, exhausted after two sleepless nights, dozed off. Lucy heard Andrea crying in the next room and opened the door to go to him but saw that his mother was already on the way and quickly withdrew. She wondered what it would be like to be Silvana tonight, a mother with a missing child, every nerve taut, every sense heightened, waiting, waiting for the news that would not come.

She sat in the big chair by Chiara's window and gazed out at the warm night and the moonlit hills and listened to the sea. She felt that her journey here, which should have been over, had barely begun. Yet in a few weeks she would have to head home or write to her school and arrange more leave. It was hardly the night to be thinking of that. What the hell was Rosa doing? Or had she, as everyone feared, come to harm?

At eight in the morning the police arrived. They had no news, there had been no sightings of Rosaria. They were going to start a full scale search.

At eight-thirty Rosaria rang. From Perugia. It was unfortunate that Paolo answered the phone because once he'd established that she was well and had not been kidnapped, tortured or sold into slavery, but was in fact in that pleasant town of her own free will, his relief turned rapidly to fury. How could she treat her family like this, worrying them half to death, none of them had slept for days, not to mention that half the police force was looking for her, wasting valuable resources on the effort, she was a selfish, immature, ungrateful child and she was to return home immediately. 'Senti, Rosaria? Subito! Il prossimo treno!'—at which point Silvana grabbed the phone, fearful that Rosaria would hang up.

Rosaria managed to tell her mother that she would not be catching the next train, or any train at all, she had no intention of returning home before her results, which were due today or tomorrow, came out—here she started sobbing so loudly that Chiara, standing next to her mother, reported on the fact. Rosaria eventually continued. She knew for sure she had failed and she could not bear their recriminations. She had done her best, just ask Lucia. It was not her fault that she wasn't academic. She would stay with her friend in Perugia until they promised she did not have to return to school.

Lucy felt once again like an intruder in the midst of this family drama and would have slipped away but Chiara, sensing her intention, whispered to her to please stay so she waited while Silvana calmed her troubled daughter, begged for some time so they could talk it all over and extracted a promise that Rosaria would ring again in half an hour. Then she hung up and crossed herself.

'Thank God she is safe.'

'Safe?' roared Paolo. 'Safe? Wait till I get my hands on her! Do we even know for sure she is in Perugia? Do we even have an address?'

'She's with her friend Giulia.'

Chiara chimed in. 'Giulia's sister works at the Università per Stranieri.'

'Fine,' said Paolo, 'then if Rosa won't catch the train, I'll drive up there and drag her home myself.'

'Don't be ridiculous, Paolo, do you want to lose her for good?' It was Michela, speaking for the first time, and for once, Lucy found herself in complete agreement with her grandmother.

'What then?'

'Talk to her, Paolo. Be reasonable. Treat her like an adult.'

Paolo threw up his hands. Then, surprisingly, he turned to Lucy. 'You've been very quiet, Lucia. What do you think?'

'I agree with Michela. You'll do better if you negotiate. Perhaps...' She trailed off, then took the plunge. 'Perhaps if Chiara could go there, to Perugia, and talk to Rosa...'

Silvana could be very decisive on occasion and now, with the weight of fear and anxiety lifted, was one such time. They would tell Rosaria, when she rang, that Chiara and Lucy—if Lucy would be good enough to agree—would go to Perugia today. Rosaria would come home and they would work out her future calmly and sensibly together. Paolo agreed reluctantly and Michela was forced to pretend that she liked the idea. Andrea begged to be allowed to accompany the girls and was refused. Lucy wondered how they would manage the restaurant but Michela insisted she'd waited on tables before and could do it again if necessary.

Rosaria, when she rang back, at least agreed to talk to Lucy and Chiara who set off shortly after on the six-hour drive to Perugia.

'How did you know she was alive?' Chiara asked. 'You don't have second sight, do you, Lucy?'

'No, thank God! No, it was just a feeling. A very strong feeling.'

'I get a strong feeling sometimes that you really are our sister. Crazy, yes?'

Lucy laughed and hoped it didn't sound forced. 'We're kindred spirits I think, Chiara, that's it. Now, how do we convince Rosaria to come home and face the music?' Neither of them knew the answer to that. They did not think Rosa would easily succumb to gentle persuasion or even to bribery.

'She'll get what she wants this time,' said Chiara. 'And what does it matter if she's safe? I think even my grandmother agrees.'

'She's a formidable woman.'

'She's had a hard life,' Chiara said. 'All her generation, you know? Here in the south, in the war and after—life was very difficult. But she is strong—she had to be. Everything she has, she fought for it.'

And no one, Lucy thought to herself, is going to take it away from her.

'So you see why she gets impatient when Rosa is lazy.'

Lucy nodded. 'Of course. I understand.'

Chiara changed the subject then. It was a long drive to Umbria, the green heart of Italy as the travel brochures called it. Maybe the Umbrians called it that too, though it seemed unlikely, Lucy mused, as she watched the clouds gathering ahead of them. Chiara chatted on. She appeared to have a thousand questions she'd been saving up for just this opportunity, when she had Lucy all to herself. Lucy had to be careful with her answers, she had to try to remember all the unfamiliar lies she had told in the past weeks. It was a tangled web and it was Geoff that undid her.

Thirty Three

North of Naples, half-way to Rome on the A1, is the exit for Cassino. It wasn't that which grabbed Lucy's attention, but the signs for the Abbazia di Montecassino. She had not realised how close it was and couldn't help exclaiming, 'So there it is!' which made Chiara look at her strangely.

Lucy smiled. 'Geoff always wanted to go there.'

'Geoff?'

Lucy tried to recover. 'My father.'

'You call him Geoff?'

'Sometimes. We're very informal in Australia.' But she couldn't lie to Chiara, not about this, she owed her something better that more petty lies. 'Actually he's my stepfather but I love him like a father, he's the only one I've ever known. I adore him.'

'I see.' Chiara was sensitive enough not to pursue it further. 'So. Why Montecassino?'

'Geoff's a bit obsessed with the place. It was destroyed several times I think?'

'Longobards, Saracens, earthquake, American bombers.'

'Yes, but always the Benedictines rebuilt it. And somehow it's survived for fifteen hundred years. Geoff says it's a testament, not just to faith but to the human spirit.'

'I think I'd like your father,' was all Chiara said.

The weather had got steadily worse and it was late afternoon when they reached Perugia. Lucy was glad that Chiara was driving now, she was sure the system of one way streets into centro would have defeated her. They left the car in a parking station, booked into a pensione not far away and then Chiara, who knew Perugia through having friends at university there, led Lucy into the surprising remains of the Rocca Paolina, a papal fort built four-hundred years earlier. Here they used the enormous escalators to ascend through a cavernous space, some of it given over to exhibitions, until finally, now high above their starting point, they found themselves in daylight again in the Piazza Italia. From there it was just a short walk down the elegant Corso Vannucci and off into one of the less-elegant, crowded side streets and the old building where Rosaria was hiding out. A fine drizzle began and in less than two minutes Lucy counted three umbrella salesmen getting into position for what could be a profitable evening, judging by the darkening sky. It always happened and it never ceased to amaze her: what did they do the rest of the time? She asked Chiara, who shrugged.

'Sunglasses? No, the Africans have got that market. I really don't know!' It remained a mystery.

It was a defiant Rosa who answered the door and let them in; her friend Giulia had tactfully absented herself and nor was Giulia's sister, who owned the apartment, anywhere to be seen. 'I don't know why you're here. I'm not going home.'

'Don't be silly, Rosa, you've got to,' Chiara said, plonking herself down in a worn leather armchair.

It was not a large apartment—just this one room with a bedroom off it and a tiny kitchenette was all Lucy could see. Bigger than her own place in Stella del Mare but not much. She wondered where Rosaria was sleeping and surmised that it must be on the small couch which didn't look very comfortable. 'What will you do if you don't go home?' she asked.

'Get a job. I've applied for one at the mensa. At the foreign university. I should be fine with all my restaurant experience.'

'You want to wait on tables all your life?' said Chiara.

'What's wrong with it? That's what Lucy's doing.'

'Lucy's a teacher. She's doing it for fun while she sees the world.'

'I'll be paid. I can live. It's better than school.'

'If you want to work in the restaurant business, fine,' said Lucy. 'Do a course, learn the whole business, one day you can take over from your dad.'

Rosaria pulled a face. Lucy thought to herself, it's like I'm back in the staffroom, trying to get a Year Twelve to stay on, to make

190

something of her life, instead of throwing it all away to join the dole queue.

'Yes, well that's the problem, isn't it?' Lucy went on. 'You don't want to run a restaurant, you want to work in fashion. Don't you?'

Silence from Rosa. 'But fashion's a world you know nothing about. You've only looked at the pictures, Rosa, you haven't read the book. You've got to start at the bottom and work your way up and study it and learn it like anything else. I'm not sure you've got what it takes.' God, stop it, she told herself. Next you'll be doling out detention.

'I thought you were on my side!'

'Only if you start to act like a responsible adult.'

'What, go home, you mean? How can I? Papà will kill me!'

'Killing hasn't been mentioned,' Lucy said calmly. 'Your parents were naturally worried. We all were. Worried to death.'

'What did you expect?' Chiara asked. 'That no one would notice you'd gone?'

It was at about that point that Rosaria's defences started to crumble. She was not made of the same stuff as her grandmother at all, she was just a rather selfish girl with a little dream of her own and no idea how to achieve it. She would look back on this episode in years to come with acute embarrassment, she sensed that already. She turned away to the small window and stared down into the alley below in a vain attempt to hide her tears.

'I'm surprised they weren't glad I had gone! I am not like you and Andrea, Chiara. I am just a big disappointment to everyone.'

Lucy, who knew quite a bit about teenage girls' propensity for self-dramatisation—she hadn't been too bad at it herself—decided to stop this performance in its tracks. 'I've got a plan!' she announced brightly, which at least got Rosa to turn and look at her. 'We ring your parents now. We tell them you'll come home with us tomorrow on condition there's no mention of school. And on the way we discuss some sensible things you might do for the next year. Deal?'

'Of course it's a deal,' said Chiara. They looked at Rosaria and waited. And waited. Until she finally caved and nodded.

'Ring your parents, Chiara,' Lucy said. 'And then can we please go and eat? I'm starving.'

By the time they went back out into the Corso Vannucci it was packed with people. And pouring with rain. As Chiara explained, nowhere did the passeggiata, the evening stroll where Italians go out to walk the street and meet and greet their friends, like Perugia. Here the ritual was elevated to an art-form. And a bit of rain, no matter how heavy, wasn't going to stop them. They put their own umbrellas up and made their way through the crowd. It was an odd mix, Lucy thought: the Perugini themselves, smart but conservative, exuding an air of middle-class prosperity as they hugged and kissed with the fervour of those who hadn't met for twenty years instead of only yesterday; and beside them, students in jeans and t-shirts from all over the world, lolling about, sitting on backpacks, squatting in circles, exchanging sodden cigarettes.

'It's so exciting!' said Rosa. 'So cosmopolitan!'

Lucy supposed it was, compared to Stella del Mare. Exciting and wet. She thought herself it was a bit like Carlton back home only with much more interesting architecture. They ate pasta in a little trattoria—not very good pasta, the foreign students were being ripped off—and Rosaria asked if they thought her options for the coming year could include going to America. Lucy and Chiara just gave her a look.

'Alright! I can ask, can't I?'

'I just wouldn't ask mamma and papà,' said Chiara. 'Not if I were you.'

They took Rosa back to the apartment, glad to see that both Giulia and her sister Anna were now there, and promised to relieve them of their guest by eight the following morning. Back at the pension, Lucy rang Stefano to bring him up to date and then she and Chiara, tired beyond belief, both fell into bed. Chiara was asleep in five minutes. For Lucy it took a bit longer; she was trying not only to find a solution to Rosa's problem, but one that Michela would think was her idea. Not easy.

They were woken at dawn by the bells. Not from one church but dozens, booming out from each of Perugia's many little hills and reminding the faithful that God was in his heaven. Lucy swore she could hear them all the way from Assisi, on the other side of the Tiber valley. 'Catholics!' she thought to herself. 'Never let it rest.'

The rain had stopped and the traffic on the autostrada was heavy. Rosaria huddled miserably in the back seat and contemplated her fate while Lucy enjoyed the scenery and Chiara took a turn at the wheel. She was a good driver, careful but not over-cautious, and Lucy felt relaxed with her. That is, until she made a last minute decision to take the Cassino exit.

'My God!' screamed Rosa in Italian, 'where are you going?'

'Montecassino.'

'I thought we'd agreed on English?' said Lucy but Rosa ignored her. 'Some boring old abbey?'

'It's not boring. Most of it's not even that old.'

Rosa sighed loudly but Lucy smiled. 'We haven't really got time.'

'We can spare one hour. So you can tell your father.'

The road up to the abbey over five hundred metres above was stomach-churning. Lucy thought once or twice that flying would have been preferable. At every hairpin bend there was, for a few moments, nothing but sky ahead. And then suddenly there was a large bus labouring in front of them. At least it blocked out the scary sky.

'Polish number plates?'

'Lots of Poles died in the battle. They are buried in the war cemetery. People come on pilgrimage.'

Lucy looked puzzled. 'I came here on a school excursion,' said Chiara, 'we learnt all the history.'

'Oh. And the Americans? The abbey itself?'

'They thought it was full of Germans. That's why they bombed it. 1944.'

'Blasted it to smithereens,' amended Rosaria.

'She's right. They did.'

'And was it? Full of Germans?'

Chiara shook her head. 'Just monks and a lot of civilian refugees.'

'Shit 'appens,' said Rosaria, in English, getting it right for once.

'And then, many years after the war ended, the Italian government paid for it all to be rebuilt. Where it was, how it was. Look.'

They had arrived. The bus veered off to a designated parking area for coaches and the abbey in all its imposing splendour stood before them. It was enormous. This would take more than an hour, Lucy thought. This would need a week.

They gave it their best shot. They walked through the many cloisters, up the grand staircase, enjoyed the view from the Paradise Loggia and entered the basilica, such a perfect baroque gem that it was impossible to believe that most of it was less than fifty years old, a meticulous copy of what had been there previously. Lucy found herself quite overawed. If this was faith in action, then she had to admit it had something going for it. Even Rosaria was impressed.

'I suppose I could always become a nun,' she said.

'Not here,' said Chiara. 'It's a monastery.'

'I don't think you're really suited to the religious life, Rosa,' said Lucy. 'Think of the clothes.'

'Better than a school uniform,' said Rosa. Exasperated, Chiara told her that school was no longer an issue, Silvana had promised on the phone last night.

Rosa was saying she'd feel better if their father had promised when, right on cue, he rang Silvana's mobile phone which she'd insisted they take.

'Where are you?'

'Montecassino. We stopped for a break, I wanted Lucy to see it.'

'Come home, Chiara, okay?'

'Something is wrong?'

'Nothing to worry about. Just come as soon as you can. Drive carefully.'

Heading south again they all worried. Rosa, thinking as usual that it was all about her, worried that they had made a decision on her future already but Chiara and Lucy both privately thought it more likely that bigger events were threatening the peace of Il Veliero and those who depended on it.

Lucy half hoped it were true; she was reaching the stage where the delegation of vengeance was becoming an option she was willing to consider. In the meantime, she decided to try out her plan for Rosaria on the girl herself. Rosa, as Lucy expected, was not impressed. Chiara, on the other hand, thought it was a brilliant idea with even a hope of parental acceptance. Somewhere south of Naples, Rosa stopped objecting. Somewhere south of Agropoli she was beginning to see it as a possibility.

'Just for a year, though.'

'Of course.'

'I couldn't stand it for more than a year.'

'Probably your grandmother couldn't either.'

'I wish you'd ask her, Lucy. Or you, Chiara.'

'Lucy's right,' said Chiara. 'Much better if it comes from you.'

'Just sort of hint at it,' Lucy said. 'Maybe she'll suggest it herself.'

'I get it,' said Rosaria. 'Give the control freak a win.' Lucy hid a smile. The kid was learning at last.

It was Silvana who came to greet them when they finally got back to the restaurant. It was closed for the couple of hours between lunch and dinner.

'I'm sorry, mamma,' Rosaria, said, and fell into her arms. 'I'm so sorry.'

'Ssh, it's alright. We'll talk about that later. I just thank God you are back,' Silvana said, holding her tightly. 'I need my family under one roof. You too, Lucy.'

Paolo came in. Rosaria held on to her mother a little tighter. Surely she wasn't frightened of him, Lucy thought? And then, looking at Paolo, who seemed suddenly grey and older and yes, sick, she realised Rosa was afraid, not of what he would do to her but of what she might have done to him.

'Papà?'

He didn't go to her. 'Your mother is right. It's a time when we need to be together.'

'What's happening?' It was Chiara who asked.

'We're not sure. Moretti wants to see me tomorrow. And Concetta has resigned. She says her sister is ill and needs her. Her sister is not ill.'

'Weird,' said Rosaria.

Lucy wondered if the two things were linked but didn't like to ask, especially as Michela had now joined them.

'Can't we hire someone else?'

'It is proving difficult so far.'

'No one needs money all of a sudden?'

'I'm still here,' said Lucy.

'You can hardly work tonight,' said Silvana. 'Any of you. You must be exhausted.'

'I'll be fine,' said Lucy and the others were quick to agree.

'Then perhaps we should talk about Rosa,' said Michela. 'Get that out of the way.'

'I think it can wait,' said Silvana. 'She's home safe, that's the most important thing.'

After glancing at Lucy, who gave the faintest of nods, Rosaria took a deep breath. 'We talked it over last night. And I had an idea. I help out here for the season—you need someone now and I'd work hard. Then you give me a year to see if I can get a start in the fashion business. I'd take anything at all, just to get a foot in the door. Somewhere up north, you know?'

'And where would you live?' asked Paolo.

'An apartment. I could share.'

A pause. Then Michela took the bait. 'You could come to Naples, you could share with me in Pozzuoli.'

'Oh, nonna, would you have me?' She was a good actor, her squeal of feigned delight was most convincing, Lucy thought.

'Someone has to keep you out of trouble, Rosaria. I think I know my duty. I have a good friend—Natalia Ficino, owns a boutique in the via Toledo—maybe she'd give you a job if I asked her.'

'And if some modelling came up...'

'Why does every pretty girl think she has what it takes to be a model? Maybe you should see an agent, then you will realise what nonsense this is.' Rosaria smiled, already on the catwalk.

Lucy and Chiara couldn't believe how easy it was. Or maybe the threat of Mario Moretti had put the problem of Rosaria into perspective.

It was a busy evening at the restaurant but thankfully not a late one. The diners were mostly young and maybe the balmy night air drew them away to other pursuits. Lucy was about to leave when

Michela bailed her up.

'It was your idea, yes? She would have had some ludicrous plan, London, New York...'

'I may have made a few suggestions.'

'Why do you care about her?'

'I'm a teacher, signora. It's my job to help mixed-up teenagers make sensible decisions.'

'There is more to it, I think.'

'I was hired to be her tutor. I couldn't help getting involved. Nothing more.'

'I see. Goodnight, Lucia.' Lucy walked home knowing that Michela didn't believe her and never would. Michela, she was sure of it now, knew who she was.

Safely back at Il Nido, she poured herself a beer because she was hot and thirsty and it made her feel homesick and sat on the balcony and rang Stefano. She told him as much as she dared about Michela, the grandmother who hated her, and he was reassuring and thought she must have it all wrong; who could possibly hate her? She told him about Mario Moretti and he was interested and concerned—he hoped it was not going to turn nasty.

'Surely not?'

'Did he get his building permit from the council?'

'For Il Delfino Nero—sorry, Blu? I don't know. There's a lot of work going on down there, it's going to be monstrous.'

'He's probably doing it without permission.'

'Isn't that normal?'

'Up to a point. Unfortunately.'

She also told him about the visit to Montecassino and how amazing and beautiful it was.

'Honestly, Stef, I'm in danger of turning Catholic!'

He was delighted. 'This is good. No problem when we get married!' She could hear him laughing as he hung up.

She finished her beer and listened to the quiet sound of the sea and tried to imagine what it might be like to live here, married to Stefano and was glad he had laughed because the idea was so absurd. A small breeze got up and she shivered. She knew that even this quiet sea must sometimes be whipped into a fury of wind and waves and remembered that Shelley himself had died sailing in just such a storm, not so very far north. The question was, really, from where would the storm come? Who would create it? Mario Moretti? Michela Esposito? Lucy O'Connell Harrington?

The answer was all of the above. And one other.

Thirty Four

T he meeting with Mario Moretti, held on Paolo's insistence in the office of his lawyer, Roberto Luccatini, did not go well. But then possibly none of the parties present expected that it would. Mario, having made the requisite enquiries about Rosaria's well-being, beat around the bush for a while. He complained about the difficulty in getting permits through council. He had hoped that certain friends might have helped to smooth the path. If allowed, the work on il Delfino Blu would assuredly create new tourist business and job opportunities for Stella del Mare. Roberto pointed out that the plans had drawn considerable opposition; many people thought they would swallow up too much of the beach.

'A few metres only!'

Roberto shrugged; he was just the messenger. It was Paolo's turn.

'You will understand that council needs time to consider all the objections.' He paused a moment. 'I see that you are, in any case, proceeding.'

'A coat of paint, some new decking. Nothing but decoration.' Interesting, thought, Paolo, this nothing was employing at least ten tradesmen at last count.

'So I have another idea,' said Mario. 'I want to make you an offer.' Paolo and Roberto exchanged a quick glance. Now they were getting to the nitty-gritty.

'An offer?'

Mario looked straight at Paolo. 'I know you are not in good health, my friend. I think to myself, you work too hard. Perhaps you would like more time with your family. I will give you a very good price for Il Veliero.'

The offer was not accepted. Mario Moretti left and Roberto poured two glasses of a fine single malt whisky, a gift from a grateful client, which he and Paolo drank without a word.

'Is it that obvious, then? Or has someone been talking?'

'You look tired, Paolo. That's all. Hardly surprising.'

'Just tired?'

'To me, yes.' Roberto, afraid for his friend, gave it a try: 'You could "arrange" for his plans to be approved. Quickly.'

'So we can live in Disneyland?'

'He'll do it anyway.'

Paolo sighed. 'Of course he will. He doesn't care about the permit, that's just an excuse. It's my restaurant he wants and we both know it.'

Lucy was in the kitchen when Paolo arrived back at Il Veliero, or rather she was at an old sink outside the kitchen, scaling fish. It was not her job, it was something Concetta used to get paid extra to do and Enrico, who had his hands full, was almost pathetically grateful when she offered to help. But the office window was open and even with the tap running Lucy could hear the conversation, could not miss the contempt and outrage in Silvana's voice.

'He's a bully. I'd burn the place down before I'd let him have it!'

'Did he threaten you, Paolo?' Michela asked.

'Not this time. No doubt it will come.'

'I wonder what made him think...' Silvana trailed off.

'That I'm sick?'

'But papà, you—' Chiara did not get to finish.

'Someone has been making up stories,' said Michela. 'I can't imagine who.' Her voice was like steel. And Lucy, who could not see her face and had never mentioned Paolo's health to anyone but Stefano and Geoff, nevertheless felt a chill and knew exactly what was coming.

All the same, nothing was said and she was starting to think she'd escaped. Then she went back home when her afternoon shift was finished and found Michela's car outside her building.

'Get in,' she said, arousing Lucy's fury more quickly than she could have imagined.

'Sorry,' said Lucy. 'I'm off duty. And very tired.'

'Then I'll come up to your apartment.'

'You're not invited.'

'Damn you, Lucia, I'm an old woman, I must talk to you! A minute of your precious time, that's all. I want to know why you did it.'

Lucy stopped then and took a deep breath. She couldn't see why she had to justify herself to this woman.

'Whatever it is, signora, I didn't do it.'

'Call me—Michela.'

She knows alright, Lucy thought, she was going to say 'nonna' and changed her mind.

'When you met with Mario Moretti the other night—what did you say to him?'

'I didn't meet him—I told you. He accosted me in the street. I recounted the conversation word for word, or as near as I could.'

'Did you tell him Paolo was sick?'

'No I did not. Is he sick? I wasn't aware. I've thought at times that he might be in pain—I'm familiar with the signs, my mother died of cancer—but I haven't discussed it with anyone. And now if you'll excuse me, signora—I need to rest. We've got a big crowd tonight.'

And she left her grandmother standing and went inside the shabby building with its peeling paint, up the stairs to safety. 'Class,' thought Michela. 'Heaven knows where she got it, but she does have class.'

Lucy, for her part, was quite proud of herself. She wasn't sure how she had kept calm; she doubted if she could do it again. She wondered about Paolo—if he were really sick, why was it such a big secret? Wasn't that carrying bella figura just a bit far? She realised, not for the first time, that she had no idea what was going on, that she was in fact way out of her depth.

For a few days things continued more or less as they had been. Michela, until she was eventually persuaded to return to Naples, watched Lucy like a hawk but Lucy was getting used to that. Rosaria, fulfilling her promise, worked hard and even Andrea, with holidays looming, was able to help. They managed quite well without Concetta who was often seen about town. Her duties in caring for her sister did not seem too onerous. And down at the end of the beach, the decorative touches to Il Delfino Blu proceeded at breakneck speed and included a car park and a terrace over a large section of the sandy shore. (The speed was especially impressive in the south, where buildings remained half-completed for decades, where bridges stopped mid-stream, where roads could end abruptly in a field of grazing buffalo.) As for Paolo, he ran the restaurant, he met with his cronies, he presided over the next meeting of the giunta, he was on the phone day and night as ever. He possibly looked more worried than usual but then he had reason to. His health, during all this activity, wasn't mentioned. He treated Lucy as he always had; if he shared Michela's suspicions he did not show it. Lucy felt at times as if it were all going on around her in black and white, as if she were playing a role in some old film by Visconti, or De Sica. The scenes of family life, picked out in such minute and loving detail, were just a dramatically necessary build-up for the approaching catastrophe. She felt confused and uncomfortable but she'd been that way since arriving in Italy so it could not explain her unease.

That, she knew, was due to the fact that she was as far as ever from fulfilling her mission; no, further because she sometimes felt, in moments of quiet honesty, that the rage was not as strong as it had been. This family—some of it—was, as Geoff had warned, getting under her skin and becoming far too important to her.

And then Mario Moretti offered her a job. She was having a quiet coffee outside a bar in Castellabate, where she'd gone to do some shopping, and he had the gall to sit down, uninvited, at her table, while the ever-present Nico hovered on the periphery. Well of course, Lucy thought, he was not the sort of man to move about unaccompanied, there had to be an underling waiting in the wings; the Paciotti shoes and the Armani suit and the diamond watch on the manicured hand would never be enough to make him feel important. Before she could tell him to go to hell he'd flicked his fingers at the waiter and then proceeded to enquire about the health and well-being of the Esposito family.

'You'd have to ask them,' said Lucy, 'I am merely an employee.'

'A very good one, from all accounts. Much experience.'

Lucy shrugged.

'Three languages.'

'My Italian is abysmal.'

'I can understand you perfectly.'

Lucy picked up her bag. 'If you'll excuse me, signore—'

'Please. One moment. I won't keep you long.'

She waited. What the hell was coming now?

What came was an offer to manage Il Delfino Blu. Starting immediately on a very large salary although she would not be needed for at least six weeks. Lucy laughed. She said she was just a schoolteacher, she wouldn't know how to manage such an establishment. She declined his generous offer. Moretti accepted her decision with apparent equanimity.

'That is regrettable,' was all he said. He made no threats. And yet they hung in the air, thick as that all-pervasive fog on Lucy's first morning in Naples. She left him and returned to her car. Once there, she started to shake. She felt as if she needed a bath.

Back at Stella del Mare, she somehow got through her shift at the restaurant. She decided that any mention of her meeting with Moretti would achieve nothing and therefore kept quiet. Unnaturally quiet apparently, because both Silvana and Chiara commented on it.

'I'm fine,' Lucy said. 'Just a bit tired.'

'I think you should take some time off,' said Silvana. 'Tomorrow is Tuesday, take Wednesday as well. Have a break.'

'You could manage?'

'Wednesday is not so busy,' said Chiara.

'And Paolo's mother is coming back.'

That settled it. The thought of facing Michela again so soon was more than Lucy could bear. Suddenly the idea of getting away became irresistible and she said that if they were sure, then maybe she'd go and see Pompeii at last or even, come to think of it, curl up in bed for two days and do nothing but sleep and read. As it turned out she did neither of those things because Stefano, when she rang him, announced the small miracle that he had some time off also.

'But how on earth...?'

'The show as I tell you is a disaster. I mean, is fine but la RAI say is disaster. It will not suit, how do you say, Italian sensibilities, yes?'

203

'But Italians are writing it, directing it...'

'This is no matter. They say it is still too Australian. Lucy, I am just stupid architect, I do not understand. So tomorrow big bosses arrive from London, from Roma, they talk a lot, they sort it all out.'

'Will they?'

'Who knows? The good news, I am not required. I leave first thing, what do you like to do?'

'It's been horrible here, I just want to get away.'

She met Stefano at Agropoli. He was beaming when he got off the Vespa, he was overjoyed to see her and swept her into a long embrace and felt her tremble slightly.

'Lucia?'

'I'm just glad you're here.'

He left the Vespa at a local garage and over coffee they argued about where to go. Stefano thought, but did not say, that Lucy looked tense and drawn and was determined that this time he would find out why she was really here because he could not see how he could help her otherwise. He wanted to take her down the coast to Palinuro, he said there was something special to see there, but Lucy had a yen to head for the hills, perhaps to visit Signora Bianchi again. He thought, 'She's afraid to be alone with me,' but aloud he said:

'You look forward to the ironing, yes? By how it will be piled up high.'

'It's beautiful country. And you haven't been there!'

'You have not been to Palinuro.'

'I bet it's just like Stella del Mare.'

'Palinuro himself was murdered there. Is historically important.'

'Except that he never actually existed.'

'Okay. We go to Monte Santa Caterina. If we have time we go also to Palinuro.'

On the way they were much too busy talking to notice the black Fiat Brava that followed them. Stefano told her about the total insanity that accompanied the production of a soap opera—especially a co-production. 'These people, Lucy—the egos! Directors think they are Fellini. Actors believe they win an Oscar. All such artists, you know? But for the Australians only speed matters, so many minutes every day, if we still there at midnight, peggio!'

'We're Philistines. In it for the money.'

'Is just a soap after all. Not exactly art.' He smiled at her. 'Still more fun than real estate.'

'Good.'

'And now it's your turn.'

So she told him about Michela's accusations and about the offer from Mario Moretti and Stefano made light of it and just said the man was an idiot. Obviously he wanted to see Paolo closed down but it was crazy to imagine that stealing his staff would achieve it.

They stopped in Roscigno Vecchio. They did not see the old lady with the donkey and the panniers but the water in the well was still cold and clear. They set Lucy's camera on time delay on the bonnet of the car and took a photo of themselves, arms around each other, and then Stefano splashed her and she splashed him back and he chased her around the crumbling old walls and when he caught her he kissed her for the second time. And found it hard to let her go, wanting her as he had never wanted any other girl but there was still this river of mistrust between them and Stefano was wise enough to know that patience was his friend now. He could wait, he told himself. He could at least wait until tonight. So there was no romantic idyll on the warm summer grass in that abandoned village square; besides, the donkey reappeared to watch their every move and rendered the scenario in Stefano's head quite ridiculous. He burst out laughing. Lucy, when she saw the animal, laughed too but in her case it was at least partly relief. It had been a close thing.

They drove on, the Brava keeping its distance behind them. Stefano couldn't resist a little gentle teasing and told her about the scripts for the soap opera.

'They are up to episode thirty-four, Lucy. I have read them, all the storylines. Still the hero and the heroine do not make love. I find this very strange.'

'Oh, well it's an old Australian custom.'

'Really?'

'Mm. No sex on the first date.'

'Or the thirty-fourth?'

'What's the hurry?'

He gave her a sideways look and she screamed. 'Stefano!' It was a pretty tight corner, where was St Christopher?

'It's supposed to keep them coming back for more. At least I think that's the rationale.'

'What?'

'The audience.'

She laughed. Stefano thought it was fairly boring himself but left it. Monte Santa Caterina looked as though little if anything had happened since Lucy's last visit. They took a chance and went straight to Signora Bianchi's house and found her in the garden, hunting for the first ripe tomatoes. She straightened up with difficulty when Lucy called her name but it took her only a moment to make the connection.

'My Australian friend,' she said. 'I did not expect to see you again!' She was delighted that they planned to stay the night, charmed by Stefano and amazed by the improvement in Lucy's Italian. She was less happy when, much later on, she discovered that Lucy was working for Paolo. They were having an aperitivo and some excellent local cheese and while Alessandra could not help enquiring after Silvana and the children, and was pleased to hear they were well, she did not think Lucy had been wise to take a job at Il Veliero.

'It's just for a while,' Lucy said. 'A holiday job.'

'Why does it worry you, signora?' Stefano asked.

'I don't trust the man,' said Alessandra. 'Never have. Did Lucy not tell you? There was a scandal.'

'I see,' said Stefano, looking at Lucy. 'No, she didn't tell me you knew him at all.'

Lucy could feel his eyes on her. She couldn't meet them. Why oh why hadn't she told him? She had truly forgotten that he didn't know. 'Signora Bianchi is Silvana's aunt,' she said. 'Some coincidence, yes?'

'And this is why you came here?' She'd heard that icy voice before, outside the hostel in Mergellina.

'Of course not! I had no idea until I came here!'

Alessandra had been watching them carefully. 'And it mattered to you, Lucy? That I was related to them? It was somehow important?'

Then it all fell into place. 'Oh,' said Alessandra. 'Of course it mattered.'

'He's my father.'

Alessandra just nodded and patted her hand. 'Such a long time ago. But some wounds don't heal. They fester.'

Stefano waited for what seemed to him like an eternity. Finally he spoke.

'Would someone be kind enough to fill me in?'

'Paolo raped my mother. That's how I came to be here. To be born. And to be here.'

He had no idea what to say. He wanted to hold her, to tell her that whatever her father had done made not one iota of difference to who and what she was. But he knew that would be wrong because he was the only one to whom it made no difference. He looked at Alessandra.

'You knew this, signora?'

Alessandra sighed. 'Not until a moment ago. But it had to be that. Something like that. It did not take much imagination.'

Stefano thought then he couldn't have any imagination at all because it was absolutely the last damn thing that he'd thought.

Alessandra watched him and felt sorry for him. He seemed a nice young man.

'Silvana's mother died when Silvana was very young,' she said. 'She came to depend on me a lot. When she fell in love with Paolo— this was two or three years after he got back from Australia—my husband was told certain things. Well-meaning people—you know how it is. And being a policeman, he made enquiries.'

'What did he discover?' It was Lucy who asked the question.

'I only know what he told me, my dear. He told me to warn Silvana that Paolo had done something dishonourable. She ought to ask him about it before she married him.'

'And did you warn her?

'No. I asked Paolo myself. And of course he denied it.'

Stefano said, 'And then you told Silvana and that was that.'

'We have barely spoken since. Guiseppe and I were not invited to the wedding.'

'You Italians!' cried Lucy, feeling Alessandra's pain after all these years.

'Yes,' said Alessandra quietly. 'So stupid. I should have gone and apologised. By the time I did, it was too late.'

Silvana, thought Lucy, Silvana should have apologised, you were only trying to save her from a monster. But of course he wasn't a monster to her, he was probably a knight in shining armour. Stefano's voice cut into her thoughts.

'...perhaps we go for a walk,' he was saying in English. 'A good idea?' He sounded like someone she barely knew, polite, detached. She followed him out and Alessandra, left alone, was suddenly glad she was old.

'The chapel you mentioned,' said Stefano, as if Lucy were a tour guide, 'where is that?' Lucy nodded towards the beech trees where the path began and they headed off without another word and walked in silence until they came to the alpine meadow where she had rested—was it only a few weeks earlier?—and there Stefano stopped. 'This will do,' he said.

'For what?'

'To talk, Lucy. Don't you think we need to talk?'

But it was a long time before either of them said a word. Faintly from a distant church a bell tolled for sext, the sixth hour, and with it a noonday hush seemed to settle on the hillside and the valley below. A multitude of bees, swarming around a clump of broom, was the only thing to be heard. Lucy stared at them, did not take her eyes off them, as though somehow their interminable buzzing would obviate the necessity for the conversation that was coming. She kept thinking, incongruously, of Yeats and his bee-loud glade, she wished she could arise and go there, go to Innisfree, go to Timbuctoo for that matter, anywhere at all away from Stefano's accusing gaze.

'I never meant it all to come out like that.'

'I am sure you did not.'

'I wanted to tell you properly. At the right time.'

'Oh? And when would this be?'

'I don't know!'

'You do not trust me, Lucy. This is the problem. Perhaps you do not trust anyone. Maybe at home but not here. Never an Italian. No matter what they do to help you.'

'You're angry.'

'I am very angry. And I want to know why you are really here.'

Why was he making her spell it out? 'Isn't that obvious? I've told you what happened. My mother was eighteen years old. Paolo raped her. And then he came home here to Italy. He left her alone and pregnant, with no one in the world to help her except some nuns. He never said he was sorry. He never suffered in any way for ruining her life. I have come to make him pay.'

Stefano stared at her for a long moment as though he hadn't really understood, as though the English he spoke so well had on this occasion let him down. 'Are you quite mad, Lucy?' he finally asked.

'I'm not mad at all. I simply want justice.'

'Oh. So you poison him, yes? Shoot him? I get you a gun?'

'No, of course not!'

'A garrote, then. Is a good choice here in the south, very popular.'

'Stop it. Stop it!'

'Then what, Lucy? What do you do in Australia?'

'I am not going to kill him!'

'Oh. I see. Then...?'

'I don't know. I'll think of something.'

The bees went on gorging themselves. Lucy wasn't thinking of Irish lakes. She was thinking of an October afternoon in Elwood. She could hear her mother's calm, measured voice, she could feel her own tears pricking her eyelids.

'You want to know what I think?' asked Stefano.

'Not really.'

'I tell you all the same. How you feel for your mother—this I understand. What Paolo did to her, yes, a terrible, terrible thing. But it was twenty-five years ago, quarter of a century.'

'So what are you saying—I should just forget?'

'To forget is not possible. But to make him pay now, you hurt a lot of other people—will this help your mother? Will it help you?'

'Please. Leave me out of it.'

'I can't,' he said. He knew from the look on her face that he'd managed to make it a declaration of love. He didn't care. None of that mattered any more, he just wanted to turn her away from what she was doing. 'Lucy. It's like the volcano. After the violence something beautiful comes. That is how life is. Can you not see?'

And even though Kate herself had said almost exactly that, Lucy remained in denial. 'You should have been a priest,' she said bitterly. 'The platitudes come to you so easily.'

Stefano spoke very quietly. 'If you want to wound your father, Lucy, perhaps your tongue is the best weapon.'

He turned and walked away, back across the meadow and on to the path again and given the steepness of the track and his furious pace, he soon disappeared from view. Lucy truly doubted that she would ever see him again. If he did love her—which she also doubted—she had treated him so badly, and made it so clear that his feelings were not returned, that he would never take the matter any further. He was far too proud to grovel. Lucy felt as she often had that Paolo's genetic influence must have confined itself to her colouring. Italy, Italians—it was not her bel paese, they were not her people, she would never feel at home here. No need to write to the school and beg for more time off. She would do what she had to do as soon as she could, however she could, and then she was going home. She sat on the grass and stared unseeing at the view while the same distant bell announced none and, much later, vespers, and the shadows grew longer. Her tears she put down to hayfever.

Thirty Five

A lessandra, when Lucy finally returned, was not deceived by her casual enquiry.

'Stefano—he came back?' Alessandra nodded. 'And got his things?' Alessandra nodded again. 'Good.'

Alessandra knew it was anything but good. She wanted to do nothing so much as to throw her arms around Lucy and, in mothering the girl, play for a few moments the role that fate had denied her. But she sensed that Lucy had already shed a great many tears and was now both exhausted and desperate not to lose control again so she contented herself with offering food and camomile tea, both of which were refused.

'I, um, I need to make a phone call. To Australia. I won't be long.'

She headed off to the phone booth in the village square and Alessandra went to the kitchen to prepare a simple pasta. She wasn't hungry but the painkillers she'd need to get her through the night sat uneasily on an empty stomach. And there was always a chance, a slim one, that the boy might return. Alessandra was romantic enough to believe in happy endings.

Lucy rang Geoff at work, she knew he wouldn't mind. Eileen, his assistant, was apologetic; he was out this morning, a deceased estate, a lot of books. Lucy hung up. She lent against the wall of the booth for a long time, her eyes closed, willing her universe to change. When a hand touched her shoulder she jumped back in fright and banged her head hard against the metal casing which held the phone itself. The owner of the hand—a man who said he'd been sitting outside the bar—was full of apologies. He'd noticed Lucy there, was worried she might be sick, had perhaps had bad news. Lucy thanked him but said she was just tired, very tired. She was returning now to Signora Bianchi's pensione where she was staying, she'd be fine. And having nowhere else to go, that is where she headed while the man, having gained the information sought by his boss, nodded pleasantly and watched her walked off.

Lucy could, of course, have rung Simone but suddenly the whole idea of trying to turn her confused thoughts and tangled emotions into any sort of coherent conversation seemed quite beyond her. Perhaps she truly was exhausted. She thought back to her childhood, to the times when she'd felt as lost and upset as she did now: when she'd had one of her rare and terrible fights with her mother, for instance; when she'd felt an outsider, as she had after the abortive weekend at Bannon Creek; when she'd had premonitions of abandonment, as all children do, of finding herself totally alone in the world. Then she had always committed her thoughts to paper, that had been the only way to calm the storm, and she wondered—feeling foolish—if it might help now.

Alessandra found her a notepad from Fabriano, where they'd been making paper for seven hundred years. Lucy protested that it was far too beautiful to use but Alessandra insisted, since she herself rarely had cause to write letters any more. A grateful Lucy took it upstairs and Alessandra, wishing she could do more to help than act as village stationer, returned to frying her garlic and tomatoes.

Lucy sat at the window where the light from the evening sun was sufficient to write by but the words did not come easily. She tried to get it all down, even in note form: why she had come, what she had achieved (very little was the answer to that one) and what she planned to do next. She examined again her feelings about Paolo and found that her anger still burned brightly; so too did her ambivalence towards the rest of the family. She did not dwell on her relationship with Stefano, she felt it was another country and her visa had expired. But she did remember his words, 'Will this help your mother?' and the answer was she didn't know.

She knew it would help her to feel that justice had in some small way been done and she passionately believed that it was what Kate deserved. She also realised, with a moment of adult clarity, that she might be pursuing Paolo as a way of coping with her loss. Having no one but Kate, that loss was enormous and showed no sign of lessening. She didn't really want it to; she didn't want the memories to fade, she wanted them all to stay hard and bright as diamonds.

And so the evening passed. Alessandra ate a little pasta and hoped Lucy might come downstairs and join her but that didn't happen. She turned on the television, softly so as not to disturb her visitor, and tried to watch a variety show which she usually enjoyed but which tonight failed to amuse her. After five minutes she turned the sound down and left the picture on for company. She thought about climbing the stairs to check on the little australiana but did not like to intrude. Had she done so she would have found Lucy still sitting by the window but in the dark now, reciting poetry to herself.

Lucy had started with some Australian stuff, bush poems from her childhood but those had made her too homesick so she'd moved on to Arnold and Auden and bits of Frost and then, with Yeats, had gone sailing off to Byzantium. And now she was doing Chesterton's 'Lepanto', an old favourite this, one that she and Kate had done in chorus and not a good choice at all for that reason but at least it was long and she knew every word. Her room was at the back of the house and so she did not see Stefano walking up to the door.

When Stefano had left her, long strides taking him back across the field and down the path, willing himself not to look back, not to break into a run, just to keep going until he was far away, he had no intention of returning on this night or any other. Lucy was right about one thing, he was proud and what she had said to him he couldn't forgive. Especially since she was not even being true to her own feelings.

Stefano knew how Lucy felt about him, whether she was ready to admit it or not. He'd known it for some time and had felt it again when he held her that morning. He'd rejoiced in it because, although he'd had many girlfriends, there'd never been one like her. It wasn't just the challenge she represented, it was because he sensed her deep unease. Stefano wanted to show her that making love—it was never just 'having sex' to him—should be a thing of passion and joy and nothing to fear.

Well that wasn't going to happen. She'd made her choice, wrong as most of Lucy's choices were. But there was something he had to

213

tell her before he went back to Naples. He didn't really think it would do any good but he had to make one last attempt to get her to see what she was doing, what she was becoming.

Stefano had already arranged a lift back to Agropoli with, of all people, the local priest, when he knocked on the door. He startled Alessandra who had dozed off in her chair and was deeply apologetic for calling so late. He wondered if Lucy might still be awake and if so, could he speak to her for just a moment?

Lucy was reluctant but Alessandra, still hoping for a miracle, persuaded her to come down stairs. Alessandra put wine and biscotti on the table and excused herself, it was way past her bedtime, and disappeared. Lucy and Stefano stood there, a chasm between them.

'I hope I didn't interrupt anything.'

'Just "Lepanto."'

'The battle?'

'The poem.'

'Oh.'

'You wouldn't have read it.'

'No. I was not at the battle either. But it changed the world.'

'Don't they all?'

Stefano decided not to answer that. 'I want to tell you a story, Lucy. It's quite short.'

Lucy shrugged. She really wanted to run away back upstairs and hide under the bed but that would hardly be a grown-up sort of thing to do. She was suddenly very aware of how she must look, the hair that hadn't been combed since morning, the circles under her red eyes.

'Perhaps you would like to sit down?'

Why did he have to be so damn polite? She pulled out a chair and sat. So did Stefano.

'This is a true story. About a family my father knew,' Stefano began. 'They came from a poor village. Had a little bit of land, not much, some olive trees, this and that, down in Reggio. There were two kids, boys, and one of them was very bright. Really clever. There was an uncle, he had some money, he decided to help this bright boy, this Luciano, that was his name. The village school was not much but

214

the teacher did her best. You are teacher, Lucy, you will understand—the pleasure to have just one boy who is clever, who really wants to learn.'

Stefano stopped and poured a glass of Alessandra's wine. He offered it to Lucy but she shook her head. She had no idea where this was heading but she thought of Liz Holden in that country school, and the joy she found in teaching Kate. Stefano sipped the wine and continued.

'But there was a problem. The teacher gave to Luciano perhaps too much attention. Some other students—one in particular—were filled with, how do you say, invidia—envy?'

'Envy, jealousy.'

'Yes. Luciano, you see, is clever, good-looking, popular. And this other boy, Maurizio, so envious?' Lucy nodded. 'He is none of those things. However... no one realise. Luciano finishes school, the uncle support him and he goes to university and he becomes a doctor. And then returns to the village. Everyone delighted, they have not had a doctor till now.'

He stopped and sipped his wine again. Lucy waited. She was hanging on every word but she was damned if she was going to ask.

'And then Maurizio shot him.'

'What?!'

'Just like that. Killed him.'

'Why?'

'He was jealous. But that was just the start. Now for the important part.'

Lucy had a horrible idea now that she did know where this was heading and could only hope that she was wrong. She tried to pour herself a glass of wine but her hand shook and Stefano did it for her. It nearly made her sick on her empty stomach but she sipped it slowly.

'You remember the uncle, who loved this boy and supported him through all his studies?'

Lucy nodded faintly.

'He wrote the names of Maurizio's family on his belt. He went into hiding and he started to kill them, one by one. He was very methodical, very clever. He murdered six, the youngest was only fourteen.'

'You are making this up,' Lucy whispered.

'It is too horrible to make up. The last member of that family— my father's friend—had carabinieri outside his house night and day. He moved up here when Luciano's uncle died.'

'How did he die?'

'Heart attack.'

'He deserved something terrible.'

'I'm surprised you think so.'

Lucy looked at him, not sure she'd heard him correctly.

'He was just making them pay for their crimes.'

'Most of that family had done nothing!'

'Exactly.'

There was a long silence, as so often happened between them. Lucy thought he had been horribly unfair but she wasn't going to say so, she wouldn't give him the satisfaction.

'You think I have been unfair to you,' Stefano said, as if reading her mind.

She wouldn't answer.

'I know you don't mean to kill anyone. But is all a matter of degree. This is the curse of Naples, the curse of Italy. Vendetta, payback, is this what you came here to learn? You want to be like Mario Moretti, you want to play at being a camorrista?'

'You patronising bastard, I just want justice for my mother! I want one man to face up to what he has done! What's so wrong with that, why shouldn't he suffer, I hate him, I hate him!'

'Do you, Lucy? Do you really hate him?'

Stefano left then, and drove with the priest through the darkness to Agropoli. The good father, a remarkably wise and sensitive man, chatted about football and motorbikes and Stefano's job at la RAI and never mentioned the girl that had been left behind in Santa Caterina.

Alessandra found her with her head on the table at three o'clock in the morning, and woke her gently and watched her go upstairs but suspected she'd already had all the sleep she was likely to get.

216

Alessandra was wrong, she hadn't taken into account the fact that people sleep when they need to heal. Broken hearts, bruised egos, the shattered remnants of self-esteem—serious cases often succumb to sleep. And Lucy was suffering from all three. It was the sun that woke her, hot on her face. It was nearly ten. She washed, brushed her hair and tossed her few things into her backpack, including the skirt and the high-heeled sandals she'd brought just in case. Definitely surplus to requirements. She picked up her phone and stuffed it into her pocket and made her way downstairs. Alessandra must have heard her moving around because the coffee was already made. They drank it together and Lucy forced herself to eat a cornetto. They did not say much though Lucy tried very hard to pretend that everything was okay.

'Lucia?'

'Mm?'

'You will go back to Stella del Mare?'

'For a little while.'

'You must do what you think is right, my dear.'

'Stefano thinks I should just forget.'

'Men see things differently.'

'Yes. They do.' She finished her coffee. 'You have been very kind, signora. I feel like you are my zia Alessandra. I hope I will see you again before I go home.'

'Yesterday, I thought you might be staying,' said Alessandra but Lucy just shook her head and hugged the old woman and then hurried out to the car before they both lost their composure.

She drove far too quickly out of Monte Santa Caterina. Had she kept to her normal pace she might have recognised the green Rover which nearly forced her off the road as the one belonging to Mario Moretti. But she was too upset to do more than swear at it. She got back to Stella del Mare in record time and could not really remember what route she had taken, only that she had deliberately avoided Roscigno Vecchio. She went straight to her little apartment, parked the car in a side street where she hoped it would not be seen, and hurried up the stairs. She desperately wanted some time alone. She closed the door behind her and threw herself on the bed and the first thing she saw on the small table beside it were Kate's picture and Stefano's angel, the one he had bought for her in via San Gregorio Armeno.

When Chiara arrived with Andrea an hour later, the angel was in a box under the bed, since she could not quite bring herself to throw it out, and the emergency litre of wine (there was always one in the kitchen cupboard), was half empty.

'I do hope,' said Lucy, 'that you don't need me to work tonight.'

Andrea giggled. Chiara, sensing a catastrophe, didn't. 'We weren't expecting you back,' she said.

'Oh. No. Just as well.'

'We've been to the shops, we happened to see the car, are you okay?' Chiara realised what a silly question it was.

'Where's Stefano?' asked Andrea.

'He had to go back to Naples.'

'Did you have a fight?' Kids, thought Lucy, could be so brutally direct. Chiara came to the rescue.

'Andrea,' she said. 'Take the shopping home? Lucy and I want to have a little chat.'

'Why can't I stay?'

'It's girl stuff, Andrea. Boring.'

He looked unimpressed. She waved two thousand lire notes under his nose and he grinned and took them and went. 'Ciao, Lucia. Ci vediamo!'

'Ciao!'

Chiara looked at Lucy and shook her head. 'You look terrible. You want to talk about it?'

'Not yet.'

'But you're alright—you and Stefano?'

'It's over, Chiara.'

'Oh, Lucy! I am so sorry. For you, of course, but I'm selfish, I'm sorry for both of us. I thought if it worked out you might stay.'

'You'll have to come and visit me in Australia.'

'But you're not going home just yet?'

'Not for a little while.' Why not? Wouldn't it be the smart thing to do, to leave right now? It would no doubt please Stefano, he'd chalk it up as a moral victory. She could ring Qantas tomorrow, this afternoon even, could give up, desert the field and run away to wintry Melbourne, to Geoff and Sim and a classroom of teenagers with no interest at all in *As You Like It*. It was wondrously appealing.

'I am glad,' Chiara was saying. 'My mother will be glad too. We need you just now. Someone we can trust.'

'Trust? Me? Why, has something else happened?'

'The thing with Moretti. It gets worse. Yesterday Marco resigned to go and work at Il Delfino Blu. The place has not even re-opened.'

'Then you will need me tonight.'

'No, no. It's your day off. And you're upset. We'll manage.'

'I'll be okay. There's something I need to tell your father.'

Chiara gave her a hug. 'See? I feel better already. There is no one like you, Lucy.' She went to give Lucy some time to rest. Chiara was right, there was no one quite like her. No one, at least, who was such a fraud. Her stomach was knotted with cramps and she even checked the calendar but as she had known her period was still a week away. Tension, then, misery, feelings of failure, feelings of loss? All of the above. And a loneliness so overwhelming she thought she might drown in it. But she wouldn't ring home until she was sure she could do it without crying.

She took some paracetamol and tried to think about the situation calmly, logically. Doubt, that was her problem. The girl who had landed at Capodichino had not had any doubt at all. It had been implanted, like a tiny embryo, with that flash of familial recognition when she met Andrea. From there it had from time to time been fed and watered: as she grew friendly with Chiara and began to help Rosa and to see Moretti as her enemy. Lucy herself had been hardly aware of this nurturing process but slowly the doubt had grown into something large and dangerous, that threatened all her plans.

Stefano was out of the picture now so it did not matter what he felt; she told herself, at any rate, that it did not matter. Still she did not know whether to go ahead or to retreat. For the first time she gave in to self-pity, and railed against her mother for dying so young and leaving her with this insoluble dilemma and even, just for a second, for having been raped in the first place. Her phone rang and she grabbed it and was shaking so much she dropped it and watched it skid across the floor. Frantically she retrieved it.

'Pronto?'

It was a wrong number. She lay on the bed and stared at the ceiling until it was time to shower and change her clothes for work. She still had no answers.

Thirty Six

W hen Lucy arrived at Il Veliero she heard angry voices coming from Paolo's office. She heard Mario Moretti's name mentioned but that was all. Her Italian was quite good now. She could follow a normal conversation, just missing a word here and there, but an argument such as this one, with four people talking at once and all determined to make their point—that was a different matter. She found a glum Enrico slapping about the kitchen, venting his feelings on the night's menu.

'It's good you came, Lucy. It's good someone turns up! That rat Marco—I will kill him!'

Michela appeared at the door before Lucy had a chance to reply. 'Lucy. Chiara said you were coming. It's kind of you.'

'Not a problem, signora.'

She did not want to get involved in a conversation with her grandmother and started to check the tables, making sure they were all set for the evening. She saw Paolo usher the three men out, heard him promise that council would do what it could.

She saw his drawn face, the grey pallor. He went behind the bar and poured himself a small grappa. And then he noticed Lucy and he smiled with genuine warmth.

'Lucia. This is good of you.' She wished they wouldn't all act as if she mattered so much. 'Have you heard what that terrible man is doing now?'

'Moretti?' said Lucy, 'I know he lured Marco away.'

'Oh, that. Annoying, yes. But a small problem. Mario has decided his terrace and his car-park are not enough. Now he wants a jetty and a boat-ramp too. It would change the beach, there'd be nothing left.'

'But surely the council—'

'Will Mario Moretti listen to the council? Wait for a permit he knows is not coming? The job will be done. And then to undo the damage...' He shrugged.

Lucy couldn't believe it. Surely they weren't just going to give in. 'Someone has to stop that man,' she said. 'You will try?'

Paolo sighed. 'You do what you can. Mostly, it is not enough.'

'I wasn't going to tell you, it was so absurd. He even offered me a job. He wanted me to manage the place.'

'Il Delfino? When did this happen?' Michela had joined them. Lucy hated the way she did that, how suddenly she was just there.

'A few days ago. I said I had neither the skills nor the interest.'

'You should have told us!' Michela's tone, as usual, was almost accusatory. Paolo was concerned.

'How did he take your refusal?'

'He said it was—regrettable, that's the word he used. I couldn't help feeling what he really meant was that I might regret. Silly.' She managed something like a laugh but noticed that Paolo wasn't smiling. 'Well. I decided you should know after all, in case anyone mentioned it. I do not intend to leave.' And she got on with her work.

They had several blow-ins that night and the restaurant was busier than expected. Lucy was glad, it took her mind off her own problems, one of which was her phone. She'd deliberately left it back at Il Nido, telling herself it would never ring again, and now she kept seeing it there on her bed, ringing constantly, unanswered. She forced herself to concentrate on the young couple trying to give her their order in Italian. They were making a valiant effort and she was wondering how long to let them practice and when to put them out of their misery. Finally, the broad Australian accents got to her.

'Would it help if we spoke English?' she asked. It helped a lot, that is, it helped the young couple; Lucy gave them all the advice she could on where to go and what to see and made sure they had a great night. She herself, more homesick than she could have imagined possible, stopped in the piazza on the way back to her flat and rang Geoff and poured her heart out. And that helped her.

'Come home,' said her step-father. 'Come home now.'

'Soon.'

Geoff, who'd been worrying because he'd not heard from Lucy for a while, was now wishing that she hadn't rung. Sometimes ignorance was bliss. He had a bad feeling about Mario Moretti— probably ridiculous but there all the same. And he thought that Lucy should just have a talk to Paolo, tell him how she felt, get it all out of her system, and leave it at that. Kate would understand. He wondered if Lucy might want to stay on in Italy for another reason but wouldn't invade her privacy to ask her outright. All the same, he suspected that she might agree with Frost when it came to accepting the end of a love or a season; he could not see her just going with the drift of things. He found the urge to buy a ticket and get on a plane all but irresistible and Simone, when he talked to her, did nothing to dissuade him. They decided if Lucy weren't back in a month, he should go.

Lucy, for her part, would probably have taken comfort from the fact that these two people cared for her so deeply. Stefano, it appeared, had stopped caring at all. Her mobile remained silent except on the rare occasions when Chiara called her instead of dropping in.

One good thing happened in the following week. The local newspaper published a story condemning the amount of construction that was going on without proper planning approval. It laid the blame squarely with unscrupulous developers and made particular mention of disappearing beaches. It couldn't have been more pointed and everyone in Paolo's camp was pleased. If the giunta, indeed the whole council, had public support, it would make their job much easier.

And then a lot of little bad things happened. All at Il Veliero. At first they seemed insignificant: the side wall of the restaurant was covered in graffiti; a guest found a couple of tyres let down; a delivery left outside the door disappeared. But when a wedding party of sixty cancelled a day before the event, Paolo decided it was more than a run of bad luck. He did not, however, have a shred of proof that Moretti was behind even one of these events.

It was a Friday morning when at last Lucy's mobile rang. She was washing one of the white shirts she wore for work, trying to remove a very stubborn oil stain, and only just managed to reach the phone before it rang out.

'Pronto?'

'I see you have achieved your aim. Well done.'

'What do you mean, Stefano?'

'It is in the paper. Yes, even got picked up by *Il Mattino*. Just what you wanted, right? I hope now you are satisfied.'

'What's in the paper? I've no idea what you're talking about!' But he'd hung up and when she tried to ring back he didn't answer. Lucy, deeply hurt and completely bewildered, grabbed her wallet and keys and dashed for the door, determined to find whichever paper it was and read—what? She couldn't imagine. She didn't have to go far. Michela was standing there about to knock, a furious Michela waving a copy of the local rag.

'Get back inside!' she hissed by way of greeting. 'And please don't argue with me, no more games. You've seen this, of course.'

'The paper? No. Someone just rang me about it, I was going to get a copy.'

'You already know what's in it.'

'Signora, I have no idea what's in it.'

'Then read.' Michela slammed it down on the table. 'And tell me that's not your doing!' She went and stood at the door to the balcony and stared out. Lucy looked at the front page and felt the knots in her stomach again and the nausea rising. There was a photo of Paolo, a most unflattering one, under a heading which read 'Is This Man Fit To Be Mayor?' Just short of outright libel, the story spoke of a long ago scandal in Australia. It was not specific. But it was easy to read between the lines. Or rather, it was easy to draw the intended conclusion from the skillfully distorted mix of half-truths and innuendo, and quotes from a 'source' who clearly knew a very great deal. Self-righteous in tone, and purporting to be in the public interest, it nowhere branded Paolo a rapist. It didn't have to. That was the impression left in the reader's mind.

Lucy was horrified. She was appalled. It was gutter journalism of the worst sort. And yet, and yet...

This was her father they were writing about. This was his crime laid bare.

It was a long time before she could look at Michela. 'I'm not responsible for this,' she said. 'You know who I am and I won't deny that yes, I did think of it. Or something like it. But I didn't do it.'

'Then who?

'I have no idea.'

'Someone in Australia?'

'It's you who have family in Australia, signora. I am on my own.'

Michela had to hand it to Lucy, she knew how to stick the knife in. Well, she had certain skills in that area herself, maybe it was inherited. 'Alright,' she said. 'Then we have to assume Moretti's behind it.'

'Moretti?'

Michela shrugged. 'The man is pathetic. But dangerous. As for your secret, Lucia—no doubt you will tell the family when you're ready. Don't wait too long, it will only cause more pain.' And she departed, leaving the newspaper behind.

Lucy put some coffee in the Moka and turned the stove on. While she waited for the little machine to bring forth solace, she tried to remember when she had last been happy and was surprised to find it was less than two weeks ago, that morning in Roscigno Vecchio. It was hard to believe how completely and utterly things had disintegrated. But what to do now? She could fold up her tent and silently steal away, a beguiling option that any sensible coward would take. Lucy knew she'd regret it if she did. Or she could stay, in spite of the risks involved, and see the whole thing through to its undoubtedly messy end. She knew she'd probably regret that too. If only she had someone to talk to, someone to confide in... but she didn't. Stefano had so little faith in her that he believed her responsible for that filthy article. She could not forgive him for that.

Lucy, obviously, was upset and not thinking clearly. She was forgetting that Stefano's attempts to dissuade her from taking revenge had met with some pretty strong resistance. She was forgetting that he had very good reason to suspect her.

In fact he didn't just suspect her, he was sure she had done it: gone to the paper and given them the story. Something must have

225

driven her to it, obviously—perhaps at last she had tried to talk to Paolo and he had denied everything. Nursing a coffee in the bar at la RAI, Stefano realised he should never have told Lucy the story of Luciano, it seemed to have had the opposite effect to what he had hoped. He should have found a better way to persuade her; he should not, above all things, have walked out and left her. But when it came to that, he did not have much choice—she had called him a patronising bastard, he'd been wrong about her feelings for him, very wrong.

Stefano had not bought into the mutterings around the studios, about how the Australians did not understand Italian culture or Italian sensitivities, how they were in fact an inferior race from the bottom of the world who dressed badly and drank too much which was of course the reason for every problem with the show. Stefano, in the warmth of his feelings for an Australian girl, had dismissed such sentiments as ignorant and chauvinistic; now he had to concede that there might be something in it. Or was it the case that this particular Australian understood Italian sensitivities only too well? No, the problem was that she was neither one thing nor the other but the worst of both and he wished that she had stayed at home. He supposed then he would never have left Falanga Immobiliare S.r.l. but maybe it would not have been too high a price to pay.

Lucy, meanwhile, made the coffee and considered Michela's warning. How and when she would break the news of her true identity, especially to Chiara—who would feel the betrayal most— was something she dreaded and had tried not to think about. But she had known from the start that she would never become a part of this family; hers was just a visiting membership.

She didn't want to go to the restaurant but she had no choice; it would look very strange if, on today of all days, she stayed away. When she got there, Paolo was in discussion with Roberto who was advising him to sue; Paolo wanted none of it. He seemed to think that ignoring the article would diminish its impact; that pretending it was inconsequential, indeed beneath contempt, would somehow make it so. He did not, at least in Lucy's hearing, ever actually deny the main points of the story; he left that to the rest of the family.

Most of them seemed to be in shock but Chiara was magnificent in her defence of him.

'How can they do this, Lucy?' she cried. 'How can they take an innocent man and destroy his good name? For what reason? My father has hurt no one! All his life he tries to help people, help his community! Why do they do it?'

Michela, Lucy knew, was watching and waiting for her response. The three of them were alone in the restaurant, setting up the tables. The clock on the wall struck eleven. Lucy thought, absurdly, that it should have been noon. She folded a napkin, placed it in a bread basket. She could answer: 'The paper is telling the truth, he deserves it.'

'Lucy?' Chiara asked again. 'Why?'

'I don't know, Chiara. Perhaps someone has it in for your father, wants to ruin his business. An old grudge, who knows, sometimes these things fester.' That's what Alessandra had said. Michela let out her breath and the clock went on ticking.

The day wore on. The restaurant was not as busy as it should have been. Paolo had friends and a few dropped in to show their support but most just made a phone call and promised to come soon. Fortunately, tourists didn't read newspapers, not local ones at any rate. Lucy found it very hard going. Stefano crept in and out of her mind but she never considered ringing him again to set the record straight. She could have done it, could have left a message with his mother, but the gulf between them had already grown too wide. She went home for her break and saw Marco lolling with a couple of his cronies in the piazza. He smirked at her and waved. She ignored him and went into the post office. He was waiting when she came out.

'Hey. This story in the paper—it's good, yeah?' In the background his friends were watching, sniggering. They couldn't know anything, they were just being boys,

But Lucy was suddenly filled with rage. This story had nothing to do with Marco Costa and his mates. It was not theirs to smirk and leer about, it was not to be the subject of their prurient imaginings and crude jokes, like the porn she'd seen Marco reading when he worked at Il Veliero. This was Kate's story and hers and the thought of Marco getting anywhere near it, to somehow sully and degrade it, was unbearable.

'I know nothing about it, Marco, I'm a stranger here. Why don't you ask your new boss? Perhaps he's familiar with the details.'

'What?'

'You heard me. Maybe Signor Moretti dreamt it up. Somebody did. Another thing, Marco. Right now, you're enjoying yourself. Well it's nice being paid to do nothing. But I've heard that Moretti's a pretty exacting boss. Not easy-going like Paolo. You think you'll be able to hack it when his place re-opens? You think you'll be good enough?' And she left him standing there and went on home, feeling rather pleased with herself, feeling that she'd come quite a way since her encounter with those other young men in Sant'Àgata sui due Golfi just a few short months ago.

The feeling did not last long. It left her an hour later as she sat on her balcony trying to write a letter home. She knew that Geoff and Sim deserved an update, a calm and reasoned account of where she was up to and what she was going to do. They'd be worried to death about her, indeed had intimated as much already and she half expected either or both to land on her doorstep. She didn't want that to happen. So the explanation, difficult to achieve with any coherence on the telephone, was necessary.

It's just that it was so damn difficult to write, requiring as it did a lot of uncomfortable soul-searching. The thing was that despite her momentary, rather petty little triumph over Marco, Lucy knew—deep in the core of her being—that her time in Italy had done nothing to make her strong. She was a different person but not a better one. The woman who had boarded the plane at Tullamarine—she was the strong one. She was confident, sure of herself, she possessed (or so Lucy had liked to think) enough of the Anzac spirit to fight for a just cause. And now? Now she was a mess, ineffectual, unable to act. All the old certainties seem to have vanished under an immense cloud of other possibilities, other ways of seeing and new, unlooked-for allegiances. She hated this new, indecisive Lucy, though had she seen the progression in one of her pupils she would have recognised it easily enough. She would have called it something like 'a new-found maturity.'

She finished the letter without ever saying what she had really intended and when it finally arrived in Melbourne it did nothing to allay the concerns of the recipients. But they had already come to some decisions of their own.

At the restaurant more unpleasantness followed, though nothing on the scale of the newspaper article. Deliveries were late. A customer, all charm at first, created a huge scene, sending Enrico's famous bocconcini di pesce spada fritti back to the kitchen. There was some trouble with the phone line which kept dropping out for no reason that Telecom Italia could explain. And then a party of ten failed to show up for dinner. Rosaria, who had taken the booking, got the blame, Silvana assuming she'd made a mistake. In fact Rosaria had double-checked, and Chiara had overheard her doing it, and much oil had to be poured on the troubled waters. Real oil, olive oil, was also a problem, when old Massimo Bellucci, who'd supplied it to Il Veliero since Paolo first opened for business, arrived with the side of his van smashed in and the news that someone, some stronzo, had run him off the road. It was getting nasty.

Lying in bed that night, Paolo wondered if the good fortune he'd enjoyed was deserting him and his world was about to start crumbling away. The thought frightened him; he couldn't understand (or would not allow himself to consider) what he might have done to deserve that, nor what he could do to stop it. Silvana reached out for him and held him and comforted him as she'd always done.

'It's nothing,' she said. 'You'll see. It will be alright, my dearest.'

But it wasn't alright.

Thirty Seven

You cannot run a seafood restaurant without fish. Lucy was just out of the shower, making coffee, when Chiara banged on her door with the worst news yet: the local fishermen were refusing to sell to Paolo. He got to the harbour at the usual time, when they'd finished unloading their boats and they claimed to have nothing left.

'Even Ernesto,' said Chiara, 'Papà has bought from him for years, he wasn't even there. Just left a message, that really hurt.' Lucy thought she could understand how much. It was clearly a conspiracy. The fishermen had been threatened—or bought off. But no one was speaking. Chiara was distraught, at this rate her parents would soon be ruined.

For a moment Lucy allowed herself to contemplate the ruin of Paolo Esposito that she had hoped for so long to achieve. Perhaps she just had to sit back and let it happen. She was even wondering, the way things were spiralling out of control, if the mere fact of her coming to Italy, to the Cilento, hadn't somehow been enough to cause a cosmic shift. It was totally irrational and she did not believe, not for a minute, in astrology or anything like that, but how otherwise to explain this string of disasters? Or was it indeed all the work of Mario Moretti? Was he even capable of it? In the meantime, there was the matter of the fish—to act or to shrug it off with words of mock outrage, that's terrible, how dare they! Chiara was looking at her, waiting for her to save the day. Little sisters can be very demanding.

Lucy suppressed a sigh. She turned off the coffee and pulled on some clothes. 'Tell me,' she said, heading for the door, 'where else can we buy seafood?'

They headed back up the coast to another seaside town, bigger than Stella del Mare, where not even Chiara would be recognised.

They were able to buy a selection of fish and some excellent mussels and calamari and they felt that Enrico would be satisfied. They paid the asking price and told the story they'd settled on—that their regular guy had been getting a bit greedy. They left with the promise that they'd be back tomorrow.

Paolo's gratitude was embarrassing and Lucy tried to make light of it.

'We can't let him get away with it,' she said. 'It is Moretti, isn't it?'

'So I've been told,' Paolo admitted.

'I don't like bullies,' Lucy said. 'I don't like people who think they can just have anything they want.' Paolo met her gaze and nodded agreement but did not reply. He found Lucy quite scary sometimes; he wasn't used to such forthright women.

The problem of the fish was solved, at least for now, though everyone seemed to be walking a tightrope, waiting for the next disaster, wondering from which direction it would come. But when it came it did not strike Il Veliero at all, at least not directly. Silvana received a message from one Carmella Rossi up in Monte Santa Caterina. It seemed that Alessandra Bianchi had been in hospital for some days and though she was now home again she was far from well. Carmella, who was Alessandra's neighbour, thought Silvana would want to know.

Lucy, who was there when this call came through, found Silvana's reaction puzzling. Surely it was no time for old feuds? Silvana had once loved this aunt like a mother, she would go to her now— wouldn't she? Forget the harsh words that had once passed between them, forget the grudge she'd borne for twenty years, pick up the car keys and go.

'Silvana?' It was Paolo.

'I'm sorry she's sick. I hope it's nothing too serious.'

'She's been in the hospital.'

'But she's home now.'

She wasn't going. Lucy couldn't stop herself. 'Would you mind if I went to see her?' They all turned to stare at her. 'I know her, you see. Your zia Alessandra. It's funny how it happened, I stayed with her the first time I went up into the mountains.'

'How come?' It was Andrea who asked the question that everyone wanted answered.

'I asked at the bar about accommodation—and she has a couple of rooms to rent. I didn't know then who she was, of course. But we got on really well, I did her ironing.'

'You what?' Michela, of course.

'Her ironing, signora.'

'You did it for money?'

'No. To help her. She has very bad arthritis. And I liked her a lot. So when I went back up there with my—with Stefano—I stayed there again. And when I told her where I was working, then she... well, she mentioned the family connection.'

'I see.' Michela again. And she didn't believe her! Well damn her. Damn the lot of them.

'It is a strange coincidence, yes. But that's what happened. Signora Bianchi was very, very kind to me. And I should like to go and see her since no one else is able to. I'm sure Chiara and Rosa can get the fish, I'll only be away one night.'

Paolo spoke quickly. 'Go if you wish, Lucy, of course.' Silvana, who for a moment had looked almost ashamed, rallied too. 'We'll send her a few things, she won't be well enough to cook, I'll get Enrico to help me. Chiara can bring it round to you.' And she fled to the kitchen.

Lucy went home, having first dealt with a request from Andrea to accompany her. He seemed keen to visit this great aunt he had never once met and Lucy herself would have quite enjoyed his company but she could see that Paolo was having none of it. Andrea was fobbed off with vague promises of a visit when zia Alessandra was better. Lucy knew there was no chance of that happening. She was quite angry. Was Silvana going to let the old woman die without ever seeing her again? Without ever effecting any sort of reconciliation? As she threw a few things into her backpack she made sure she included all the photos she'd taken of the family. They were no real substitute but they might be some comfort.

Chiara arrived without the hamper—it was downstairs in the car, she said, she couldn't possibly carry it up Lucy's steep stairs.

'Mamma has gone overboard.' Lucy gave her a look. 'You think she should be going herself.'

'It's not for me to say, Chiara. I was a bit surprised that she didn't want to.'

'I don't know what happened between them. It was long before I was born. It does seem such a pity.'

'Yes.'

The hamper, which Lucy had trouble heaving into the boot of the Punto, was in two parts, a cool bag and a basket. Silvana had indeed gone overboard. There was antipasto of every sort and fish and cheese and frittata and fresh pasta sauce and a dish of pasticcio ready for the oven. In addition, there was a fruit tart, an apple cake, a container of sugary crostoli, a bottle of Paolo's aniseed-flavoured grappa and one of the very best limoncello. It was, Lucy thought, a good way to assuage your guilt. Aloud, she said, 'I think Alessandra and I might have a party tonight. Invite all of Santa Caterina.'

'Did you really do her ironing?'

'Yes! She was tired and in a lot of pain, I had nothing better to do. But Stefano thought it was strange too, he said it was very Australian.' She couldn't quite keep the bitterness out of her voice.

'You and him, Lucy—there is no chance?'

Lucy shook her head. 'We hurt each other too much. I think we are just too different. There has to be trust, Chiara. Without that— what is the point?'

'I'm sorry.'

'Yeah. Me too. I'd better get going.' Anything was better than standing there talking about Stefano. They hugged briefly and Chiara stood and watched Lucy drive away. Like Andrea, she would have relished the chance to visit this great-aunt, known only as a signature on a Christmas card, but she was needed elsewhere.

Lucy headed off once again to Monte Santa Caterina. She knew the way well enough and found the drive quite easy. Which was just as well because nothing that followed was easy at all. For one thing, she was about to find out exactly what Mario Moretti was capable of. This visit, like her previous ones, would prove to have a profound affect on her life.

When she pulled up outside Alessandra's house, a woman was just leaving. She introduced herself as Carmella and shook her head when Lucy enquired about the state of Alessandra's health.

'The doctor came this morning. He wants her back in hospital but...' An expressive shrug. 'You know what it's like in this country.' Lucy actually had no idea, she certainly didn't know that families provided much of the patient care in Italian hospitals and if you had no family, then it could be pretty tough.

'What's the problem, exactly?'

'Her heart. She had some sort of attack. Her niece—she is coming?'

Lucy had to explain that Silvana wasn't coming but had sent a lot of beautiful food and seeing Carmella's look of disappointment—or was it disgust?—found herself making excuses, about the busy season and the difficulties they were having with staff. Carmella was not impressed.

'You do not leave your own flesh and blood to die alone, signorina. That is what I think.'

'Is she really that bad? Dying?'

'I think you will find that she doesn't want to live.' But she saw that Lucy was distraught and softened. 'Alessandra has talked about you. At least you've come. This food—I don't know what we'll do with it, she's barely eating at all. But let me help you.'

Carmella, who was surprisingly strong, helped Lucy to lug it all into the kitchen. Inside the house her eyes needed time to adjust to the gloom; the shutters were all drawn and the darkness, which should have come as a welcome respite from the burning sun outside, seemed already on its way to being a permanent fixture. Carmella was right. This house, so warm and welcoming just a couple of weeks ago, was waiting for death. Carmella went to warn Alessandra she had a visitor. Lucy tried to pull herself together. She told herself it was superstitious nonsense; Santa Caterina was playing tricks on her again. She would cook a good meal tonight for herself and Alessandra; they would talk; she would cheer the old lady up and she would get better.

Carmella came back and said Alessandra wanted to see her. She herself would be next door if she were needed. Lucy thanked her again and took a deep breath and went into the bedroom. Somehow she hid her shock. She kissed the pale figure, lost in the white sheets on that great big lumpy letto matrimoniale. As she sat down she touched the pillowcase with its roses and love-knots and she managed to laugh.

'I remember that,' said Lucy. 'It was a bugger to iron.' And then she took Alessandra's hand in hers. 'We're going to get you well.' It did not get the response Lucy was hoping for. Alessandra's eyes filled with tears and she turned her head away and spoke so softly it was hard to hear her words.

'I have done a terrible thing,' she said. 'The priest says God will forgive me but I can't forgive myself. If only Giuseppe had still been here, then I wouldn't have said a word. But I was alone. He frightened me, Lucia. He and his henchman...'

Like a scene from a film, a green Rover sprang unbidden into Lucy's mind, passing her on the steep road out of Santa Caterina. Who in these parts but Mario Moretti drove a Rover in British racing green? And the man at the phone booth in the piazza, so solicitous... Lucy cursed herself for her stupidity. Was she then no smarter than Marco or Concetta? Would they be surprised to know that Moretti would threaten a defenceless old woman?

'Of course he frightened you, zia, can I call you that? You mustn't blame yourself, I would have been frightened too, anyone would. I'll make some camomile, yes? And then we'll talk.'

Lucy made the tea quickly and poured herself coffee from a pot on the stove, thanking the absent Carmella. She chose a few tempting morsels from Silvana's largesse, arranged them on a plate and returned to the bedroom, straining to maintain her composure, her attitude that this was really not such a very big deal, it could all be sorted out quite easily and everything would go back to normal.

'Try to eat something, you want to get your strength back. Silvana sent the most amazing hamper, we could feed the whole village. Of course she would have come herself, but they are having a bad time. Moretti is making things difficult everywhere.' It was only partly a lie. Lucy wasn't sure if Alessandra bought it or not.

'I want to tell you what happened, Lucia.'

'There's no need. I think I know already.'

Alessandra ignored her. 'When you left the last time, I felt sad. You and Stefano—so happy when you arrived and then so quickly it all went wrong. I went and lay down for a while and when I woke up there is loud knocking, bang, bang. I thought you'd come back but it was two men. Next thing, they're inside. Uninvited.'

'Mario Moretti.'

Alessandra nodded. 'Not that we were introduced.' She sipped her tea. She was finding it hard and Lucy wanted her to stop.

'This is my fault. I led that bastard straight to your door.'

Alessandra shook her head. 'Everyone knew already that I was Silvana's aunt. This was common knowledge.'

'Ah yes. But when I turn up, the Australian connection, and come here to Santa Caterina—they don't know it's coincidence, do they? They don't know I'm just looking for somewhere to sleep. They think I'm here for a reason, something sinister maybe—they think at the very least they can dig up some dirt!'

It was just a whisper from Alessandra. 'They were right,' she said.

There was a long, long silence. In a way, I've done it already, thought Lucy. I gave the tools to Alessandra and she did the job for me, was forced to do it. It was botched completely, not her fault, and now it's all just a terrible mess, un casino grande...

'I did try, Lucia. I tried so hard not to tell them anything. They wanted to know who you really were and I said you were just a tourist, another Australian, but they didn't believe me. Moretti got nasty then. He said you must be Paolo's daughter. I just laughed, I said it was rubbish. He wanted to know about the scandal in Australia. I pretended I know nothing. And then...' She couldn't continue.

'Who did he threaten, zia?'

'The children.'

'Silvana's children?'

'Yes. He showed me pictures of Andrea. And then I told him.'

Her hand was shaking too much now to hold the teacup. It rattled as she put it down on the bedside table. 'And then Carmella brings me the newspaper with that terrible story, and I see Moretti will stop at nothing to ruin Paolo and get this real estate he wants. And I think, Alessandra, what have you done?'

Lucy, who was asking the same question of herself, said: 'You tried to keep Silvana's family from harm. You did the best you could.'

'He hurt them anyway. And who's to say he won't do it again? That's what happens when you give in to a bully.'

Lucy did her best to be reassuring but the words sounded hollow, even to her. She hated seeing Alessandra so distressed, it didn't seem fair, this was nothing to do with her, she was the victim here and why weren't the police handling it? She too wished that the sensible-looking Giuseppe were still around to sort it all out. Damn Mario Moretti, damn him to hell—and Paolo along with him, since he'd started it all. And damn her own hubris, thinking she could just waltz in here and somehow, with the wisdom of Solomon, dish out justice, hurting not a single innocent bystander.

'Lucia? You are crying.'

This wasn't supposed to happen, she was here to look after Alessandra. 'I'm sorry. I've made a bit of a mess of things, haven't I?'

'I am starting to think your Stefano was right. You and I—we must let the past go.'

'I'm not sure I can.'

'Silvana didn't come today. I will die without seeing her again. I should have gone long ago and asked for her forgiveness.'

'She could have come and asked for yours.'

'Who does the asking—what does it matter?' She sighed, a long deep sigh that was full of regret. 'When you are old—then you finally learn what is important. It has taken me a long time.'

Lucy wanted to ask her what she meant, what it was she had learnt, but Alessandra had closed her eyes and looked so tired and frail, lying back there on the pillows among the rosebuds and love-knots, that Lucy didn't like to disturb her, so she just said, very quietly, 'Can I get you anything?'

'I might sleep for a while. Will you stay tonight?'

'Of course.' Alessandra smiled and Lucy picked up the tray with its untouched food and went out and closed the door behind her.

She realised she hadn't produced the photos she'd brought from Stella del Mare and spread them out now on the kitchen table: Chiara behind the bar, checking the bookings, serious, thoughtful; Rosaria struggling with her English vocab, gorgeously petulant; Andrea of the green eyes, triumphantly winning at table soccer. Paolo's children. Paolo's other children. Lucy sat there looking at the photos for a long time in the cool, still room. Sat there until the shadows had crept up from the valley below and reached Monte Santa Caterina, and the darkness outside the house matched that within. By then she was getting an idea of what she had to do. Like a print slowly developing from a negative, it was gradually becoming clear.

Thirty Eight

Lucy checked on Alessandra periodically and each time found her sleeping, apparently peacefully. She was in two minds about waking her and was glad when Carmella came, all calm practicality.

'Perhaps wake her a bit later? The doctor said fluids and her medicine is all that matters. Here's my number, the phone is by my bed. You need me, you ring, okay? Three in the morning, not a problem.'

'You are very kind.'

'Alessandra's my friend. And you, poor child—eat some of that food, yes? We don't want you sick as well.'

She went and Lucy did as she'd been told and ate some bread and tomatoes and some very good mozzarella, which she knew would not be very good tomorrow so it seemed a pity to waste it. She even had a glass of Alessandra's wine.

Around ten Alessandra awoke and although she wasn't hungry Lucy took her some of the mozzarella and a tiny piece of Enrico's beautiful frittata and she ate a mouthful or two and had her medication. And then, strangely, she said she would like a tiny glass of Guiseppe's special grappa, the one flavoured with anice, which he always said was the very best medicine there was. Lucy, doubting the wisdom of it but in no mood to deny Alessandra any small pleasure, poured two glasses. Lucy herself was not expecting to like it, she was no fan of grappa, but was pleasantly surprised by this.

'Good, yes?' asked her hostess.

'Like drinking black jellybeans.' Alessandra smiled but looked rather vague and Lucy suddenly realised she had never seen jellybeans in Italy so the comparison was probably meaningless. 'Delicious,' she said. 'Smooth as silk,' and that Alessandra did agree with.

After a while Alessandra spoke again. 'I've been thinking,' she said. This afternoon, I wasn't asleep all the time. There is something I want to tell you.'

'Tomorrow, zia. It can wait till tomorrow. You'll feel stronger in the morning.'

'I'll sleep better if you know. It's about your father.'

Lucy put her glass down and waited. Whatever it was, she wasn't at all sure she wanted to hear it. Her plans were so close to being finalised, she didn't want anything to change them, she didn't want to go back to the doubt and confusion she'd been experiencing. On the other hand, perhaps it was best to find out everything, she would never get another chance. Alessandra sipped her grappa again, as though she needed the strength of the very best medicine there was.

'You have heard of the Irpinia earthquake?'

'Stefano mentioned it. 1980 was it? I know it was very bad.'

'More than two thousand people killed. Ten thousand injured. Some towns were totally destroyed. Teora was one of them. And Paolo was there.'

'In Teora? No one has ever mentioned this.'

'I've been told they do not talk about it.'

'Well. I suppose it was a long time ago.'

'Not so long really. Not if you were best man at a wedding and your friend the groom was killed.'

'Is that what happened?'

'Yes. They were at the church, the bride hadn't arrived yet. Paolo got out alright but he went back to try to rescue Davide—he wasn't to know the poor man was already dead. That's when he was injured. By the time they got Paolo to hospital it was touch and go for him too. They tried—the press, you know—to make a hero of him but he wouldn't talk about it. He suffers still.'

'How do you know all this, zia, when you have no contact with them?' Lucy hated herself for asking.

If Alessandra was hurt, she hid it well. 'You misunderstand me, Lucia. I tell you this so you know that your father has done something fine in his life. He has also done evil, and one does not cancel out the other. But none of us are all good or all bad. That is what you learn when you get old. And you learn that it is better always to think about the good.' She reached for Lucy's hand. 'Ornella Lucattini,' she said. 'Ornella came to see me now and then. The first time after the wedding. Paolo is her cousin and she loves him. But she knew a great wrong had been done and I had suffered because of it.'

She was exhausted. 'I'm sorry,' Lucy said. 'I just thought, maybe...'

'I would never lie to you, Lucy. Not even to make you reconcile with your father. I want only that you know him for what he is. All of what he is, you understand?'

Lucy could only nod.

'Call your Stefano. Talk to him.'

'Maybe.'

'You must learn to trust people, Lucia.'

Alessandra closed her eyes then and Lucy smoothed the sheets around her and tiptoed out. She had wanted to thank her, wanted to tell her she couldn't ring Stefano because it was too late, there was something else she had to do that was even more important, but she couldn't get the words out. She opened the shutters and let the moon shine its pale light into the kitchen. It was a gibbous moon tonight, it looked like a golden sail filled by some heavenly wind. Everything was strangely quiet, no Credence Clearwater booming out, no hopeful tenor murdering *Tosca*, only the distant murmur of voices from the bar in the piazza, the occasional bark of a dog. Lucy thought about trust and how it kept coming up, how Stefano had accused her of not trusting him and no doubt he was right because hadn't she said as much to Chiara? And now here was Alessandra repeating the message, she must learn to trust people. Did it all go back to Kate then, whose trust had been violated so completely that even her daughter was still feeling the aftershocks? Lucy wanted to ring Stefano, wanted nothing more than to hear his voice. Such a pity the time for that was gone.

She didn't want to go upstairs in case Alessandra called so she tried to doze on the couch in the living-room. She was tired—she seemed always to be tired—and she knew that the next day was going to be a hard one. Sleep, however, did not come easily and when it did, she was troubled by dreams, caught in an earthquake with Paolo and trying to save him from a yawning chasm which opened up in front of them. Soon after two o'clock she checked on Alessandra and all seemed to be well. Lucy wondered if she were really asleep or just pretending again but she touched the knotted old hand and got no response so was reassured that one of them at least was getting some rest.

Wide-awake now, she went to the kitchen where she resisted the temptation to hit the grappa again and instead made some more camomile tea. She smiled at the realisation that she was becoming addicted to the stuff and wondered what sort of response she would get if she tried to introduce it to her friends back home. Well let them mock; she found it did more to induce sleep and a sense of calm than most of the drugs, legal or otherwise, that she'd ever tried. She filled a big mug with it and took it and stood at the open kitchen door and gazed out at the night. The bar was shut now, the silence unbroken. Santa Caterina slept. Lucy felt she was alone with the moon and a million glittering stars.

No night bird called, no meteor fell to earth, there wasn't even the whisper of a wind in the beech trees. But Lucy knew the moment when Alessandra died. She put down her mug of camomile tea and went and sat by her bed and checked her pulse and found it still. She closed Alessandra's eyes and kissed her forehead and held her hands for a long time and wondered about the havoc that she, Lucy, had wrought since she came to this country. And then she went and phoned Carmella.

The doctor told Lucy that since nothing would have kept Alessandra's heart going but a bypass operation which she refused to have, it had only been a matter of time. The priest—the same priest who had given Stefano a lift to Agropoli—told her that Alessandra was tired of this world and, having no desire to fight on, had been begging God for some time to reunite her with her Giuseppe. Which God, being merciful, had duly done. Neither of them mentioned Mario Moretti's part in helping the Almighty. Lucy should have felt absolved of all responsibility but didn't.

Lucy reported the death to the family at Il Veliero. She spoke to

Silvana and couldn't tell if the news affected her or not. Lucy didn't ask for time off; she said straight out that she'd be staying for the funeral in two days time and would return to work after that.

The tiny village church was filled with mourners but Silvana was not amongst them. Ornella Lucattini, however, was, and once the mass was over she helped in the house, when all that food from the restaurant was finally put to good use. At last it was just her and Lucy.

'I expected Silvana,' said Lucy.

'And not me?'

Lucy smiled. 'Oh no. I knew you'd come, signora. Alessandra talked about you.'

'Call me Ornella, Lucy. After all, we are family.'

Lucy looked at her coolly. 'Did Michela tell you?'

'No. I told Michela.' She flicked a crumb of crostoli from her skirt. 'Delicious but so messy!' She ate another mouthful. 'I went to Australia when I was young. I stayed with my aunt Grazia. She has a photo, I think you've seen it?'

Lucy nodded.

'There you are then. Are you going to tell the others?'

'Soon. First there is something I must do.'

'You're not comfortable here, are you?' asked Ornella conversationally. 'In Italy, I mean.'

Damn her perception, thought Lucy. She didn't want Ornella probing and prying, not now. 'Not really, no. It's harder than I expected.'

'I can understand that,' said Ornella. 'I can understand it very well I think. The choices are just too hard.' Lucy didn't think for a moment that she was talking about day trips, or museums. She wondered if Roberto Lucattini had any idea how smart his wife was.

'I was very fond of Alessandra,' Ornella was saying, 'I'm so glad you were with her.'

'Family would have been better.'

'Don't be too hard on Silvana. She has her own cross to bear.'

'Paolo. His health. I've noticed.'

'He does too much, the man thinks he's still twenty. At least he's

243

got today off, they're closed out of respect.' Lucy thought that coming to the funeral would have shown greater respect but wisely kept quiet. 'You are coming back to Stella del Mare?'

'I'll be at work tomorrow,' Lucy said, not wanting to commit herself any further than that.

'Good. Though business is so bad... the rumours, you know, since that article?'

'It will pick up eventually,' Lucy said with some certainty. 'People will see through the lies.'

That struck Ornella as a very strange thing for Lucy to say and she thought about it all the way home without finding any satisfactory reason as to why she should have said it. Ornella dearly wanted to know what Lucy's agenda was and felt she had missed an opportunity to get close to the girl and find out. Upset as she'd been during the service, there was something about Lucy that made you keep your distance—though clearly Alessandra had not felt any such constraint.

Lucy saw Carmella again before she too left. She offered to help put the house to rights but Carmella said no, she and Lina, the neighbour from the other side would do it. And then it would be shut up to await the arrival of Giuseppe's nephew from America. And he, no doubt, would sell it and the Bianchis would be gone from the village forever because sadly, that is what happened. Carmella had a little present for Lucy. It was something which Alessandra, on the last evening of her life, had made her promise to find in the big old linen cupboard. It was a pair of new pillowcases, the same as the ones on Alessandra's bed, the same as those Lucy had ironed, but kept perhaps for a daughter who was never to be, kept anyway for 'best,' kept for a whole lifetime. Lucy took them and hugged Carmella and could hardly see the road as she drove away from Monte Santa Caterina for what she knew would be the last time.

On the way back to Stella del Mare, she took a slightly different route, stopping at an inland town where she had an appointment. Not far from Stella del Mare, it was considerably bigger but missed out to other places north and south by not being on the train line. It did, however, have a number of amenities such as secondary schools, a library and a local newspaper. It was to the last of these that Lucy was headed. The interview which followed took more than an hour and given the emotion of the last few days, and the difficult subject matter, she was glad that it was carried out in English. Even so, she felt completely drained at the end of it and the journalist, a middle-aged man who was also the paper's editor, felt concerned enough to offer all the usual restoratives: coffee, camomile, grappa, even Scotch. Lucy thanked him and refused. She could hardly tell him that what she needed was absolution and a long, cleansing shower.

She got the first, in some small measure, from Geoff. She rang him from the town post office before she attempted the drive home. He actually approved of what she had done, or said he did. More than that, he was of the firm opinion that Kate would approve. While Lucy did not believe that for a second, she drew great comfort from talking to him and this was a good thing, because she was close to breaking point.

Somehow she did get back to Stella del Mare but like the trip home from the mountains after she broke up with Stefano, she had no recollection of the journey. Lucy had never in her life driven under the influence of any drug but she was starting to understand what it must be like and to appreciate the dangers. Perhaps heightened emotions, like grief and euphoria (though she hadn't had much experience with the latter) should also be banned while behind the wheel.

Safe in her apartment, she put Alessandra's pillowslips into the box next to Stefano's angel. It was, she realised, fast becoming a repository for things that, left lying about, would only make her cry. And then cry she did, for an hour or more, under the shower; cried for failing the mother she had loved so much, cried for failing herself.

Afterwards, she had intended to go down to Il Veliero. It had been her plan, discussed with Geoff, to warn the family of what was coming. But she did not have the strength to face them then. So she went to bed and spent the night hoping against hope that some good might come out of what she had done; that, after all, was why she had done it: because Alessandra had told her to let go of the past;

because there were certain people she could not bear to hurt; because she wanted to part on good terms with Stefano.

Thirty Nine

Tired as she was, Lucy got up very early next morning, went down to the kiosk in the piazza and bought the local paper. It was already very hot but there was a faint breeze off the water. She thought of getting a coffee and reading the story there but she felt—or imagined—that a couple of people looked at her oddly and she changed her mind and went back to the apartment instead.

The journalist had done a good job. The mayor, so recently a man of loose morals and near-criminality, had become honourable again overnight. 'Sindaco Uomo Onorevole' boomed the front-page headline while the story went on to explain how no less a source than Paolo Esposito's long-lost daughter had come forward to set the record straight. What had happened in Australia all those years ago was described as nothing more than an indiscretion on the part of two young people...

Lucy pushed the paper aside for a moment there and took a deep breath before forcing herself to go on reading. They were almost her own words. Vittorio, the editor, had not changed much. Signor Esposito's daughter, the paper said, had come to Italy after the death of her mother to meet the father she had never known and make the acquaintance of her Italian relatives. The paper—Vittorio had suggested this himself—apologised unreservedly to Signor Esposito for any part it might have played in spreading what were clearly malicious rumours about his early life and was glad to have this opportunity to set the record straight.

There, she thought. It's done. I can only hurt Paolo now by going home and that's what I'm going to do. But at least I've paid Moretti back, just a tiny bit, for Alessandra. She suddenly felt a sadness beyond telling, a heaviness of heart that scared her. She was twenty-four and she felt as old as time. Lucy, who rarely thought about her health, actually wondered if she were getting some illness. And then she told herself, sternly, not to be ridiculous. It was nothing but stress. That, and the fact that Stefano hadn't rung. She'd hoped—no she was counting on the fact—that he would see the story. But then again, a rebuttal was never as big as the original dirt, it probably hadn't been picked up by *Il Mattino*. That had to be the case because the thought that he had seen it and read it and still hadn't rung her was more than she could bear.

(In fact the story was in *Il Mattino*, but Stefano never saw it. Stefano spent the day in bed, when he wasn't in the bathroom. The night before, while Lucy lay agonising over what she had done, Stefano was at a restaurant. It had been a good week on the show, with five excellent episodes completed and to show their appreciation, the Australians had taken everyone out to dinner. But the set menu included cassuola di pesce and it did look exceptionally good and just about everyone else was having it so he did too. And now he was paying for it. Or paying for a bad mussel. For the first time since that terrible night in Monte Santa Caterina, Stefano was glad that Lucy wasn't around.)

Lucy, staring at the shining sea while she finished her coffee, thought about the day ahead and wondered how she would ever get through it, how she would face the family. She wondered if she couldn't lock the door and hide for a couple of days. Except that it was so unbearably hot. And someone was bound to come knocking. The water beckoned. She could hide there, in that blueness.

She put her bathers on under her jeans, grabbed a hat, towel and sunglasses. She left the car, a dead giveaway to her whereabouts, and headed for the beach. Ten minutes later, she was floating a hundred metres from the shore. She was just a little shaken. The beach was almost deserted at this early hour but she was sure she had seen Nico, Moretti's sidekick, dart among the few parked cars as she approached. Not so strange that he should be there but why conceal himself unless, in his clumsy way, he'd been attempting to follow her? Oh well, she thought, let him follow her out here; he'd no doubt sink like a stone. After a while she trod water and glanced back at the beach; no sign of the burly Nico but a smaller figure, unmistakeably

Andrea, stood there waving. Damn it. She pretended not to see him and swam further out, another fifty metres, a hundred, in the strong breast-stroke which had won her medals in her schooldays. The water was seductive; so easy, Lucy thought, to lose yourself in its embrace. Some poet had said it, Swinburne, unfashionable now like so many of the poets she liked:

> *Softer than sleep's are the sea's caresses,*
> *Kinder than love's that betrays and blesses...*

Yes, it would be easy to stay here, but if she did, if she dived down into those clear depths, past the shafts of sunlight, then she ran the risk of drowning. She was not a schoolgirl any more and she was out of training and a long way from the shore. She was being an idiot, trying to put off the inevitable, a pointless exercise. She stopped and turned around and there was Andrea still, his waving quite frantic now. She waved back to show him she wasn't drowning yet and headed slowly to the shore.

Andrea came to meet her, holding her towel. He held it out to her.

'Thank you, Andrea.' She usually spoke to him in English, giving him the practice.

'That's okay. Sister. Sorella.' Getting used to the word in both languages.

'Half-sister. What do you say in Italian?'

'Sorellastra.'

Lucy repeated it. 'Sorellastra. Now we both have a new word.'

He watched her dry herself. He was awkward, he didn't know what to say.

'You swim a long way out. Not frightened?'

'No. All Australians swim.' She pulled on her jeans and shirt and finally Andrea plucked up his courage.

'I think they like to see you. The others.'

'Fine. I need to go home first.'

'I come with you, sister,' said Andrea and Lucy could not find a good reason to stop him. As they walked, she kept an eye open for Nico who seemed, however, to have given up surveillance. Perhaps he realised it wasn't his forte.

'Is important you come,' Andrea went on. 'Everyone act very strange.'

'Oh?'

'They wonder why you not tell us before. And I said, is because you want first to see if we are nice people. Is this right?'

'That's just about spot on,' Lucy said and he slipped his hand into hers.

'Another sister is okay,' said Andrea. 'But pity you aren't a boy.'

Half an hour later, Lucy presented herself at Il Veliero. Andrea rushed in ahead of her, announcing her arrival as if she were a visiting rock star or minor foreign royalty.

'She's here!' he yelled, 'It's Lucy!'

It was the hardest entrance Lucy had ever made. They were all there: Paolo, Silvana, Michela, the children, even Ornella. Fortunately, Enrico hadn't arrived yet. The newspaper was on the bar, another copy on the main table.

'Andrea tells me you've all read the story then,' she said foolishly.

'Yes,' said Paolo. 'This family is in your debt, Lucy.'

'The rest of the family,' Ornella was quick to correct him.

'Of course.' He smiled. 'We'll soon get used to that.' He was quite at ease, Lucy thought, he was sure this was going to go alright. It was Michela who was on tenterhooks, she and Ornella both, while Silvana looked weary, as though some ordeal had ended. Only Rosaria and Andrea seemed genuinely happy about the new state of affairs. Chiara, quite clearly, felt betrayed.

'I'm sorry you had to find out like this,' Lucy said. 'I meant to come round last night and warn you but I couldn't even remember driving home. I hope you'll forgive me, it's not been a good week.' She looked straight at Chiara but got no response. Oh well. She ploughed on. 'There's something you should know. Mario Moretti visited zia Alessandra before she became ill. There's not much doubt the two events are related. He threatened her until she told him who I was.'

'She knew?' Chiara.

'She guessed. When I was there with Stefano. We talked about a lot of things, Australians do that, and she guessed.' Alright, Chiara was hurt. On the other hand, it was Lucy lying through her teeth to save the good name of Chiara's father. Silvana had an arm around Chiara now, trying to calm her down. Silvana herself looked quite distraught, regretting too late that she hadn't made the trip to Santa Caterina. So many regrets, Lucy thought, the air was thick with them. She went on.

'Anyway, as we know, Moretti went to the press with his version of the story and did a lot of damage. He also left Alessandra broken-hearted. I thought, well at least I had the means to make him pay for what he had done, and possibly stop him in his tracks.'

'You have to wonder if a bullet might not have been better,' said Ornella.

'Indeed,' said Lucy, 'though it's not the way we do things where I come from.'

'No,' said Chiara, 'you just lie and cheat to get what you want, isn't that right?' And she turned and ran for the stairs.

'She'll be okay,' said Rosaria. 'It's because she was always saying you were just like sisters and you never told her, you know? Me, I think it's really cool.' And she hugged Lucy who, for once, accepted her superficial view of the world with gratitude.

Paolo's views were harder to stomach. 'This should at least give us some breathing space,' he was saying now. 'I don't know how we can ever repay you for setting the record straight.' Straight out of the paper: the record has been set straight.

Lucy thought the silence lasted for an eternity but it was probably just a second or two. Long enough for her to feel Ornella's eyes on her. Long enough for her to hear the familiar intake of breath from Michela. Long enough for her to wonder how much Silvana knew. She thought, I can't expect him to acknowledge the truth to anyone but me. In private, to me. I'll wait for that, it will have to be enough because it's all I will get.

'Paolo is right,' his wife said. 'Already the phone has been ringing.'

'So quick to change their tune.' It was Michela, finding her voice at last. 'Now they're saying, 'Of course we always knew Paolo was innocent!'

'It's human nature,' said Paolo, 'we mustn't let it upset us. Especially not today.' No, thought Lucy, not today, not any day. Just pretend that everything is absolutely fine. Suddenly she wanted to get out of there. Out of there, on a plane, home. The phone was ringing now and she wished with all her being that somehow it would be Stefano, though why he should ring the restaurant she couldn't imagine and what point it would serve she couldn't imagine either, except that she needed someone outside this family to talk to. It was a booking for the evening.

'We are going to be busy again!' said Rosaria.

'I wonder, Lucy,' asked a tentative Silvana. 'Could you possibly work tonight?'

'I said I would,' said Lucy. 'Did Ornella not tell you?'

'She needs a rest.' Lucy began to wonder when Ornella had been appointed her guardian.

'I'll be here tonight,' said Lucy. 'Tell Chiara... no. I'll see her later. I'll see you all later.' She had nothing else to say to them, not now, certainly not as a group, though if Paolo had asked she'd have talked to him. But he didn't. As she walked out she saw tears in Silvana's eyes; she wondered if they were for the suffering of a once-loved aunt or did Silvana somehow know about the lies that had been told to the world that morning?

She went back to the apartment once known as Il Nido. She didn't call it that any more, it wasn't a deliberate change, just part of the subconscious letting go of anything that reminded her of Stefano. She thought now that throwing her damn cellulare away would be a good idea but of course she couldn't bear to do that, not while she was almost holding her breath, waiting for it to ring. Ring it did, with Ornella on the other end, thanking her for being so brave and magnanimous. That was the word she used and it surprised Lucy; but then Ornella did know more than anyone except Paolo himself. Disappointed as she was that the call was not from Stefano, Lucy appreciated the small show of support because she did not feel that the meeting with her new family had gone all that well.

In spite of Andrea's best efforts, she had never expected to be welcomed like some prodigal into the bosom of the family. But only he and Rosaria had shown any real warmth towards her. The others had seemed awkward, embarrassed even. And as for Chiara... well they had hurt each other.

She suspected that as a family, they thought yes, Lucy had got them out of a hole. But as she had also got them into it, then that was the least she could do. Completely overlooking the fact that Paolo had dug the enormous pit in the first place.

Lucy had two more visitors that morning. The first was Silvana who had never before been to Lucy's apartment. She looked around.

'It's nice. Like a little nest.' Lucy just nodded and looked out the window and Silvana realised that for some reason she had said the wrong thing. 'I know you think badly of me,' she went on. 'And you're right, I should have gone to see Alessandra. I will never forgive myself.'

'Alessandra had regrets too, Silvana. She spoke of them. How she wished she had come to see you, to say she was sorry. She loved you still. Let the past go, that's what she said. And I'm the last person to judge you.' She looked straight into Silvana's brown eyes and thought, she does know, I'm sure of it. That's why she never went to see Alessandra, she'd have had to admit it. But she'll never say a word, she'll protect her children from the truth till her dying breath. And that's alright. After all, it's what Kate tried to do. Lucy made coffee then and told Silvana what the doctor and the priest had said about Alessandra and described the funeral in detail and they both felt a little better when Silvana left. But then Chiara came and that followed the general trend of the morning in not going very well at all. She spoke English as she always did with Lucy; spoke it better that Rosaria ever would.

'I thought we are close like sisters. Now I find we truly are and you have treated me like shit, Lucy! I deserve that?'

'I know you're hurt, Chiara. And no, you don't deserve that. You've been a friend to me since the first day I came here.'

'So why you couldn't trust me? It was you who said it, remember? We were talking about Stefano. You said—'

'I know what I said!'

'Without trust, what is the point.'

'Yes.'

'I don't understand you, Lucy. Why did you come here, if not to find your father? Why you didn't walk in the door, open and honest, hello, I am Lucy?'

Lucy almost laughed then realised she was probably close to hysteria through lack of sleep. But she knew she didn't want to go home having lost both Stefano and Chiara. She had to make an effort. 'Chiara,' she said, 'the trust thing—it works both ways. There are things you don't know about, that I can't and won't explain, they are ancient history now. I came to Italy to find my father but it was never going to be like they do it on television, the beautiful reunion and everyone lives happily ever after. It was never going to be like that.'

'Why not?'

'We were strangers. Total strangers.'

'In Italian we have a saying. "Il sangue non è acqua."'

'In English too, almost the same: "Blood is thicker than water," we say.'

'You did not feel this?'

'You made me feel it. You and Andrea, and Rosa too after a while.'

'But not papà?'

'We barely know each other.'

'But you will! You will get to know each other in time.' She paused. 'If you try.'

'I will try.'

'This is good. Whatever happen, he is your father. It just need time.' Chiara was almost hopeful now. While she sensed that dark things lay hidden in the past she had the feeling they had been laid to rest and it was all going to be alright.

Lucy did not want to risk deceiving her again. She was about to say that time was the one thing she didn't have for this getting-to-know-you stuff with Paolo because she was going home. But she hadn't actually booked yet; it might take a week or two. She'd tell Chiara the minute she had a date. Chiara departed a little happier than when she'd arrived. Lucy sighed. She had not expected that she

254

would be the one mending fences. She finally fell on to her bed. The mobile phone under her pillow did not ring. And Paolo, of course, did not come. As she dozed off, she thought she would try to make the most of the few days she had left and just enjoy having a sister— two sisters and a brother, in fact—for the only time in her life. At least, that was the plan.

Forty

Human nature being what it is, the restaurant was busy for the next few days. Those of Paolo's acquaintances who had been quick to disassociate themselves from Il Veliero were even quicker to renew their custom once the little unpleasantness had been cleared up. The excuses given for their absence were awarded points for creativity by the younger members of the family. The weather was also kind and Stella del Mare was still full of tourists.

But the air of bonhomie which prevailed was just a little forced. For one thing, no one, from Andrea up, could help wondering how Mario Moretti might react to the sight of the full car-park at Il Veliero, especially given the fact that only the bar at Il Delfino Blu was open, the grandiose renovations haven taken longer than expected.

Lucy had other concerns. Between herself and Paolo much remained unsaid. She waited for her father to approach her but two days passed and then three and still he hadn't said a word. He treated her, in fact, much as he had before—with friendly courtesy, even respect, except when he was forced to introduce her to his friends. On those occasions he played the role of the proud father and made a fuss of her and Lucy, to keep faith with what she had said in the interview, went along with it and was utterly charming to everyone and cringed inside and went home afterwards and wept. Silvana watched these little charades and knew they could not go on.

Lucy knew it too. With Stefano she had tried to be rational; tried to tell herself that really, it was all for the best, no point would be served by seeing him one last time. But Paolo was different, his cowardice—that's how she saw it—in not talking to her was incomprehensible, an unforgivable insult.

She could not help thinking how naïve Chiara had been. Get to know Paolo? How? More importantly, why? Filled with nostalgia—it sounded so poetic in Italian but was still gut-wrenchingly painful—Lucy rang Qantas and booked a seat. At about the same time Silvana confronted her husband. 'Confronted' was perhaps not the right word. Silvana had her own way of approaching difficult subjects.

'I was talking to Chiara this morning.'

'Oh yes.'

They were having coffee in the garden behind the restaurant, surrounded by the beds of herbs and vegetables which supplied much of its needs.

'Just look at those San Marzanos,' Silvana said, and Paolo duly looked at the tomatoes, knowing his wife well enough to understand that she had not changed the subject but had merely chosen a roundabout route.

'An amazing crop,' he said.

'Lots of sauce,' said Silvana. 'I wonder if Lucy will still be here when we make the sauce.'

'Why wouldn't she be?'

'Chiara is worried about her, Paolo. So am I. So should you be.'

Paolo drank his coffee. 'You haven't talked to her.'

'No.'

'You must.' She was right. When it came to the things that mattered she was always right. And Paolo knew it. But he didn't always do what she said.

Chiara was worried about Lucy. She understood her new sister was unhappy and wanted to offer comfort and had failed to do so because she still hadn't really forgiven her. And then Lucy, who'd been agonising over the timing, asked Chiara if they could meet somewhere and Chiara opted to come to the apartment and Lucy dropped her bombshell. It did not go down well.

'Home? You can't go home!'

'Well I can't stay either. For one thing, your government won't let me.'

'Is rubbish! Roberto—he could fix that, not a problem!'

'If I stay much longer, I'll lose my job.'

'You get another job when you want one. You've got a job here!'

'I'm a teacher.'

'We need teachers.'

'I teach English literature, Chiara. And then there's the car. The lease is nearly up. I really can't afford to renew it.'

'You just make all these excuses!'

Lucy shook her head. Why was Chiara making it so hard? Why couldn't she just accept that Lucy was going, that she had the best of reasons for going, and leave it at that?

'Oh! Of course. Che stupida!' And Chiara slammed her palm into her forehead. 'I am sorry. Is Stefano, yes? You want to be far away to forget him?'

'It's not him, Chiara. Well. Maybe a little bit. Him and—' She broke off. She could not say 'and our weak bastard of a father.' Instead she said 'I think I'm just homesick,' and burst into tears. Chiara wrapped her arms around her and hugged her and after a few minutes Lucy got control of herself, not without difficulty.

'You know, except for when my mother died, I hardly ever cried. I mean, I just didn't. I wasn't a weepy sort of person. And since I came to Italy, I cry all the time. It's not me.'

'How do you know this, Lucy? Is half you, surely.'

'Not a half I like.'

'Is wrong to show your emotions?'

Lucy felt uncomfortable now. 'Wrong for me.'

'You get used to it. To many things,' Chiara said sadly. 'But now is no time left.'

'I still have ten days. And I will come back, you know.'

'Promise?'

'Giuro.' And Lucy crossed her heart.

So it was Chiara who told the rest of the family of Lucy's impending departure. Andrea, like his elder sister, was heart-broken. Rosaria, genuinely sorry, reported the fact to her grandmother up in Naples who heaved a private sigh of relief. Silvana felt the timing was all wrong; both she and Ornella, without discussing it, feared that Lucy would be leaving with less than happy memories and weren't comfortable with that. As for Paolo, he knew that he was running out of time and wished he could find the courage he'd been able to summon up in Teora all those years ago. He wasn't sure he knew where to look.

And Stefano? On the evening the news got out, when everyone at Il Veliero treated Lucy with the care and consideration usually accorded someone just diagnosed with terminal cancer, Stefano was trying to forget he'd ever met her. He was out to dinner with one of the storyliners on the show. She had suggested going to Marechiaro and he had taken her instead to a noisy restaurant halfway down the hill in Posillipo. The food was good and the view was nice, there were lots of lights al di là del mare, she was a nice girl and he tried to give her a pleasant evening but she wasn't fooled for a minute. He ended up crying on her shoulder but he did not take her advice to give Lucia one more try. It was over, he told her. They were too different. She did not love him as he loved her. She was probably back in Australia by now. It would never have worked. So he did not pick up his cellulare and make the phone call that Lucy had wanted so much to receive.

At Il Veliero, where the food and the view were also good, the night was busy and they finished quite late. Even so, Paolo asked Lucy if perhaps she could stay and have a drink with him afterwards and Lucy agreed. Perhaps Silvana said something because the others all seemed to find urgent business elsewhere and the place was soon deserted except for the two of them.

'What will you have?'

She surprised him by asking for beer but the night was hot, almost oppressively so, and besides, beer sounded Australian. She couldn't help it, she was already on the defensive. Paolo got the drinks, a Scotch for himself, and they sat down and clinked glasses.

'I should have done this days ago,' Paolo started.

'Yes.'

'I didn't know what to say.' He was sweating. His own daughter, and he almost wished another earthquake would swallow him. 'And then I realised it wasn't that hard. I just had to say thank you.'

Lucy thought, 'I'm having déjà vu.' She felt sure she was going to be sick. It was like the first night she walked into this place and saw him. She pushed the beer away, afraid she'd knock it over. She heard

Palo's voice coming from a long way off, sounding a little disconcerted, trying to make her understand.

'What I mean is, I knew that was a good place to start. To thank you for being so—adult. For being able to accept the past for what it was. Of course I knew you hadn't come here to hurt me. But to know you've forgiven me, that we can move on and have a—'

'Forgive you, Paolo! Move on? What in God's name are you talking about?'

'But I thought...'

Lucy just shook her head. 'You still don't get it, do you? How can I forgive you? For what? For the fact that I was born?' And then at last Paolo realised how much he'd misjudged her and how misplaced were his hopes for glossing over the past.

'Why did you come, Lucia?'

'To pay you back. For what you did to my mother.'

'Why didn't you?'

'Because zia Alessandra and—and someone else—made me realise I'd end up like Mario Moretti. Doing harm to people who have never harmed me. And my mother would never forgive me.'

There was silence. Lucy got up. Then Paolo spoke, just a whisper, not looking at her.

'Did she ever forgive me?'

'She wouldn't even tell me your name.' Somehow Lucy walked out of the restaurant and was glad she hadn't brought the car and sorry too, because she was nervous walking home but no one followed her, not that night. Back at the apartment she thought about Paolo's last words and wondered if they could in any way be construed as a confession but she doubted if he was capable of making one. She was angry and upset and so desperately alone that she even thought of ringing Stefano but she realised she had left her mobile phone at the restaurant. Just as well, she would no doubt have caught him with some other woman at this hour of the night and how humiliating that would have been.

Paolo sat over his Scotch for a long, long time. He thought about the young man who'd gone to Australia and wondered if he had learnt very much in the intervening years. He thought about the daughter, so recently found and so quickly lost. And he wondered if the damage done could ever be repaired and did not see how it could without losing his other children in the process. Then he crept up to bed and accepted, as he always did, the solace offered by Silvana who knew that he had messed up what should have been a very simple thing.

The next day began quite normally. The sun came up, hidden behind deep banks of cloud over the mountains, and the oppressive heat continued. The sea did not shine, it was burnished like metal. In the camping grounds along the Cilento coast, a few old hands folded their tents and crept away. The less knowing applied more sunscreen and headed for the beach.

Being a Tuesday, the restaurant was closed. Lucy was glad because it meant that with luck she would not see Paolo. She would have to go and collect her phone at some stage. She remembered leaving it in the kitchen where she'd been talking to Enrico and had ended up helping him with the alici. But that could wait. She needed to disappear early or she'd find herself on a trip to Salerno with Chiara and Rosaria. They were going to collect Rosaria's new contact lenses, they'd have lunch and go shopping and all the time there'd be a million questions Lucy didn't want to answer, questions about her tête-à-tête with Paolo. She hadn't said yes or no last night but now the whole idea was unthinkable. She made a quick decision to go for a drive on her own instead, to see a bit more of the country before she left. She dressed in five minutes, forgot about her cornflakes and was out the door. Her heart skipped several beats when she saw a black Vespa parked nearby but then she realised that it was a newer model that Stefano's. And wasn't that Nico Barone walking towards it? She wondered what it had cost him: just serious boot-licking or something more sinister? She quickly got into her car.

For some reason Lucy headed inland first and stopped as soon as she was able to ring Chiara and explain what she was doing. Chiara forgave her when she said she wanted to go to Palinuro because Stefano seemed to rate it so highly.

'And go to Velia,' said Chiara. 'The Greeks ruins, Lucy, almost as good as Paestum. You should see.'

'I'll try and do that too, then.'

'You have left your cellulare in the kitchen.'

'I know. I'll get it later. Then you can show me all the stuff you've bought. Have a good time.' Lucy drove on, ignoring the clouds and the heat and the lump of lead that seemed to have settled in her stomach. She told herself firmly that it was good to be alone and away from Stella del Mare, good that her business here was finally finished and she would soon be home. She had no idea how wrong she was.

While she drove south in blissful ignorance, Chiara and Rosa drove north, bickering. Rosa was certain that Lucy and their father had enjoyed a nice bonding session the previous evening but Chiara was not convinced. More sensitive than her sister, she felt if that were the case, then Lucy would have joined them this morning. Chiara was troubled on many fronts. Rosaria, with her move to Naples only a few weeks away, was happy. Andrea, having decided to make the best of things, was happy too. He was already looking forward to visiting Lucy in Australia and intended telling his mate Dario about it when he met him down at the harbour. They were hoping to earn some pocket money by helping the fishermen. Not even the sight of that stronzo, Nico, who nearly ran him down on a brand-new Vespa, could put a dent in Andrea's good mood.

Which left Silvana and Paolo on what was supposed to be their day of rest. It didn't start well, they'd barely finished their coffee when Michela rang. Silvana took the call.

'I think I'll come down.'

'Oh. Why?'

'I don't know. Just a feeling I should.'

'There's no need, Michela, truly. Everything's fine.'

'Paolo—he's spoken with Lucia?'

'Last night.'

'And?'

'It went well. Really well.'

'Hm. Well I'm here if I'm needed.' Michela hung up. Silvana looked at Paolo and shrugged.

'She's not coming down?'

'I talked her out of it.'

'Thank God.' His thanks were actually a bit premature but for the moment Paolo still thought he could avoid any discussion of his talk with Lucy. With his mother, that is, his wife was a different matter.

'So what will you do next?' Silvana was asking.

'I don't know. I can't undo the past, Silvana, can I?' Then he left her and went into the office and closed the door. She knew he must be in pain, he looked old and grey and she wished he would let her drive him to the doctor but knew better than to suggest it.

Lucy, meanwhile, in no real hurry to get anywhere, had stopped to indulge herself with coffee and two cornetti, knowing that before long she'd have to make do with toast and Vegemite again. She did like some things about Italy. She decided to take Chiara's advice and headed back to the coast over a very dodgy road and down to Velia, where she admired again the handiwork of tradesmen whose gates and towers and walls and drains had stood, at least in part, for two and a half thousand years. It wasn't as grand as Paestum but it was interesting and Lucy wandered around trying to decide whether or not to go to Palinuro and sort of hoping that, if she did, she would find it very dull and boring, further proof that she and Stefano had nothing at all in common. The risk being, of course that it did indeed have something special. She couldn't make up her mind so loitered amongst the ruins instead.

Back in Stella del Mare, Paolo emerged from his office, no less grey but a little calmer, and sat down to lunch with his wife. He enquired about Andrea's whereabouts and learned that his son was spending the day with Dario's family. Since Dario's dad was a member of the giunta and his parents amongst the few who had not deserted Il Veliero, this was okay. Paolo was making an effort, Silvana could see that, pretending that everything was fine, but she'd prepared an insalata caprese and he barely touched it, so nothing was fine. After lunch they tried to rest for a while and then Paolo said he was going out. He didn't elaborate, Silvana didn't ask but she touched the cross around her neck as he left.

Further north in Naples, Michela was fretting. She wasn't normally the fretting type and put her restlessness and irritability down to the heat, which she hated, and to the unsatisfactory phone call she'd had with her daughter-in-law. Michela had been awake for most of the previous night and had spent it thinking about Lucy. She might have been glad that Lucy was going but like others in the family, she was also troubled. The girl was her granddaughter, damn it. She didn't want to feel glad. She wanted to get to know her. She wanted them to like each other, since love seemed out of the question. Nor did she believe for a minute that Lucy and Paolo were reconciled. When Michela itched, she scratched. So now she threw a few things into a bag and got into her car.

Silvana, to take her mind off where her husband might be and what he might or might not be doing, decided to spend the rest of the afternoon in the garden. It was a place where she could get her thoughts in order and bid her heart to be still and as she pruned and weeded and re-staked the over-laden San Marzanos, she wished she'd asked Paolo to help her. That might have kept him at home. She would have been surprised, no stunned and amazed, had she known where Paolo was.

The Saracens had managed to beat the Catholics to the best spot in town so the parish church of Stella del Mare stood further inland, on the aptly named via della Chiesa. This street ran uphill at right-angles to Lungomare, the road by the sea on which stood Il Veliero, but the church fathers had chosen the site well and it still had a commanding view of the ocean. Paolo was in the church now, for the first time in a very long time, weddings and funerals excepted, and the local priest was sitting beside him. Paolo had hoped to slip into the church unnoticed but had been sprung by, of all people, his cousin Ornella, who was taking a short cut through the churchyard. She was about to tease him, to ask what mortal sin had brought him to the church but she saw his face and bit her tongue. 'Are you alright?' she asked.

Paolo attempted a smile. 'Fine. Just some council business with Father Francesco.' Ornella sighed and watched him enter the church. She had hoped he might be there to deal with the other, much bigger lie which had cast a shadow on all their lives. Ornella had found the last few days difficult. She continued on her walk, thinking she might call and see how Silvana was bearing up.

In the church, Paolo was telling the priest a long and involved story. It did not take Father Francesco long to realise that what he was really seeking was forgiveness. Fortunately that was something the church, while not able to offer directly, could certainly facilitate.

Lucy had also been receiving heavenly instructions. She'd almost decided to go to Palinuro. But then, sitting in the car in Castellamare di Velia, eating a slab of okay pizza, she noticed several locals giving the sky some serious attention. She peered out the window and saw how very black it was getting and how quickly the wind was picking up. You didn't need a degree in meteorology to know it wasn't looking good. Convincing herself that if you'd seen one southern seaside town you'd seen them all, she finished her pizza and turned the car around.

Forty One

When Lucy got back the sea was dark with white caps and the first spots of rain were starting to fall. She decided to go straight to Il Veliero and collect her mobile, then head for home. She doubted if the girls were back but she had her own key, Silvana had given it to her weeks ago. She parked the car and got out, bracing against the wind.

Andrea was also heading home. He'd had a row with Dario, who didn't believe his story about going to visit his sister in Australia. He made a dash for the front door, just ahead of Lucy, who saw him and smiled, she wouldn't need her key after all.

It was then that she saw the Vespa. Saw it slow down right outside Il Veliero, saw Nico Barone raise his arm. The old Visconti film—the one Lucy felt she'd been starring in for months—was finally reaching its climax.

Andrea went on putting his key in the lock. Lucy tried to scream but no sound came. She realised that Nico, too keen to get the job done, had missed his target. The bomb, instead of going through the window, had landed on the balcony. Lucy hurled herself on top of Andrea as it went off and the whole structure—the concrete, the white pillars, the tangle of bougainvillea vines—came crashing down on top of them. The Vespa disappeared. Il Veliero itself remained intact; from the rubble on the terrace a cloud of dust rose thickly, blown about in the rising wind.

Silvana was putting her gardening tools away when she heard the explosion. She started to shake even as she tried to run towards the sound. Fortunately others had heard and even seen it so by the time Silvana arrived at the front of Il Veliero neighbours and tourists in bathers were already at work lifting the fallen masonry and someone had called the ambulance and Vito, the young cop, had appeared and was doing his best to summon more help. Everyone seemed oblivious to the increasing wind and rain. Silvana went to Vito.

'Please, signora, stay back. We will get them out.'

'Them? Who?'

He shrugged.

The Comandante arrived at the same time as Michela. Neither had any trouble in pushing to the front of the crowd. Michela wrapped an arm around her daughter-in-law and together they watched while the debris was cleared and the paramedics made ready.

In the church, Paolo and the priest were still engaged in matters spiritual. They had not heard the explosion, or perhaps had put it down to thunder.

As the weather drove the tourists from the beach, the bar of Mario Moretti's big hotel filled rapidly. But it was Marco, the recent recruit, who brought the news. Mario expressed his shock and retired to his office to consider what to do about Nico who, in trying to make himself indispensable, had become a liability. Mario was tempted to feed him to the fishes but you couldn't do that to a half-wit. Maybe a miserable winter with Mario's cousin in the damp and fog of the Po Valley could be arranged. He made some phone calls then headed off to play the role of concerned citizen.

The tableau that greeted him was enough to make his expressions of shock sound almost genuine. The damage, for one thing. And then the Australian girl, the long-lost daughter, half-dead she looked, being lifted into an ambulance. Michela got in too and it moved off. A protesting Andrea, clearly not badly hurt at all, was helped into a second ambulance. Silvana and Paolo embraced, then Silvana accompanied Andrea and they too were driven away. Oddly, there was a priest with Paolo, and his friend Roberto of course. Thick as thieves, those two. Mario forced himself to go forward.

'Terrible business,' he said. 'My condolences. I hope your children make a full and rapid recovery, Paolo.'

'We pray God,' said the priest.

'Fortunately, there was a witness,' said Roberto. 'At least we'll find out who did this.' Paolo said nothing.

'That's something,' said Mario. 'A little bit of good news.'

'Yes,' said Roberto. 'An English lady from Naples, saw the whole thing. Lucia threw herself on to Andrea and saved his life. Otherwise we might be looking at murder here. Of course if Lucia doesn't recover...'

'She will,' said Paolo fiercely.

Roberto gripped one shoulder. The priest patted the other.

'We will all be praying for such a brave young woman,' said Mario Moretti and wondered how quickly he could decently get away.

Chiara and Rosaria had had a good day in Salerno. Rosaria was wearing her new contact lenses and was amazed at all the things she could now see, like road signs. Just as well she'd got them before she started her driving lessons. They'd also done some shopping and had bought Lucy a farewell present of a really beautiful bag. And then Chiara, who still hadn't spent the money she'd been given for her birthday months ago, had for once in her life done something impulsive and bought herself a mobile phone—egged on by Rosa, who could see herself borrowing it on occasion. Now, on the way home, while Chiara drove, they nearly decided to christen it and call Lucy but the weather was bad and people were driving erratically and Chiara decided she didn't need the distraction. So they were totally unprepared when they pulled up outside Il Veliero and were directed by Vito, still on duty, around to the back entrance.

Paolo was on the phone so Ornella and Roberto told them the story, or as much as was known; thanks to the English woman, this was quite a bit and there was no doubt that Lucy was a heroine. They had finished a brief outline when Paolo came with his update, the good news being that Andrea, with little more than cuts and bruises, could even be discharged tonight from the local hospital in Castellabate. Lucy, however, who'd been taken to Salerno, was a different matter. Michela said she was in surgery, they did not yet know the extent of her injuries. They must get in touch with her stepfather in Australia.

'Geoff,' said Chiara, forcing herself to think. 'Geoff Harrington. His number might be in her passport. Next of kin.'

'Her bag?' Ornella asked.

Roberto went outside. He and Vito searched and eventually found

Lucy's bag where she'd dropped it, hidden now under the remains of one of the balcony lights. The passport was in a zippered inside pocket and Chiara's hunch had been right. Geoff's name and contact details were there.

Chiara looked at her father and something told her he could not make that call, not tonight. 'I spoke to Geoff once, to say hello,' she said. 'I'll do it. You go to mamma.'

Ornella was quick to endorse it. 'Good idea, Roberto will drive him. We girls can hold the fort here.' Paolo did not protest. He just thought how quickly his elder—no, his *middle*—daughter was growing up. He suggested however that Roberto follow him in the BMW.

'You're alright to drive?' Chiara again, worried for him.

'I'm fine. And it might be as well to have two cars.' He kissed her and Rosaria and Ornella too and told them not to worry and left Il Veliero with his friend.

Chiara made the difficult call to Australia. She played up Lucy's bravery and tried to play down her injuries but the fact was she had no idea of the extent of them at all. She gave Geoff numbers and the name of the hospital. He thanked her and hung up. He rang the hospital in Salerno and got nowhere. He rang the Australian Embassy. And then he started ringing around the airlines until he got a seat the next night on a plane to Rome, albeit via Frankfurt.

Chiara had no sooner hung up the phone than it rang again. This time it was her grandmother.

'There's no news,' Michela said quickly, forestalling any questions. 'Lucia is still in surgery. They tell you nothing.'

'Oh.'

'It's about whathisname.'

'Sorry.'

'That boy of hers. You know, Chiara, don't be obtuse. I saw her with him in Naples. They were besotted.'

'Stefano.'

'Stefano! Has anyone rung him?'

'It's over, nonna. They broke up.'

'Oh nonsense, Chiara. A misunderstanding. Lucia can be so

stubborn. At least ring him. I'll be in touch when they deign to tell me anything.' She hung up. Ornella and Rosa looked at her. Ornella nodded.

'She's right. It wouldn't hurt to ring.'

'I don't have his number.'

'Won't it be in her cellulare?' Damn Rosa, thought Chiara and she went to the kitchen wondering why she got all the shit jobs. She found the phone and called the last number. It was him alright.

'Stefano? It's Chiara, Lucy's friend. I don't know if you remember—'

'Chiara, of course I remember, how are you? How's Lucy, is she alright, is she still there? I've been meaning, you know, to ring... Chiara?'

'There's been an accident.'

'Oh my God, no!'

He still loved her. Not a doubt. 'It's okay, I mean, she's alive...'

At the hospital in Castellabate, Paolo and Silvana were reassured by the doctor who talked about possible after effects and told them what a lucky boy Andrea was. Then Paolo had a moment alone with Silvana.

'Is it alright if Roberto takes you and Andrea home? I think I should go to Salerno.'

'Today? She is having surgery.'

'I want to be there when she comes out.' He paused, he was afraid of her reaction when she knew that the inadmissible was being dragged into the light. 'I went to confession today.'

'She is an atheist, Paolo.'

'I think she will understand.' He was almost begging. 'I hope you will understand.'

Silvana didn't want him to go. She wanted her family safely around her in what remained of their home. But she thought if it would bring him peace then she'd be wrong to stop him. She glanced through the door at Andrea, Roberto was chatting to him, making him laugh. She knew that Lucy deserved peace as well. She embraced Paolo and told him to drive carefully because the weather wasn't getting any better, already there had been accidents. Paolo went in to say goodbye to his son.

They wheeled Lucy out of surgery and into recovery. Her left arm was in plaster, her left leg swathed in bandages. There were several smaller dressings. She was still unconscious, attached to drips and pale as a ghost. They allowed Michela to sit by her bed and wait for the doctor. When he came, kind and weary, he said how lucky Lucy was, the arm was bad, they had to put a pin in her elbow, but it would heal, she was young and fit, she'd get all the movement back. The leg too, a scar yes, but not too bad, much could be done these days. The bleeding had caused the most trouble, they'd been forced to remove her spleen. But you can live without a spleen. As he said, lucky when you think what damage those things can do—some sort of home-made bomb, the paramedics said?—but a terrible thing to happen, terrible. Still, that was the Mezzogiorno, wasn't it? His pager sounded.

'One of those nights,' he said. 'Your granddaughter will be alright, signora. She will recover well.' Michela thanked him, she had more questions but they could wait. He was right, as these things go, Lucy was lucky. The last time she'd listened to a doctor like him, standing by Silvana's side, the prognosis had been less sanguine.

While they had been talking Lucy had swum up from the depths of a dark sea, fighting to reach the light. She thought for a brief moment that she saw her grandmother but that couldn't be, her grandmother lived in Far East Gippsland. She thought she heard voices but they sounded strange and it took Lucy a while, and quite a lot of effort, to realise they were speaking in Italian. Then she remembered she had recently acquired a second grandmother who was, indeed, Italian. Which explained it. Exhausted, she drifted back down into the deep.

It was not a good night in the Mezzogiorno and the weather affected both Stefano, riding south on his Vespa, and Paolo, heading north in his Fiat Ulysse. Storms lashed the countryside, bringing relief from the heat but otherwise causing havoc. The high winds brought down trees and power lines and torrential rain loosened the unstable earth on hills and cliffs. Vesuvio slept on but the rest of the earth rumbled and people—as Chiara and Rosa had noticed—

behaved erratically.

When the rain finally stopped and the clouds parted, there was a bad moon rising once again. It revealed a multi-vehicle pile-up on the A3 north of Salerno while further south, emergency workers were putting out signs on the road out of Castellabate. 'FRANA!' they read. 'PERICOLO!' The workers reckoned it would take a week to clear the road, so large was the landslide.

In the hospital in Salerno, Lucy's eyes were fluttering again.

'I think she might be coming round,' Michela whispered. 'I'll leave you for a while.' Stefano smiled his thanks and watched her go. He thought she was opinionated and stubborn and difficult but there was a lot to like. Most assuredly, he had reason to like her. Actually, he could see a lot of Lucy in her. But the big question was, how did Lucy feel? He was nervous, sitting there waiting. It didn't matter what Chiara had said, about the interview he'd missed, about how Lucy had waited for him to ring. He had to hear it from Lucy herself. If only she'd wake up! It must have been one hell of an anaesthetic they'd used.

Michela rarely smoked but she'd felt the need for a cigarette and went to the waiting room to have one. There was a middle-aged man there, with the haggard face of one who has given up hoping for good news, and a younger man trying to amuse a fractious toddler with some Lego. The television was on, a news service, with coverage of the chaos all over Campania.

A mother does not have to be clairvoyant to know when her child has died. Michela had been preparing herself to lose Paolo for some time now. But she'd expected it to happen in a place like this, in a hospital, when all the options for treating his condition had been exhausted. She had not expected him to die in his car, crushed to death under a load of falling rock. But that car she could see on the screen, or what was left of it, that Fiat Ulysse caught in the Castellabate landslide—that was Paolo's. She could even read some of the number plate. She thought how strange it was, that he should survive an earthquake, only to be crushed to death like this... it didn't seem possible. For one family to go through so much in one day, that wasn't possible either, nature didn't behave like that, the odds were outrageous. But people won the lottery. And anyway, what had nature to do with Nico Barone?

Michela stubbed out her cigarette.

'Would you turn that off?' she asked the younger man and he took one look at her face and complied.

'Are you alright? Shall I call someone?'

'Thank you, no.' She knew she should go and find a telephone but it could wait for a while. She fought back her tears. They too would have to wait. She hoped the news hadn't reached Stella del Mare. She hoped they were all still rejoicing in the fact that Andrea and Lucy had survived. But that's not what was happening.

The Comandante had enlisted the aid of the priest and together they had gone to Il Veliero. It was through them that Silvana and her children were learning that their blackest day was not yet over.

Lucy, still unaware that all debts had been paid, that a line had been drawn in the ledger and the account closed, came up for air again. She opened her eyes and saw Stefano sitting by the bed. She had no idea why he was there. She tried to speak but her mouth was too dry. She tried to move her hand towards him but her arm was too heavy. He reached for her hand instead.

'It's alright,' he said. 'Everything's going to be alright.'

She knew she had to tell him that wasn't true, it was far from alright.

'Don't talk,' Stefano said. 'Listen.' And he told her what had happened and how she had saved Andrea and come here to the hospital in Salerno with Michela. He told her that Chiara had rung Geoff, who was on his way, and she had also—at Michela's suggestion—rung him. And here he was. And he hoped she was pleased to see him.

Lucy found her voice then. 'When the interview was published—I waited and waited for you to ring.'

'Chiara told me. Lucy, I never saw it.'

'It was in *Il Mattino*.'

'And I was in bed, like you say, sick as—what do you say?'

'A dog.'

'Esatto. Sick as this dog. There was a dinner, Australians like to do

273

dinner. And everyone was eating—please do not laugh, it will hurt you—cassuola di pesce. So I too, just for politeness. Never again, Lucy, mai, mai più!' Lucy did not laugh. She just held his hand a little tighter and wished she could change the world.

'It was very brave, Lucy. The interview. Then what you did today. You amaze me.'

'The interview was hard. Today...' She shrugged. 'Instinct, that's all.' It should happen now, she thought. In that soap he was working on, it would. The big love scene, right here in this hospital room with nurses hovering in the background and never mind her plastered arm and the damn drip and whatever else was wrong with her. Stefano would somehow manage to take her in his arms and the past would be forgotten and undying love declared and they would be together forever or at least for another forty episodes. But this wasn't a soap opera.

'Stef,' said Lucy. 'I have to tell you something. I'm going home.'

Stefano looked at Lucy lying there, tears sliding down her bruised and scratched cheeks, and wondered why it always had to end like this. He'd thought the storm was over, that they'd come through it safely, and now here they were on the rocks again.

'You know why I came, Stefano. So surely you can understand why I have to go.'

'No. I can't.'

'Paolo never once said he was sorry. He's never once admitted to what he did. He acts as though what I said was the truth. If I stay I will betray my mother's memory.'

'And what about us?'

'He raped her.'

'And she wants that you pay for it? What sort of mother was she?'

'The best. The very best. I let her down. I did everything I could but it wasn't enough.'

'You know something, Lucy? We talk about this when you're well. I don't think this is what Kate would like at all. A mother wants for her child only happiness. This I can give you. Perhaps only me. If you will open your eyes and see.'

Stefano left her then. He wasn't giving up, not a chance. He would get Geoff on side. He would find Paolo, he would force him to his knees in front of Lucy, he would make him admit to every sin he had ever committed. And then he saw Michela, sitting in the corridor, looking like an ice carving. He hurried to her and she looked up at him from where she sat.

'It just goes on,' she said. 'Paolo was killed by a landslide. I saw it on the television and then Silvana rang. He was coming to see Lucy.' Stefano had never rejoiced in the death of another human being. He did not do it now. But he did think, foolishly, that this death would change things. He was wrong.

Forty Two

Paolo's funeral did not take place for six days. In the interim, everyone tried to keep busy. The restaurant closed, reportedly for repairs though in fact Silvana had no idea about her plans for the future. Members of the clan started to gather from all over Italy and each had a view to express. Silvana gave Roberto and Ornella the job of family P.R.

The children handled the loss each in their own way. Chiara, outwardly a tower of strength, fretted through each long night for things left undone and unsaid. Rosaria chose martyrdom; she would give up Naples and go back to school and get her maturità as papà had wanted. To her relief, Silvana told her that Paolo just wanted her to work hard and be happy and she should still go to Naples, though perhaps a month or two later than planned. As for Andrea, he tried pathetically hard, as young boys will, to be the man of the house until the day when it all got too much and he broke down and cried like a baby.

Michela stayed with Lucy until Stefano said he'd been given leave from work, she should go to Stella del Mare. Lucy said they'd kick her out soon anyway, she didn't need lots of people waiting on her.

'It was good of you to come with me in the ambulance.'

'I'm your grandmother,' said Michela. 'What else would I do? We'll see you in a few days then, all being well.' She turned to Stefano. 'I leave her in your hands, Stefano. See that she does what they tell her?'

Stefano nodded and Michela turned to go then realised she was still holding something. 'I'm getting old. This was left for you, apparently.' She handed the parcel to Lucy, kissed her and left. Stefano undid the wrapping, It was a copy of Shelley's *Collected Poems*. He handed Lucy the accompanying note and she read it aloud:

Life is full of co-incidences. We first met in the Protestant Cemetery in Rome. And then I saw you again less happily yesterday when I witnessed your heroism at Il Veliero. I hope this small volume gives you some pleasure during your convalescence. Perhaps you will come to visit me one day in Naples, where I live. It is still a bel paese.

With best wishes,
Eleanor Sinclair

'Oh, how lovely of her! I'll write to her. Perhaps one day...'

'And who is this person?' So Lucy told him about her second day in Italy, and how she had cried by the graves of those old English poets and thought of her mother and talked to a pleasant English lady.

'This poetry thing. Is very important to you.'

'I couldn't live without poetry. It's the glory of English literature.'

'I thought that was Shakespeare?'

'Most of Shakespeare is poetry.'

Stefano got a little defensive. 'Italian also has great poets. Dante, Petrarca, many fine modern poets.' And then realised he'd dug himself a hole.

'Recite some for me,' Lucy said.

'Later,' said Stefano. 'You need to sleep. Geoff will be here in the morning.' He stood on the hospital balcony, where you could just glimpse the bay, the gulf of Salerno, and wondered again for the thousandth time about the gulf between him and Lucy and how he had thought, so stupidly, that love would bridge it. Well it almost had, and he was willing to learn the whole of the *Commedia* off by heart if that would clinch it but he knew that Paolo and Kate would still be there, both dead and both of them standing in the way.

Stefano collected Geoff himself from Fiumicino and took him back to Salerno. By the time they got there, Geoff understood Stefano's view of things perfectly. But he suspected that Lucy's heart would prove more complicated by far.

'Please,' Stefano said as he parked the car. 'Tell me this one thing.

Would her mother have wanted this? That she give up everything?'

Geoff didn't know how to answer. 'Try to understand,' he finally said. 'Her mother would not have wanted her to come here at all. But Lucy felt she had no choice. She felt—driven, yes, that's the word, compelled to come.'

'And make Paolo pay for what he did.'

'Yes. And she thinks she's failed. Lucy can't bear to fail. She thinks, too, that she's let her mother down. She can't bear that either.'

'I don't see it,' said Stefano. 'How has she failed? Paolo had to acknowledge her. He had to say to everyone, yes, there was Kate in my life and this is my beautiful daughter. Why is that not enough?'

'It will never be enough for Lucy.'

'"I will not give up, Geoff. Not ever.'

'Nor should you. Besides, we're Catholics, aren't we? We believe in miracles.'

With that, Geoff went in to see the daughter he knew so well; the daughter that Paolo had only got to know at all in the last few hours of his life.

When Lucy saw Geoff she clung to him like a ten-year-old. He came with the comforting arms and the smells of home. Sim, who had rushed around to help him pack, had made up a surprise pack of Tim-Tams and Twisties and Vegemite and sprigs of gumleaves and a copy of *The Age*, the Melbourne daily, and although Lucy tried to share it all with Stefano he felt she was, at that moment, far away from him, Lucia luntana, he could barely even follow the conversation. He was quite sure he would lose her but he'd forgotten about the possibility of, not a miracle exactly, more like a slight realignment to put the stars back on their proper courses.

Four days later, Lucy was allowed out of hospital and transferred to the care of the local doctor in Stella del Mare. Il Nido, with all those stairs, was for now out of the question but Ornella had taken it upon herself to find a suitable ground floor apartment with views of the Tyrrhenian Sea where Lucy and Geoff could stay and where Chiara or Rosaria could come to help. It was Stefano who camped at Il Nido, feeling for some reason more comfortable with that arrangement.

The reunion with the girls, and with Andrea, was teary and—for Lucy—embarrassing. She did not want to be thanked, even less to be treated as a heroine. She had, she told them again and again, acted on instinct as anyone would have done. She changed the subject and told them about Eleanor Sinclair instead, only to learn from Michela that Eleanor was well-known in Naples, where she'd lived for forty years, that she was a writer and lectured at the university. Lucy also learnt that Eleanor's eye-witness account of the bombing had led to the arrest just that day in Vercelli in the Po Valley of Nico Barone. The idiot was still riding the same Vespa. Mario Moretti, needless to say, knew nothing about anything, niente di niente.

Chiara, looking at Stefano, finally asked the question to which everyone wanted an answer. 'Are you still going home then, Lucy?'

'Not quite so soon,' Lucy replied. 'The doctors said to put it off for a couple of weeks so I've done that. At least Geoff will get to see a bit of the country, it's twenty years since he was here.'

'I'm looking forward to it,' Geoff said, practising his newly-acquired Italian or what there was of it. No one else said anything. No one looked at Stefano or Lucy again at all.

That evening, Silvana turned up at the apartment. She asked if she might have a word with Lucy in private and Stefano decided to take Geoff to the local bar for an aperitivo.

'I'm sorry I wasn't able to visit you in the hospital, Lucia,' Silvana began. 'I would have, of course, if...'

Lucy reached out and touched her hand.

'There is something I have to tell you.' Silvana went on. 'This is painful for both of us so I will be brief. The night your father was killed, did Michela tell you? He was on his way to see you. I didn't want him to go, not in that weather, but he was afraid that if anything happened to you...'

Lucy could not help that little tiny beat of hope from starting up.

'Did he have something to tell me?'

Silvana nodded. It was a moment before she could finish. 'He had been to confession. That's what he wanted to tell you. He said to me, that he knew you were an atheist but he thought you would understand. Do you, Lucia? Do you understand?' And Lucy could only say, with a lightness in her heart that she had not felt since she first set foot in this country, that yes, she did.

The two women talked for a long time. Silvana said she'd tried not to believe the story about what had happened in Australia. But after the Irpinia earthquake she'd had to accept that it was true. She'd accepted it but couldn't, because of the children, admit to it.

'I'm sorry—the earthquake? You mean when Paolo tried to save his friend?'

Silvana looked surprised.

'Alessandra told me what happened.'

'Paolo said it was God's punishment but God had got it wrong, it was he and not Davide who should have died. They say survivors suffer guilt. What happened with Paolo was that it made the guilt worse.'

'Alessandra said he was badly injured.'

'He was. He had two operations on his back. But he just took medication and carried on, we were not allowed to talk about it. Never. And then, quite recently, he learnt about the cancer. Just like your poor mother.'

'I did wonder. I know the signs.'

'He was dying anyway, Lucia.'

'Are you saying, I did not have to come?'

'I am not. I think perhaps you are now at peace. You have a family. And Paolo died in a state of grace. I am glad for all these things.' She was a much stronger woman than Lucy had realised.

'Brave as he was,' Silvana continued, 'he dreaded what was coming. I should be glad that he's avoided it but I'm not. He was a good man who did one terrible thing and I don't know what I will do without him.' She paused and looked at Lucy. 'You are very like him, Lucia.'

Lucy wanted to cry out, no, I am not, I'm not like him at all, if I'd done that terrible thing I would have owned up to it, I wouldn't have waited for twenty-five years! But she knew that it was true. She was the sum of them all: Kate and Paolo and Michela... she supposed even Stan and Joy had left a genetic marker somewhere, though she hoped it was too faint to be discernable.

'I lit a candle for your mother today,' said Silvana. 'She would be so proud of you. I hope she will rest in peace now.'

'Thank you,' said Lucy, and made a gesture that Kate would have been proud of. 'Let us hope they can both rest in peace.'

Paolo was buried next day in the style befitting a man who was not only sindaco but a well-known and highly-respected member of the community. It was standing-room only. The priest spoke of God's mysterious and merciful ways, of how Paolo had sought confession on the very day he died, as if he had perhaps foreseen the end. Lucy found it all hard to swallow but responded to Geoff's gentle promptings and managed to keep her place. As the coffin left the church, the mourners broke into applause just as they had at the simpler funeral for zia Alessandra, a strange custom but one that Lucy rather liked; after all, the performance was over, surely the star turn deserved some final acclamation.

That evening, when it was all at last done, when the friends and relatives had mostly dispersed, Michela suggested to Geoff that he and Stefano should quietly take an exhausted Lucy away. Sometimes a plastered arm and a swathe of bandages are a useful prop.

Back at the apartment, only Stefano had any energy left. Lucy went to lie down and Geoff collapsed in a chair on the terrace.

'Today was rather full on.'

Stefano agreed, though he had found it quite disturbing. He hadn't had more than a moment or two alone with Lucy but he sensed there was something different about her and he couldn't put a finger on what it was.

'Something has happened,' he said. 'Perhaps she is just glad she will soon be home.'

Geoff knew no more than Stefano but he was not so sure. 'I think you need some time alone,' he said. 'Could I borrow the Vespa one day soon?'

'You know how to ride it?'

'I think I can manage.'

Stefano checked with Lucy next morning: did she think Geoff would be alright?

'On the Vespa? Of course. He's got a Harley at home. Didn't he tell you?'

Damn Australians, thought Stefano. 'I suppose you ride it too.' He was relieved when Lucy informed him that it scared her to death.

'How about a very slow, sedate drive down the coast?'

'Palinuro?'

'Too far. You must not get tired.'

'Stefano! At home we drive that far to get an ice-cream.'

'Perhaps, then. When you feel up to it.'

Epilogue

Summer had returned to Campania and although the storm had left its mark all along the coast, the sun was warm and sky and sea met and melded together on a hazy blue horizon. Geoff enjoyed his ride to Pompeii on the Vespa, it made him feel like a kid again; he was looking forward to a couple of days on his own, poking around the ancient ruins. He reminded himself that he must ring Simone that evening, as he'd promised to do. He wondered if her passport were up-to-date, it might be wise to mention it.

Stefano drove very carefully, avoiding bumps and sudden stops, but even so he and Lucy pulled up by the beach in Palinuro at lunchtime. Lucy laughed out loud.

'What?'

'It's just another Stella del Mare. Fishing port. Beaches. Lighthouse. Sort of newer, though.'

'Not when Palinuro came.'

'If he did.'

'I choose to believe. Is more fun. There are sea caves too. Very beautiful. But not today, you in a little boat is not a good idea.'

'Probably not.'

'I like this place. We came here when I was a small boy.'

'That's nice. I just don't see what's so special, you know?'

'For me it has good memories. And when I thought that maybe you would stay—then I wanted to bring you here. Another time we go to Capri and Positano but first here. Somewhere simple. What you call laid back, yes? I thought you would like it. I thought—this is a Lucy sort of place. I have misunderstood you again.'

'Stefano,' said Lucy, 'I'm starving. Can we have some lunch? There was a little hotel as we drove in, they had a lovely terrace, perhaps we could go there?'

They went there. They ate spaghetti alle vongole and sarago. Stefano had no idea what she was thinking, whether or not he had somehow offended her. She chatted about the food and drank some wine and did not actually say very much at all. Then she had a glass of limoncello and she looked at him and knew that she had to take the risk. So finally she told him what Silvana had said.

'So I might just stay a while after all,' she said. 'And I was wondering about the show, you know? What episode are they plotting?'

'Fifty-eight,' said Stefano.

'Really? And the hero and heroine, have they made love yet?'

'No.'

'The audience will give up.'

'I thought it was old Australian custom.'

'No, there's a limit, this is too much. I noticed they have rooms here, there are vacancies. Do you think perhaps we could stay? Because you're right, it is my sort of place. It really is.'

It was uncanny how she had chosen the Albergo Bel Paese but even so, it wasn't quite the way Stefano had been imagining it for all these months. For one thing, he hadn't counted on the plastered arm and the bruised face and the bandaged leg, which rather precluded the sort of sex that he was accustomed to. He would have liked the heady perfume of lilies and violets and the dazzle of fireworks, and Verdi in the background. He had wanted to show her how romantic and tender Italians could be for he was aware above all things that this girl he loved so much had to be treated, even without her injuries, like eggshells.

But it must have gone alright. By dinner time—strangely, they both refused the cassuola di pesce—they were arguing about whether or not the children would be brought up Catholic.